"...on the missile range," the defense secretary said. "Suddenly, strange new life forms are destroying our roads. The stuff is spreading—the entire Southern corridor is threatened!"

"*We* are not happy about the situation either, Mr. Secretary," Tate replied. Then he adopted a more aggressive posture. "Can I ask you one thing? Where is the secretary of the interior? I should think this is more in his jurisdiction. Are we at war, Mr. Secretary?"

"Humpf!" was the response Carp offered. "Maybe."

Praise for MARK LEON's previous novel
MIND-SURFER:

"SURREAL . . . AMUSING . . .
Intriguing imagery and ideas"
Locus

"A MAGICAL MYSTERY TOUR
OF THE COSMOS"
San Francisco Chronicle

"COWABUNGA! . . .
Leon has a wide-ranging mind
and a good story sense . . .
He's a real ho-dad"
Austin Chronicle

Other AvoNova Books by
Mark Leon

MIND-SURFER

Avon Books are available at special quantity discounts for bulk purchases for sales promotions, premiums, fund raising or educational use. Special books, or book excerpts, can also be created to fit specific needs.

For details write or telephone the office of the Director of Special Markets, Avon Books, Dept. FP, 1350 Avenue of the Americas, New York, New York 10019, 1-800-238-0658.

The Gaia War

MARK LEON

AVON BOOKS • NEW YORK

If you purchased this book without a cover, you should be aware that this book is stolen property. It was reported as "unsold and destroyed" to the publisher, and neither the author nor the publisher has received any payment for this "stripped book."

THE GAIA WAR is an original publication of Avon Books. This work has never before appeared in book form. This work is a novel. Any similarity to actual persons or events is purely coincidental.

AVON BOOKS
A division of
The Hearst Corporation
1350 Avenue of the Americas
New York, New York 10019

Copyright © 1995 by Mark Leon
Front cover art by Eric Peterson
Published by arrangement with the author
Library of Congress Catalog Card Number: 95-94311
ISBN: 0-380-77873-4

All rights reserved, which includes the right to reproduce this book or portions thereof in any form whatsoever except as provided by the U.S. Copyright Law. For information address Donald Maass Literary Agency, 157 West 57th Street, #1003, New York, New York 10019.

First AvoNova Printing: November 1995

AVONOVA TRADEMARK REG. U.S. PAT. OFF. AND IN OTHER COUNTRIES, MARCA REGISTRADA, HECHO EN U.S.A.

Printed in the U.S.A.

RA   10   9   8   7   6   5   4   3   2   1

CHAPTER 1

"I am talking about the secret of life and death." There was a passionate tone to Alan's voice and a bright gleam to his gaze. He was staring straight at Lew with a deep intensity.

"I don't suppose you would like to go out for a beer?" Lew said uneasily, looking away from Alan and scanning the shelves full of books on philosophy, religion, chemistry, physics, and assorted esoterica.

"Really the secret of life," Alan continued, apparently oblivious to Lew's suggestion, "the secret of death follows. Death is really just the flip side of life, the other side of the coin. The important thing, Lew"—Alan became even more intense—"is that it is *the same coin*!"

Lew shifted in his chair during the awkward silence that followed this pronouncement.

"Beer," Alan said finally. "They say the Egyptians invented beer. You know they were really after the same thing. But they lacked modern scientific methods. Not that those will suffice. The Egyptians had the necessary *imagination*. The modern biologists have lost that, the physicists, too, the whole bunch of them. It requires both—soaring imagination, a dreamlike capacity to aspire to godhood, and the scientific knowledge to make that vision a reality!

"Let me tell you something, Lew," Alan continued. "Knowledge is one thing. The technique to apply knowl-

2 Mark Leon

edge is another. But neither will amount to anything without something else. I call that skill. Not skill in the mundane sense of ordinary know-how. That is merely knowledge coupled with technique. Skill in the ability to attune to and modulate one's own life force. Only then can knowledge be directed to the supreme goal!'' Alan ceased abruptly and then, in a totally different tone of voice said, ''By all means, let's go get a beer.''

Later that evening, back in his upstairs garage apartment, Lew thought about all Alan had said. He was worried about his friend. Alan Fain had not lived a normal life, nor was he about to, as far as Lew could tell. Was it insanity or genius? Lew had too much respect for Alan's intelligence to dismiss his ideas as lunatic raving. But the secret of life? Who could take that sort of thing seriously? And what *exactly* did Alan propose to *do*? Lew still did not know. He was afraid to ask.

I wish the professor were here . . . Lew thought. He had not seen the man for two years. It was a mixed blessing. The white-haired old man had turned his life inside out, had caused a lot of trouble. But it had been interesting, and life was starting to get boring again for Lew Slack. Certainly the professor would know whether or not Alan was crazy or onto something important. Lew looked up to see his reflection in the window, and the realization (a memory really) which followed did little to ease his anxiety. The professor *was* there. And Lew felt none the wiser for it.[1]

''You ever get the feeling, Lew, that something new is about to happen?'' Skinner, Lew's boss, asked.

They were having coffee in Skinner's office. It was a fairly regular thing. Skinner liked Lew's company and Skinner's office was the most comfortable in the building.

''What do you mean?'' Lew said, gazing out the twenty-third story window. The air was clear and the view unob-

---

[1] A full account of Lew's adventure with the professor is given in Volume 1 of the series, *Mind-Surfer*.

THE GAIA WAR

structed. Lew could see the river in the distance, the blue-green water flanked by the lush growth of oak, pecan and cypress trees.

"I mean the feeling that something extraordinary is on the verge of breaking through to the ordinary—all this!" Skinner gestured to indicate his office, the company, all the trappings of stability and security. "Have you ever been to India?"

"India? No, I . . ."

"Neither have I. But someday . . ." Skinner's voice trailed off. "Soon it may be too late," he said softly.

"Too late?" Lew responded. "Why?"

"I don't know!" Skinner sounded impatient. "The year 2000 will be here soon. Anything could happen. Use your imagination. Sometimes I think that's what's wrong with you, Lew. You just don't have enough imagination."

"I didn't know you were my analyst," Lew said.

"Oh come on, Lew. I didn't mean anything by it. You are the best programmer we've ever had, but don't you ever dream? I mean a comfortable, middle-class life is one thing, but . . ."

"You don't pay me enough to live a comfortable, middle-class life," Lew said, "much less to dream."

"You're touchy today, Lew," Skinner said. "I think you feel it, too."

"Feel what?"

"I don't know . . . but something is going to happen, Lew. Maybe it has something to do with the approach of the third millennium. Isn't the Mayan calendar due to run out sometime soon? I read about it. Some people think that the Mayans knew the cosmic schedule of time, and that is why their calendar ends when it does, because that is just as far as time goes."

"Jeez!" Lew muttered to himself on his way back to his office. Alan was one thing, but Skinner, too? The man was a corporate executive for God's sake!

But Lew had to admit that he did want something to happen. When he took the job at NatCo it was a welcome return to mundane reality, after what he had been through. But as time passed the depressing thought began to haunt

4 Mark Leon

him that this could be it. Twenty or so more years of work, then a pension and then . . . Was that the way to live a life?

Back in his office, Lew logged on to the system. He checked the parameters and activity log. It was redundant work. The entire network practically ran itself. Lew had programmed it to do its own diagnostics, print a daily set of reports, and flag anything that looked suspicious. Lew was particularly proud of an antiviral immune system that he had written.

In short, Lew Slack had practically programmed himself out of a job. He was bored. He leaned back and propped his feet up on the desk, which was littered with papers. *Wish I had a newspaper*, he thought, *or a good book*. He closed his eyes.

The phone jolted him awake. His right leg had gone numb and he sat up stiffly, grabbing the receiver. "Slack," he said thickly.

"Lunch," came the low voice.

"What . . . ?" Lew said, still groggy.

"Lunch in half an hour. Meet you at the usual place," Alan said.

"But . . . listen, Alan, I'm really busy here . . . big project deadline . . . I really can't . . ."

"No you're not," Alan said. "And yes you can. Listen Lew, this is important, a lot more important than your nap. See you in half an hour." Alan hung up.

"Damn!" Lew said, and slammed the receiver down.

"What's wrong, Lew?" Meagan, Skinner's perennially cheery secretary, poked her head in at Lew's door.

"Oh nothing," Lew said. "Just a nasty system bug. I might have to shut the network down tonight and run some tests."

"OK." Meagan laughed. "Go back to sleep . . ."

"I can't," Lew said. "I've got to meet someone for lunch."

"Tough *break*." She smiled and went back on her way.

"Jesus!" Lew muttered as he grabbed his jacket and stood up stretching. "I've got to get *out* of here!"

Lew strode down the hall, hands thrust inside his denim

THE GAIA WAR

jacket, his head down. Skinner blindsided him at the elevator. "Lunch, Lew?" the boss asked.

Lew looked up, surprised to see Skinner. The man looked fresh and well pressed as ever.

"Yeah," Lew said.

"Where do you want to go?" Skinner asked.

"Oh no," Lew said. "I mean, I can't. I'm meeting someone."

"I see," Skinner said, and winked at Lew. "One of your girlfriends, I suppose." Despite all evidence to the contrary, Skinner nurtured his own fantasy that Lew was a playboy with several young female companions. Skinner, a married man who kept a private penthouse for his occasional affairs, apparently got an additional charge from the fiction.

"I'll understand if you're not back by one." Skinner winked again.

"No, it's nothing like that," Lew said glumly as he stepped into the elevator.

"Oh I *see*," Skinner said. "Well in that case—"

Lew sensed that his boss was about to invite himself along. "I'm meeting Alan," Lew interrupted quickly.

Skinner's voice lowered. "OK, Lew, I'll be seeing you." They got off the elevator. Just as Lew was about to make his getaway, Skinner stopped him, putting a hand on Lew's shoulder. "You know how I feel about Alan Fain, Lew," he said. "Now don't take this the wrong way. Who you associate with on your own time is your own business. But when it starts to affect your work it becomes my business, too. All I'm saying is watch yourself. Alan Fain is not the most . . . how should I put this? He *rubs off* on people. He has made a mess of his own life, and I would hate to see him screw up yours as well." Skinner let his hand drop from Lew's shoulder.

"Alan and I are old friends," Lew said sullenly.

"Of course. Of course. Don't take it the wrong way, Lew. Just some friendly advice. You have got a great future here at NatCo if you play your cards right." He winked again, turned his back on Lew, and walked toward the revolving door.

"I *really* have to get the fuck out of here," Lew said

6   **Mark Leon**

out loud, drawing a few unfriendly stares from secretaries on their way to lunch. He lowered his head, jammed his hands back in his pockets, and charged out to the street.

"Lew, do you have any idea what a *curse* it is to be taken *seriously*?" Alan's intensity had not abated from the previous evening, and the effect on Lew was the same. He was drawn to the source of it even while it made him extremely uneasy. He tried to bury his head in the menu.

"Do you? Lew, *listen* to me. This is important. Get the enchilada special. Today is shrimp. Do you understand what I am trying to say?"

"No."

"OK, listen. I am serious. Do you have *any idea* what a curse it is to be taken seriously?"

"No."

"All my life I thought it was what I really wanted. I took myself seriously, but no one else did. I was convinced that it would be a blessing when my time came. Well it is. A blessing in disguise. Disguised as a curse."

The waitress made her presence known.

"Two specials," Alan said.

"Anything to drink?"

"Two teas," Alan said. "OK, Lew?"

"Sure, why not? Tea, coffee, beer . . . what's the difference!" Lew folded his menu and slammed it down on the table.

"Sorry." Alan smiled at the waitress. "He's had a bad day at the office."

"At least it is an office," the waitress said, shooting Lew a mean look as she gathered the menus and retreated into the kitchen.

"Disguised as a curse, I tell you," Alan repeated. "You should be more sensitive, Lew. Don't antagonize the waitress. Our lunch is in her hands. *Literally.*"

"So who's taking you seriously, Alan?" Lew asked.

"No one," Alan said, "but they will soon enough. Remember *this*." He pulled a small vial from his coat pocket. Alan still liked to wear suits even though he had no regular

THE GAIA WAR 7

job which required it. The vial was filled with a pale blue liquid. He held it up at eye level, midway between them.

"The empathetic aether,"[2] Lew said, almost whispering.

"I have been doing some analysis," Alan said. "This stuff is the key to the next millennium."

"What are you talking about, Alan?" Lew asked.

The waitress arrived with their teas and set them down, eyeing the vial suspiciously.

"Watch this." Alan pulled the stopper from the vial and poured a tiny drop into his water glass. Then he picked up his tea and took a long, slow sip.

Nothing happened at first. Lew looked around. The usual clientele were present. Lawyers, office workers, some doctors—mostly professionals who could afford the excellent, but overpriced, ethnic fare.

"Look." Alan drew Lew's attention back to his water glass. The blue tint had faded. Lew could discern a motion which grew in intensity as he watched.

At first it looked like a particulate precipitate, but then he realized the individual particles were moving, wiggling, squirming, and—growing.

"Oh no," Alan said.

"What?" Lew asked, his eyes glued to the intense activity in the liquid.

"I think I used too much," Alan said. "It's hard to calibrate the dosage. This could be embarrassing."

The waitress arrived with two plates of steaming shrimp enchiladas. As she set Alan's plate down, the water from his glass splashed over the rim, and something slimy and green flopped from the puddle onto Alan's plate, where it began an agonized thrashing in the heat of the sauce. A peculiar, fishy, vegetative smell mingled with the aroma of shrimp and chilies.

The waitress, calling on all her professional skills, said, "Should I bring another plate?"

---

[2] Described in *Mind-Surfer*, the empathetic aether is an extradimensional substance with miraculous healing powers.

8 Mark Leon

"No, no." Alan was busy mopping up the mess. "I'm very sorry. If you could just bring a small towel . . . and maybe some disinfectant."

She set Lew's plate down. "Sure," she said in a tone of voice that hid more than it revealed.

"Maybe we should get out of here," Alan said as soon as she left.

"But what about our food?" Lew protested. He was beginning to get quite hungry in spite of the weird smell.

"Look." Alan gestured to his plate. The slimy thing was rapidly decomposing, and his rice, shrimp, and beans were shot through with green, funguslike filaments.

"Mine's OK," Lew said.

"Good, then we can share." Alan moved his plate aside and put Lew's between them. He began to eat with an animal-like voraciousness. "Excellent," he said, motioning with his fork for Lew to follow suit.

The waitress returned, carrying a towel and another plate of shrimp enchiladas. She set it down in front of Alan as he pushed Lew's plate away.

"Hey!" Lew barked. "Why do you get the new one?"

"Trivial concerns, Lew," Alan said. "Very trivial. What's the difference?"

"But you already started eating . . ."

"I know," Alan said, "you like to feel that you control your own destiny. That is a dangerous illusion, Lew. You need to learn to go with the flow of things."

"Alan, we are talking about lunch!" Lew said.

"I quite agree," Alan said. "A trivial concern. Like your job."

"My job!" Lew practically shouted. "Without my job . . ."

"I know, I know . . ." Alan said, raising his palm in a gesture of peace. "Calm down, Lew. Please."

"It's just that you don't seem to appreciate my position at all," Lew said.

"But I *do* appreciate it." Alan smiled. "You sell yourself daily for a handful of dimes . . ."

"Forget it," Lew said miserably.

"Don't *despair*, Lew," Alan said. "That is the worst

THE GAIA WAR 9

thing you can do, no matter how pathetically hopeless your situation."

"Thanks a lot," Lew said.

"I wouldn't be saying this to you, Lew, if it weren't for the fact that I have a way out . . . for both of us. I don't understand it all yet. In fact I'm just beginning to appreciate the totally awesome magnitude of it, but—"

"What was that green thing?" Lew interrupted. "It seemed to be alive."

"That's the part of it that I do understand," Alan said. "It will change the face of the entire planet . . . not to mention that it will make us both rich."

"Rich?" Lew's eyes opened wider, flashing a little as he echoed the word.

"I *thought* that would get your attention," Alan said. "You're so damn materialistic, Lew. But anyway, what I have discovered will turn modern day biology on its head— it is more significant than the Watson-Crick discovery of DNA structure. DNA, it turns out, is not the storehouse for all the information that makes you, me, or that plant over there what it is."

"It's not?" Lew said. He took a resentful bite from his half-eaten enchilada.

"No, it is not," Alan said.

"So?"

"So I don't know the rest of it," Alan said. "DNA is just one of many possible structures which serve as a conduit for the information that literally *is* life itself. This stuff"—Alan pulled the vial from hi. pocket—"is *another* such channel for the life vibrations. The empathetic aether, the *elixir* of life."

Lew was looking nervously at his watch.

"Did you *hear* what I said?" Alan asked emphatically.

"Yeah. Listen, I've go to be getting back to work . . ."

"Fuck work!" Alan said loudly enough to attract some stares. "Lew, you are seriously in danger of losing the last spark of imagination from your poor, tortured soul. You could easily become one of *them*." Alan gestured at the restaurant crowd, many of whom were restlessly eyeing their meal checks, fumbling with credit cards, and looking

10   **Mark Leon**

at their watches. A few were looking at Alan, who did not seem to care.

"OK." Lew sighed. "So you have the elixir of life . . ."

"Bullshit!" Alan said.

"What?"

"Bullshit! All that alchemical crap! It has nothing to do with science. I am a scientist. This"—he held the tube where it caught the feeble fluorescent light—"is Nobel Prize material." The blue liquid seemed to respond with an inner illumination casting a rainbow of warm, pastel Day-Glo colors on the faded plastic tabletop.

"Wow." The waitress came with the check. "That's pretty. What is it?"

"Liquid ecstasy of life," Alan said softly, looking the waitress in the eye.

"Gosh," she giggled, blushing. She returned his gaze and then turned away nervously.

"Gets 'em every time." Alan smiled at Lew.

"What are you talking about?" Lew asked.

"Just one of my discoveries," Alan whispered. "The aether has a powerful sexual potential. I think it actually enhances the sexual field energy surrounding any living system."

"You have completely lost me now," Lew said.

"The cosmic aether that the physicists in the early part of this century sought . . ." Alan said. "That's what I'm talking about. They abandoned the search with the culmination of Maxwell's work on electromagnetism in the early 1900s. But they shouldn't have—they were merely looking in the wrong places. The aether exists. The physicists made a serious *conceptual* mistake."

"What was that?" Lew asked.

"They put *life*, and specifically consciousness, in some subordinate, *secondary* category . . . as if these things were mere *accidents* of nature, *afterthoughts* in the cosmic drama. But they were wrong. Life and consciousness are primary. They transcend the basic categories of matter and energy. What, after all, is the name which God gives Himself?" Alan asked.

"What?"

THE GAIA WAR 11

" '*I am*,' " Alan said. "That is God's own, God-given name . . . '*I am*.' "

"Oh," Lew said. "Listen, Alan, could we pay up? I've got to get back to the office."

Alan gave a sigh of resignation. "Sure," he said.

Alan and Lew met Skinner in the lobby. "Rather long lunch, eh Lew?" Skinner asked, looking at his watch.

"Just getting back yourself, are you then?" Alan shot back, fixing Skinner with a sharp stare.

"Hello, Alan," Skinner said. "How *are* you?"

"Fine."

"If you will excuse us," Skinner said, "Lew has work to do."

"And you?" Alan said with a smile.

"And me too, Alan. Not all of us have the luxury of doing—uh, whatever it is you do." Skinner said this with clear distaste.

"I excuse you," Alan said. "The question is whether or not you can excuse yourself—therein lies the *real* challenge." Alan turned and walked easily through the revolving door, without a backward glance.

Skinner let out a long breath. "I will never understand . . ." he said tightly.

"What?" Lew asked as they got on the elevator.

"Why some people *refuse* to serve."

"Serve?" Lew asked.

"Yeah," Skinner said. "Take what we do here . . . We provide a service to society. You, in your limited capacity as a programmer, are part of it, part of the great engine that drives us all, drives the economy."

"Maybe Alan hasn't got much respect for the engine, the economy. We are, after all, choking to death on our own wastes," Lew said. "Every day we lose more species, the complex ecosystem of the planet is further degraded. And we continue to destroy . . ."

Skinner turned to look at Lew. It was a cold look, expressive of an ancient wound that refused to heal. "So he *has* gotten to you. Listen, Lew, that kind of thinking is the real danger. It is Alan Fain and people like him who are poisoning our minds and destroying this country, our very way of life!''

''Maybe it isn't such a good way of life,'' Lew said.

Skinner's brow was covered in perspiration.

''Oh, change *is* coming,'' Skinner said. ''But it won't be the kind of change Alan Fain will like.'' Skinner said this with a vacant, absent expression.

Back in his office Lew ran the usual routine diagnostics. *I need something good to read*, he thought, contemplating a long, uneventful afternoon.

He got an unexpected error message. A record-locking routine had failed. This meant that data had been written over by one user while it was being accessed by another. It was the sort of thing that should never happen in the execution of a well-written database program.

Lew was both annoyed and stimulated. It meant work. Such an error could not be ignored for long without serious corruption of data. But it was interesting since it presented an unusual challenge. For the first time in recent memory something was wrong with the system, and Lew did not have the slightest idea what it was.

He worked all afternoon. He found nothing—no trace of the bug. He was scanning a software manual when the phone rang. It was Alan.

''What's going on, Lew?''

''I'm busy, Alan.''

''Sure.''

''No. Really. This is serious.''

''Well it is five o'clock. Time to knock off. I'm inviting you for dinner.''

''Can't. I may have to be here into the night.''

''I have something to show you. Something which I am sure you will find very interesting.'' Alan said this with an air of mystery that seemed both genuine and overly theatrical.

''But I really am busy,'' Lew said.

''Alright. But if you can drop by around seven, I promise you will not be disappointed.''

''If I can,'' Lew said and hung up.

THE GAIA WAR   13

Two hours later Lew was about to give up. In desperation he decided to check the source code. There was no possibility of error there, but he could think of nothing else.

When he finally located the record-locking subroutine he was astonished to find that the main section had been erased. In its place was a string of alien-looking symbols, vaguely familiar but completely unreadable.

Clearly that was the problem. It was inconceivable. Even if some hack could penetrate the system security, the graphics interface was not capable of producing weird symbols such as he had found. He copied the strange sequence of characters and then replaced the code from a backup disk. Within fifteen minutes he had recompiled the database program and the problem was fixed.

It was seven-thirty and Lew was hungry. He decided to stop by Alan's, hoping there would still be food.

"Sambhar-curried lentils, rice, and various delectable side dishes," Alan said. "It should be just about ready."

Lew detected exotic, pungent aromas coming from Alan's kitchen. "I actually learned this from a master cook in Benares," Alan said.

"India?"

"Yeah, Benares, India. The most sacred city in all of Hinduism, on the banks of the holy Ganges River. I met a *sadhu* there who drank from the river daily. The water is supposed to be holy, but it is actually full of the nastiest bacteria and intestinal parasites. The guy never got sick, though. Makes you wonder . . .

"Oh well, God bless America! Right, Lew? At least here you can drink the water. Let's eat."

"Something strange happened with the system this afternoon, Alan," Lew said.

Alan seemed not to hear. "My guru in Benares was also a cook. It's really unusual for a guru to do his own cooking. Swami-ji is a real progressive guy."

"Swami-ji?" Lew asked. The food was hot, spicy, and delicious.

"That is just his nickname," Alan said. "His real name

14 **Mark Leon**

is too complicated to mess with. Lew, if you don't mind my saying it, you seem awfully lifeless these days.''

''Lifeless?''

''Yeah.''

''I *feel* hypersensitive,'' Lew said.

''That's a bad combination,'' Alan said. ''Lifeless and hypersensitive, the worst of both worlds. One could describe the present state of the planet in just that way. While the ecosystem retreats into shock, the biosphere shows increasing sensitivity—ozone depletion, greenhouse warming, etcetera.

''You are familiar with the Gaia hypothesis, aren't you, Lew?''

''More or less. You mean the idea that the planet is an organism, like a cell?''

''Yes, and more. It has an intelligence which regulates the biosphere. On the Gaia view, the planet will clean itself up, take care of acid rain, deforestation, etc.''

''Do you believe that?'' Lew asked.

''Yes,'' Alan said, ''but . . .''

''But what?'' Lew asked. Alan had grown suddenly silent.

''The problem with the Gaia hypothesis is that we *can't* just assume earth will heal itself. We are causing too much harm as human beings, so we must act. But what even the environmentalists miss is the one most obvious fact. Namely, we, you and I, are part of Gaia. So Gaia, as the living intelligence of the planet, will likely use human beings to clean up the mess that human beings created. *I* have been selected!'' Alan's eyes were shining.

''What do you mean?'' Lew asked.

''I mean that Gaia has chosen me, imparted certain information to me. And this information is what has led me to my discovery. You witnessed a small demonstration today. But that was nothing, just a minor trick. The real work is to *reclaim* the planet in the name of life!''

''How?'' Lew asked, stuffing his mouth with hot, steamy naan bread and a spicy eggplant/potato dish.

''Not so fast,'' Alan said. ''Let's talk about you.''

''Me?''

THE GAIA WAR 15

"Yes. You. Which side are you going to choose?"

"Which side?"

"You can't stay neutral in this, Lew," Alan said passionately, tearing a piece of bread and using it to scoop up a fragrant mess of yellow curry.

"The lines are drawn. You are either with us or against us."

"Who is 'us'?" Lew asked uneasily, shifting in his chair and looking down at his plate.

"The friends of life. The friends of the earth. The *agents* of Gaia."

"How do you know which side you're on?" Lew finally asked.

" 'Ye shall know them by their fruits,' " Alan said. "And who they *work for*, I might add."

"I take it you don't think NatCo is on the right side," Lew said.

"NatCo and your boss, Larry Skinner, represent the forces of death. NatCo alone is responsible for the clearing of thousands of acres of the last remaining tropical rain forests in Indonesia. The indigenous tribes were conveniently relocated and put to work in paper and textile mills. You work for these bastards, Lew. What creative energies you have left are contributing to the destruction of the earth."

"I agree with you, Alan, but I have to make a living," Lew said in a pathetic tone of voice.

"What irony!" Alan laughed. "A *living* you call it. A living out of death. And what you really have for yourself is a living death. You know it's true."

"What is it all about, Alan? You tell me you have discovered the secret of life and death. You show me a . . . I don't know what . . . some biological trick, and now you want me to walk away from my job to embark on God knows what crazy adventure . . ."

"Can't tell you anything more about the project, Lew. Not while you are in league with the enemy." Alan cleaned the last smudge of rice, lentils, and vegetables off his plate with a swipe of his bread.

"OK. So I am trapped in a living death. What do you

want me to do?'' Lew raised his hands in a gesture of helplessness.

"Nothing. You don't have to do a thing," Alan said. "Just make sure that you're speaking the truth now. Your resolve must be clear. You are with us or against us. There is no middle ground."

"OK," Lew said, "I am with you."

"Good. Maybe I exaggerated a bit—all that stuff about the secret of life and death. I don't quite have all the answers—yet. But I do have something *really interesting* to show you." Alan led Lew to a bedroom in the back of the house. There he opened a closet door. Alan pressed on one of the slats of wood paneling inside the closet where the wood showed a small knot. A secret door opened inward on silent hinges, revealing a staircase which led down. "Follow me." Alan started down the steps.

It was an underground laboratory, all the more unusual since houses in Lew's part of the world rarely had basements. The underground chamber was bigger than the entire house above and very nicely appointed. The walls were painted a mellow yellow, which reflected the recessed ceiling lighting in such a way as to fill the space with an even, warm glow. At one end, near the staircase, were a comfortable sofa and coffee table, which rested on a beautiful Persian carpet with intricate design. At the other end was a lab bench. It looked well used, but orderly. An abundance of chemical glassware was evident.

Alan went to the sofa. "Sit down, Lew," he said, easily falling back into the soft cushions. He put his feet up on the coffee table.

"Where do you get the money for all this?" Lew asked as he sat down.

"Always money," Alan said. " 'Consider the lilies of the field . . .' When you have something worth doing, you will find the means to do it. Why do all those idiots up there slave away at meaningless jobs, many of which are degrading as well as destructive? Why do they do it? Because they have never found anything worth doing. *This* is my sanctuary, where I work and find meaning." Then Alan lowered his voice and fixed Lew with a penetrating stare.

THE GAIA WAR 17

"And this is also where we, if you will join me, will find the means to save the world from the forces of doom, which are spreading like a cancer even as we speak."

"How are you going to do this, Alan?"

"We, Lew, *we*."

"OK. How are we going to do it?"

"You remember Asklepios?" Alan asked.

"Of course I remember," Lew said. Project Asklepios, in which Lew had been propelled into nouspace and nearly killed, was something he could never forget.[3] The strange, colorful, and dangerous visions of that journey were dormant now that he had returned to the world of mundane American reality, but Alan's mention of the project stirred them to life.

"Well the Asklepian wave is more than the professor ever told," Alan continued. "It is not just the fundamental vibration of consciousness. What, after all, is consciousness?" Alan asked.

"Am I supposed to know the answer?" Lew responded.

Alan laughed. "The answer . . . I'm not sure it is an answer. Maybe *we* are the question."

"Yeah," Lew said. He had heard all this sort of thing before. It no longer had the power to excite him. In fact, it was downright boring.

"Ever get the feeling life is passing you by, Lew?"

"All the time . . ." Lew sighed.

"Well take a look around," Alan said. "Take a good look."

Lew looked down at the Persian rug. The intricate pattern seemed momentarily to come alive and the truth hit him like a white-hot bolt out of the blue. The time was now—life cannot pass you by unless you stop living it.

"You see," Alan said, "very little of what you normally see as important actually matters. Your job, social standing, etc. Life, on the other hand, is now. You are in it, actually living it, if you could only wake up."

"How do you wake up?" Lew asked.

---

[3] Described in *Mind-Surfer*.

18 Mark Leon

Alan laughed again. "Who knows? We are always waking up. Or trying to. Life is a free-flowing ecstasy, Lew. You worry too much. Lighten up."

"But you're always judging me, Alan. Maybe there are reasons why I do what I do. You can't just evaluate everything from your own perspective."

"And what perspective is that?" Alan asked. His eyelids were half-closed, giving him an inscrutable air.

"You left it all a long time ago, Alan. You left us. You ran away to the Far East, India and Tibet. You missed the trials and tribulations of coming of age in America. It hurt to have my best friend suddenly disappear. I was just a sophomore in college. I leaned on you. Looked up to you. And then you were gone. Then you suddenly came back a few years ago—just materialized out of nowhere—You should try and understand those of us who stayed behind. You sat at the feet of your guru for years and years. For what? What did it gain you to abandon your life like that? Did you learn the secrets of the universe? I think not, in spite of what you say. Do you think that you are smarter than anyone else?"

"No, Lew, I did not learn the secrets of the universe. But I did learn patience and control. I came back because I realized my real work was here. The time in the East was all mere prelude. I'm sorry I abandoned you, but now we can begin anew. The real adventure of our lives is about to start. We are on the threshold of a future beyond our wildest imaginations. Do you see?" Alan concluded passionately.

"You make me nervous when you talk like that," Lew said.

"Good—nervous is good," Alan said. "Courage, Lew! We really have no choice but to cast ourselves into the wave, which is the flow of time. Let go of the dross that drowns, have courage to swim and surf the waves of time!"

This was the Alan Fain who had won Lew's heart so many years ago. The old magic was still there, and Lew, despite his grave misgivings, felt his blood come alive and his spirit quicken.

"Now it is time to show you what I promised," Alan

THE GAIA WAR 19

said quietly. "Once I do there really will be no turning back. Are you ready?"

"Yes."

Alan got up and motioned for Lew to follow him across the room. They approached a long, highly polished wooden box. It reminded Lew of a coffin more than he would have liked. His sense of foreboding grew and he became convinced that once he looked inside there would, indeed, be no turning back.

Alan unscrewed the stainless steel clamps. Apparently the thing was hermetically sealed; a pale vapor began to seep through the seal formed by the lid and the body of the box. The cool mist spilled onto the floor. It had a peculiar scent that reminded Lew of desert sagebrush and morning dew. Alan slowly raised the lid.

At first he could see nothing inside—the vapor was so thick. But slowly it cleared and settled. The vision before Lew's eyes took his breath away. He felt a terrible awe, which was at once both sacred and profane.

"Do you like her?" Alan asked, a confident pride in his voice.

"Alan . . ." Lew gasped. "How . . . I mean who . . ."

"Don't worry, Lew," Alan said. "There is no kidnapping or murder here. I grew her myself."

"You *what*?" Lew could not take his eyes off the creamy smooth skin, the beautiful, pink-tipped breasts, and the long, wavy, black hair. Her face wore a mask of serene repose. The eyes were closed.

"Is she . . . alive?" Lew asked finally.

"Oh yes," Alan said, "but she is not quite finished. I think her mind requires a longer gestation than does her body. But that is no surprise—is it?"

"This isn't possible, Alan," Lew said. "I can't believe that you . . ."

"Could grow a woman," Alan finished Lew's thought. "We shall see. It won't be long now. Only a matter of days I should think. But things look promising, do they not?" He looked at Lew with a mad, mischievous twinkle. He replaced the lid and began to bolt it back down.

Lew found himself staring at the yellow walls. There was

20   Mark Leon

a paisley print cotton bedspread hanging on one of them—the patterns seemed like living cell tissue, moving and pulsating with his confused thoughts. He followed Alan back to the sofa—Lew noticed that the cushions were upholstered in even more intricate Indian print designs.

"Great stuff, eh?" Alan asked.

Lew stared blankly back at his friend, not sure if the face he saw belonged to a genius or a madman. "What?" Lew asked.

"This Indian paisley. Great stuff. I love it."

"It reminds me of something," Lew said.

"Yeah, I know," Alan agreed.

"Know what?" Lew almost shouted; the tension was too much for him to contain.

"Take it easy, Lew . . ."

"Alan, you have a corpse in there and you . . ."

"She is *not* a corpse. She is alive. Soon she will be as alive as we are. Maybe more so. In fact, I am counting on it."

"Counting on it?"

"Yes! She will be more alive, more aware than either of us, than anyone else on earth. You think this is just a game?"

"Hardly."

"Why do you think I am doing this?"

"You really . . . *grew* her?"

"I couldn't possibly engineer such a thing myself," Alan answered. "I had help. I used the empathetic aether to channel the life pulse, the Asklepian wave that is universally broadcast throughout the cosmos. Surely you haven't forgotten about that?"

"No . . . I . . ."

"The Asklepian wave is far more rarefied than any electromagnetic radiation. That is why no physicist has ever detected it. They never bothered to look, they are so hung up on light, electricity, and radio waves. I used the empathetic aether, along with some DNA I got from a young woman . . ."

"Who? What young woman?" Lew asked.

"Don't worry. She never suspected a thing. Just a wait-

THE GAIA WAR   21

ress in a coffee shop. She happened to cut her finger on a glass she dropped on the counter. It was easy to get a little blood sample. Completely harmless.''

"So this *experiment* is a clone?'' Lew asked.

"No. Not at all. I used the waitress's DNA as a receptive matrix to guide the general structure of formation. But the actual morphology comes from outside, from the Asklepian vibrations themselves. Our little friend in the box doesn't look much like my waitress. Same hair color, though.''

"But why?''

"Why not? Why not grow a fantastically beautiful woman in your basement? She is beautiful, isn't she?''

"Yeah.'' Lew sighed.

"Imagine, Lew. A fully formed woman with a brilliant mind, untainted by social conditioning. She will have no traumatic childhood, no crazy adolescence, no screwed-up marriage, etc. She won't have a head full of TV-driven consumer madness or affected intellectualism. No political indoctrination.''

"What *will* she have?'' Lew asked.

"I don't know,'' Alan said, "but she will be *pure*. And that purity could save the world—provided it is given the right direction, the proper training.''

"Proper training?''

"That's where *we* come in Lew,'' Alan said excitedly. "Now do you see why I need you?''

"Not exactly.''

"Look at this.'' Alan picked up a newspaper from where it lay on the coffee table.

"What?'' Lew took the paper.

"The story about waste dumping,'' Alan said.

There was a story in the paper about New York City's last sludge barge to dump liquid waste in the Atlantic.

"Yeah,'' Lew said, "I know. It's a mess and now that they can't dump in the ocean anymore, they will probably just start filling our backyards with it.''

"Not that,'' Alan said.

"What then?''

"Read the *name* of the sludge barge.''

"*Spring Brook*,'' Lew read.

22 **Mark Leon**

"Surpasses irony doesn't it?" Alan said. "A barge headed out to sea for the express purpose of dumping a load of liquid shit—and they call it *Spring Brook*." He laughed.

"I don't see what this has to do with—*her*." Lew gestured toward the incubation chamber.

"It has everything to do with her," Alan said. "She will lead the fight—she will bring back the vibrant, lush sphere of life that is our birthright, our home."

"How?"

"Don't you see? I have channeled the life frequency of the Asklepian wave into a receiving matrix. That matrix is programmed to take the form of a woman. A woman pure, born of the aether of life, the cosmic breath of creation. She will quite naturally be the messiah of the biosphere. *Now* do you understand?"

"Sure," Lew said, deciding that it was best to agree. "And you and I will have the responsibility of 'educating' her."

"Educating her in what she does not know," Alan said. "She will know more than you or I about astronomy, physics, and chemistry. She will speak English, Greek, Sanskrit, Japanese . . ."

"Japanese!" Lew said. "How?"

"I am able to program the receptivity to some extent. All language is just modulation of the universal language which is present in the aether at all times. Anyway, she will know more than you or I can ever hope to learn. But she will be ignorant of the ways of our sorry little world. I mean the social, political, and economic hell we have created. That's where we will need to teach her."

"How are we going to do that?" Lew asked.

"That is just where I need your help the most," Alan said. "I would say you are an expert on trouble in paradise."

"Thanks," Lew grumbled. "Thanks a lot."

Skinner paced nervously in his office. When Alan Fain had disappeared all those years ago it had served to validate what Skinner had chosen—the inside path. Skinner was a

THE GAIA WAR

consummate insider—he had built his business up by playing ball with those who had power and capital.

Lew Slack was another matter—a man adrift, in Skinner's view, a man to be recruited. Rebels like Fain were doomed to failure, or so Skinner needed to believe—that is why his disappearance had been so welcome. How could a guy who threw all his obvious talents away by running off to the Far East in search of God, enlightenment, or whatever it was, ever amount to anything? Lew, a man of not-so-obvious talents, was the kind of guy Skinner needed to dominate. Alan was the sort Skinner needed to defeat.

That is why it was so troubling to Skinner when Alan had come back. It would have been OK if he had returned a disillusioned failure. But Alan Fain was as bright and full of life as ever—and as scornful of the status quo.

Skinner picked up the phone and dialed. "Roger?"

"Speaking, Mr. Skinner."

"I have a little off-duty assignment for you."

"Off-duty?"

"Yeah. NatCo cannot be involved, strictly speaking, if you get my meaning . . . there is a personal element."

"Oh . . ."

"And there is a big bonus in it for you if you can operate in absolute confidentiality. I am commissioning you as a *private* security agent . . . Do you understand?"

"Absolutely," the NatCo security chief answered—the promise of a bonus was all the explanation he needed.

"Good."

CHAPTER 2

Lew noticed a change in Skinner. Ever since the encounter with Alan, the man had grown moody. "Did I ever tell you about the time Alan and I mixed up a batch of nitro?" Skinner asked. They were having coffee in his office.

"No," Lew said.

"We were classmates in college, you know."

"Yeah," Lew said. "You guys were two years ahead of me."

"Funny how I ended up here at NatCo with you working for me," Skinner mused. Lew did not think it was funny at all, but he kept quiet.

"Yeah," Skinner continued, "we were in organic chemistry together. Alan was way ahead of the game—knew more than our poor professor. I felt sorry for the guy. He was just a kindly old man waiting to retire. He hadn't learned anything new since the fifties. Alan kept hounding him about the latest developments in molecular orbital theory. The guy was helpless.

"Anyway, I suggested we make a bomb. Alan only did it because he was bored. We blew the face off the big clock on the main building."

"That was you!" Lew said. "I remember that. It had the whole campus freaked out. They finally blamed it on 'terrorists.' "

"Alan really did all the work. He even built a guided

THE GAIA WAR 25

balloon delivery system. We were miles away when it went off. They never had a prayer of catching us. Still, it scared me shitless.''

Lew laughed, but Skinner remained grim. "The days of college pranks are long gone, Lew," he said.

"I guess so."

"You know what I was talking about the other day?" Skinner continued.

"What?" Lew asked.

"The changes that are coming! Don't you ever listen, Lew? Don't you realize that there is a world beyond that little computer system of yours!"

"Sure, I do. I'm just not sure what changes you are talking about," Lew said, trying to control his temper.

"Well they're big, and we at NatCo are at the center of it. We are going to be major players, Lew. Can I take you into my confidence?" he asked suddenly.

"Sure. I mean, I guess so."

"You guess so! I have to be sure, Lew. I have to know where your loyalties lie. I am beginning to wonder."

"What do you mean?"

"I mean the company you keep," Skinner said. "I have enormous respect for Alan Fain. He is a genius. Unfortunately he is a failed genius, and he's on the wrong side."

"Oh," Lew said. "Well I . . ."

"You work for us, Lew!" Skinner interrupted. "Do we have your loyalty?"

"I am not sure I know what you mean." Lew was alarmed by Skinner's excited state. "I won't reveal corporate secrets or anything like that."

Skinner sighed. "I guess that will have to do. I was hoping that we could come to a deeper understanding about these things, but maybe I'm asking too much from a man with such limited capacity." Skinner said this as if to himself, as if Lew were not even present.

Lew shifted uneasily in his chair. He wanted to resign right then and there, but some crazy kind of prudence compelled him to silence.

"Sorry, Lew," Skinner said, appearing to snap out of a momentary trance. "I didn't really mean that. I've been under a lot of stress lately. I need someone to talk to. Will you listen? That's all I ask. Just listen.''

"OK."

"We are developing a new technology here. If it's successful, it will revolutionize agriculture. It will change the global economy. In fact we are on the verge of a New Age in which man will finally triumph over the forces of nature.'' Skinner stood up abruptly and turned his back on Lew to face the large, floor-to-ceiling window behind his desk. The midmorning sky beyond was bright blue and streaked with high cirrus clouds.

"Do you know your history, Lew?'' Skinner spun around and fired the question off like a shot.

"A little. I mean, I always liked history. I've read some historical novels . . .''

"Novels! Dreams of dreamers! I'm talking about the truth! Do you know what the truth of it is?''

"No, I guess not.''

"The struggle to rise out of a bestial existence. The urge of man to transcend the animal, to shake off this mortal coil and aspire to godhood! That is what is really behind all of human history, all wars, all religion, all our political and economic striving. These environmentalists! Like your friend Alan—they want to turn back the clock, make us mere animals again . . .''

"I don't think that's exactly right . . .'' Lew began.

"Hear me through!'' Skinner shouted, and then regained some control of himself. "They have you and half the public duped into thinking that we have to save the trees, save the whales, or whatever. I'm telling you that the goal of human evolution is something else entirely. We are on the brink of a new dawn for humanity. You know our company got started back in the seventies. A few ex-hippie idealists founded the *Nature Company* as they called it. They were dedicated to producing permaculture products.''

"Permaculture?''

"It means biologically sustainable and renewable—or something like that,'' Skinner said with disdain. "Fortunately greed got the better of those entrepreneurs and they sold the company as soon as it became profitable. I think

THE GAIA WAR 27

they retired to a commune in Oregon or some other God-forsaken wilderness. The new owners had the good sense to scrap all that socially conscious stuff and concentrate on market research and product development, not to mention their hiring of me. They changed the name to NatCo and we are now poised to lead the way into the coming New Age.''

''How?''

''This is where I need your loyalty, Lew. I need to know that you will not reveal what I'm about to tell you.''

''OK,'' Lew said with a sense of dread.

''We have a new product,'' Skinner said softly. ''Actually it's more than a product. It's a new technology. Are you concerned about toxic waste disposal?'' Skinner suddenly asked.

''Well, sure.''

''I thought you would be.'' Skinner smiled. ''Well, we have developed a system to take care of all that. We have a contract with the Feds. Testing starts next week. Imagine the most inhospitable desert environment turned into productive land. Highly productive, yielding ten times the agricultural output of prime Midwestern farmland. And imagine that this land is also a waste dump, where we dispose of almost unlimited quantities of heavy metals and toxic hydrocarbons.''

''A waste dump?''

''Yes! And the beauty of it is that the super productivity happens because of, not in spite of, this dual use.''

''How can that be possible?'' Lew asked.

''It is possible because of the cyberion process. It works like this. Tons of the most deadly chemicals are plowed into desert land. These are the by-products of our great industrial engine. The engine that has been crippled, I might add, by whining environmentalists, who have managed to get limits and controls placed on these substances.''

''But they're dangerous,'' Lew said.

''Danger is a relative concept, Lew. Bear with me. Phase one of the cyberion process is complete when the deposit of these materials kills most of the indigenous life-forms. The test site is located on the White Sands missile range

28   **Mark Leon**

in New Mexico. So the only life-forms that will be affected are the scrawny desert flora and maybe a few jackrabbits. But the process should work anywhere, from the Sahara to the most lush tropical rain forests. Anyway, I digress. Most of the native life will perish since it cannot tolerate the foreign substances coming into the environment. Then we will have a clean slate, and phase two can begin.

"This is where we here at NatCo stand poised to revolutionize the world. *And* make a great deal of money, I might add. Our biotechnology division has come up with some extremely clever microbes. They thrive on the toxic chemicals we will be dumping out there in the desert. This is nothing extraordinarily new. Bacteria and fungi have been used for several years now to help break down pollutants and speed the cleanup of dump sites. The power of our new patented organisms is twofold. First they metabolize a much wider class of chemicals. There are virtually no major pollutants that they cannot eat. But the big news is the fact that they can be tuned to excrete most of the proteins and carbohydrates necessary to sustain human life!"

"That's great," Lew said. "You mean these new organisms can turn toxic waste into food."

"We have had test subjects living on the stuff for a year now," Skinner said. "No serious side effects have developed."

"How does it taste?" Lew asked.

"We are still working on that. The stuff has to be processed, of course. It needs to be molded. With proper adjustment of sugar and salt content the stuff is palatable. Of course it has to be detoxed as well."

"Detoxed?"

"Yeah, our little bugs are not able to neutralize completely all the bad stuff. Some of it inevitably gets into the product. But as long as the farmers wear protective gear and take suitable precautions, the whole procedure is relatively safe.

"Imagine, Lew. No more worries about overpopulation. A conservative estimate is that the planet can sustain twenty billion people. Of course we will have to convert most

THE GAIA WAR 29

farmland and all available desert regions into cyberial factories. There is plenty of land in Africa . . ."

"What about the elephants?" Lew said.

"We won't need them anymore. Don't you see, Lew. With this process we won't need any life-form that is not functional in the cyberion process. Even the oceans. We have almost perfected a new kind of algae that is capable of producing all the oxygen we will ever need. It lives on seawater and one of our microbes. We will clean the planet up!"

"Clean it up?"

"Yes. There are too many species competing for limited resources right now. The cyberion process will allow us to take charge, clear out the redundant and ineffective plants and animals. Eventually there will only be us and a few very efficient microbes. And we will totally control those."

"But what about forests, and jungles and coral reefs, and . . ." Lew said.

"Forget about the past," Skinner said. "You've heard of the Gaia hypothesis, haven't you?"

"Yeah." Lew sighed.

"Well, the environmentalists think it means that Gaia, or mother earth, wants all this raucous life to go on indefinitely. But that is nonsense. The earth is like a big organism. Our role in that organism is to clean it up, get rid of all the unnecessary stuff. Gaia, if you want to use that term, will be eternally grateful for a well-regulated, orderly planet."

"But what about beauty?" Lew asked. "I mean, doesn't the variety and complexity of life have some intrinsic beauty?"

"Beauty is in the eye of the beholder," Skinner said with a thin smile. "We are the beholders, Lew. We also have the brains and foresight to make the planet into an orderly machine. Think of it! Cities will encompass whole continents. The industrial output will all go to cyberial farms. There will be an abundance of food and an abundance of manufactured goods and services, all part of a nice, self-regulating mechanism. That is why we call it the cyberion process—after cybernetics, the science of self-regulating systems. The earth will be one giant factory, and we will be the lords of this new creation.''

"But the biosphere is already self-regulating,'' Lew said. "How can you be sure that we have the wisdom to do a better job . . .''

"Have you been listening, Lew? Have you heard a word of what I am saying? We will do an infinitely better job! No more waste! We can even build giant engine cities!''

"Engine cities?'' Lew asked.

"Yes! Cities carefully positioned and primed to produce enormous power—enough power to shift the earth on its axis or even modify its orbit around the sun. We can regulate climate that way. Make the days shorter or longer. Some say that maybe''—he had a mad gleam in his eye—"someday we will generate enough energy to break free of the solar system. The earth a giant spaceship!''

"But why?'' Lew asked.

"Why? Why! Because we have the power to do it. Because we can! Something else I have not mentioned.''

"What?''

"The cyberion research is on the verge of unlocking the door to immortality. Those of us in control—you could be one of us, Lew—will not have to die. Our labs have discovered a virus which appears to infect the cell nucleus with a virulent strain of its own DNA. This new DNA has amazing side effects. It neutralizes the aging process. Aging is not inevitable, you know. It's programmed into our DNA. We're close to finding the means to shut down that program. For the lucky few here on the inside—we will live forever to cruise the galaxy in spaceship earth! Are you with me, Lew?''

"I think so,'' Lew said, trying to pacify the manic element which had consumed Skinner.

"Good!'' Skinner exhaled, and all his crazy energy seemed to flow out of him in one breath. "That's all, Lew,'' he said calmly. "I just wanted to let you in on this because NatCo is going to need allies. If you play your cards right, you could become one of the most privileged

THE GAIA WAR 31

persons to ever live—a virtual god. Are you religious, Lew?''

''Not really,'' Lew said.

''Neither was I,'' Skinner said. ''But I have been doing a lot of thinking lately. We are going to fulfill prophecy, Lew. Read the Book of Revelation. It's all in code. The whole Bible is a code. God is just an abstraction. God really does not yet exist outside of that abstraction. That's what we are doing here. We are going to bring God into being. I mean the men and women who are bold enough to seize the moment are going to become, quite literally, the God of the Old and New testaments. I am offering you a chance to get in on the ground floor.''

''Thanks,'' Lew said.

''Don't mention it. Now we had better get back to work, hadn't we?''

Lew jumped at the chance to get away from his boss. Meagan was watching him as he carefully closed the door behind him.

''Long coffee break,'' she said.

''Yeah.''

''Is something wrong, Lew? You look sort of washed out.''

''No. Stress is all. Too much stress.''

''Maybe you need some help,'' she offered.

''Oh no, I'll be alright. I don't trust doctors anyway.''

''I didn't mean that kind of help,'' Meagan said softly.

Lew was startled by her tone. At first he thought she was coming on to him. But then he saw her incline her head toward the book she was reading. It was a Bible. Meagan was very devout. She belonged to a nondenominational, charismatic Christian church. She tried to get Lew to go once or twice, but had long since given up on him.

''Thanks, Meagan,'' Lew said. ''But I don't think that would help either.''

''You'd be surprised,'' she said.

''Meagan, what do you people think about environmentalism?'' Lew asked.

''Environmentalism?''

''The earth, I mean. What should our relationship to the

32   Mark Leon

earth be? Is it ours to do with as we please?''

"Well, God did entrust all the animals to Adam," Meagan said.

"So it is OK to take over the whole thing, remake it however we see fit?''

"Well," Meagan said, "I'll have to ask my pastor about that. But after the Fall I think we sort of disqualified ourselves to do anything like that. Only God has that kind of wisdom.''

"Who is God?" Lew asked.

"You have to get to know Him personally," Meagan said. "And once you do . . ."

"What if we just got rid of most of the plants and animals and turned the earth into one giant factory?" Lew interrupted.

"Sounds horrible," she said. "The plants and animals come from God, too.''

"Thanks," Lew said. He started back to his office.

"It's a sign," Alan said. He was looking at the strange figures which had disrupted Lew's computer system. "You should have shown it to me the other night.''

"I tried to tell you about it," Lew said, "but you were too caught up in telling me about your little experiment." Lew pointed down. They were in Alan's dining room. The remnants of another excellent dinner were strewn about the table.

"Yes, but this," Alan said, "this is a mystery. Clearly a sign. Do you know what it says?''

"How could I?''

"This is Sanskrit, the ancient language of India. It is the closest thing to a root language ever discovered. Most European languages are derived from a common mother tongue, and linguists now think Sanskrit is a close approximation to that language of languages.''

"What does it say?''

"Curious," Alan said. "I'm not sure what it means. The closest translation I can come up with is something like, 'Roads divide the land and kill the life.' ''

"Roads divide the land and kill the life?" Lew echoed.

THE GAIA WAR

"Yeah. Any ideas? I confess that I'm baffled. But I'm certain that it is intended for us. It's one more clue to the puzzle."

"Puzzle?"

"The Gaia puzzle," Alan said. "My creation is just one piece. I still don't know how to best utilize her when she wakes up. We are treading on new ground here. This is virgin territory. No one has ever done what I have done here."

"But, Alan," Lew said, "I can just barely believe that a strange message, written in Sanskrit, could penetrate security and get into my system. Hackers can do all kinds of amazing things these days. But how do you know it has something to do with your plans, with . . . her?" Lew still had difficulty in referring to Alan's experiment as a person.

"Synchronicity, Lew." Alan seemed to think this was explanation enough.

"Sure," Lew said. "Speaking of coincidences, I had a weird conversation with Skinner yesterday. It reminded me of some of the things we've been talking about."

"Really?" Alan became suddenly curious. "What did he say? What are they up to at NatCo?"

Lew wanted to tell Alan that Skinner was also talking about remaking the world, but the boss's vision was radically different from Alan's. But Lew had promised Skinner to keep quiet about it. "Oh nothing," Lew said. "Just some of Skinner's New Age fantasies. A lot of bullshit about the millennium—that sort of thing."

"I get the feeling you are not leveling with me, Lew."

"Don't worry about it, Alan. It was really nothing." Lew really did not want to honor his promise of loyalty to Skinner. But at the same time he was hoping that Skinner was just spouting nonsense, and that the whole thing really would amount to nothing.

"OK, Lew. I won't press you. But remember what I said. You are either with us or against us on this one. There is no middle ground."

When Skinner heard the tape he was pleased that Lew had not revealed the substance of their discussion. He was

34 Mark Leon

also slightly annoyed with himself for having told Lew so much. Too much enthusiasm, he told himself. He did want to recruit Lew. They would need a database expert eventually—soon, if things went as well as expected.

But what really interested him about the tape Roger had made was the reference to Alan's plans—specifically to "her." Skinner called Roger. "Did you see anything unusual when you planted the bugs, Roger?"

"Not really, Mr. Skinner. It was a fairly straightforward job."

"No signs of a laboratory, electronic equipment, anything like that?"

"No."

"I want you to get back into Fain's house. Something is going on there. Did you see the entire place last time, all the rooms?"

"Yes."

"Either Fain has a place somewhere else or he has a hidden room somewhere in that house. Put a tail on him and search his place thoroughly."

"Alright . . ." Roger sounded uneasy.

"What's the matter. Can't you handle this kind of work?" Skinner asked testily.

"Sure," Roger said. He had worked for the FBI and run a private investigation agency. The agency had been so successful that he had retired at age fifty. Boredom and the lucrative salary at NatCo had persuaded him to come off the golf course. "This kind of thing gets expensive, Mr. Skinner."

"Don't worry about the money, Roger. I promised you a nice bonus."

"Yeah, I know, but I'm going to have to bring in someone else now," Roger said. "We need to talk specific amounts."

"I'm listening."

"Three thousand dollars a week, plus expenses."

"Sounds a little high."

"You can get folks cheaper," Roger said.

Skinner steamed in silence for a moment. Roger was a pro with solid experience. NatCo would not have hired any-

THE GAIA WAR

35

thing less than the best. The money was going to have to come out of his own funds. He could afford it—for a limited time. It infuriated him that Alan Fain was going to cost him so dearly, but the urgency of the situation could not be ignored. He needed to know what Alan was up to. There was too much riding on the cyberion project to take any chances. "OK," he said tightly. "I want a report as soon as possible."

"Absolutely, Mr. Skinner."

Two figures sat in front of a computer terminal in Benares, India. They were not looking at the screen. They were both Indians. One, Alan's old guru Swami-ji, was a Sanskrit pundit, born in Benares, the most sacred city in all of Hinduism. The other was a full-blooded Apache Mescalero from New Mexico.

"Do you think our message got through?" the Apache asked.

"I'm certain of it," Swami-ji said.

"How can you be sure?"

"You worry too much, Paul."

"Maybe we should have been more explicit. How do we know that Alan will figure out what to do?"

"It may be just as well that he does not," the guru said. "Things could actually go very badly."

"It needs to be done," the Apache named Paul said. "It needed to be done a long time ago, before the Europeans destroyed my world."

"They were not so very kind to mine, either," Swami-ji said. "I share your concern. I merely point out that this could easily spin out of control. We cannot know, until after the fact, whether or not it was wise to encourage Alan."

"But if it works, we will have saved the world."

"Don't be so sure," the guru said. "My world is much older than yours. We have seen some world saving before and it does not always work out so well. But I agree that it is a risk worth taking."

"Why did we have to be so cryptic?" Paul asked. "I mean, the message was sent through a maze of computer security blocks and spliced into an obscure portion of a database program. It was written in Sanskrit, and to top it all off we can't even be sure Alan will figure out what it means.''

"I know Alan Fain," Swami-ji said. "Any other way would have been too direct. Now, once he does put it all together, you can be sure he will act promptly. If we had been more direct, he would surely waste precious time in overanalyzing every little detail. By that time it might be too late."

"What about the woman?" The big Apache got up and turned to look at the holy Ganges River, which had begun to rise with the monsoon rains. The water was already lapping at the door to the temple, which sat beneath Swami-ji's office. Soon the temple would be flooded, and the only way to enter the office would be by boat.

"She should awake soon." The old Hindu smiled. "That should prove to be really interesting."

Skinner read through the report from Roger again. He had already grilled his spy repeatedly. He simply could not believe it. A synthetic woman! Either Alan had completely flipped out or things were more serious than he had feared. He let the sheaf of papers fall back into the folder and locked it away inside his desk. There was only one way to proceed. He did not like the idea of breaking and entering—he was already in over his head—but he could see no other option. He got Roger back on the phone.

"Are you sure he's gone?" Skinner asked, later that evening. They were parked in front of Alan's house in Roger's black Ford Taurus.

"I saw him leave," Roger said. "He probably went out to eat. He does that often—when he decides not to cook one of his elaborate Indian meals. Don't worry. He probably won't be back for a couple of hours. He usually spends a lot of time browsing in bookstores and newsstands after dinner."

"Probably . . ." Skinner said. "What if we're caught?"

"Don't worry. We won't get caught. And if we are, I can handle him."

THE GAIA WAR

"No violence!" Skinner hissed.

"I won't do any permanent damage," Roger said, "but wouldn't you rather have him roughed up a little than spend the night in jail?"

"Yeah. OK," Skinner said. "Let's go."

Roger had little trouble with Alan's door. They were in quickly. "How do we get to the basement?" Skinner asked.

"I don't know."

"You don't know! What the fuck am I paying you for?" Skinner yelled.

"Hey!" Roger's voice took a commanding tone. "Calm down. You're going to get us busted. You're paying me to do a professional job. Which I am doing. Now you don't like it, just tell me and we'll get the fuck out of here."

"Sorry," Skinner said.

"I'm pretty sure the entrance to the basement is in Fain's bedroom. But I didn't have time to locate it last night. I have a sonic probe that should do the trick." He led Skinner to Roger's bedroom and began scanning the walls. "Bingo," he said when they got to the closet. "There's a big hollow spot here. It has to be the entrance." Soon they were descending the stairs.

"I knew it," Skinner said after the lights had been on a few moments. "I knew the guy was up to something. This lab is serious. Do you think it's here?"

"What?"

"The . . . woman . . . or whatever it is."

"I don't get paid to think that much," Roger said. "You read my report and heard the tapes. They say that *something* is down here."

"This has to be it," Skinner said after they found the box. He was running his hand along the seam. "Let's take a look." They set to work unscrewing the clamps.

"What do you think, Roger?" Skinner asked. They were both staring at the naked woman.

"I'd say this is serious," Roger said. "I refuse to get mixed up in murder or kidnapping. Surveillance is one thing . . ."

"Too late!" Skinner snapped. "We are here and you are

38 Mark Leon

going to help me. If I know Alan Fain, this is neither kidnapping nor murder."

"Who is she, then?" Roger asked. "His sister who just happens to sleep in a coffin."

"No," Skinner said. "I think we have something really new here." He pulled a syringe from his coat pocket.

"What's that?" Roger asked uneasily.

"Relax. I'm just going to take a blood sample for later analysis." Skinner wiped the needle with a sterile alcohol pad. Then he pinched a portion of her thigh. He was surprised at the firmness of the flesh. The skin was extremely smooth. This was deceptive because it was also very tough. It was not easy to get the needle to penetrate. Skinner finally had to jab with a vicious thrust. Even then the needle flexed, threatening to break before it popped under the surface of her skin. Skinner filled the chamber with a few cc's of blood and withdrew the needle. He wiped the puncture with another sterile pad and was amazed to see the tiny wound practically vanish before his eyes.

"That should do it, Roger," Skinner said. "Let's get her crated up again and get out of here." Skinner was momentarily preoccupied with unscrewing the needle and sealing the chamber in a sterile carrying case so Roger's silence did not immediately register. "Roger," he finally said, "come on. Let's get moving."

"Uh, Mr. Skinner . . ." Roger said.

"What?" Skinner looked up to see Roger's eyes practically bugging out of his head.

"Look," was all Roger could say.

The woman's eyes were open, and she was staring straight at Roger with an expression of awesome intensity. When Skinner looked down her eyes quickly darted to meet his gaze. It literally took his breath away. A moment ago she had seemed comatose. Now her face was full of life—and those eyes! They mesmerized with a cool fire that flashed and flowed with the power of a million unanswered questions.

Skinner had pondered the question of what a synthetic woman might be like after he had read Roger's latest report. He had assumed that she would be like a newborn baby—

THE GAIA WAR 39

ignorant and innocent. Her mind, he reasoned, would be a blank slate. When he imagined what she might look like, he had supposed a face of slack-jawed wonder and doelike eyes, all vacuous and simple. But the image before him was nothing of the sort. It recalled to his mind images of the goddess Athena which he had gleaned from his undergraduate study of *The Odyssey*. Athena, daughter of Zeus, was said to have sprung fully formed and worldly-wise from her father's forehead.

For a moment Skinner was speechless. Finally he spoke. It seemed an absurd thing to say, but he said it anyway. "Hello."

"Are you the one who hurt me?" Her voice was profoundly feminine and surprisingly deep and resonant.

"What?" Skinner stammered.

"My leg," she said, rubbing her thigh where Skinner had jabbed her.

"I'm sorry, I . . ." Skinner said, trying to keep the fear out of his voice.

"Don't hurt me again." This was said without any trace of threat. It was more like a command. She obviously could not even imagine that it would ever be disobeyed.

"No . . . I won't," Skinner said. "I'm sorry."

She sat up with an easy, fluid grace and looked around, all but ignoring the two men. She climbed out of her box, lacking any self-consciousness about her nudity. After exploring the room for a few minutes she walked over to the sofa and sat down, crossing her legs.

Skinner walked slowly over to her. She did not seem to feel any need to speak. This made him extremely uneasy. He thought furiously for something to say, but anything that came to mind seemed so ridiculous that he could not get it out. So instead he just stood before her with his head slightly lowered and shifting from foot to foot.

Finally she looked up at him and spoke. "I'm hungry."

This so completely baffled Skinner that he had to sit down beside her on the sofa. "Hungry?" he said.

"Don't you ever get hungry?" she asked.

"Well, yeah, I guess so."

40 Mark Leon

"You guess so? What an odd thing to say. I can guess about a great many things, but not hunger. There is no guessing about that." Then she did something completely unexpected. She laughed. It was a sound as light as air, but full. And when she stopped it was absolutely over. She did not show the slightest concern over whether anyone else shared in her mirth. "I'm starving," she said quite seriously. "I want something to eat."

"Just a minute," Skinner said. He got up and went back over to where Roger was standing. A plan of sorts was beginning to take shape in his mind.

"Just a minute?" she echoed. "How strange. One cannot eat time."

"Roger." Skinner practically whispered. "Roger, look at me, dammit!"

"What?" Roger's face was pale and his voice sounded far away.

"I have an idea. She's hungry."

"Hungry?"

"Yes! And she seems fairly trusting. Let's get her to my penthouse. We can send out for pizza and . . ."

"And then what!" Roger snapped back to the present. "Then we'll be involved in a kidnapping. And what are you going to do with her . . ."

"Shut up!" Skinner said. She was staring at them with an expression that indicated both curiosity and sublime indifference. "Once we get her back to my place you can split. Let me worry about the rest of it. And it won't be kidnapping if she comes voluntarily, which I think she will."

Skinner walked back over to the sofa. "We haven't been properly introduced," he said. She laughed quite loudly. This infuriated him, but he fought to conceal it. "My name is Skinner," he said, "Larry Skinner. You can call me Larry." He held out his hand.

She laughed again. "Alright, I will call you Larry. Larry, Larry!" she said gaily. "Now, Larry, can you tell me where I might find some food?" She ignored his outstretched hand and got up to walk around, apparently searching the premises for signs of anything edible.

THE GAIA WAR 41

Skinner turned red and took a deep breath. Then he went after her. "Uh, miss, if you will come with me, I think we can get you some food."

Her eyes lit up. "Oh, that would be wonderful!" she said. "I will come with you, then."

Skinner smiled to himself, surprised at how easy she was to manipulate. "Just a moment," he said to her. He then enlisted Roger's help in lifting the heavy lid back in place on top of her box. It slipped out of Skinner's hands and nearly hit his foot as a corner smashed into the floor. "Idiot!" Skinner yelled at Roger.

"But you . . ." Roger stammered.

"Look," Skinner said, pointing to the corner of the lid. The wood was damaged. It was a small area, but quite noticeable.

"Can I help?" She was suddenly standing between them. She bent down and grabbed the heavy burden. With a flexing of thighs and a swinging motion of her back and arms, she hefted the lid back into place. A small breath escaped her in the process, but she obviously had not exerted herself much.

The two men just stared at each other.

"Well?" she said.

"Well what?" Skinner asked.

"When do we eat?"

Skinner and Roger quickly bolted the top back into place. Then they left the basement, followed by the beautiful woman.

"We have to get you some clothes," Skinner said. They were in Alan's bedroom.

"To eat?" she asked.

Skinner did not answer. "Roger," he said, "find some pants and a shirt, some old things that he will not miss too easily."

"Find them yourself," Roger said.

Skinner furiously started rummaging through Alan's closets and drawers, determined to fire Roger as soon as possible. He finally found an old pair of jeans and a cotton work shirt. "Put these on," he said.

42   **Mark Leon**

"No," she said simply, not a trace of obstinacy in her voice.

"Why not?" Skinner asked desperately.

"Why should I?" she said. "I thought we were going to eat."

"Yes," Skinner said, "we are going to eat. Follow me." He took the clothes under one arm and led her to the front door. "Now listen," he said. "There's a car outside. We're going to have to run to get to it."

"Why?" she asked.

"Because we want to hurry and get to the food," he said.

"Alright," she said neutrally.

"Just follow me. Close the door behind us, Roger." He opened the door and looked outside. It was dark. Their car was parked down the street, about a block away. Fortunately it was not close to any streetlight and there were no neighbors in sight. He made a mad dash. She ran behind him. It was a ludicrous sight. Skinner, who prided himself on staying in shape, looked awkward in comparison to the nude woman. She ran like an Olympic athlete and had to slow down to stay behind him.

He motioned for her to get into the backseat, nervously scanning the neighborhood for any sign that they had been seen. He got in behind her and Roger took the wheel.

"Can I possibly persuade you to put this shirt on?" Skinner asked her when they were under way.

"Why?"

"It's difficult to explain. But if you put it on, we will be able to get food much more quickly."

For the first time her face showed an expression of distrust. It was not hostile, just open suspicion. "That makes absolutely no sense," she said.

"I know it doesn't," he said, "but you must believe me."

"I do not believe you," she said, "but I will put the shirt on."

When she was covered from the waist up he breathed a sigh of relief. "Stop at the Pizza Palace, Roger. Then let's head for my penthouse."

THE GAIA WAR

"Sure," Roger said.

She ate hungrily, passionately. Skinner could not take his eyes off the way she devoured slice after slice. What fascinated him was the combination of animal food lust with human grace. There was nothing sloppy or unseemly in her eating, yet her grace employed none of the false reserve that we so often mistake as "good manners." She did not offer any to the two men. When she had eaten half the pizza she put the box down on the seat.

"Good?" Skinner asked.

"Not really," she said, wiping her mouth with the back of her hand. "Much too high in fat, the vegetables had no taste, and the bread was not worthy of the name."

"You ate it," Skinner said in a whiny tone of voice.

"I was hungry," she said.

When they arrived Skinner asked her to put the pants on.

"I am thirsty now," she said.

"That is why you need to put these on," Skinner said. "I have drink inside, but you need to wear pants before we can go in."

"Nonsense," she said, and got out of the car.

Skinner ran after her, clutching Alan's jeans in one hand. "Wait." He pleaded.

She ignored him and walked into the building. A guard in the lobby gaped at her. "Uh, miss . . ." he said.

"I am thirsty," she said.

Something in her tone of voice made the guard gesture to a water fountain. "Over there," he said.

She was fumbling with the mechanism when Skinner came up behind her. He held the button down for her and she drank greedily. The guard called out, "Can I help you, Mr. Skinner? I mean do you . . . need anything?"

"No!" Skinner barked. He hurried over and handed the bewildered man a fifty-dollar bill. Then he punched the elevator button. The door opened and he was relieved to see that it was empty. "Come on!" He grabbed her arm and led her into the elevator. Thirst sated, she allowed herself to be drawn in. She studied the claustrophobic surroundings with a curious expression that also seemed oddly

44   Mark Leon

bored. Skinner breathed a sigh of relief when he got her into his penthouse and shut the door.

"I think it's time," Alan said to Lew. They were drinking beer up in Lew's apartment. The sparse furnishings and beat-up old sofa always helped Alan to relax, and he was somewhat tense.

"Time for what?"

"To wake her up. She's ready. I examined her today. The gestation period is over. Frankly I'm a little scared."

"What are you scared of?" Lew asked.

"I just don't know what to expect. I'm counting on her for so much and I really have no idea what sort of creature she will be."

"But you seemed so confident," Lew protested.

"All bluff," Alan said. "One has to put on a good show to play the game we're playing, but when you get right down to it, I'm as clueless as you are."

"I see," Lew said.

"Not to put you down," Alan added hastily. "I just meant that as ordinary mortals, we . . ."

"Spare me," Lew said. "I've heard it all before. Just don't forget that you asked me to help you with this."

"I'm just a little uneasy," Alan said. "Tonight is the night."

"For what?"

"We need to wake her, Lew. Rouse her from her slumber, bring her fully into her new life."

"How?"

"It shouldn't take much," Alan said. "A little cold water on the face, a slight stimulus to the epidermis, something like that. You will help me, won't you? Now that the moment of reckoning has come I just can't face it alone. I mean it's one thing to pretend that you are creating a new life, but to actually pull it off, that ups the ante a bit. What if she hates me?"

"Why would she hate you?"

"I don't know. She didn't ask to be created. I don't really know what her life will be like, and I do have high

THE GAIA WAR 45

expectations of her. It could all go wrong. It could all be a disaster.''

''Can you abort?'' Lew asked.

Alan's expression got very dark and he said in a low voice, ''That would be murder, Lew! Don't even think about it. Now do you see why I said there is no turning back.''

''Yeah, I suppose you're right.''

''Are you ready?'' Alan asked.

''No.''

''Neither am I. Let's go.''

Alan drove them back to his place. They descended into the basement with an air of ritual solemnity. As they approached the box, Alan's face took on a worried expression. ''What's this?'' he said, examining the damaged corner.

''What?'' Lew asked.

Alan was already unscrewing the lid. ''Someone has been here, Lew!''

He cursed loudly when they removed the lid to see the empty chamber. Then he stared for several moments in deep silence, thinking hard. ''Come on, Lew!'' he said finally. He led Lew quickly back upstairs and out to the car. They got inside and sped away. He drove them out of town to a deserted farm road and insisted that they get out and walk.

''Someone is onto us, Lew,'' he said. The full moon cast shadows on his face, making it appear more angular and gaunt than it was. ''My house is probably bugged. They've kidnapped her! Someone is onto us and I think I know who it is!''

''Who?'' Lew was having a hard time keeping up. Alan's long legs were going at a feverish pace.

Suddenly Alan stopped and turned. Lew nearly collided with him. Alan put his hands on Lew's shoulders. ''Lew,'' he said softly, eyes boring into his friend's, ''you have to tell me everything. What did Larry Skinner say to you the other day?''

''Skinner?'' Lew asked.

''Yes.'' Alan's breath hissed out between his tightly clenched jaws. ''Skinner.''

CHAPTER 3

Skinner knew that Alan could not call the police. How do you report the kidnapping of a woman with no established identity? His immediate problem was how to make the best possible use of the woman herself. So far she had been content to stay in his penthouse and read. She devoured books like candy. She also ate voraciously. And she refused to wear any clothes other than the work shirt, only donning that when she consumed food in his presence. It seemed to represent a complicated joke of which he was the butt.

His line buzzed. "Skinner here."

"Mr. Skinner, this is Pete down at the lab. I have the analysis you requested on that blood sample."

"Good. Anything to report?"

"Well, I would like to know the origin of the sample before I tell you anything."

"Confidential," Skinner said. "Just tell me what you found."

"OK, but I really need more information."

"Too bad," Skinner snapped.

"All I can say is that the sample *appears* to be human blood. Female."

"Appears?"

"Yes. There are proteins that we have never seen before. In addition to hemoglobin there are other, more exotic oxygen transporters. Molecules that you could dream up in a

THE GAIA WAR   47

theoretical analysis of life, but none of which have ever been seen or even synthesized. But the most unusual thing—I really don't know what to make of this . . .''

"Yeah, go on." Skinner's anxiety was getting the better of him.

"Well the DNA is not really human as we know it."

"Not human? What the hell is that supposed to mean?"

"There are several extra genes and a few extra chromosomes—I guess your other research team beat us to it."

"Beat you to what? What are you talking about?"

"Didn't you get this from an X-life test subject?" X-life was the NatCo code name for the life-extension project. The goal of X-life was to augment normal human DNA with an alien strand of genetic material that would have the effect of slowing or stopping the aging process.

"There is no other X-life research team. You guys at the lab run the only one," Skinner said, and immediately regretted it. The researcher had supplied Skinner with a perfect cover story for the origin of the woman's blood, and Skinner had failed to take advantage of it. "Just get to the point," he snapped.

"Well," the scientist said, "this stuff has a very advanced form of the X-life gene that we have been working on. My guess is that the subject will easily live for several hundred years. In fact, I would say that she is virtually immortal."

Skinner could not keep the excitement out of his voice. "Can you duplicate it?" he asked. "I mean, can you develop the necessary techniques to splice this new gene into normal human DNA?"

"I'm afraid not. We need to examine the subject more closely. There is a lot here we don't understand. Can I ask you a question?"

"What?"

"Was this sample taken from a live specimen?"

"Why?"

"Because in order to do a thorough analysis, we would need to completely dissect the organism."

"I'll get back to you," Skinner said, and hung up.

*   *   *

48 Mark Leon

That evening he began to look at his guest in a new light. She was ignoring him as usual, reading from a stack of encyclopedias. He had given up trying to make conversation. The woman just did not see any reason to talk unless she wanted something. Her nudity was difficult for him— her body was exquisitely beautiful. But her remoteness made her seem more chaste than a nun. And Skinner had never forgotten her great strength.

Curious to see just how strong she was, he managed to persuade her one evening to try his bench press. She could easily handle four hundred pounds. She had expressed some interest in the weights by asking what they were for. When Skinner tried to explain it she became very bored and finally just laughed. "What a silly thing to do. I thought maybe there was some purpose to it."

When he asked what her name was she got very quiet and thoughtful for a moment. "You can call me Gaia," she said, and then added, as if it were a highly significant caveat, "for *now*."

She was beginning to disturb him deeply. He wanted to be rid of her, and the image of her body stretched out on a dissecting table became a soothing balm to his distress.

He laid out the Chinese takeout on the dining room table and was about to inform her that dinner was ready when a noise at the door caught their attention. His head jerked around as if pulled by an invisible wire. She merely looked up calmly from the sofa where she lay in a pose that could easily have been mistaken for wantonness until one noted the ease and the lack of passion.

A key was slowly turning in the lock. Skinner sprang to the door. He got to it just as a head poked through. It was Meagan, and she was staring, gaping at the nude woman.

"Didn't I tell you to always call first!" Skinner shouted. He had already grabbed her by the arm and was attempting to roughly shove her out the door. Meagan cried out. His grip was hard, and she was badly startled by the abruptness of her rude ejection.

"You're hurting me! Please!"

Skinner was about to slam the door when he felt a hand

THE GAIA WAR 49

restraining him. "What are you doing?" his nude guest asked in a cool, forceful voice.

"Stay out of this!" Skinner said.

"Out of what? You are hurting the woman." Gaia pushed Skinner away and opened the door to let Meagan in. Skinner's secretary just stood there, humiliated and shocked. "Come in," Gaia said.

The authority in her voice got the better of Meagan and she did as she was told. Skinner was standing to one side rubbing his shoulder where Gaia had grabbed him.

"Meagan," Skinner began, voice shaking.

"Don't bother," Meagan said. "I don't own you. I just wanted to see you. But I guess you're busy." She looked at Gaia.

"It is not what you think," Skinner said.

"How do you know what I think?" Meagan shot back. "My name is Meagan," she said to Gaia.

Gaia said nothing for a few moments. Then she looked toward the dining room. "I smell food," she said, turning to face the source of the odor. "Pardon me while I dress." She went to the sofa and retrieved the shirt.

Meagan watched as Gaia buttoned up. "We always dress for dinner around here, Meagan," Gaia said with a trace of sarcasm. "Larry insists." Meagan followed her to the table.

"No pants?" Meagan asked as Gaia sat down.

"Who needs pants?" Gaia laughed. "I think you should take yours off, too."

"Why not?" Meagan said. She quickly removed her slacks and underwear before sitting down. "Tell me," she asked, "what exactly is your relationship with Mr. Skinner—I mean Larry?"

"None," Gaia said, shoving fried rice into her mouth.

"You're not his mistress?"

Gaia laughed so hard at this that she nearly choked. "You *are* funny," she said to Meagan. "I did not even know the meaning of the word 'mistress' until yesterday. You really mean am I his 'fuckpiece' don't you?" She began laughing again. This time Meagan could not help but join in.

50   Mark Leon

"I *am* his 'fuckpiece,' " Meagan said. They both laughed again at this.

"Why?" Gaia asked between ravenous bites of food.

"Good question," Meagan said. "I've been asking myself that for a long time."

Skinner was watching this absurd display with a growing sense of hostility. "Meagan," he said, "you are not to reveal the fact that I am keeping this woman here—to anyone. Do you understand? This involves corporate matters that you would not understand."

"Do you work for NatCo?" Meagan asked Gaia.

"Work?" Gaia said in a voice so purely innocent that Meagan just stared at her in awe.

"Yes, work," Meagan finally said.

"I have also just begun to read about work," Gaia said. "But it is not nearly so easy to understand."

"No," Meagan said, "I don't suppose it is."

"Meagan," Skinner said, "did you hear me?"

"What? Oh sure, Larry," Meagan said. "Your secret is safe with me. I keep your little secrets pretty well. Or don't you remember?"

"I remember," Skinner said. "Now I think you had better be going."

"But I think not, Larry," Meagan said. She looked at Gaia. "Should I go?"

"Go. Go where?" Gaia asked.

"Out. Away from here."

"Oh, no. You should stay," Gaia said.

"Why?" Meagan asked, transfixed by the deep, gray pools of the other woman's eyes.

"Because you want to," Gaia said.

"That's right," Meagan said. "I do." She looked up at Skinner. "I think I'll stay, Larry," she said.

"Suit yourself," he said angrily, and stalked off to his study.

"What's his problem?" Meagan asked.

"Larry is not himself," Gaia said, and laughed. Her laughter was beginning to take on more depth—it was not the pure innocent delight of a few days earlier. There were now undertones of recognition in it, recognition of dark

THE GAIA WAR 51

things that she still did not understand and was not eager to learn.

Meagan had just come from church. Her mind was full of the charismatic trappings of the Holy Spirit. When she looked at Gaia these feelings grew. She was beginning to think that she knew this strange woman. She was beginning to think that this was the Mother of God, and that the final days promised in the Book of Revelation were nearer than she dared hope.

Skinner, in the privacy of his study, was on the phone talking to a biologist at the NatCo research lab.

"I'm not sure I understand, Mr. Skinner," the biologist was saying. "You have a large animal that you want to poison?"

"Not poison! I mean not exactly. This is very confidential you understand."

"Yeah, I understand. Just tell me what you want." The biologist's tone was neutral.

"Well, we have created a large tissue sample," Skinner said. "It is not exactly alive, but we have reason to believe that a thorough dissection of the tissue could shed light on the X-life research. But we need to terminate all its vital functions. It is very important that we do this in a way that will not damage the genetic material. Do you have any 'substances' that would be suitable?"

"Sure. Can you be more specific? How much does this 'tissue sample' weigh?"

"About 120 pounds," Skinner said. Then he recalled Gaia's great strength. "I mean 200 pounds."

"Is this anything like a complex organism?"

"Yes. Very complex."

"Does it have a nervous system?"

"Yes."

"Is it as sophisticated as a—primate?"

"Yes."

"OK, Mr. Skinner." The man sounded cool. Skinner was grateful for that. At NatCo they tried to choose employees who would follow orders and not ask too many questions. "Call me tomorrow. I think I can whip up something suitable. Of course, it would be best if I could examine this specimen.''

"Impossible," Skinner said. "Sorry. You know how it is."

"Of course."

Skinner felt better immediately, but dreaded the prospect of facing those two women again. There was something creepy about the way Meagan and Gaia had immediately established an intimate bond that excluded him. He made a mental note to dump Meagan when this was all over.

He went to the kitchen and poured himself a drink. They were sitting on the sofa, both still naked from the waist down. Meagan was reading from her Bible, and Gaia was listening with rapt attention. The sight made him gulp his drink. He quickly poured another. *Just one more day*, he thought.

Lew sat at his desk pondering his awkward situation. After Gaia's disappearance he had told Alan everything he knew about NatCo's cyberion project. Alan was convinced that Skinner had stolen the woman. And Skinner knew that Lew and Alan were in close contact. Lew was caught in the middle of a game that was turning ugly and dangerous.

He looked up to see Meagan walking by. "Hi," he said.

"Hello, Lew." Meagan looked radiant, strangely peaceful.

"You certainly look happy," Lew said.

"Happy? No I wouldn't say happy. Happiness is something I try not to think about much anymore."

"What do you mean?" Lew asked.

"I mean that when the rapture comes it will not matter. The final judgment does not have anything to do with happiness. It all just comes down to one thing, Lew."

"What is that?"

"Do you genuinely thank God for the gift of life . . . or not?"

"Seems pretty simple," Lew said.

"It is. But it's hard when you have to live in this world."

"Why?"

"Because"—Meagan came into Lew's office—"this

THE GAIA WAR

world is Babylon, and the distractions here make us forget what's really important. The danger is that we will be so confused by those distractions that we will not be ready.''

''Ready for what?''

''Oh, Lew!'' Meagan said. ''You know what I mean. God is coming. And now I *know* it for sure.''

Something about the way she said this caught Lew's attention. He knew Meagan was sincere in her beliefs, passionate even. But now she was talking as if she had recently witnessed a miracle. It did not sound like the usual Bible study stuff that she was so ready to recite.

''You *know* it?'' Lew asked. ''How? What have you seen?''

''I have seen *her*,'' Meagan said, her whole face glowing.

''Who? Who have you seen?''

''The Mother of God. She is here, Lew. And that can mean only one thing.''

''What?''

''The Lord is coming. Soon.'' She walked out before Lew could say anything.

''Skinner is not spending any time at his house,'' Alan said at lunch.

''That doesn't surprise me,'' Lew said. ''His wife and kids are away. I told you about his penthouse.''

''Yeah,'' Alan said. ''I can't get up there. I've tried, but the security is too tight. I *know* he has her.''

''How can you be sure?'' Lew asked.

''Who else could it be?'' Alan said. ''And after what you told me about the cyberion project . . . Lew, the situation is critical. I found out something interesting last night.''

''What is that?''

''I was watching the front of the building where Skinner has his love retreat. I saw that cute little secretary from your office go in. You know, the religious freak. What's her name?''

''Meagan,'' Lew said.

''Yeah, Meagan. Well she had no trouble getting past the guard. He seemed to know her. I stayed until 4:00 A.M. and

54 **Mark Leon**

she still had not come out. Now I doubt if Meagan can afford an apartment in that building on her secretary's salary. I would say our little Bible thumper has got something going with your boss.''

''Impossible!'' Lew said, realizing that it was actually quite probable.

''Why do you say that? Because it is against the Ten Commandments? Come on, Lew. She may be devout, but she's still human.''

This bothered Lew more than he cared to admit. While he found Meagan's religious fervor trying, he did respect her faith. There was an innocence and purity about it that he almost envied. But he knew Skinner, knew what kind of man his boss was. It just did not seem right that Meagan could be involved with him. But his conversation with Meagan that morning began to take on a new meaning, and he had to believe that Alan was probably right.

''Can you get to her?'' Alan was saying.

''Who?''

''Meagan! Can you talk to her? She must have seen something last night.''

''Yeah,'' Lew said. ''I think she did.'' He proceeded to relate his encounter with Meagan.

Alan laughed. It was a nervous sound with an unwholesome edge to it. ''The Mother of God! I had no idea that I was so talented. But in a way she is right.''

''What do you mean?''

''If things go according to plan, she *will* be something like the Mother of God. We need her, Lew. Without her we are lost and the earth is doomed. Talk to Meagan this afternoon. Find out all you can! I have a bad feeling that time is running out!''

Skinner went to visit the lab that afternoon. He got what he wanted. It was approximately 30 cc's of a clear liquid in a small bottle. He pocketed the stuff and returned to his office. The thought occurred to him that he was about to commit murder, something he had never done before. But then he reminded himself that she was not really human, at least not in the usual sense. With that thought he

THE GAIA WAR 55

was able to convince himself that she was not really alive either.

Lew met Meagan at her church that evening. It was the only way he could persuade her to talk to him outside of work. "We are the army of the Lord!" the pastor was saying. "We must be prepared to march in His righteousness. How long, Lord? How long? If He comes this day, this hour, we are ready. And if the Lord tarries . . ."

"Ah key wisom begom!" Meagan suddenly lifted her head and began to speak loudly. There were no words that Lew could recognize, but the sounds issuing from her mouth did sound eerily like a language. Standing next to her, Lew felt all eyes of the congregation turn in their direction. *"Nai shay besam besam! Hai! No rei, no rei reison."* Her voice was getting stronger, and the words were flowing faster. Lew felt a tingle at the base of his spine. He wanted to run. There was an energy in the room that frightened him. Suddenly, without any noticeable change in tone or cadence, Meagan's utterances shifted into English. "She has come, brothers and sisters! The Mother of God is here. The Son is not far behind. Selah!"

There was a long moment of silence. Then the pastor began to lead the congregation in another round of singing. Meagan nudged Lew in the ribs and pointed to the words which were being projected on the wall behind the pastor. Dutifully Lew also began to sing, "God is the strength of our hearts!"

After the service the pastor stopped them at the door. "That was beautiful prophecy, Meagan," he said.

"Thank you, Pastor Lee," Meagan said. "This is my friend, Lew."

"God bless you, Lew," Pastor Lee said as they shook hands.

"Thank you," Lew said, feeling extremely awkward.

"Don't thank me," Lee said. "Thank the Lord."

"OK," Lew said.

Lee laughed. "I can see this is all rather new to you, Lew."

"Yeah, I guess so," Lew said.

56   **Mark Leon**

"You must think we're all crazy here."

"No, I . . ."

"It does probably look that way, but I assure we know what we're doing."

"I'm sure . . ."

"But don't take my word for it," Lee said. "Ask the Lord. Do you know the Lord, Lew?"

"I can't say that I do," Lew replied.

"Well, Praise God!" Lee said. "It is time you two got acquainted. Come back, won't you, Lew? All people are welcome here."

"Sure," Lew said, grateful that Lee was letting him off the hook.

The pastor had turned to Meagan. "Be careful, Meagan," he said.

"Yes, I . . ."

"I know that you have seen signs," the pastor continued. "Just remember that the powers of deception are mighty. There are signs and there are signs. There are spirits and then there is the one true Holy Spirit. Be careful."

"Thank you," Meagan said humbly.

"Meagan, we have to talk." Lew was driving with Meagan beside him.

"I'm sorry if things got a little weird for you in there, Lew," she said. "But there really is something to it. If you would just open yourself to the Lord . . ."

"Not about that," Lew said.

"What then?" Meagan said defensively.

"Skinner."

"Larry?"

"Yeah, our boss. Larry Skinner."

"What about Larry?"

"Don't take this the wrong way, Meagan"—Lew turned to look at her—"but I need to ask you about your relationship with Larry."

"What relationship! What do you mean, Lew? Larry and I are just friends. I work for him, I never . . ."

"Take it easy," Lew said, "I'm not trying to pry into your personal life. And I am not judging you. It is fine with me if you and Larry are . . ."

THE GAIA WAR   57

"Are what!"

"Are having an affair."

"How could you, Lew? You really just can't go saying things like that to a person you know, you really can't . . ." She had started to cry. At first she seemed to have it under control. But then the dam burst and great sobs began to break through.

"Hey," Lew said, and stopped the car. He reached for her, but she pushed him away. "I didn't mean anything, Meagan. It's OK. I just need to talk . . ."

"I know it's a sin!" She was still sobbing. "But I needed somebody! And he seemed so nice at first. And then . . . after I got started I just couldn't stop! Oh, God forgive me!"

"He does. He does forgive you, Meagan." Lew took her hand. "Weren't you listening tonight? God forgives you. God loves you." This calmed her down a little. "How about some coffee?"

"OK," she said. "I'll be OK now."

In the restaurant Lew tried to explain the situation to her, but whenever he began to talk about Skinner's penthouse she got very quiet, and he was afraid of provoking another crying spell.

"Hi," Alan said. Lew looked up from the booth, surprised to see his friend.

"Alan, what are you doing here?"

"Just saw you two sitting here," Alan said. "Mind if I join you?"

"No, I guess not," Lew said. Meagan remained quiet and watched Alan with deep suspicion.

"Meagan, isn't it?" Alan said as he sat down across from her, next to Lew.

"Yes," Meagan said. "I know who you are. You're Alan Fain."

"Just so," Alan said, and picked up the menu. Meagan's stare and her tone of voice had made him extremely self-conscious.

Alan ordered apple pie and tea. Then he looked at Mea-

58   Mark Leon

gan and said, "Meagan, we have to get into Larry Skinner's apartment."

Meagan grabbed her purse and started to get up.

"Meagan wait!" Lew said. "Alan and I want to help!"

"Then stay out of my personal life!" she shot back.

"Will you just listen a minute?" Lew said.

"We know about you and Larry . . ." Alan began. He was starting to get angry.

"Let me handle this, Alan," Lew interrupted. "Meagan is right. Her personal life is none of our business . . ."

"It is when the fate of the world is at stake," Alan snapped.

"Shut up!" Lew said. A few heads from the counter turned to look. "Please," he said more softly, "we are not going to get anywhere unless we can talk rationally. Now, Meagan, you did see someone else at Larry's didn't you? We really don't want to cause any trouble for you, but this other person is very important. And we think she may be in danger."

"Danger?" Meagan's eyes flashed for an instant.

"Yes," Lew said. "Larry has kidnapped her. He may even want to hurt her."

"Kidnapped? But she . . ."

"So you did see her!" Alan interrupted. "I knew it!"

"She did not seem to be in any trouble," Meagan said. "She is . . ."

"We know what you think she is," Alan said. "And you may be right. But if Larry Skinner has his way, she may not live much longer. He took her from my house last week. And I know he means her no good."

"From your house?" Meagan seemed shocked. "I don't believe it!"

"It's nothing like that," Alan said. "There is nothing of that sort between us. This woman is special."

"I know," Meagan said passionately.

"Then will you help us to get her back? Will you help us to set her free?" Alan locked eyes with Meagan. Lew sensed an intense battle of wills, each fortified by passionate belief.

*   *   *

THE GAIA WAR 59

"Dinner is served." Skinner walked into the living room, where Gaia was reading *The Odyssey*—in Greek.

"Oh my, I had better get dressed, hadn't I?" She was now openly sarcastic with him.

"Do what you like!" Skinner snapped.

"Keep your shirt on, Larry!" She laughed as she put hers on. "I think I will dine out tonight."

"What?"

"I'm going out. I am sick of this place, and I am sick of you. There is something rotten in Denmark, as they say."

"They don't say that," Skinner said coldly.

"Whatever." She was walking toward the door.

Skinner began to panic. "Won't you at least have some wine?"

"Wine?"

"Yes, I have a bottle of excellent Bordeaux. Surely reading all those classics has whetted your appetite for some good wine."

"Yes"—she stopped—"it has. What is that line from Homer about the 'wine-dark sea'?"

"Yes," Skinner said, " 'the wine-dark sea.' " He was already fumbling with the bottle.

"Tell me, Larry," she asked, "will I really need to wear pants in order to go out?"

"What?" The cork had crumbled in his clumsy effort. There were little bits floating in the bottle. "Pants? Oh yes. Pants. If you don't wear pants, you'll be arrested."

"Arrested? As in those ridiculous mystery novels you keep around here?"

"Exactly."

"Get me some pants," she ordered.

"And then you will have some wine?"

"Sure. And after that I'm going out."

Skinner, sweating, went to get some pants. He returned with the jeans he had stolen from Alan's house.

She had a hard time squeezing into them; her hips were much fuller than Alan's. "What a curious feeling," she said after she got them zipped. "Almost sexy." She was running her hands over the tight denim stretched across her beautiful ass.

Skinner was now sweating profusely, and his hands were shaking. "Why, Larry, what is wrong?" She was standing behind him as he poured the wine. He spilled a considerable amount. Then he thrust his hand into the pocket with the poison. He got the rubber stopper out without spilling too much.

"Look!" he shouted, and pointed out the window opposite the dining table. She eyed him curiously and turned to look.

Skinner jerked the bottle out of his pocket and spilled about half the contents in the process. He dumped the rest into her glass just as she was turning back to face him.

"What is that?" she asked pointing at the empty bottle, which he was trying to get back in his pocket.

He picked up her glass and handed it to her. "Nothing," he said.

"Well you just dumped the contents into my wineglass," she said. "It must be something."

"Flavor enhancer," he said.

"Really, Larry," she said. "If I didn't know better, I would say you are trying to poison me. Just as in those silly books."

"Don't be ridiculous," he managed to say.

"No," she said, "I won't. That sort of thing never happens outside those stories. I can't believe you read that stuff." She took a drink.

Skinner breathed a long sigh of relief. "Yeah," he said, "pretty ridiculous." He stirred his drink with his index finger as he watched her drain the glass. Only when she finished did he allow himself to drink. The lab tech had assured him that there was enough poison in the vial to kill an elephant. But Skinner, knowing very little about her physiology, had decided to use it all on her. In spite of the fact that he had spilled half the toxin, he was sure it would kill her. It was fast acting. He expected her to drop any second.

She was standing in front of the window and looking down. She watched with detached curiosity as a car sped

THE GAIA WAR 61

to a halt on the street below. The door opened and three figures, two men and a woman, dashed out. They ran into the building.

Skinner suddenly fell to his knees. His legs simply would not work. He could not see over the counter. He tried to call out to her, but as he collapsed, facedown on the floor, he realized with a creeping horror that he could barely whisper.

"Larry," he heard her say, "I feel terrible all of a sudden. I think I will lie down." He heard faltering footsteps as she walked slowly to the couch and then a soft plop as she let her body drop onto the cushions.

Suddenly it dawned on him that he had spilled the poison all over his fingers, the same fingers he had put into his wineglass. He had dosed himself, and he was almost totally paralyzed. At least he could still breathe. He could only pray that it had not been a lethal amount.

"You know Mr. Skinner left instructions that I should have access to his apartment," Meagan was saying to the security guard.

"Of course, but he didn't say anything about your two friends," the guard said.

"I work for Mr. Skinner," Lew said. He showed the man his NatCo ID card. "And Mr. Fain here is an old college friend of Mr. Skinner's. We are invited to dinner." Alan managed a smile.

"Alright," the guard said. "I guess it's OK. Go on up."

Skinner's breathing was ragged but holding. All he could do was open his eyes and look at the little pool of drool that was forming under his mouth. He heard a sound. It was a key in the door. *Meagan!* he thought, with a mixture of anger and hope.

"Oh my God!" Skinner grimaced as he recognized Alan's voice. "What has he done to her?"

Alan rushed to the sofa and knelt beside Gaia. "Is she alive?" Meagan asked.

"I don't know," Alan said. "She isn't breathing, but . . . I just don't know. We have to get her out of here, back to my lab. I may be able to do something there."

"Alan!" It was Lew. He had gone to the other side of

62 Mark Leon

the bar, which separated the kitchen from the living room, to find Skinner lying facedown in his own spit.

Alan quickly came around. "Larry!" he yelled. "What have you done? Talk to me, dammit!" Alan got down beside Skinner and rolled him over. Skinner was obviously still alive. His eyes were registering fear. "Can you talk?" Alan asked.

Skinner struggled to move his lips. He was barely able to whisper. Alan lowered his ear to Skinner's face. "What are you saying, Larry?"

"Poison." Alan could just make out the word.

"What kind of poison, Larry?" Alan demanded.

"In . . . my pocket."

Alan found the bottle in Skinner's coat pocket. He sniffed the contents and winced. There were a few drops clinging to the bottom of the bottle. "This will have to do," he said, pocketing the bottle. "Come on, Lew. Help me get her out of here."

"What about Larry?" Lew said, looking down at the helpless, terrified man on the floor.

"Fuck him," Alan said. "Did you hear me, Larry?" Alan was standing up now. "I said fuck you!"

"But Alan . . ." Lew started to protest.

"He tried to kill her, and he accidentally dosed himself, too," Alan said. "I'm not going to help him. Anyway, from the looks of it he'll be OK. He may have an unpleasant time of it on the floor, but I think he'll recover." Alan got quiet for a few moments, and then he said slowly but loudly, "We could easily kill him right now, Lew. If we suffocate him, it will still look like poison—the poison that he administered to himself, I should add."

"Alan!" Lew said.

"Relax, Lew," Alan said. "We're not going to kill him. I just wanted to watch his pupils dilate with fear—which they did rather nicely. Scared you, huh, Larry?" Alan was looking straight down at Skinner, who stared back in impotent fear and fury.

Lew and Alan carried her down to the basement. Meagan helped with the elevator. There was a loading entrance that opened from the inside. Alan went back up to the lobby

THE GAIA WAR 63

and exited to get the car. He brought it around to the alley and they managed to get her into the backseat.

"Is she going to be alright?" Meagan asked. They were back in Alan's lab. Gaia was stretched out on the sofa. She was utterly motionless.

"I don't know," Alan said. He had just finished an analysis of the poison. "If this was even half-full"—he held up the empty bottle retrieved from Skinner's jacket—"there was enough poison to kill all three of us—several times over."

"She isn't breathing!" Meagan said, agonized.

"No, she isn't," Alan responded, "but she's not dead either. There isn't much I can do for her. The poison is a fast-acting neurotoxin for which there is no antidote. I can only hope."

"Hope for what?" Lew asked.

"I expected that she would have remarkable powers of regeneration," Alan explained. "It is just possible that she also has a high-level immune system, one that detects toxins as well as microbes. She may have gone into a sort of suspended animation, a yogilike trance. If so, all of her life energies can be directed toward neutralizing the poison. About all I can do is give her an IV drip to supply fluids and carbohydrates. The rest is up to her."

"Oh, please . . ." Meagan was kneeling beside the woman. Gaia was still dressed in Alan's jeans and work shirt. She looked peaceful and very, very still.

"What do we do now, Alan?" Lew asked. They were upstairs. Alan had prepared dinner. Meagan refused to eat and was still downstairs with Gaia.

"Now?" Alan echoed, sipping a glass of wine.

"Yeah," Lew said. "I can't very well go back to work. Not after this. And Larry might . . ."

"Might what?" Alan asked, setting his glass down. He poured another round for Lew and himself.

"Might press charges or something."

"I doubt it," Alan said. "What could he say? That we poisoned him? He would have some explaining of his own to do. No, if she survives, I think this will be a stalemate."

"Except I have lost my job," Lew said.

"Do you really want to work for that asshole now?" Alan asked.

"No, I guess not."

"Listen, Lew," Alan said. "You said that the cyberion process is due for a major test at White Sands next week, right?"

"That's right."

"Well, if Gaia survives, then we should also be ready to launch a counterattack by then."

"Counterattack?"

"Don't kid yourself, Lew. Larry Skinner and NatCo are planning an all-out assault on planet earth, on the biosphere that sustains us all. I can't do much about it by myself, but with her help"—he gestured down to the basement—"I think we can fight back."

"How?" Lew said.

"You remember that cryptic message you got?" Alan asked, smiling.

"Yeah. 'The roads divide the land and kill the life,' " Lew recited.

"I still don't know where it came from," Alan said, "but I think I'm beginning to understand what it means."

"How does that relate to the NatCo cyberion test?" Lew asked.

"I have an idea, Lew," Alan said. He tapped his temple. "I think I have a very good idea."

CHAPTER 4

Skinner was able to crawl to the sofa after six hours of agony on the kitchen floor. He slept there for another four hours, plagued by dreams full of primitive lust and violent jealousies. When he was finally able to stand he did not feel grateful for the life that still carried him. There was a taste like burning metal in his mouth. His head hummed with an emptiness so profound that he seriously contemplated suicide.

There was nothing wrong with him. The poison, which had nearly shut down his autonomic functions, left almost no physical side effects. He drank several glasses of water and took a shower. When he emerged from the stall he heard himself speak. The words seemed to come from a forgotten part of himself. "What have I got left?" he asked. He felt tears begin to flow. He wanted to fling himself down and weep, let all the pain out in a flood. But something held him back. It worked its way through him with icy, deliberate stealth. It was a realization which shocked and horrified him, even as he embraced it, welcomed it, made it his one reason to keep on living. "I still have my hate," he said between clenched teeth. "I still have that."

Had he taken the time to reflect, Skinner might have been sufficiently disturbed by the experience to seek a change in his life. But he had decided many years earlier that self-examination is for the feeble-minded. It paralyzes the will.

66 Mark Leon

So he took heart in the energy that was renewing him and thought only of shaving, dressing, and of how he might wreak vengeance on Alan Fain. The man had humiliated him, and for Larry Skinner humiliation was worse than death.

Meagan would not leave Gaia's side. At first Alan was furious with her. "She is not the Mother of God!" he said, holding Meagan's face in his hands, forcing her to look at him. "I *grew* her for Christ sakes!"

"We are all instruments of the Lord," was Meagan's only response.

Finally Alan gave up on her. "You're too hard on Meagan," Lew said to him. They were having dinner in Alan's dining room. "She may be naive, but she is sincere."

"Yeah," Alan said, "I guess she can't hurt anything, and she is keeping a sharp watch. I suppose I should be grateful for her help. It's just all that religious stuff. It makes me uneasy."

"Why?" Lew asked.

"Why?" Alan seemed genuinely perplexed by the question. "Doesn't it bother you?"

"A little," Lew admitted. "You aren't afraid, are you?"

"Afraid of what?" Alan snapped, surprised at his own terseness.

"Afraid that she may be right," Lew said. "What if we are only tools in a larger scheme of things. What if . . ."

"Alright, alright," Alan said, passing a bowl of steaming pasta seasoned with olive oil and enormous quantities of garlic. "Knock it off. You will reduce us both to quivering blobs of superstitious angst. That we are part of some larger scheme I do not doubt for one second. But it simply does not follow that my creation is the Holy Virgin."

"But all myth is an expression of deeper truth, isn't it?" Lew asked.

"You have been watching too much public television, Lew," Alan said. "Get a grip. Things are extremely weird

THE GAIA WAR 67

and they are going to get weirder. You remember what the good Doctor Thompson[4] says, don't you?''

'' 'When the going gets weird the weird turn pro,' '' Lew quoted.

"That's right," Alan said. "Don't forget we are professionals. We have been prepared by the forces of the cosmos itself to fight the good fight."

"You sound like Pastor Lee," Lew said.

"Who?"

"Meagan's pastor. I went to church with her the other night. He was saying that his mission was to provide a spiritual training center for the armies of the Lord, so that when Armageddon arrives . . .''

"OK. I get the idea," Alan said. "Jesus, Lew, sometimes I wonder about you."

"So what happens now?" Lew asked, trying to change the subject.

"That depends on her," Alan said. "If she recovers, then we'll take a little trip out West."

"West?"

"White Sands, New Mexico," Alan said. "I have a little surprise planned for Larry Skinner and NatCo."

"What if she dies?" Lew asked.

"If she dies," Alan mused, "I suggest you go back to Meagan's church."

"Meagan's church?"

"Without Gaia, I cannot do anything to stop Skinner," Alan said. "And if Skinner has his way—God help us all."

"But corporate has only authorized a limited test, Mr. Skinner," the lab technician was saying. "The cyberion bacteria for the test are programmed to die after two weeks. If I remove the control gene, that won't happen. In fact, I don't know what will happen. It could be dangerous."

"Listen." Skinner fought for control of his voice. He had to sound convincing. "You know the cyberion project has operated on a strict 'need to know' basis.' ''

---

[4] Hunter S. Thompson from *Fear and Loathing in Las Vegas*.

Mark Leon

"Of course," the tech said.

"It has been determined that the test will be more effective if we remove the control gene."

"But I haven't been notified . . ."

"*I* am notifying you," Skinner said.

"But all my previous orders came from corporate . . ."

"This is very sensitive," Skinner said. "Corporate has determined that the remainder of the project should be controlled from here. That way corporate protects itself. You have heard of *plausible deniability*, haven't you?"

"Sure, but . . ."

"Well, that is what is going on."

"This could be dangerous, Mr. Skinner." The tech sounded deeply disturbed. "If we can't shut the cyberion process down, it could run wild. You haven't worked with this stuff like I have. It's scary."

"We know what we are doing," Skinner said. "There is an external control mechanism which was developed at our California lab . . ."

"California! I was told we were the only ones working on cyberion!"

"Need to know, need to know. You had no need to know about the California operation. I only just learned of it," Skinner lied easily. "So you see there is really nothing to worry about. Just do your job. I will take full responsibility. Trust me. We would not risk the reputation of the company. I should add that there is a substantial bonus for all you folks here at the lab if the test is successful. And I do mean substantial."

In the end Skinner got what he wanted. The tech promised to deliver a new strain of the bacteria, minus the control gene, by the end of the week. The prospect thrilled him. In his opinion the moguls at corporate were a bunch of chicken shits. They had never fully appreciated the potential of the cyberion process, and they were overly cautious.

Caution in this case, Skinner reasoned, made sense only for the timid. He picked up the report marked SENSITIVE that was lying on his desk and again opened it to his favorite section. He read:

THE GAIA WAR

The cyberion bacteria show a robustness never before seen in an organism. We have tested various strains in several controlled environments. They always win. And they win in a way not seen before. Other new organisms succeed by establishing a niche, thereby achieving a balance with the other organisms and the ecosystem as a whole. The cyberion microbes succeed by totally wiping out all other life-forms. This does not seem to bother them at all. The more the environment is reduced to a feeding and breeding ground for them alone, the more they seem to like it.

The prospects for experimentation in uncontrolled environments are frightening. From what we have seen in the lab, the microbes are capable of consuming the entire biosphere. In time they would probably exhaust all the available nutrients and perish themselves, but by then it would be too late—all higher life-forms, and possibly all life, would be gone from the earth.

Skinner closed the report and locked it back in his file cabinet. He leaned back in his chair, propped his feet up on his desk, and smiled. The next few weeks promised to be very interesting. He was looking forward to a brave new world, one in which the fainthearted would be swept aside forever.

She lay in what appeared to be a coma for three days. Alan insisted that she was really in deep *samadhi* trance. "The most adept of my Tibetan gurus were able to suspend nearly all autonomic functions for hours at a time. But they were not unconscious. In such a state the mind achieves a quiescence. It is like the surface of a pond unbroken by ripples. The ripples are the thoughts of normal, everyday existence. When those are stilled, the radiance of pure mind shines through."

"How do you know that's what is going on with her?" Lew asked, looking down at the supine form.

"Having seen it and experienced it for brief moments, you just know. I can't explain it, Lew. It's an intuition that

I trust more than most ordinary perceptions. She is there. I am sure of it.''

"Will she live?"

"That depends on her body's ability to process the poison. If she had not instinctively gone into her present state, she would have been dead in seconds. By suspending nearly all her vital functions, she was able to halt the spread of the poison to her most sensitive autonomic systems. I can only guess at how sophisticated her bio systems are. If she can neutralize the toxin by an alternate route that bypasses the nervous system, she should make a full recovery. Otherwise, she is only prolonging the inevitable and her death will take days rather than moments.'' Alan sounded cool and analytical.

"Can't you *do* something?" Meagan asked. "We can't just let her die.''

"I am doing all I can," Alan said. "I suggest you go and get some sleep. You've hardly eaten anything and you're exhausted.''

Meagan glared at him. "How can you be so cold?"

"Alan is right," Lew said to her. "Go upstairs and get some sleep. We'll call you the moment there's any change.''

Lew's more gentle tone finally prevailed, and Meagan went to the spare bedroom to take a short nap. She fell into a deep sleep almost as soon as her head touched the pillow. She dreamed of ascending to heaven. There was a radiant white light ahead and she was soaring toward it. The act of flying felt wonderfully natural. It was as if she had finally remembered how to do it, and it was the easiest thing in the world. She was approaching the gates to the celestial city when her attention was drawn by something to her left. It was a display of brilliant color and intricate, overlapping patterns. When she turned to look she saw Gaia, surrounded by a riot of organic shapes and forms. Instead of continuing on, Meagan changed her course and flew toward the lush, flowing landscape.

"Are we really here?" she asked.

Gaia smiled at her. "Where do you mean?"

"Heaven," Meagan said.

THE GAIA WAR 71

"Oh no." Gaia laughed. It was an innocent sound tinged with regret. "This is not heaven."

"Oh." Meagan was clearly disappointed.

"Don't worry," Gaia said. "Everything will be fine." She turned and vanished into the beautiful tapestry of color and light that grew all around.

Meagan woke up. She had slept for ten hours. After a trip to the bathroom she went to the kitchen, where she found Lew fumbling with a blender. "What are you doing?" she asked sleepily. Her dress was terribly wrinkled and her hair a disheveled mess. Her appearance had an odd effect on Lew. For the first time he found her attractive, sensual-looking. He had to force himself not to stare at the long, tangled waves of hair that played around the top of her dress, which was unbuttoned to reveal the top of a modest bra. She smelled of sweat and musky perfume.

Lew cleared his throat and Meagan shifted from one bare foot to the other as she leaned lightly against the doorframe. "Are you making a smoothie?" she asked.

"Yeah." Lew spooned some concentrated protein powder into the mixture of bananas and yogurt.

"Looks good," she said.

"I'll make you one, too," Lew said. "You need it."

"I am hungry," she said, sitting down at the table.

Lew ran the blender, poured the mixture into a large glass, and made another one for Meagan. He set the two glasses on the table and sat down opposite her. She began to drink slowly, but was soon gulping the stuff. "That was great. Thanks, Lew. Aren't you going to drink yours?" she asked, noting that Lew had not touched the other glass.

"It's not for me," he said.

Something in his voice made Meagan's eyes flash. All traces of sleep were suddenly gone. "Who then?"

"Our guest is awake," he said. "Alan thinks she's going to be OK."

"Why didn't you tell me?" Meagan asked sharply.

"You were beat, Meagan," Lew said. "We didn't want another casualty on our hands. Anyway, she is only now able to sit up and speak."

Meagan was already starting toward the basement. Lew

followed with the smoothie. "She's still very weak," he said. "Don't lean on her too hard. She needs to eat and rest."

Gaia graciously accepted the drink from Lew. Her brush with death had clearly made an impact. It was not just her physical appearance, although she was pale and gaunt. Her eyes and expression had an older look. "He tried to kill me," she said after a few sips. Her lips were wet with white foam.

"Yeah," Alan said.

"Why?" She wiped her mouth with the back of her hand.

"I'm not sure," Alan said. "He's afraid of you."

"Afraid?"

"Larry Skinner is playing a very dangerous game. He perceived you to be an unexpected problem, one that might throw him completely off his plan."

"I don't understand." She looked at Alan, her eyes boring through him with an intensity that made him blink.

"It *is* hard to understand," Alan said. "There's a battle shaping up."

"A battle."

"Yes. We are on one side and Skinner is on the other. The fate of all life on earth may very well hang in the balance. I need your help."

"*My* help?"

"You do want revenge, don't you?" Alan could not keep the anxiety from his voice.

She laughed at this. It was a weak sound, made so by her frail condition. Even so, all three of them were struck by the weird combination of delight and bitterness in her amusement. "How can this be? It is just like those silly books I read at Larry's. Murder? Vengeance? I thought it was all just for fun. It was a peculiar kind of fun even when it was only in words. But I don't see any kind of fun in it when it really happens."

"It is not fun," Alan said.

"Then why are you doing it?" she asked, taking another sip. Her big eyes shone over the rim of the glass.

"Many things we do in this world are not for fun."

THE GAIA WAR 73

"Why do you do them?"

"Because we have no choice," Alan said with clenched teeth.

"No choice! How very odd. I will have to think about this a long time."

"There is not much time to think, I'm afraid," Alan said.

"I'm tired." She set her glass down on the coffee table and lay back on the sofa.

"Please, we desperately need your help." Alan moved closer. Her expression registered something like pain at his pleading.

"Can't you see she needs rest?" Meagan shot Alan an ugly look. Gaia looked at Meagan and smiled.

"Meagan," she said.

"Yes, Mother?" Meagan responded.

"I now know what you think about me, Meagan. I must tell you that I am not who you wish me to be."

"But I know the signs . . ." Meagan protested.

"Yes, the signs. There are many signs. Don't you remember the dream? I tried to show you then . . ."

"We were ascending to heaven! Yes! Then it was not a dream," Meagan said with delight.

"It *was* a dream, Meagan. A shared dream. But you do not understand the meaning of it yet. Be patient. Don't worry. Everything will be fine."

After she finished her drink Gaia declared that she needed more rest. Alan reluctantly led the other two back upstairs. They were having coffee in his living room. "How did she survive?" Lew asked.

"I told you," Alan said. "She went into deep meditation and was able to prevent the poison from being absorbed into her nervous system, which would have been the usual path and would have certainly killed her. Her body must possess an awareness that is unlike anything known to modern physiology. Somehow the poison was processed by an alternate system, perhaps the lymphatic. It took time—the stuff was extremely potent—but you see the result. She is tired and malnourished, but otherwise she is fine."

"What was all that about down there, Alan?" Lew

asked. "I mean the stuff about a battle shaping up and so on."

"We have to move," Alan said "Soon "

"Move? Where?"

"White Sands. Skinner is probably already on his way. I have a pretty good idea what he's planning."

"What?"

"From my experiments with the aether I have discovered that there is a dark side to the forces of life. My research has focused on biodiversity, the celebration of differences and the ever increasing complexification of the tapestry of life."

"I saw it!" Meagan said. "I saw the tapestry!"

"What?" Alan sounded genuinely baffled.

"In my dream," Meagan said. "And *she* was there. Standing in the middle of the most beautiful tapestry of form. It was alive, growing and changing and . . ."

"You *dreamed* this?" Alan interrogated.

"Yes."

"Is this the dream that she mentioned?"

"Yes."

"Good," Alan said. "She knows then."

"Knows what?" Lew asked. "What are you talking about?"

"Gaia sent Meagan a dream," Alan said. "I don't know why, but the content of the dream is prophecy. It is her destiny. And she obviously knows it on some level. Now it is our job to make her fully wake up to it. We can only hope that we are not too late."

"I still don't get it," Lew said.

"Remember the message, Lew?"

"The roads divide the land and kill the life?"

"Yeah? We need her to unleash the tapestry of life in the roads. In the process we can also stop Skinner. He has also tapped into the life force, but the cyberion process is the dark side. NatCo has designed a microbe that threatens to destroy all the marvelous diversity and complexity of life. If I know Larry, he will not wait to test it. He is planning to unleash its full force as soon as possible. Once the process takes hold it has the potential of destroying all other

THE GAIA WAR

life-forms on the planet. Only those in positions of power, like Larry, will be able to protect themselves.''

''But it sounds like madness, suicide,'' Lew said. ''Why would anyone want to do such a thing?''

''Because Larry thinks he can control the process,'' Alan said. ''That would give him unlimited power. He sees himself as a lord of the earth. All nations, all governments would have to negotiate with NatCo, with him, in order to gain access to the technology necessary to extract food from the only life-form remaining on the planet.''

''So it is power he's after,'' Lew mused. ''But who would want that sort of power? I mean, what would be left to rule? A barren wasteland of bacteria and the few humans willing or able to subject themselves to the authority of Larry Skinner and NatCo.''

'' 'Better to rule in Hell than to serve in Heaven,' '' Alan said.

''I don't think *you* have any business quoting scripture,'' Meagan said, indignantly.

''It's not from the Bible,'' Alan shot back. ''It's Milton. *Paradise Lost*.''

''So what do you want her to do?'' Lew asked, trying to deflect some of the hostility in the air.

''We need to mount a large-scale demonstration,'' Alan said. ''And it must be powerful enough to contain the horror that Larry is about to unleash. I don't have the expertise. I am certain that she possesses the knowledge required to turn my laboratory experiments into a full-scale riot of biological forms that can literally devour the highways and give the life back to the land. That is what was behind the message we received. But I need her help in order to design the protean virus.''

''Protean virus?''

''For want of a better term. It is really a primitive form of DNA. And far more versatile. You could say it is a precursor to DNA, and therefore it has the power to spawn hundreds of new life-forms. These will be capable of metabolizing concrete, asphalt, and silicon. I've got it all planned. Here, take a look.'' Alan put a map of New Mexico on the coffee table.

Mark Leon

"Here is White Sands," he said. "We'll plant the protean virus at Las Cruces, Alamogordo, and north of White Sands National Monument. The stuff will grow like wildfire. Oh it will be beautiful! Imagine a tropical rain forest of hundreds, thousands of new plant species devouring the highways. It should easily move at ten miles per day. Maybe faster. We will accomplish two things. First we will start the process of reclaiming mother earth for the living. Once all the roads and highways are gone, life can begin to renew itself. No more cars. No more noxious exhaust. We can begin to live the way we were intended to live—in a garden. Paradise Regained! Modern civilization has transformed the world into a supermarket, and the roads and highways are the key.

"In addition we will be able to surround and contain the cyberion scourge that Larry is planning to unleash. The protean jungle that will sprout out there in the desert will be, I think, the only life capable of resisting and conquering those horrid little microbes from the NatCo labs."

"Won't the destruction of the roads cause massive hardship? I mean, people depend on . . ." Meagan said.

"A small price to pay!" Alan shouted. "Don't you understand that this is the final showdown. The battle between the forces of life and death has begun. Sure we depend on the roads to supply us with all the things that our mass-market culture has convinced us that we need. But the time has come to rise above all that. The time has come to change the way we live and take the planet back from those who only want to carve it up and *sell* it. This is no time for petty concerns, Meagan."

"But the welfare of millions of people is not petty," Meagan said.

"And what will be the fate of those people if Larry has his way?" Alan demanded. "It is my way or his. It is that simple."

Lew could see that Meagan did not think it was so simple. She had an innate distrust of Alan. Lew understood Meagan's eminently reasonable concerns. But he was mildly surprised to find that he did not share them. He was thrilled by Alan's vision of a new world transformed into

THE GAIA WAR

a garden. Even if it were only fantasy, the vision was more appealing than the reality of modern life. A world full of new life, without cars or roads, sounded like a world of adventure, and Lew longed for adventure.

Later Alan went back down to the basement. He waited patiently until Gaia opened her eyes. "Have some food," he said, and warmed a potato curry dish in the microwave.

"This is delicious," she said. "I was beginning to think that all the food here tasted like the pitiful stuff Larry kept dragging home."

"We have to talk," Alan said.

She said nothing, watching him with wide, innocent eyes while she ate.

"I need your help," he prompted.

Still no response.

Alan fought to control his frustration at her intractable nature. It was, after all, part of what made her so valuable. That and her innate knowledge. He patiently explained his plans. He also described the cyberion project. She did begin to show interest when he described the havoc that modern civilization had wreaked on the environment.

"That is terrible," she said at one point.

"Precisely," Alan said. "That's why I need your help. The protean virus needs to be engineered at a molecular level." He showed her the plastic models he had built.

She held one of the helical structures, examining it with a critical eye, noting subtle sequencing patterns. Finally she spoke. "This will work, but only if you insert a new strand here." She pointed to a spot on the model. "That will give the various organisms the ability to metabolize asphalt and concrete."

"And the cyberion microbes?"

"We don't know much about Larry's little bugs," she said. "But I think our protean life-forms can at least contain them, if not wipe them out entirely."

They worked for several hours. Alan was astounded by her knowledge and skill. With her help he was able to design a protean virus that exceeded his highest expectations. For the final step in the synthesis he needed to use the last of the empathetic aether. "Are you sure this will work?"

he asked her. He and Lew had obtained the stuff quite by accident. The chances of getting another batch, should the synthesis fail, were remote.

"Of course it will work," she said calmly.

Alan poured the last of the precious stuff into the flask. There was nothing more to do but wait. The reaction would take several hours. Exhausted, Alan said good night.

"Good night," she said, and stretched out on the sofa like a young cat. She was almost instantly asleep. Alan watched her for a few moments. Strange emotions and forbidden desires began to crowd his thoughts. He was startled by their force and quickly retreated upstairs.

CHAPTER 5

Alan, Gaia, Meagan, and Lew were on their way to White Sands, New Mexico, when they hit the United States Immigration checkpoint. The agent asked each one to declare citizenship. It was a routine procedure and the agent could see that no one in the car appeared to be Hispanic. The checkpoint had been established to slow the tide of illegal immigrants coming up from Mexico. But when it was Gaia's turn to answer she just smiled and said, "That is an interesting question."

"Out of the car, please." The immigration agent sounded bored.

Alan was extremely nervous. "She's with me," he said. "We're both just tired."

"Miss," the agent said, "are you, or are you not, a citizen of the United States?"

"What do you mean?" Gaia asked.

"Listen," the agent said, "this is no game. Do you want me to search your car? Do you want to spend the rest of the day here and possibly go to jail?"

"Jail?" Alan said. "For what? I told you we are all citizens . . ."

"But I need to hear it from Miss *Wise Girl* here," the agent interrupted.

"Look," Alan said softly, as if he were taking the man into his confidence, "Gail is not really herself these days.

79

80   Mark Leon

Her family has a history of schizophrenia. I am starting to worry about her. She doesn't mean anything by it. You can see that she isn't an illegal. I promise you she was born and raised in North Dakota. She's a citizen alright. She's just a little confused right now. If you press her too hard, she may have a breakdown. Believe me, you don't want to deal with that. I have seen her strip naked and fling herself down on the highway, screaming and tearing her hair.'' Alan held his breath while he waited for the officer's response.

"Well," he said, "are you sure she is not making fun of me? I mean, I represent the US government, and . . ."

"No, nothing like that. She is seriously disturbed. Just look at her," Alan said quickly.

The agent did. Then he pulled Alan to one side. "I see what you mean," he said, trying to sound very authoritative. "Her eyes are just too bright." Then, as if it had just occurred to him, "You folks aren't on drugs, are you?"

"Search the car if you want," Alan said, sweating profusely. If they found the protean catalyst virus cultures, there was sure to be trouble. They would probably be confiscated and the cultures would die if not properly handled.

In the end his suspicion that the agent was really too lazy to bother with searching the car paid off. "OK," he said, "go ahead, but get some help for that young lady."

"Whew!" Alan was shaking as they drove on.

"Where are we going?" Meagan asked, sounding angry. She had overheard some of the conversation between Alan and the agent and did not like the demeaning references to Gaia's nonconventional attitude and appearance.

"I told you," Alan snapped. "Alamogordo. We'll get some rooms there. We all need a good night's rest. Tomorrow you and Lew will drop Gaia and me off inside the White Sands National Park area. Then you will take the car and inoculate the roads marked on your map. You will pick us up at the park entrance in the afternoon."

"What are we doing out here?" Meagan asked. "I don't like it."

"We are ushering in a new age," Alan said. "The new

THE GAIA WAR 81

Eden is upon us. Or will be after we're done with our work tomorrow.''

Skinner, in spite of himself, was appalled by the rapid growth of the microbes. After two days they had totally taken over ten square miles of the gypsum sand desert on the White Sands missile testing range. The smell was hideous. He was standing on a dune at the perimeter of the ever expanding area, and his eyes were streaming tears at the noxious vapors that poured up from the newly blackened desert floor. A jackrabbit hobbled up beside him. It actually turned its eyes up to look at Skinner before it succumbed to violent convulsions. It took a massive amount of self-control to dismiss from his mind what he had seen in those watery eyes. Never before had he beheld such pure terror, such absolute pain.

''I have to get a gas mask,'' he muttered to himself as he climbed back into his off-road vehicle. It was growing too fast. In a few days it would start to encroach on the national park's boundary. He was going to have to be ready for all the publicity. The boys at corporate were not going to like it. But he felt sure that once they understood that there was no turning back, he would win their support. After all, within weeks they would control the entire state of New Mexico, and soon after that—the world.

He was euphoric as he drove back to his hotel in Alamogordo. Had he been more observant, he would have noticed a familiar, baby blue Ford as it turned into the motel ahead of him, and the sight of the four occupants would have turned his euphoria to something far more urgent and dangerous. But Skinner's head was too full of dreams to see Alan park the car and emerge into the orange evening glow of the desert sunset.

Alan was too intent on getting them safely situated to notice the man in the suit, driving the Cherokee, who pulled into the hotel barely two blocks away. Had he seen Skinner, he would not have been willing to wait until morning. As it was, both parties managed to get some fitful sleep before dawn sent streaks of red through the morning sky.

''They call this food!'' Alan said. They were having

82 Mark Leon

breakfast the next morning at the Wagon Wheel Waffle House.

"I think they call this breakfast," Gaia said.

"What's the matter, Alan?" Meagan asked. "Not up to your gourmet standards?"

"This stuff sucks," Lew said. His egg burrito tasted like cardboard stuffed with sponge.

"Yeah, it sucks." Gaia laughed. "I have been waiting for a chance to say that."

"You got your chance," Alan said. "Come on, let's get out of here."

A few blocks away Larry Skinner was having breakfast difficulties of his own. "What do you mean you don't have toast?" he demanded.

"Sorry, sir, but . . ."

"This is a breakfast buffet, for God's sake. And you don't even have toast!"

"I'll speak to the kitchen staff, sir . . ."

"Never mind." Skinner paid his bill and set out for the test site. The growing horror in the desert had a strange grip on him. It was even more disgusting than he had imagined.

"Alright, does everyone know what to do?" Alan asked when they were back in the car.

"Meagan and I are supposed to inoculate key points on Highway 70 and Interstate 25," Lew said.

"Right, and Gaia and I will go on a little hike through the dunes," Alan said.

Lew drove deep into the park and stopped in front of a large white mound of gypsum. "This place is weird," Lew said. "Miles and miles of white dunes, out here in the middle of . . ."

"Nowhere," Meagan said.

"It's not nowhere," Alan said, getting out. "It's New Mexico."

"Land of Enchantment." Gaia laughed.

Alan gave her a funny look. "Where did you learn that?"

"I can read license plates," she said.

"Of course." Alan handed her a pack. He donned his

THE GAIA WAR 83

own and turned to Lew. "You guys be careful. Remember that it's not all that important exactly where you plant the stuff. Just be discreet, and make sure you get the highway and the interstate. We have to surround Larry's little mess as best we can." He waved and turned to begin walking up the face of the dune. Gaia followed him. In her boots and khaki pants she looked like a female adventurer, an explorer out to discover the new frontier.

"Will they be OK?" Meagan asked, watching them disappear over the top of the white hill.

"They have plenty of water," Lew said. "They'll be fine."

"But what if they get lost?"

"Don't worry, Meagan," Lew said, his brow creased with anxiety. "We had better get going ourselves."

Six hours later they returned to find Gaia waiting for them. Alone.

"Where is Alan?" Lew asked.

"He went that way." Gaia pointed west. "He asked me to give you this note." She handed him a folded piece of yellow, coarse paper. He read:

Lew,

I have to inoculate the San Andres mountain range. The only way to get there is on foot. Don't worry about me. I have plenty of food and supplies. This is the only way we can really surround Larry's test site. I should be back sometime tomorrow. Wait for me at the motel. If for some reason you do not hear from me by tomorrow night, here is what you need to do.

Call the newspapers at Las Cruces and Albuquerque and give an anonymous tip. Tell them that the strange growth on the roads is due to the NatCo cyberion test project at the missile range. This will keep any investigators off our backs and should give Larry a nasty surprise. Then get out of the state as fast as you can.

Alan

84   **Mark Leon**

"Oh man." Lew sighed.

"What's wrong?" Meagan asked.

"Nothing—I hope," Lew said. They drove back to Alamogordo in silence.

Alan was able to hike the fifteen miles to the San Andres range by sunset. He was too exhausted to pitch his tent. After a quick meal of trail mix and a granola bar, he unrolled his sleeping bag and climbed in. When he looked up he was glad not to have a nylon roof over his head. The stars were brilliant and thicker than he thought possible. A brief meteor shower added some dynamics to the show. At one point he thought he saw a bright object streak across the sky, abruptly stop, and streak back in the opposite direction. *UFO?* he thought. Before he could speculate any further on the mystery he was asleep.

The morning was surprisingly cold. Alan's fingers did not want to respond to his commands as he struggled to make coffee. But the steamy warmth of the brew made the painful exertions worth the effort. He sat sipping with his sleeping bag draped around his shoulders. Soon the sun was heating up the foothills, and he stood up to stretch. His plan was to skirt the western side of the range, planting the protean virus along the way.

Things went well until late afternoon. He had planted the protean seeds in nearly all the ground that he had planned to cover when he saw the telltale cloud of dust to the south that indicated a vehicle approaching. He quickly stashed the remaining vials of inocula, digging a shallow hole and covering them with dirt and several large rocks. He made a mental note of the surroundings, hoping that he could find the spot again. Then he continued walking down the trail.

A few minutes later, Skinner's Cherokee bounced up the jeep trail. He stopped and got out. Alan was looking down on him from the more rugged hiking trail several meters above. "Hi, Larry," he said.

"Well, well," Skinner answered in a high-pitched, nervous voice. "Alan Fain. So we meet again."

"So we do."

"What are you doing out here?" Skinner's tone became menacing.

THE GAIA WAR

85

"Hiking."

"Hiking, is it? Well I advise you to do your hiking elsewhere."

"It is public land, Larry," Alan retorted.

"So it is, so it is." Skinner reached into the car and turned to point a gun at Alan. "You had better come with me."

"You wouldn't shoot me." Alan turned his back and continued down the trail.

A shot rang out. Alan fell forward and hit the trail with a thump. He got up slowly and removed his backpack. The bullet had lodged in the alloy frame.

"Sorry," Skinner said, climbing up to the trail, still pointing the gun at Alan. "That was meant to be a warning shot. You're lucky. Now get in the car. You can drive."

"Where are we going, Larry?" Alan asked as they skidded and bounced down the barely discernible road.

"Don't worry about that."

"But you can't keep that gun pointed at me forever," Alan said. "Are you going to kill me?"

"I've thought about it," Skinner said. "Just keep driving."

The next morning Lew and the two women drove back to White Sands.

"I don't know what you expect to find," Meagan said, as they were wandering around the dunes. "He is obviously not coming back."

"Don't you think we should follow his instructions?" Gaia asked after two hours of futile searching.

"I guess," Lew said dejectedly. A lush, slightly sweet smell assailed his senses suddenly. "What was that?"

"What?" Meagan asked.

"Nothing. Let's get out of here."

They were stopped by a roadblock at the junction with the interstate. "License, please," the state trooper said.

Lew handed it over. "What's going on?" he asked, trying to keep the sound of his rapid heartbeat out of his voice.

"Some kind of disturbance on I-25 a few miles north.

86   Mark Leon

We're checking all outbound vehicles. Where you coming from?''

"Alamogordo," Lew said.

"What were you doing there?"

"Just wanted to show my wife and sister White Sands. They've never been out this way before."

The cop seemed satisfied. "OK, you can go. Be careful."

"Wife and sister!" Meagan said.

"What was I supposed to say?" Lew asked. The experience had been totally nerve-racking.

They stopped in Las Cruces and Lew went to a phone booth. He called the Albuquerque paper first. "I need to speak to a reporter," he said.

"Rafferty here," a voice said, after a short wait.

"You know that disturbance on the interstate?" Lew said.

"The jungle? Sure. What about it?"

Jungle? Lew thought to himself. *What had they started*?

"I know who's responsible," Lew said.

"Oh yeah." The reporter sounded skeptical.

"Just check out a certain research project at the White Sands missile test site. It's a company called NatCo—you familiar with it?"

"NatCo? Sure. What have they got to do with this?" Rafferty was starting to sound more interested.

"They are testing a new life-form out there," Lew said. "The code name for the project is cyberion. It's top secret, but they know about it at corporate. A guy named Larry Skinner is running the test. He should be out there."

"Who are you?" Rafferty asked.

"I can't tell you any more," Lew said. "Just go check it out." He hung up. Then he made a similar call to the *Las Cruces Sun-Times*.

"Take a look inside, Lew." It was Meagan, grabbing him as he came out of the booth. She led him back into the convenience store. The patrons and the clerk were all staring up at the television screen.

"What the hell is going on?" one of them said.

It was live footage from a helicopter hovering over the interstate about sixty miles north. The screen was a riot of

THE GAIA WAR 87

color. You could actually see the growth as the creeping vegetation devoured the road surface. Where highway had been there was now a jungle of various trees, vines, flowers, and plants for which Lew had no name.

"Botany professors from the university are on their way," the newscaster said. "So far, the most potent herbicides don't seem to have any effect on the stuff. Highway department officials estimate that at the current rate it will move at least ten miles a day."

"Hey," a customer said, "I saw a UFO out in the desert last night. I'll bet . . ."

"You're always seeing UFOs, Joe," the clerk said.

"And now maybe someone will believe me," Joe said indignantly.

"Come on," Lew said. "Did you pay for the gas?"

"Yeah," Meagan said. "You owe me twelve bucks."

Lew felt relieved to be back on the road. Even so, the high visibility of law enforcement officers made it impossible for him to relax. It wasn't until they were really in the middle of nowhere, out in West Texas, that he began to feel more secure.

By the time they got back the news was full of the *Genesis Bomb*, as the media dubbed it. Lew was watching TV in Alan's house. An interviewer was talking to an Apache Mescalero Indian. The Mescalero reservation was close to White Sands and the Indian, Paul Rainwater, was a self-proclaimed environmental activist.

"What do the tribe members think about the *Genesis Bomb*?" the correspondent asked.

"There is no consensus in the nation," Rainwater said. "As you know, we run a large commercial ski operation out here. If the roads are shut down, there will be no ski revenue this season. That will affect our schools, hospitals, all our human services. So many of the tribal leaders are working with the various US government agencies to halt the spreading jungle that is devouring our roads and highways."

"What is your position?"

"My position is somewhat different," Rainwater said. "I have felt for a long time that the North American con-

88 **Mark Leon**

tinent was a better place before the Europeans came here. Now you must understand one thing. It is not because the Native Americans were better people than the European settlers that things got so screwed up. It is simply a matter of technology and point of view. It would never have occurred to the native peoples to carve the continent up with so many highways and roads. These concrete and asphalt strips have gradually choked the life out of our very home. I can put it very simply.'' At this point Rainwater stared straight into the camera. His long black hair glistened and his big dark eyes seemed to be staring straight at Lew. ''The roads divide the land and kill the life.''

Lew fell limply back in his chair. The words matched perfectly the mysterious message that he and Alan had received. It could be no coincidence. He had to try and get in touch with this Apache Indian.

''It sounds as if you approve of what is happening,'' the interviewer said.

''Let us just say that I do not despair over it,'' Rainwater said. ''I realize that a great many people will suffer because of it. I do not enjoy human suffering.''

''Do you have any idea who could be responsible for the *Genesis Bomb*?''

''Absolutely not,'' Rainwater said, easily. Lew was almost certain that he detected something hidden behind that denial.

''There is a lead on tracking the culprits. We have just received word that the Albuquerque newspaper got an anonymous tip about a top secret biological project being conducted on the White Sands missile range. Law enforcement and military personnel are investigating this lead. There are unsubstantiated rumors that they have found something, a bizarre growth in a large area of the test range. We will keep you informed as the story develops.''

Lew switched the set off. It was all happening too fast. He needed to think, even though he was not confident that thinking would help.

Skinner drove Alan to a deserted building on the test range. It was a bunker which had obviously taken some

THE GAIA WAR 89

hits. The interior was lit by a single bulb dangling from the ceiling. The windows were narrow slits. There was a wood table, heavy and bare, and an old, stuffed armchair. The upholstery was worn through in several places, but it looked comfortable enough. Skinner motioned Alan to the chair. "Sit down."

Alan obeyed. "What are you going to do, Larry?"

"Nothing." Skinner smiled. "I'm leaving. I think you will find some water and maybe some food in the pantry. They use this place for observation sometimes. Anyway, I don't think you will suffer too much. Certainly not for long."

"What do you mean?"

"The door bolts securely from the outside. You did notice the heavy iron assemblage? Before long this little bunker will be completely . . . I don't know quite how to put it, absorbed?"

"What are you talking about?"

"The cyberion process. I assume that Lew, that little *traitor*, briefed you on it?"

Alan remained silent.

"Well it doesn't matter now," Skinner said. "Do you smell anything?"

Alan had started to notice a particularly foul smell coming from the east. It smelled like sulfur, nitrogenous wastes, and some of the open city sewers he had seen in India.

"Those are my babies." Skinner smiled. "It won't be long before they get here. They're cleaning up the desert."

"Cleaning it up? Smells like they are doing something else."

"It's all relative," Skinner said. "It's starting to smell kind of sweet to me. There's too much life on the earth, too much wild, crazy, out of control life. Come to think of it, that's what you are, Alan Fain—an animal out of control. So it is only fitting that you be consumed with all the rest of it."

"You are really insane," Alan said, calmly.

"Sanity, like sweet, is also a relative term." Skinner smiled. He was backing toward the door. He held the gun level with Alan's chest. When he closed the door, Alan

90 Mark Leon

leapt up and hurled his weight against it. But it was too late. Skinner had thrown the large bolt. Alan listened with a sinking heart as he heard Skinner fumbling with several locks.

It took several calls to information before Lew was able to get the number for the Apache Mescalero tribal headquarters in New Mexico. "I need to speak with Paul Rainwater," he said to the woman who answered.

"Who?"

"Paul Rainwater. The guy on TV last night," Lew said.

"Is he an official of the nation?"

"I don't know," Lew said.

"I don't see his name in the directory," the woman said. "If he were on the school board or any of the governing councils, he would be listed."

"All I know is that he's a member of the tribe," Lew said.

"It is a large nation," the woman said.

"Yeah. Well, can I leave a message?" Lew asked despairingly.

"How will I deliver the message?"

"The guy was on TV last night," Lew said angrily. "He must be well-known around there . . ."

"Leave your message, sir," the woman said diplomatically. "I'll see what I can do."

"OK. Here it is. 'The roads divide the land and kill the life,' " Lew said, and gave his phone number.

"That's all?"

"That's all. Thanks." Lew hung up. "What are we supposed to do?" Lew asked. The two women were with him in Alan's living room. "Alan may be in serious trouble."

"*We* could be in serious trouble," Meagan said, throwing the morning newspaper down on the coffee table. There was a huge color photo on the front page showing a tangle of colored life tearing up Interstate 25.

"Why is everyone so disturbed by what is happening?" Gaia asked. "Clearly the network of roads and highways is bad for the complex ecosystem on this continent. They have transformed millions of square miles into parcels of

THE GAIA WAR 91

isolated homogeneous areas. The amount of exhaust that the internal-combustion engines dump into the atmosphere is shameful. And the slaughter and maiming of innocent people in traffic accidents is a disgrace. Surely it is obvious that we have done a service to ourselves and life in general."

Lew sighed. "That's not the way most people think," he said.

"How do they think?" Gaia asked simply.

"In very strange and complicated ways," Lew said.

There was enough water in the bunker to last for at least a week. There were also some emergency rations. Alan could only hope that someone would find him. The more acute problem was the awful smell, which got stronger every hour. It made him nauseous. He moved the table close to the east-facing window and climbed up to look out. He could see a black line in the desert. Beyond the line was a sea of what appeared to be sludge. Except that it was obviously alive. The stuff appeared to be boiling, seething. Suddenly the wind picked up. The air that buffeted Alan's face made him cry out. The noxious fumes assailed his taste buds as well as his olfactory apparatus. He quickly jumped off the table. He grabbed the bandanna from his head and held it over his nose and mouth as he crouched in the corner opposite the window. He waited until the sound of the wind died down before he returned to the armchair. He sank into the cushions with a feeling of impending doom. He was certain from his brief glimpse of the stuff outside that it was growing. It was, at best, a quarter mile away. Alan did not want to die. But the fear of death paled in comparison to the contemplation of being engulfed by the horrid, creeping blackness outside.

"What the hell *is* this stuff?" The state trooper stood on the eastern front of the advancing cyberion sludge.

"We had better be careful," an army officer from the missile test range said. "It looks like it's alive." The assembled state and federal officers all wore gas masks so their voices were extremely distorted.

92   Mark Leon

"Oh my God!" the trooper said. "Look."

A large jackrabbit, the size of a small deer, had been bounding along the periphery of the stuff. Apparently its den had been engulfed and it was looking for a way in or around. It got too close. It was subtle, not an easily detectable motion, but there was movement of sorts. Somehow the microbes, acting in a disturbing unison, managed to catch the rabbit's left hind leg in a sticky brown slime. The powerful thumpers could not dislodge the poor animal. It seemed to the onlookers that the rabbit actually turned its big, watery eyes in their direction, as if imploring them to bear witness to this outrage. It was over quickly, the creature was gone, and the microbes claimed a few more square feet of desert.

"This doesn't look anything like the jungle that is devouring the roads," an FBI agent said.

"I'd feel better if we moved closer to the helicopters," the state trooper said.

"Gentlemen." A tall man in a suit spoke. "We are here to assess the situation. I assure you the choppers are safe, ready, and waiting to get us out of here."

"But sir," the FBI man said, "this stuff is clearly not what is tearing up the roads."

"You're FBI aren't you?" the tall man said.

"Yes, sir. Special Agent James Creel, sir."

"Well, Agent Creel, there is no need to be so formal. As secretary of defense I'm not your boss. Call me Jack."

"OK . . . Jack," Creel said, "but like I said, this stuff isn't the same stuff that we saw out on the interstate, is it?"

"Doesn't appear to be, no," Jack Carp, secretary of defense, said.

"So what are we doing *here*?" Creel said. "Shouldn't we be tracking down the source of the *Genesis Bomb*?"

"*Something* is going on here," Carp said. "It may be that this *stuff*, whatever it is, goes through various stages of development. The destructive life-forms on the highways may be a later stage. So we may be dealing with the same basic phenomenon. But our job here is to gather samples for analysis. You saw what just happened to that rabbit, so

THE GAIA WAR 93

be careful." Carp disappeared over a dune. He went down the other side to a large army tent.

"How are things going?" a man asked as the the defense secretary entered the tent.

"Things are going about as well as can be expected. Are you sure there isn't something else you want to tell me? Men could easily die out there," Carp answered.

"Mr. Secretary, I told you that we at NatCo don't know anything more."

"Bullshit!" the secretary of defense yelled and slammed his fist down on the table. "What you really mean is that you don't want to reveal corporate secrets. My president, *your* president, is not too happy about this, Mr. Tate. You claim that one of your people, a Mr. Larry Skinner, went a little too far. Damn right he went too far! I suggest that you tell me how to destroy the stuff out there or we will seriously think about destroying NatCo."

"I doubt you can do that," NatCo's dapper CEO said.

"You *have* heard of antitrust, the EPA, the Department of Energy?" the defense secretary said. "We can bring all that and a lot more to bear on the situation, make things rather uncomfortable for you."

"I think you are overreacting a bit," Tate said.

"Like hell! Do you realize the large-scale disruption of the economy that will result if we don't stop that stuff from tearing up the roads. I-25 is already shut down south of Albuquerque. The stuff is spreading south to I-10—the entire Southern corridor is threatened! We are talking about the kind of economic disaster that can trigger a major depression."

"I told you that NatCo is not responsible for what is happening out on the highways," Tate said.

"You decide to test a bizarre new life-form on the missile range," Carp said. "Suddenly, following your *experiment*, strange new life-forms that seem to originate from the vicinity of your test site are destroying our roads. What is your explanation? Coincidence?"

"Yes," Tate said.

"Where is this Larry Skinner?" the secretary asked, trying a different tactic.

Mark Leon

"I don't know. All we know is that he produced a new strain of the cyberion bacteria and decided to test it on his own authority. *We* are not happy about the situation either, Mr. Secretary."

"I'm glad to hear that."

"Can I ask you one thing, Mr. Secretary?" Tate said, adopting a more aggressive posture.

"Hmpf!" was all the response Carp offered.

"Where is the secretary of the interior? I should think this is more in his jurisdiction. After all, White Sands is a National Monument . . ."

"Secretary Fields is not well suited for this sort of thing!" Carp snapped.

"And what sort of thing is that?" Tate said. "Are we at war, Mr. Secretary?"

"Maybe."

Skinner boarded the plane at Los Angeles International Airport. He was loath to do it. His empire was just in its embryonic stage and he was abandoning it. But he had no choice. He had learned through his corporate spy network that the head honchos were after him. Someone had tipped the press about NatCo's involvement. Worse, they had leaked his name.

When Skinner had first seen the reports of the strange new growth that was destroying the roads of New Mexico he was genuinely perplexed. But with a little reflection it had all become clear. Alan had succeeded in his laboratory quest for a Genesis-type substance. Skinner was concerned about the inevitable showdown between the cyberion microbes and Alan's creation. Which life-form would prevail?

But what really infuriated Skinner was that he was now linked to the so-called *Genesis Bomb*. That was clearly Alan's doing as well. No matter that the cyberion microbes were totally innocent in the large-scale destruction of the nation's Southwestern highways. It would be a long time before the press or the various investigative agencies were able to sort out the true complexity of the situation. In fact, Skinner realized, in this case the truth was probably too

THE GAIA WAR

95

bizarre to ever reach the light of day. No one would believe it even if the facts could be discovered.

In spite of himself Skinner had to admire Alan's devious ingenuity. *Too bad he was on the wrong side*, he thought. *Alan Fain would have made a powerful ally.*

Skinner decided there was only one option. He could flee the country and wait. Hopefully this *Genesis Bomb* of Alan's was only a minor distraction. Either it would peter out on its own or Skinner's microbes would consume it along with all the other unwanted animal and vegetable life on the planet. Then, Skinner reasoned, he could emerge from hiding and establish the perfect world order with himself at the helm. As the only one in the world, besides a handful of NatCo scientists, who could exercise any control over the cyberion microbes, it should not be too difficult. Meanwhile he would go far away. Someplace he had always wanted to visit, yet where no one would think to look for him.

"*Namaste*, ladies and gentlemen," the flight attendant said. "Welcome to Air India."

Alan tried to chip away at the mortar around the windows. It was a slow process. He had only a pocketknife with which to work, and after several hours he had failed to loosen even a single brick. He did, however, see something to give him hope. Looking out the western window he could see a mass of junglelike growth advancing. When the wind shifted from that direction it brought a refreshing scent that stimulated the imagination with images of gardens and spaces where life ran wild and free. The protean virus had worked. Alan could only wonder at what would happen when the complex blossoming protean lifeforms met the creeping cyberion bacteria.

The more immediate question was which would reach him first. The cyberion sludge was closer but moving more slowly. It was beginning to look as though Alan would be at the center of a clash between two new and utterly incompatible forms of life.

He was grateful for the western breeze when the sun set. Sleep would have been impossible had he been forced to breathe the stench coming from the east. Alan closed his eyes on the floor that night and found himself actually petitioning the heavens for deliverance. He found this only mildly surprising. Not particularly religious, he did realize that there was absolutely nothing he could do but wait.

It was the smell which woke him. The slimy dark obscenity from the NatCo labs had begun seeping through the floor vents. Alan backed up against the western wall and tied his bandanna around his face. The putrid air still made him gag. It was an eerie, horrifying sight. He faced the beautiful light of dawn, which was spilling in through windows and falling on the mass of bacteria that made its slow advance. Alan could see that the stuff was not really all black or brown. There were colors on its shiny surface. They were all variations on earth tones, not at all unpleasing to the eye if one could ignore the primary substance underneath.

Alan had no doubt that the stuff would kill him as soon as it made contact. He was beginning to think that his only reasonable hope was for a quick death.

He felt a pressure on the wall behind him. The wall was actually bulging out slightly, pushing him toward the nemesis creeping from the other direction. He resisted, but the pressure became irresistible. A gaggle of long, green tendrils came shooting through the window above where he stood. They quickly wrapped themselves around his neck, torso, and legs. At the same moment he felt the wall give and saw the roof begin to collapse. He realized with despair that death would not come from any exotic source, but that he would be crushed by the heavy bricks that were beginning to fall.

They did fall, but not en masse, nor with any great force. This was because the protean vegetation working through the roof and walls was so dense and advancing so quickly that Alan was engulfed in a network of branches, vines, and blossoms before he could be buried by the collapsing structure. In fact, the structure did not collapse at all. It was subsumed by the exploding jungle. Parts of the ceiling were actually pushed upward into the tangle of growth that arched overhead for a dozen yards or more.

THE GAIA WAR   97

Alan felt a sharp pain in his left heel where he had come in contact with the cyberion bacteria. Reflexively he dug the heel into the green stalk that was lifting him off the floor. There was a burning hiss and the pain subsided. When Alan looked down he could see the brownish black sludge bubbling and frothing as tendrils of green shot through it. Many of the tendrils shriveled and died, but it was clear that the cyberion organisms were no match for the prolific explosion of colorful life that was still wrapping itself around Alan and lifting him into the sky.

CHAPTER 6

Paul Rainwater watched with satisfaction as Interstate 25 slowly crumbled before his eyes. He was one of a crowd of spectators who had gathered in the Albuquerque suburbs.

"Can't anybody stop it?" a woman asked.

"This stuff is alien," a man said. "The government found the seeds out in space."

"Who says? I haven't heard anything about that." another voice challenged.

"Surprise, surprise!" the conspiracy theorist said sarcastically. "We don't hear anything about what is *really* going on."

"Why would the government want to destroy our highways?" The woman sounded genuinely perplexed.

"They were testing the stuff to use as a weapon. But now it's out of control, and there ain't nothing or nobody gonna stop it."

Rainwater smiled. He was amused and impressed. It had been a stroke of genius on Alan's part to link the *Genesis Bomb* to NatCo. The news accounts were now so garbled and confused that it was extremely unlikely that anyone would ever figure out what had really happened. It looked to the public like another giant, impenetrable conspiracy that involved both the government and corporate America.

"Hey!" a TV newsman said. "Aren't you the guy that came out in favor of all this the other night?"

THE GAIA WAR

Rainwater turned to face the reporter. "I gave an interview," he said mildly.

"Yeah, but you said that the Indians were happy about this," the reporter pressed.

"That is not what I said."

"Can I get a statement from you?" The reporter called his cameraman over.

"Sure."

"This is Jason Sharp reporting from Albuquerque, where the *Genesis Bomb* is rapidly approaching the city. I am talking with Paul Rainwater, an Apache Mescalero Indian, who has come out in favor of what is happening. Mr. Rainwater, aren't you aware of the economic chaos that will ensue if this strange new life-form is not stopped?"

"I think it is actually many new life-forms," Rainwater said. "Notice the tremendous variety of plant species that are eating up all that asphalt and concrete. And to answer your question: Yes, I realize that the disruption will cause temporary problems. Serious problems. All I meant to say was that I think we will all benefit in the long run."

"Why?" Fields asked.

"Because"—Rainwater again looked into the camera—"The roads divide the land and kill the life."

Tana Strand was watching the local news later that evening. When she saw the segment with Rainwater she remembered her conversation two days earlier with Lew.

The next day, back at her desk at the central offices of the Apache Mescalero nation she found the message that Lew had left, the one with the same words that she had heard on TV.

She began to ask around the office if anyone knew this Paul Rainwater. Finally she found someone. "Oh, you mean Mr. Mystic," Linda in accounting said. "Yeah, I know him." She sounded bitter.

"What can you tell me about him?" Tana asked.

"He taught philosophy and English at the Mescalero high school for several years. Then he had some kind of vision. He claimed that the visions of the old medicine men were correct, but that the elders lacked the knowledge of the world that was required to make those visions clear. He said, in effect, that the tribal seers didn't understand their own visions. He pissed a lot of people off. Then he left.''

"Left? Where did he go?"

"No one is sure. Rumor had it that he went off to India. It was a joke. The Indian going to India. But they say he was going to study with some holy man, guru or whatever it is that they have over there. And now he's back. I saw him on TV the other night. How embarrassing! He's causing trouble for the entire nation, talking about how great it is that our roads are being eaten up from underneath us! Do you have any idea what this is going to do to our revenue? If people can't get to the ski lifts, the winter will be a financial disaster. We'll have to shut down the schools.''

"Do you know how I can find him?" Tana asked.

"Why?" Linda sounded suddenly suspicious.

"Were you two . . . like involved or something?" Tana asked.

"Does it show that badly?" Linda laughed. "Yeah, I guess you could say that I got dumped for a bunch of empty dreams. Oh well, that was a few years ago. I'm over it.''

She did not sound "over it" to Tana. "I just want to give him this message." Tana showed the message to Linda.

"Who left this?" Linda asked.

"I don't know. He only left his number.''

"Well," Linda said, "I think I can find him. Why don't you leave this with me. It will give me an excuse to see how Mr. Rainwater is getting on these days." A wry half smile graced her face.

Tana gave her the message and went back downstairs to her desk, glad to be free from the business which had turned out to be rather more complicated than she had expected.

Upstairs in accounting Linda gazed at the pink message slip for several minutes before she picked up the telephone. She dialed a number with slow deliberation.

"Hello." There was no mistaking the voice.

"Paul?"

THE GAIA WAR 101

"Linda! I'm so glad to hear from you. I've been meaning to call. I . . ."

"I have a message for you," Linda said.

Lew was worried about Alan. The reports from the desert indicated that their efforts had been remarkably successful. And so far there was no indication that they were in danger of being found out.

"This is not right," Meagan was saying. All three were staying at Alan's house. "So much destruction . . ."

"Destruction possibly," Gaia said. "Surely you have read the Book of Revelation. Destruction of that which is inimical to life is not necessarily a bad thing."

"Meagan doesn't need to hear that sort of thing from you," Lew said, looking at Gaia.

Gaia turned her eyes down. She realized that Lew was right. She was playing right into Meagan's belief that she was somehow divine.

"I'm worried about Alan . . ." Lew began.

"He can take care of himself," Meagan snapped. "Anyway, this whole thing is his fault."

Later that night, after Meagan had gone to bed, Lew and Gaia were talking. "Do you have any memories—before your 'birth'?" Lew asked.

"Birth? Was I born?" she asked, innocently.

"Well not exactly," Lew said. "Your situation is unique. That's what makes me curious. Some people think that we come from somewhere, that we exist in a state of perfect knowledge before we are born, and that birth causes us to forget."

"Do you believe that?" she asked.

"Not necessarily . . . I . . ."

"Not necessarily?" she mused. "What, I wonder, is a necessary belief?"

"I just wondered if you have any recollection—from before," Lew said. "It would be fascinating. I mean to find out about . . ."

"About what?"

102 Mark Leon

"I don't know," Lew said. "Eternity, I guess . . . or something like that."

"I am afraid that I can't tell you very much," she said. "It does seem as if I existed somewhere, somehow, before I met Larry, and all of this silly business started. It feels both vague and definite at the same time. But it certainly isn't the sort of thing I can put into words. Either I don't have the words or the memories are just impossible to describe."

"But you do remember *something*?" Lew pressed.

"Yes, something. But no thing that I can say." They were interrupted by the telephone.

"Hello," Lew answered.

"I am trying to reach a Mr. Lew Slack," the voice said.

"I'm Lew Slack."

"I received a message from you earlier this afternoon, Mr. Slack. I apologize for not getting back to you sooner, but the phone lines are overloaded out this way—what with all the trouble."

"Trouble?" Lew was suddenly suspicious, afraid that someone was on their trail.

The man just laughed. "OK, I'll stop playing around. Did you not leave the following message for me: 'The roads divide the land and kill the life'? This is Paul Rainwater."

Lew breathed a sigh of relief. "Yeah, that was me," he said.

"Where did you get that particular line?" Rainwater asked.

"It was an extremely peculiar message that showed up on my computer system at NatCo." Lew immediately regretted mentioning NatCo. He was not sure how far he could trust Rainwater, and his employer was rapidly becoming quite notorious owing to the "trouble" in New Mexico.

"Don't worry, Mr. Slack," Rainwater said, as if reading Lew's mind. "I'm on your side. We sent you the message. That is why I gave that little television interview. I hoped you would see it and get in touch. Where is Alan?"

THE GAIA WAR

"I wish I knew. The last time I saw him he was headed into White Sands."

"White Sands," Rainwater said, "is rapidly being transformed into the most fantastic jungle the world has ever seen."

"So I hear," Lew said. "Is there any chance that someone could survive in there?"

Rainwater laughed.

"What's so funny?" Lew asked, annoyed.

"Sorry. I am concerned about Alan, too. But I think his chances of survival are excellent."

"Why do you say that?" Lew asked.

"I think it would be better if we could get together to discuss this," Rainwater said. "One can never be too sure about the telephones, you know."

"Where?" Lew asked.

"Suppose I come to you? Things are a little too hot out here."

After they made the necessary arrangements, and Lew had put the phone down, Gaia asked, "Who was that?"

"That was another piece of the puzzle," Lew answered.

CHAPTER 7

Skinner was not prepared for India. He arrived in New Delhi at 2:30 A.M. The officer who checked his visa was dressed in an olive drab soldier's uniform of a style from a bygone age of colonialism. He opened Skinner's passport and appeared to check it with a curious sort of suspicion. Then he completely unnerved Skinner with an ironic smile. For a moment Skinner thought that he had been found out. "How long are you planning to stay in India, Mr. Williams?" the officer asked.

"Uh—I'm not sure," Skinner answered.

"What is the purpose of your visit?"

"Well, I've always wanted to see India . . . I . . ."

"Destination?" the officer asked in a neutral tone.

"Benares," Skinner answered.

"Yes, Benares," the officer echoed. He pronounced the name of the city as if it were the punch line to a private joke. "The sacred city. The city of Lord Shiva." He paused and looked deeply into Skinner's eyes. "The city of light?"

The clear questioning tone of the officer put Skinner in an even more defensive posture. "The city of light?" he repeated.

"Did you not know this other name for our most holy of cities, Mr. Williams?" The officer seemed to be enjoying himself. "Benares is also called Kashi, which means the city of light. Enjoy your stay in India, Mr. Williams." The

THE GAIA WAR 105

officer suddenly stamped Skinner's passport with such violent force that the window bars in front of him shook. Skinner nearly jumped into the air at the sound. The officer then handed the passport back to Skinner with a lazy, quiet gesture that was completely incongruous with his action of a moment before.

Skinner collected his one bag and headed for customs. He walked past a man in a military cap with a cigarette poised immobile in the corner of his mouth. The next moment, without realizing it, he was outside in the steamy New Delhi night. He was immediately surrounded by taxi drivers and boys grabbing at his bag.

"Taxi! Where you want to go, sir? I am giving the best service!" a man with a mustache was screaming into his ear.

"Sorry," Skinner said. "I need to go through customs. I must have gone out the wrong door."

He hurried back into the airport and went up to the man in the cap who appeared to be some sort of official. "Excuse me," Skinner said. "Can you direct me to customs?"

"Yes," the man said—amazingly the cigarette did not appear to move as he spoke. "I am customs."

"Oh—well you see I have just arrived from California and ..." Skinner had no idea what to say. He, in fact, had no idea what he was doing.

This did not seem to bother the customs agent in the least. He slowly took the cigarette from his mouth and said, "Do you have any American cigarettes? I will give you a very good price."

"Cigarettes? No, I ..."

The agent appeared very disappointed at this and immediately lost interest in Skinner. Suddenly the officer focused on an Indian Sikh man in a business suit and turban who was carrying two large suitcases. *"Mut Kero!"* the customs agent barked in a deafening voice.

The Sikh stopped and looked at the agent and yelled back, *"Keyonh? Meri Desh heh!"* This precipitated a lengthy shouting match. Skinner was convinced it would come to blows, so passionate was the exchange. Finally the Sikh opened one of his bags. The customs agent suddenly appeared very bored and merely poked halfheartedly at the garments packed within. Then he waved the Sikh on. A dumbfounded Skinner watched the man disappear into the madness of the night as if nothing at all had taken place.

Skinner's ride into New Delhi was terrifying. His taxi, an Indian Ambassador, seemed held together by wire and chewing gum. Its one headlight was extremely dim. There were no interior lights. The cabdriver's assistant, a young boy, kept flicking a cigarette lighter and holding it to the dashboard. It took several minutes for Skinner to figure out that the boy was trying to get a good look at the fuel gauge, which hovered precariously a hair above empty.

They careened through a small group of cows, which had wandered into an intersection, and then abruptly stopped. The driver got out to study the street sign. Skinner was amazed. It appeared that the man did not know the way into the city. The driver's young sidekick got out and they both stood there in the middle of the road, surrounded by cows that were eating garbage and swishing their tails. Ignoring the cows, the two began an intense discussion in Hindi.

Skinner poked his head out and asked, "What's wrong?" This question seemed to totally baffle them, even though Skinner knew that the driver spoke passable English. A number of other cabs came screeching by, missing them by inches. Finally the two jumped back into the front seat and they were off again at a reckless pace through the unlit streets and boulevards of the New Delhi suburbs.

The next morning Skinner ventured out into the New Delhi day. He walked past a spice stand. The exotic aromas served to lift his spirits. Suddenly a man put his hand on Skinner's shoulder. "Watch your step," the man said in excellent English.

"What . . ." Skinner mumbled.

The Indian merely pointed to the sidewalk in front of them. A concrete slab had been removed to reveal a clogged sewer line that ran only a few feet underneath the pavement. The stench of human waste and nameless debris was overwhelming. Skinner had been about to step right into it. "Oh," he said, "thanks."

THE GAIA WAR 107

"No problem," the man said. He was dressed in traditional Indian garb of loose *pajama* pants and long *coorta* shirt. "You don't want to be walking into the sewer line."

"Why don't they put up a barricade or something?" Skinner asked.

"They are fixing it," the man said, as if that were explanation enough. "It is all jammed up, you see."

"Oh. Where are the workmen?" Skinner asked.

"The *muzdoori*?" the man said. "They must be having tea, coffee, or something."

"But . . ." Skinner began, recalling the delightful odors of just a few yards back while staring into the pile of stinking filth. "I don't understand."

"Don't worry about it," the man said. "This is India."

Skinner walked around the dangerous hole and continued on toward Connaught Circle. He was beginning to wonder if he was in the right place.

A week later, still suffering from the wrenching jet lag that results from traveling to the other side of the globe, Skinner was sitting on the main burning *ghat* in Benares. The *ghats* lined the city's crescent border with the Ganges river. They consisted of broad steps that led down to the water. Each *ghat* had some particular significance to the Hindu faith. Many housed temples devoted to various gods and goddesses.

The burning *ghat* was the site of cremations. Bodies burned and smoldered there from dawn late into the night. Families brought corpses from all over India to see their loved ones return to the elements on the banks of the sacred river.

Skinner was watching a Brahmin family as it placed the shrouded body of a father on a pile of wood. "What is death but the end of breath? Eh *Sahib*?" A wandering *sadhu*, or holy man, spoke these words to Skinner.

Skinner had learned to ignore all beggars and *sadhus* (often it was difficult to tell the difference). But this man was persistent. His English was impeccable, which did not jibe with Skinner's previous experience. "I don't want any money," the man continued. Skinner did not believe him for a second, but the fact that the man had explicitly refused money was surprising. Life for an American in India, Skinner had learned during his short stay, consisted in large part of dealing with people who assumed they could get some cash from you.

But after his cryptic remarks this man, dressed in saffron robes, sat quietly beside Skinner. Together they watched as the son lit the funeral pyre and the patriarch's body was engulfed in flames.

They were startled by a dog that ran straight at them. The mangy street cur had a charred human hand in its mouth. The animal was being chased by a young boy with a long stick. The poor, starving creature had learned, like many others of its kind, that free meals of cooked human flesh were available on the burning *ghats*. But they came at a price. The dog, momentarily confused, had halted in front of Skinner and his mysterious companion. This gave the youth time to reach the dog. He lit into the beast's hindquarters with a savage brutality. The dog yelped piti- fully and dropped the hand. It ran between the two men and escaped into the narrow streets, called *gullis*, of the adjoining neighborhood.

Skinner had been badly shaken by the ordeal. The young boy left the blackened, gnawed human flesh where it lay on the *ghat* and returned to tend his funeral pyre. Skinner's companion said, "It is a difficult thing to see, is it not? The ways of this culture are sometimes not the most aes- thetically pleasing. Why don't you come with me to have some tea? It is only a short distance."

Skinner was surprised to find himself following the man as he led the way along the *ghats*. They walked for about a half a mile and stopped by an ancient temple. The man opened a small door, a door in the side of the temple. It was really only a narrow, cloth-covered opening in the an- cient brickwork. Skinner had to duck to follow inside.

They sat on a mat covered with thick white cotton. Skin- ner had removed his shoes, which lay next to his host's sandals just inside the door. The room was small but clean. A servant, emerging from the adjoining kitchen, brought their tea. It was heavily spiced with cardamom and clove.

THE GAIA WAR 109

"You may call me Swami-ji," the man in saffron said after taking a cautious sip. The tea was extremely hot. "All my friends do." Skinner did not volunteer his name, nor did his host express any curiosity on that matter.

"We are but breathing dust, you know," Swami-ji continued. "That is what fascinates me about death. Not that I am of a morbid nature. Life is where it's at, don't you think?"

"Sure," Skinner said.

"Yes. But here in India death is so much a part of life. Sometimes I think too much. When you watch the bodies burn you cannot help but be struck by the delicate nature of it. The combustion returns the elements of the body to the air. That wispy smoke seems to summarize what we really are after all. Our bodies are powered by combustion of various elements with the air we breathe. What is life but the temporary internalization of that combustion? We are, each moment, carried on the wind. This is not metaphor, but the actual nature of things. It gives one pause."

Swami-ji fell into a silence so deep that Skinner was drawn into it. It made him decidedly uncomfortable. He uncrossed his legs and extended them. He sipped his tea and examined the patterns on the wall hangings. Finally Swami-ji raised his head and spoke. "India is not an easy place. I am sure that you have learned this."

"Yes."

"There is great beauty here. A deep richness. But, alas, it is so hard to see nowadays. The misery of our people weighs more heavily than ever. And I am afraid that no one knows what can be done about it. But that is not why you have come to India, is it?"

"What do you mean?" Skinner was suddenly suspicious.

"I mean that you are obviously not one of those 'do-gooders' who has come to help us. Don't get me wrong. Many of those people are dedicated and do much good. But unfortunately it is never enough, and some of them are very misguided. You are not a tourist either, are you?"

"Not exactly," Skinner admitted.

"No matter." Swami-ji stood and pulled a wall hanging aside. He opened a door and started up a narrow staircase,

110 Mark Leon

saying, "Follow me. I have space that will perhaps be more suitable for our discussion."

They emerged into a spacious room on top of the temple. It was light, airy, and well appointed. What most surprised Skinner was the personal computer on the large desk by the window, which commanded an excellent view of the river. "Please." Swami-ji sat in a comfortable armchair and motioned for Skinner to take the one opposite.

Skinner ignored his host and remained standing in front of the window. He stared at the ancient *ghats* and the long curve of the Ganges. There were several wooden boats, mostly full of tourists. The boatmen strained at oars that could have been as old as the river itself. He turned to face Swami-ji and took a slow sip of his tea. "So I gather you are not a wandering *sadhu*?"

His host laughed. It was a soft sound that would have been barely detectable were it not for the animated light of Swami-ji's eyes. "I suppose I am what you might call a 'high-tech' guru," he said.

"This is your . . . office?" Skinner asked.

"Yes. My office. The computer is not state of the art, but it suffices."

"Suffices for what?"

"Various things. I use it for writing mostly. I am doing a book, you know."

Skinner just stared. He was trying to figure out how old the guru was. Swami-ji's face had the lines of an old man, but he carried his body with a youthful, limber grace.

"I hope to develop a philosophical system to rival those of the greatest minds—both East and West. Our two cultures have a great deal to learn from each other, don't you think?"

"I wouldn't know," Skinner said flatly.

"Enough of all this banter. Please, be seated. Make yourself comfortable."

Skinner took the other armchair.

"So how do you like India?"

"It makes me tired," Skinner said.

"Yes, I know. The rewards of the Indian experience can

THE GAIA WAR 111

be great if you have enough tolerance and patience. West erners are so impatient.''

''Are we?''

''Please don't take it personally. I only meant that we Indians have an ancient tradition of waiting and watching. Sometimes this works to our disadvantage—as you can plainly see when you look at the human misery that has grown up around us while we just wait and watch. But it can be a very useful thing as well.''

''How is that?''

''Results are tricky things. One doesn't always get the result one wants. If a person goes to great extremes, sac-rifices *everything* for a dream—that person will be in a very bad way if things do not turn out as planned. This is the way of it in the West. You have many spectacular success stories to be sure. I am, for example, extremely grateful for my computer. It has made life so much easier for me. I would like to think that given enough time we would have developed computers on our own here in India. But I cannot convince myself that this is so.

''So you have much of which to be proud. Dreams have come true in your world. But for every dream come true there are many broken dreams. Broken dreams make for broken lives.'' Swami-ji's eyes flashed for a moment, and Skinner felt as if the man were staring right through him.

''And you do not have broken dreams here?'' Skinner asked.

''Of course we do. And many broken lives, as you can easily see for yourself. I am rambling and babbling as is too often my habit. The easy thing to say is that you live *for* dreams in your country, and here we live *in* dreams. But silly sorts of things like this have been said about India all too often. And what do they reveal of the truth?''

''What is truth?'' Skinner asked.

Swami-ji laughed again. This time the sound actually seemed to generate light. But Skinner quickly convinced himself that it had been an illusion. The room was no brighter than before. ''Your philosophers have been trying to answer that question for a very long time,'' Swami-ji said. "You know what your Jesus said when asked the same thing?"

"What?" Skinner said.

"Nothing. He did not answer. Why do you suppose that is?"

"Because he didn't know," Skinner said.

"No, it was because he was not a philosopher." Swami-ji smiled.

"Maybe he should have been," Skinner said.

"I don't know if that would have done him much good," Swami-ji said. "The authorities also executed Socrates, your greatest philosopher."

"A scientist then?"

"Now that is quite a funny image," Swami-ji said. "Can you just picture it? Jesus a scientist. Searching for truth in the laboratory—perhaps a corporate laboratory, like the famed labs of the NatCo Corporation." Swami-ji shot Skinner a knowing glance.

Skinner was caught completely off guard by the sudden reference to his employer. "How did you know . . ." he blurted out before he could restrain himself.

"I know a great deal about you, Mr. Skinner," the guru said.

CHAPTER 8

Alan was all aglow, on fire. It was a cool radiance that bathed his body inside and out. The more he relaxed, the more he felt a strange new tension that began at the base of his spine. It was working its way up, slowly, deliciously translating itself into new sensational possibilities of feeling. Any attempt on Alan's part to focus on what was happening only resulted in ever more new and delightful somatic messages.

But when the warmth reached his stomach he began to wonder, *What if this stuff is eating me?* He was still being borne by the prolific growth of plant life. His eyes were closed and he imagined tendrils of vegetation and strands of fungal mycelia creeping into his limbs, invading his nervous system, lulling him into acceptance through a false sense of ecstasy, even as it devoured him, digesting from the inside out. He dared not open his eyes even as he became convinced that he was dying a horrible death.

The comfortable warmth in his stomach turned to nausea. He tried to sit, surprised at how easy the motion was—he had expected to feel thousands of tiny strands binding him, like Gulliver among the Lilliputians. But instead the jungle tangle surrounding him responded to his desire, shifting subtly to facilitate his change of position. *Don't fear.* The voice was gone from inside his head before he could convince himself that he had really heard it.

114   Mark Leon

At first all his attention was entirely consumed by the rapid beating of his own heart. The pressure of soft stems and padded leaves on his back served to calm him, and he began to look around. The jungle met his gaze and looked back with a splendor that would have been insolent if it were not so beautiful. The sheer beauty of it took his breath away and actually forced him to forget his panic. Any fears he might have had were made to look petty in light of the new life that greeted his astonishment.

"I had no idea," he said aloud, surprised by the sound of his voice. The silence which followed was full of laughter and music. The quiet was bursting with song and delight—so full that it contained its own paradox: any single sound would diminish the silence from which it sprang.

"Far out," Alan said, and immediately regretted the absurdity of this pronouncement. But before any further judgmental thoughts could lay hold of his mind he was seized by a fit of laughter so violent that he would again have feared for his life were it not so wonderfully pleasant, in a wild and wicked way, just to give himself over to the experience. The thought of death by laughter conjured the image of his skeleton sitting and laughing still, the bones rattling with each new convulsive burst. This sustained his sense of humor through any dread notions of his own demise.

The last chuckle rippled through him and left his body feeling renewed, relaxed and invigorated. He wiped the tears from his cheeks with the back of his hand and took a long, slow, deep breath. The air was positively intoxicating. Wild, exotic scents swam like ribbons of texture through the jungle's atmosphere. Each breath brought something new to his olfactory sensibilities. And something old. Just as an ordinary smell can often trigger long-forgotten memories, the extraordinary aromas surrounding Alan hinted at memories of ancient experiences and civilizations of which he could logically know nothing but to which he nevertheless felt intimately connected.

Feeling more centered, he began to examine his surroundings with a more critical eye. He was supported by a

THE GAIA WAR 115

dense thicket of vines about twenty feet from the jungle floor, which he could only dimly perceive. It was impossible to tell how many different species were present. All the new life seemed incredibly diverse yet marvelously interconnected so that, for all Alan knew, the growth might represent one single species or thousands of different ones. There was at least another twenty feet of growth above, through which he could see a few small patches of blue New Mexico sky.

He decided to descend and was again helped by the leaves, vine stalks, and tendrils that seemed to anticipate his every move and adjusted themselves accordingly. He jumped the last five feet to the soft, sandy gypsum floor. Looking back up he saw that the jungle was more open than he had supposed. In places the growth was extremely dense—the spot that had supported him was one such place, but in general there was a remarkable openness to the lush foliage. There was no geometric regularity to the empty spaces, and yet they conformed to an integrity of design that Alan could only describe as artistic for lack of a better term. The empty spaces served to enhance the beauty of the rest.

Alan wandered aimlessly, traversing a square mile or two. By his most conservative estimates the jungle covered an area of several hundred square miles. He did not know if it would ever stop. They had designed the protean virus to metabolize gypsum sand, concrete, and asphalt, but Alan suspected that the stuff was infinitely adaptable. It might sweep the entire surface of the earth with an acceleration that would follow a geometric progression. "Today White Sands, tomorrow the world." He laughed.

Suddenly, on the periphery of his vision, he detected a silvery, shimmering motion. Seeking out the source of it he found a plant which stood waist high on a single green stalk, about one inch in diameter. The top of the plant was a single leaf that opened in a nearly perfect conical shape about one yard across and two feet deep. The remarkable thing was the water that filled it. The plant was a living fountain. Alan could see little bubbles percolating up from the bottom, the apex of the cone where the big leaf joined

116 Mark Leon

the stalk. The plant must have had an incredibly long and complex root system in order to go deep enough to find water and then pump it back to the surface. Alan cautiously took a small sip. It was deliciously pure, with a subtle tang that came from the fountain plant itself. Abandoning all caution, Alan took great gulps, finishing by submerging his head. Finally he shook his hair out and splashed more water into his eyes. With this refreshment came a new yet familiar sensation. He realized that he had become quite hungry.

Wandering farther he found a tree. It grew in a small clearing. Looking up, Alan could not see its top. The tree disappeared in the tangle of growth that formed the roof of this strange new world. The trunk was smooth, the bark had a paperlike texture. The lowest branches started about ten feet up, but some of them were so laden with a turquoise fruit that they hung down far enough at the ends for Alan to pick one. At first it tasted like guava, but then the flavors seemed to subtly change, as if the fruit were actively trying to offer a taste both familiar and new. After identifying shades of pineapple, orange, grape, watermelon, and banana, Alan gave up and decided it was delicious.

He sat down on the soft carpet of blue grass, resting his back against the tree trunk. Again he was impressed by the feeling of quiet fullness. He imagined that he could feel the life of the tree in his spine. Then he was convinced it was more than imagination. He *could* feel it, a vibration that transmitted warm waves of energy directly into his central nervous system. It was both pleasant and exciting.

Looking about Alan decided that the jungle did consist of many different species; hundreds were visible within a radius of ten yards from where he sat. Even the blue carpet of grass was shot through with tiny flowers of a seemingly endless variety. And there were things which he would have called weeds, but they were so intricately formed that to do so would have seemed an injustice.

He woke to endlessly dappled evening sunlight. Wandering westward toward the warm, jungle-filtered glow, he found a very strange-looking plant that drew him like a magnet. "What have we here?" he murmured to himself

THE GAIA WAR　　　　**117**

as he knelt to examine the creamy yellow leaves. They grew out of a short, knee-high stalk in a pattern that struck Alan as curiously inorganic. They were bunched together in a lateral, symmetrical pattern and produced an acrid smell that made Alan think of green bananas and new-mown grass. On closer examination Alan saw that the yellow color of each leaf was shot through with black patterns, which he first took for veins. But the dark squiggles were far too regular—they reminded him of Arabic writing.

He brushed the edge of the bunch with his fingers and a few leaves flapped open like the pages of a book. Did the squiggles move? They were beginning to look more like text, but he could not make out the language. One moment he thought he saw Sanskrit characters, the next Egyptian hieroglyphics. He stared hard at the patterns and had the creepy feeling that they were trying to make themselves intelligible, trying out different scripts, searching for one he could understand. He thought he saw Greek, French, Russian, but before he could be sure he found himself staring at English text.

He could understand nothing of it. Starting was easy. The words flowed off the page, playing with his imagination. But what began as intelligible prose quickly turned into something else. Each sentence led his mind into an ever-deeper labyrinth of meaning from which there was no return. And when he tried to start fresh he could not be sure that the words were the same. When he tried to flip to a new page he was frustrated by the stickiness of the leaves. And only the outer pages at the beginning were accessible. In order to pry the volume open at its center Alan would have had to do violence to the plant.

Alan stood and shook his head. The experience, while interesting, had been disturbing. He had witnessed a depth of confusion that was positively eerie. For the first time he began to doubt the wisdom of the project. Standing in the midst of his own creation, he felt the implications of what he had done wash over him in dizzying waves. *Could it really be possible?* he wondered. *Billions of years of planetary evolution completely wiped out by the protean jungle?* It made him feel very small.

This actually eased his conscience a bit. He began to feel so small that he could no longer think of the new world around him as his own creation. "Clearly I am just one of the agencies by which it came into being," he said aloud. Was it his imagination or did he detect laughter in the surrounding silence? In any case the thought that he was really not responsible, that he was merely one small actor in a plan greater than anything of which he could conceive, gave him some comfort.

I wonder what is going on out there? he asked himself, thinking of Lew, Gaia, Meagan, and Skinner. "I hope that bastard is in big trouble," he mumbled. He was somewhat surprised to realize that these thoughts did not interest him very much. They seemed out of place where he was, and he really did not want to be anywhere else, at least for the time being. "Far out," he said, again feeling the inadequacy of his powers of expression. So he vowed to read more literature in order to improve in that area. But the thought of literature brought to mind another world, one of libraries, buildings, streets, and cars, and that world was fast becoming a memory, a memory that seemed to come from a dream of a possible world that might have existed long ago and far away.

Night was coming on fast. The red glow in the west was gone, leaving a purple smear that faded quickly into black. Alan could see only patches of these colors through the dense growth, and they made him suddenly afraid. He had no sleeping bag, nothing with which to insulate himself from the bitter, night cold of the desert. He quickly began to dig a shallow pit in the sand. Then he went in search of leaves, grass, any suitable material that he could use for warmth. He ripped up piles of the blue grass and lined the pit. He tore bundles of leaves and vines, racing against the approaching darkness. He worked for some time arranging each type of vegetation according to his estimate of its insulating properties. He became obsessed with the work, convinced that his survival depended on it, so that it was only his overwhelming fatigue that forced him to pause briefly.

He slowly became aware of two facts, both improbable,

THE GAIA WAR 119

yet undeniable. The first was that he was very warm, actually hot and sweating profusely. The second was the light. He could see clearly that the blackness of the desert night had failed to materialize. The light consisted of a soft, phosphorescent-like glow which emanated from various plants. Alan noted several different species which were responsible. The heat, he assumed, must also come from the flora. It was a pleasant warmth when he relaxed.

He made a bed by filling the pit with the soft stuff that he had gathered. He lay down on top of it and again had the sensation that the material was shifting to accommodate his weight and shape. He stared up through the canopy for a while, content to listen to his slow heartbeat and to feel his breath coming in and going out. He closed his eyes for a moment and relaxed even more. When he opened them briefly the surroundings looked darker, as if the luminescence were in tune with his need to see. *Impossible*, he thought. But he immediately realized that until quite recently he would have thought the whole thing impossible. *Who knows?* He breathed softly as a slow exhalation escaped him. The answer seemed to be all around as he drifted off to sleep. He did not see the pair of eyes that were watching him from behind a nearby tree, nor did he hear the soft footsteps approach.

Alan's sleep was both deeply satisfying and strangely electric. He had dreams of shimmering, tubular growing things that exploded into fractal patterns of infinite complexity and wild beauty. He woke quite rested yet feeling that the night had been extremely busy. One lingering image from his dreams was particularly compelling. It was a face, almost human. What made it alien was no strangeness of physical feature; the face was, in fact, quite beautiful. Rather it was an expression of embryonic wonder, a childlike innocence which would have appeared simple had it not been for the obvious intelligence behind those big, blue-green eyes. In Alan's dream the face had watched him for some time and then turned away. It was then that he realized the creature possessed a beautiful female body. He watched her walk away, the full curves of her naked behind glowing in the soft, nighttime luminescence. Was it a trick of the light or had her pale, creamy skin given off a faint, greenish glow of its own?

What a dream, Alan thought as he stood and stretched. The morning air had a slight chill, not harsh, just enough bite to stimulate the muscles and the appetite. He went in search of breakfast, confident that he would find some delicious morsel. The ground around Alan's sleeping nest was in a small clearing. The blue grass covered most of the area although there were patches of bare, white sand. As Alan moved toward the denser jungle growth in search of food, he looked down to notice the tread marks his hiking boots had left in the sand. He knew the sand was quite soft and the grass appeared more so, luxuriant and inviting to the tread of bare feet. He contemplated shedding his boots and was about to sit down to do so when he noticed something which made him stop and stand very still for a moment. Then he knelt to study it more closely. It was a footprint, not his own. Its maker had gone shoeless and had smaller feet. The print indicated that the foot was quite narrow and had a deep arch. The toe marks were particularly interesting. They were open and quite distinct. Whoever it was had almost certainly never worn shoes, had never forced toes to cramp together in the unnatural fashion to which most of us are accustomed.

The realization that he was not alone had an unexpected effect. Alan was curious and a little afraid. But he was also disappointed. He had, without realizing it, begun to think of this new world as his. He felt a selfish resistance to the idea that he might have to share it with someone else. The print also stimulated fear tinged with sexual excitement because it made him suspect that the vivid dream had been no dream. He could no longer easily dismiss that compelling face as fantasy. He was being watched by someone, and she was not necessarily human.

Alan found a perfect breakfast fruit. It was only slightly sweet and somehow managed to remind him of toast and a mushroom omelette. The fruit was shaped like eggplant and was white with black, spiraling stripes. He had found a cluster of them growing on a vine that wrapped around

THE GAIA WAR 121

the trunk of a large tree and disappeared in the upper foliage.

The slight morning chill did not last long, and Alan was again beginning to feel uncomfortably warm. By this time his clothes were quite dirty and he longed for a shower and a change. He had been wandering for about an hour after breakfast when he heard the unmistakable sound of flowing water. Brushing his way past a particularly dense stand of bright green and orange shrubs, he discovered the source of the sound. Water was flowing in abundance out of the top of a tree some thirty feet high. The tree was surrounded by plants that appeared to be larger versions of the small fountain plant from which he had drunk. The effect was spectacular. Right there in the midst of the jungle was a series of waterfalls that cascaded into small pools. Each tier of pools emptied into the next level until finally spilling onto the ground.

Alan quickly stripped and ran to stand underneath the nearest waterfall. He screamed with delight. The water was cool, bracing but not really cold. He was able to climb easily to a leaf basin pool about ten feet off the ground. It was just large enough to float him, and he lay back to look at the top of the waterfall. He realized that the main trunk was more like a giant vine than a tree. It was brilliant green. The root system must have been awesome in order to tap such a large quantity of pure springwater and pump it to the surface. The root system must have also provided the energy to bring the water up to such a pleasant temperature.

He washed his clothes and hung them on a giant golden fern to dry. Then he lay down on a soft patch of grass where the filtered sunlight was relatively unobstructed.

As he basked in the warmth, Alan noticed a change in his thought processes. "The ordinary mind is a tyrant," he muttered. It seemed to Alan that most valuable thoughts and perceptions occur obliquely, by which he meant that real insight is normally filtered out by ordinary, familiar thoughts. His mind was remarkably free of those, and it left room for things which had always been there but to which he had seldom paid much attention.

The result was that he felt his mind to be functioning as

it was meant to function, for perhaps the first time in his life. This did not involve spectacular, mind-blowing revelations about the ultimate nature of life, death, and the universe. Those things remained an impenetrable mystery to him. Rather his mind had subtly, almost without his noticing, taken on a new role. His thoughts were no longer always judging his behavior and weighing him down with "shoulds" and "should nots." Instead, thinking was a pleasure which enriched experience instead of diminishing it.

Lost in these esoteric speculations of dubious meaning, Alan did not at first notice the shadow which passed over his naked body and settled a few feet from him. His eyes got very wide when he finally realized that he was staring at the midmorning silhouette of a naked woman. He was very still for a moment, afraid to look up in search of the real thing of which the shadow was only a dark image. In that moment the shadow abruptly withdrew, as if its owner had suddenly become aware of detection.

Alan sat up and looked hard in the direction of the sun. He saw pale, strangely luminous skin and the glimpse of a profile before the face was turned fully away. She was fast, and the jungle swallowed her straight back and beautifully curved hips before Alan could get to his feet. He went crashing into the dense growth. A vine snagged his foot and he pitched headlong onto the soft ground. He continued the chase for several minutes, even as he realized the futility of it.

He was hopelessly lost. He tried for an hour to retrace his steps to the waterfall clearing and gave up. Now he was naked, which gave him an unwelcome sense of vulnerability. But with that came a strange, new, sensual excitement. His body felt full of a secret kind of knowledge that could only be expressed when it was free of clothing. Alan almost believed that the jungle had conspired to rid him once and for all of his second, "civilized" layer of skin, so that the real stuff could do its thing.

He felt his way farther. One direction was as good as another. The shadows gave him only a vague indication of which direction was south, and, as far as he knew, there

THE GAIA WAR

was no end to the mysterious realm in which he now wandered.

By midafternoon his anxiety, rekindled by his nudity, had grown. He stood in a small clearing where the blue grass grew and took a slow, deep breath. Once again he felt the strange, live quality that permeated the silence. It gave him a claustrophobic feeling. But his yogic training served him well. He was able to achieve a degree of mental detachment which allowed him to analyze the situation. From this he gleaned that the close feeling was not inimical, it was only his own resistance to it that caused fear. He surmised that it was his job to coexist with the fullness. It was not a particularly easy thing to do, as accustomed as most people are to either intrusive company or isolated privacy. This was simultaneously both and neither. Conscious of the source of his anxiety, he found that he could control his fear by modulating his attitude.

He looked down, surprised to find that he was standing in front of the book plant. At least he assumed it was the same one; the surrounding jungle looked familiar. The plant had changed. The outer leaves had spread out a little. They were not so sticky as before, and he could now read the title page.

The Book of the New Creation, is what it said. He turned to page one.

> You may wonder how it is that you come to be reading this. Why you? Why now? The easy answer is to say that some questions cannot be answered. This is the way of mysticism. The mystical truth is beyond questions and answers, it just is.
>
> But we have come too far for that, haven't we, my friend? That sort of thing is fine for childhood, but simply will no longer satisfy. We must have answers. Unfortunately the search for answers leads directly to philosophy which is ultimately as disappointing as mysticism. Where the mystic reduces all to an unfathomable mystery, the philosopher reduces things to trivial answers that depend on tedious arguments.
>
> As always we must search for the middle path. ''Avoid

extremes,'' is what Aristotle said, but it is a little late for that, too. The fact that you are now reading this indicates that extremes have been exceeded. Clearly you are not one for perpetual moderation; extremes are too much a part of your nature.

What you see around you is the new creation and you need to know something about it. So this, that you now read, is *The Book of the New Creation*. Doubtless you have heard many things, stories of paradise, why paradise was lost, and what is to be done about it. There is some truth to all these tales and myths. And many lies. But their appeal is the result of a very real resonance with the truth.

"What is truth?" Some say it is the correspondence between what we think and what actually is. Some say it is a story big enough to include us all and compelling enough to convince us each. But this is philosophy, and we want to avoid the endless swamp of metaphysical and epistemological debate.

So don't worry about truth. Instead be satisfied that for the present this is enough. There is some sort of evolving plan here. It involves all life on the planet, which includes your species. You are at a crossroads. If you blow it, the future is dismal, a lingering horror of half life before a final death. On the other hand your future could be bright, brilliant even. You are destined for the stars. Surely you have sensed this—it is a theme which echoes down the millennia in many of your more edifying stories and myths.

This text is largely a handbook for your future life, a stellar life which is really only the beginning of a journey that will last for millions of years and take you to the center of your galaxy. It is a book of beginnings. Until now your race has been too concerned, obsessed really, with endings.

It is time you learned how to begin . . .

"Damn!" Alan muttered as he turned the page and was again confronted with text that was absolutely incomprehensible. And he could not get past the first few pages without meeting the same sticky green resistance that stopped him the first time.

The text had captured him, promised the answers that he craved. He could no longer pretend that this was his own private science project. It was more than that, but he was clueless as to the real meaning of what was happening. *The Book of the New Creation* promised to reveal that meaning and it was a closed book. "Not ripe yet," Alan said softly as he stood up.

CHAPTER 9

Special Agent James Creel was not happy with his new assignment. He was checking the records of the Apache Mescalero nation to look for suspicious characters. The council leaders had granted the FBI unprecedented access to their files. "None of us are thrilled about having the government poke around the nation," one of the council members had said at the critical meeting, "but this *Genesis Bomb* is going to kill us financially if we don't stop it. We depend on the revenue from our gambling casinos and our ski operation. People have to get here, and they aren't going to walk. We need the roads as much as the rest of the state."

It was a long shot, but the Feds were desperate. Skinner had vanished without a trace, and if the NatCo boys at corporate were lying, they were doing a damn good job of it. Creel's boss had been straight with him. "There are all kinds of rumors, Jim. Just be glad you aren't on the UFO detail."

"UFO?"

"We can't afford to ignore anything. There was a 'sighting' around the time this whole business started. I have Bill and Rick on it. We have also had reports that some crazy Apache Indian or Indians are involved. Trying to reclaim North America for the natives or something. Got to check it out. We have clearance from the tribal leaders. They are

THE GAIA WAR 127

as upset about this thing as anybody else. More, possibly. It's going to cost them a shitload of money if the roads aren't reopened in time for ski season.

"I don't need to tell you to take it easy up there on the reservation, James. Even though we have permission to access most of their tribal records, civil and criminal, you are not going to be too popular."

"Don't worry, Chief," Creel said.

He had met with resistance and some not-so-subtle hostility, but for the most part the Mescaleros had been cooperative, even friendly. He was seated at a terminal, scrolling through a huge file that listed the names of people who had left the reservation. He stopped at one record. The name had come up before in a civil file. Nothing serious, but the individual had distinguished himself as a radical of sorts, an Indian schoolteacher who preached the old ways a little too strongly for the tribal school board.

He printed the name off the screen. "Ever heard of this guy?" he asked the woman at the next desk.

She looked at the name. "You might ask Linda up in financial," she said.

Creel walked into Linda's office. "Can I help you?" she asked. He was struck by how pretty she was—long black hair, high cheekbones, and big dark eyes.

Her smile faded when he identified himself. He was surprised at how much this bothered him. "I need information on this person." He showed her the printout and noted the startled look that momentarily crossed her face.

"This person?" she asked, sounding a little tense.

"Yeah. Paul Rainwater. I was told to ask you about him."

"I don't know why," she said tightly. "What has he done, anyway?"

"Nothing as far as I know, but his name came up in a couple of files. He got in trouble with the school board a few years back and then left for India or something."

"So?"

"So I don't know. I'm just checking out anybody that seems suspicious."

Mark Leon

"What is so suspicious about somebody speaking his mind and then taking a trip?" she snapped at him.

"Probably nothing," he said. "Are you sure you don't know this guy?" He looked her in the eye.

She met his gaze with a look of defiance. "I've heard of him. I remember the business with the school board, but I've never met him," she said. "Now if you will excuse me, I have work to do."

"OK. Thanks for your time." Creel backpedaled out the door. On his way downstairs he made a note to watch Linda Lightfoot. He had barely taken his seat at the terminal when he caught a glimpse through the window of someone moving very fast in the parking lot. It was Linda. She was practically running to her car.

Creel was up in a flash and out the door. He followed her through the town of Rui Doso and up the Sierra Blanca mountain road. It was difficult to remain inconspicuous on such narrow, twisting terrain, but he was confident that he had not been noticed when she turned off on a dirt road. He waited for a few minutes and then turned in after her. The road went into a narrow canyon and ended at a house. Creel parked on a little hill overlooking the house, behind a stand of pine trees.

Lying down behind some shrubs, he got out his binoculars. He could see Linda talking with a tall man outside. The man was listening to her very carefully. After a few minutes he became agitated. They disappeared inside his house.

About an hour later Linda emerged. They embraced in the doorway, and she got in her car and drove off. The man (he was certain it was Paul Rainwater) was busily loading the trunk of his car, a late model Subaru. Then he, too, sped off down the dirt road toward Creel, leaving a trail of dust.

Creel waited for him to go by and then ran to his car. He was determined to follow Rainwater to the ends of the earth if necessary.

* * *

THE GAIA WAR 129

"I still don't understand," Gaia said. "You are telling me that you don't always act freely, nor is what you do always supposed to be fun."

"That's right," Lew said.

"Then why do you do it?"

"Good question," Lew said.

Later, after Gaia had gone down to Alan's basement sanctuary to read, Meagan said to Lew, "You really aren't helping her to understand when you answer her by saying, *'That's a good question.'*"

"What am I supposed to say?" Lew responded, clearly irritated.

"You could try to explain the roots of evil, original sin . . . things like that."

Lew looked at Meagan with an expression of hopelessness mixed with incredulity. "*You* tell her about all that stuff," he said. "That's more in your line, don't you think? I don't profess to understand or believe it, but if you want to indoctrinate her with your fundamentalism, go ahead. She's going to hear even crazier nonsense before all this is over."

"Oh, Lew," Meagan said. Lew was taken aback by her tone of voice. He had anticipated anger, but instead she sounded as if she felt sorry for him. *He* was the angry one.

"Don't patronize me . . ." he said.

"I'm not!" Meagan interrupted him. "What you think is your own business. I can't help thinking it's pathetic."

"You don't know what I think! How dare you . . ."

"OK, Lew, I'm sorry. This is getting us nowhere. Let's just forget it, alright?"

"Yeah, sure." Lew got up and went to get a beer. It required all of his will to yell from the kitchen, "Want a beer, Meagan?"

He was surprised when she said, "Sure."

He returned carrying two bottles, which he set on the coffee table. "Cheers," he said, picking his up and taking a long drink.

"Amen," she said, and grabbed hers.

* * *

130 Mark Leon

Gaia was deep into *Paradise Lost* when the lights went out. She put the book down and lay back. She welcomed the unexpected darkness as a friend that gave her some respite from the weight of world. "What was it that Miranda, that other innocent, said in *The Tempest*?" She tried to remember. "Oh yes. 'Brave new world that has such creatures in't,' " she recalled. She shared only part of Miranda's sentiments. A beguiling, new world, yes, but not brave.

I suppose what we did out there in the desert was brave, she thought, but the notion was without passionate conviction. There was too much she did not yet understand about herself to be sure of many things beyond the immediate facts of her existence.

She scarcely noticed the lights descending the stairs. When they were almost upon her she looked up, startled out of her musings. She gasped.

"Gaia?" It was Lew.

"Are you alright, Mother?" Meagan asked.

"Please, Meagan," Gaia said, "don't call me Mother."

"What should I call you, then?"

"Why not Gaia?" Gaia said.

"But that's not your name," Meagan said angrily. "That is just something Alan calls you for his own perverted reasons."

"What's in a name?" Gaia said, sounding tired.

"Are you OK?" Lew asked again.

"Why shouldn't I be?"

"The electricity went out. We thought you might be afraid."

"Of the dark?" She laughed.

"Yeah," Lew said. "I guess."

"Your skin!" Meagan said suddenly. She was staring at Gaia's face.

"What about my skin?" Gaia said.

"Turn off your flashlight," Lew said, flicking off his own.

Meagan's light went out and she gasped. "Wow," Lew said softly.

"What?" Gaia asked.

THE GAIA WAR

"Your face is glowing," Lew said.

"Green," Meagan added.

"Green?" Gaia asked. "My face is green?"

"Only a light green," Lew said quickly. "And I don't think you can see it in daylight. It's like some kind of natural phosphorescence or something."

"Oh," Gaia said thoughtfully. She was not at all worried. In fact this newly discovered feature gave her a strange comfort. She had the distinct impression that it was the beginning of something—something good, possibly great. The really odd thing was the conviction that it was something she would *remember* when the time came. It made her feel suddenly lighthearted. Then she said something that surprised both Lew and Meagan. "Far out. That's really cool, isn't it."

"Uh, yeah," Lew stammered, worried but not sure why. "Cool."

"Cool? What do you mean 'cool'? This could be serious," Meagan said.

"Uh, Meagan," Gaia said.

"Yes?"

"Could you leave Lew and me alone for a while?"

"Alone?"

"Yes. Please. We will talk soon, I promise."

"Well, sure. If that's what you want I . . ." Meagan was disturbed by the prospect of leaving the two alone in the dark.

"Thank you," Gaia said. Her voice carried a note of finality that actually turned Meagan around and sent her back up the stairs.

Meagan closed the door at the top of the stairs and left them in almost total darkness. The only light was the pale green glow emanating from Gaia's skin. "Sit down, Lew," she said.

"OK." Lew was worried and scared. He felt terribly alone and vulnerable.

"We need to talk," she said. "I am beginning to remember a little of why I am here and what I need to do. You can help me."

"Help you? How?"

132 Mark Leon

"Make love to me, Lew."

"Here? Now?"

"Why not?" she said.

Lew tried to think of a reason. After a few seconds he gave up.

Lew sleepily stumbled into the kitchen the next morning. Meagan was reading the paper, which was full of the latest from New Mexico. She looked up, fixing Lew with an icy stare. "'Morning," he mumbled.

She said nothing, but continued to bore into him with her cool, gray eyes.

"Uh ... Any coffee?" he asked, struggling for some semblance of clear articulation.

"Aren't you *something*," she said.

"I wouldn't know."

"Yes there is coffee. I made it extra strong, just the way you and Alan like it. What *is* it with you guys, anyway?"

"What do you mean?" Lew asked absently. His attention was all on the coffee he was pouring.

"I mean you have no respect for society or anything else as far as I can tell."

"What the hell is that supposed to mean?" Lew sat down and poured some Half & Half into his brew.

"Or God," she continued, ignoring his question.

"Meagan, it's a little early in the morning for you to be giving me the third degree. Have some respect yourself." He took a slow sip and began to relax a little.

"It's ten-thirty!" she said. "I've been up for hours."

"Good for you," he said. "You know Sir William Harvey, the English physician who pioneered the science of cardiology, held a coffee bean between his thumb and forefinger right before he died. He raised it up to the light streaming through his window and said, 'In this little bean lies the soul of happiness and wit.' "

"How poetic."

"What is the matter, Meagan?"

"What happened between you and Gaia last night?"

"She doesn't want to be called Gaia anymore," Lew said.

THE GAIA WAR   133

"What?"

"Yeah, I guess your little speech got to her. She officially changed her name."

"To what?"

Lew took another sip. "This is pretty good, Meagan. Kick-ass coffee for sure."

"What's her new name?"

"Miranda," Lew said, looking at the big branches of the pecan tree that grew outside the kitchen window.

"Miranda," Meagan repeated. "Oh well, at least it's her own name, not something Alan Fain dreamed up."

"You really should lighten up about Alan," Lew said.

"I don't like him, and I don't trust him."

"I know, but he's my friend and he may be in trouble. Where is your Christian compassion?"

She shot him a wicked look. "You didn't answer my question. What happened last night?"

"I don't think . . . ." he began uneasily.

"You don't think it's any of my business," she finished for him. "In general, maybe not, but the circumstances here are different."

"How?"

"She's an innocent creature thrust into a sinful world. She needs someone to protect her."

"And you have taken on that responsibility?"

"There is no one else."

"Don't you thing you should ask Gai . . . Miranda?" Lew said softly.

"I told you she's an innocent. She doesn't know what she needs or what the dangers of this world are."

"And you do?"

"Forget it, Lew. I don't want to argue about it. Can't you tell me what happened? Did you . . . ."

"Have sex?"

"Yes." She hissed the word.

"I guess so."

"You guess so! Did you or not?"

"Yeah, I fucked her," Lew said. He immediately regretted his indelicate phrasing when he saw the effect on Meagan. She fought valiantly to control herself, but the

134   **Mark Leon**

trembling at the corners of her mouth gave her away.

"Oh Lew!" She started sobbing. "How could you? She . . ."

Lew thought, *She is one hell of a sex machine*, but he did not say it. Instead he reached out and took Meagan's hand. "Try to understand," he said. "It wasn't my idea. She wanted to. I couldn't refuse."

"No, I guess not." Meagan regained some composure. She took her hand slowly from Lew's. "Never pass up a good piece of ass, isn't that right? It's the male code of honor or something, I think."

"Oh Meagan! It wasn't like that. I told you. She seems to think that the sexual experience is necessary to some kind of process."

"Process?"

"Yeah. In her development. I don't know. I respect who and what she is . . ."

"You don't even know who she is," Meagan said.

"Don't be so sure that you do either," Lew said. "I'm sorry for what I said—I mean the way I put it. It wasn't like that. Believe me. In fact if anyone is the innocent in this, it's me. Truth be told, I feel kind of used. I don't think she particularly cares for me—as a *man* I mean. I was just convenient. And I don't mean that she was just horny if you will pardon the expression. She went about it all with a cool deliberateness that was uncanny, like she was performing a ritual or a scientific experiment. Don't you see? Neither you nor I really know what is going on here. Remember that before you get all bent out of shape."

In spite of herself, Meagan saw some sense in what Lew was saying. She thought, *God works in mysterious ways.* Gaia, or Miranda, had to get pregnant somehow. No reason why the Holy Ghost had to perform the deed again. Could Lew be the unwitting vehicle for the Second Coming? She didn't voice any of this, but it made her feel a little better.

The doorbell rang. Lew, still a little slow, got to his feet. He walked through the living room and opened the door to face an intense, dark man with long, straight black hair. They just stared at each other for half a second.

"Lew Slack?" the man said.

THE GAIA WAR

135

"Yeah."

"I'm Paul Rainwater."

"Oh," Lew said. "You got here fast. I thought you were out in New Mexico."

"Circumstances have taken another turn," he said enigmatically. Then, after another brief pause, "May I come in?"

"Oh yeah. I mean sure. Come in." Lew stood aside and held the door open a little wider. "Coffee?"

"No thanks," Rainwater said. "I've been driving all night. I'll want to get some sleep soon. But we have to talk."

Lew sat down in Alan's big green armchair. Rainwater took the couch. "You have to go to India," Rainwater said.

"India?" Lew set his cup on the coffee table and stared at Rainwater.

"Yes, India."

"Why?"

"That's where all this started," Rainwater said.

"All what started?" Meagan had just entered the room.

"This is Meagan," Lew said. "A friend of mine."

Rainwater got up and extended his big hand. "Pleased to meet you," he said.

Meagan took his hand and continued to stare at him. "What do you know?" she said.

"Not all that much," Rainwater admitted. "But I do know that soon it will be too dangerous for you here. We sent you that message. It had the desired effect. The roads and highways of southern New Mexico are being devoured by the *New Creation*. I really don't know how Alan did it. I think Swami-ji does, but he won't explain it to me."

"Swami-ji?" Meagan said, barely concealing her sarcasm.

"Alan's guru," Lew said, as if that explained everything.

"Oh," Meagan said. Her sarcasm had turned to contempt.

"I just wanted to reclaim the North American continent. Get the US out of it. Make it a place for the living again," Rainwater said, as if this were a conservative ambition, like wanting to paint the kitchen in an old house. "Swami-ji's

136 Mark Leon

got other ideas, and I'm damned if I understand them. They have something to do with the end of the *Kali-Yuga*."

"The *Kali-Yuga*?" Lew said.

"Yeah, that's Sanskrit for Dark Age. According to Hindu cosmology the universe goes through cycles. We are currently in a bad cycle, the *Kali-Yuga*. Some gurus and Sanskrit pundits think it is about to end. They think it is no accident that the year 2000 is almost here."

"The Age of Aquarius," Lew said wistfully.

"Yeah, something like that." Rainwater laughed.

It was a good laugh that made Lew think of falling water. He had the flashing thought that Rainwater's laugh must be the source of the Apache's name. That he had probably gotten the name before he could laugh did not, at that moment, seem to present any serious challenge to this theory.

"This is madness!" Meagan said. "A lot of recycled hippie nonsense from the sixties."

"How would you know about any of that?" Lew retorted. Her remark had angered him.

"You think because I'm religious I'm *stupid*?" she said. "This stuff about a New Age or *New Creation* is a lot of occult nonsense that borders on the satanic."

"And Christians don't believe in a coming New Age?" Lew said.

"That's different," she said, lowering her head a little.

Lew laughed scornfully. "I see."

Rainwater uncrossed his legs and leaned forward a little. "Do you have a passport, Lew?"

"I think so," Lew said. "I was planning a trip to Europe last summer, but it got canceled at the last minute. Now it looks like I'm headed much farther east than that."

"West, actually," Rainwater said, pulling a packet of airline tickets from his inside coat pocket. "I've got you booked on Thai Airlines. You fly out of Seattle."

"Seattle? How am I going to get to Seattle?"

"Relax, Lew. I've arranged for your connecting flights. It's all here." He handed the tickets to Lew.

Lew was absently thumbing through the stuff and suddenly said, "That's today! At noon! It's already . . ."

"Eleven," Meagan said, looking at Rainwater curiously.

THE GAIA WAR 137

"Better start packing," Rainwater said. "You won't need much. It's warm over there this time of year. Just some light clothes and a toothbrush. Maybe a book to read on the plane."

Lew was staring, openmouthed. "But . . ." He couldn't think of anything to say.

"Here is Swami-ji's address in Benares." Rainwater handed Lew a card. It was engraved with an image of Ganesh, the elephant-headed god of good fortune. The card read, "Delectable curries for the mind," and gave an address.

"I don't have much money . . ." Lew began.

"Here's five thousand dollars." Rainwater handed Lew a stack of bills. "That should do you nicely. You can live cheaply in India. But don't overdo it. Eat at the best restaurants if you want to avoid all those nasty intestinal parasites."

"What about Alan?" Lew asked.

"I wouldn't worry about Alan," Rainwater said in a way that made Lew wonder but also prevented him from probing further on the subject of his lost friend. "You need to think of yourself first."

"What do you mean?" he asked.

"I mean I don't think I've been followed, but I can't be sure. In any case it's only a matter of time before they're onto you."

"They?"

"The government, the corporate goons, FBI, CIA, you name it. We have meddled with the foundations of the power structure. These are dangerous times. The worst thing you can do is sit around and wait to get nailed."

"What am I supposed to do in India?" Lew said.

"For one thing, it will buy you some time. But more importantly, Swami-ji can probably help to put some perspective on this whole thing. You just might be able to see the forest for once."

"I guess I better get going," Lew said, not quite believing that he was allowing a strange Apache Indian to pack him off to South Asia for dubious reasons on barely an

138 Mark Leon

hour's notice. *But I have done stranger things*, he told himself.

Rainwater got up. "I have to go. Wait ten minutes in case I was followed. Then have Meagan drive you to the airport. OK?"

Lew nodded. Meagan said nothing. As much as she distrusted Rainwater, she was secretly glad he was sending Lew away. It meant she would have Miranda to herself.

"This is the beginning, Lew," Rainwater said.

"Of what?" Lew said.

"I don't know. That is what we're trying to figure out."

"Oh," Lew said.

"Take it easy." Rainwater opened the door and was quickly gone.

Creel was exhausted from the long night drive. "Oh God." He sighed when he saw Rainwater emerge from the house and jump back in his car. He looked back at the house and caught a glimpse of Lew in the doorway before he took off after Rainwater.

They stopped at Lew's place to get his passport. Meagan was silent the rest of the way to the airport. "Aren't you going to say anything?" he asked, as she pulled up to the terminal.

"Bon voyage," she said.

"Take care of Miranda," Lew said, getting out of the car. He was carrying his one bag.

"Don't worry about that," Meagan said. Lew turned his back and started into the airport. Meagan watched him for a moment and then called out, "Lew!"

"Yeah?" He turned around.

"We *were* friends before, weren't we?" she said.

"Uh, yeah. We were," he said, and looked down at the pavement.

"Take care of yourself, Lew," Meagan said.

"You too, Meagan." He tried to smile.

She actually managed one. "I'd like to see you get back safely."

THE GAIA WAR 139

"Don't worry. I've always wanted to go to India. From what I hear it's not a dangerous place."

"Danger is in the heart. Take care," she said, and drove off.

"What the hell did she mean by that?" Lew said too loudly. A mother pulled her child closer as Lew walked past. The glass doors slid open and swallowed him up.

"Dammit!" Creel said. He couldn't believe it. After following Rainwater for seven hundred miles the man had disappeared. There was no use denying it, he had failed. *Unless there is something to learn back at that house*, he thought, turning his car around. He drove back to Alan's house.

Miranda was monitoring the changes in her body. The sexual experience with Lew had awakened dormant energies deep within. She felt something growing inside. It was as if she were pregnant. Pregnant not with child but with herself.

She could feel the warmth spreading from her womb, bathing her limbs with a golden light. She could almost see it when she closed her eyes and emptied her mind. "This is the future," she said softly to herself. "And for me the future is now."

The sound of Meagan's footsteps descending the stairs brought Miranda out of her meditation. "Mo . . . Miranda?" Meagan said.

"Yes." Miranda opened her eyes and sat up on the sofa.

"Lew left," Miranda said.

"Left? Where?"

"India. He went to India."

"Of course," Miranda said, as much to herself as to Meagan.

"I was watching CNN just now. The jungle seems to have stopped spreading," Meagan said. "It covers White Sands and has eaten up Interstate 25 north almost to Albuquerque and south halfway to Las Cruces, but is no longer advancing. It's not retreating either."

"Oh," Miranda said.

140 Mark Leon

"You don't really care...one way or the other, do you?" Meagan said.

"I don't know. You have made a hideous mess of the planet. In some ways the spread of your species could be compared to the growth of a cancer on the earthly biosphere. So I guess anything that helps restore a balance is a good thing..."

"What will we do now?" Meagan said.

"Now?" Miranda said, as if the question were unintelligible.

"Yes. We're alone here. I don't have a job anymore... I..." Meagan burst into tears. "I don't know what to do. I'm scared."

Miranda reached out to her. "Don't worry. There is no need to worry. Everything is going to be alright, Meagan. You still believe in..."

"God?" Meagan said, her eyes brightening behind the tears.

"Uh, yes, I guess that's what I mean," Miranda said, warily.

"Of course. I know I'm being weak, but things are so crazy and it's hard to have faith when you don't understand what's happening."

"Just don't worry. Understand what you can and leave the rest to your god."

"Thank you," Meagan said.

"I'm starving," Miranda said. "How about some lunch?"

They were busy with peanut butter and banana sandwiches and coffee when the doorbell rang again. Meagan went to the living room and opened the door.

"May I speak to Mr. Alan Fain?" Creel said. He had checked the county tax records and assumed the man he had seen in the doorway was the owner of the house.

"He's not here," Meagan said, anxiety breaking through a layer of forced calm.

"Can you tell me when he'll return?"

"No, not really." Meagan was starting to panic. The man had an air of menace about him.

Miranda came to the door. "Can I help you?" she said.

THE GAIA WAR 141

"I'm looking for Alan Fain," Creel said.

"And who are you?" Miranda said.

"Look, this is all rather awkward," Creel said, flashing a professional grin. "May I come in?" Before either woman could answer, Creel stepped inside.

"I'm calling the police," Miranda said.

"That is what makes this awkward, miss." Creel said. "I *am* the police."

"Show us your ID," Meagan said.

Creel flashed a fake badge that identified him as Lieutenant James Finch of the Los Angeles Police Department. "We are investigating a possible connection between Alan Fain and a Mr. Paul Rainwater." Creel was watching both their faces closely. He noted the dilation of Meagan's pupils and widening of her eyes at the mention of Rainwater's name. "Rainwater is wanted on a murder charge in California."

"You're lying," Miranda said. "Why? Why do you do it? Don't you know that the truth is your only hope? You are killing yourself with lies. All of you!" She could not keep the indignation out of her voice.

The words hit Creel like a splash of cold water in the face. He actually stepped back toward the door. He wasn't sure why he had lied. It seemed the prudent course of action. He had used the LAPD ruse before. People were often more willing to talk to a Hollywood cop than to an FBI agent. He blamed the movies. But this woman had burst his bubble. Why *did* he so often lie when the truth would serve just as well? *And how had she known*?

Miranda was also surprised. The words had leapt out of her mouth. It was only on reflection that she could identify the subtle cues in Creel's voice and manner that had so completely betrayed him, cues that she would not have noticed the day before. "I think you had better go," she said in a tone so cold that Meagan gasped.

Creel panicked. Years of trained discipline deserted him, and he drew his gun. It wasn't just the woman's uncanny perception. There was something more than human about her. Here eyes were too bright and her skin too radiant.

142 Mark Leon

Suddenly all the rumors of UFOs and alien life-forms came alive for Special Agent James Creel.

"This is serious," he said, fighting for composure.

"I can see that," Miranda said, staring at the gun.

"Do you have a warrant?" Meagan stammered.

"This is a national security matter," he said. "Normal regs don't apply."

"By 'normal regs' I assume you mean the Bill of Rights?" Miranda said. Creel did not answer. "What do you intend to do with us?" she said.

It was the worst thing she could have said as far as Creel was concerned. His head was spinning. He had never lost his cool before. This was worse than being in the line of fire. She had hit the nail on the head. What was he going to do? He would be in big trouble if this turned out to be a false lead. But he felt certain it was not. The woman had to be involved. He made a quick decision. There was no backing down. "Come with me," he said.

"Where?" Miranda said.

"I'm taking you in for questioning."

"Questioning?" Meagan said. "About what?"

"I think you know," he said. "Now let's go." He waved the gun toward the door.

Miranda acted before she knew what she was doing. She grabbed Meagan's hand and lunged out the door.

"Stop!" Creel yelled. He automatically dropped to a kneeling position in the doorway. He fired a warning shot, but Miranda kept going. He leveled the gun at her back. She stopped and turned, but instead of assuming a submissive posture of surrender she pulled Meagan close and clasped her in a tight embrace.

Creel stood. "Don't do that again," he said, unable to produce the authoritative sound he wanted. Then his gun hand went limp and he stood there gaping at what he saw.

Miranda, taking Meagan with her, was ascending to the sky. By the time he could recover enough to point his gun after them and say "Stop" (it was practically a whisper), they were soaring, an impossible target in a bright blue sky.

CHAPTER 10

The jet lag one experiences on a trip to the other side of the globe really deserves another name, Lew thought as he strolled the campus of Benares Hindu University. It was interesting—night turned into day, the whole world turned on its head. And then there was India herself.

"*Saray Jahanh Se Achaa, Hindustan Hamare, Hamare!*" A group of schoolchildren, on a guided tour of the campus, were singing these Hindi lyrics to a melody that seduced Lew with haunting modulations from major to minor. He approached the teacher in charge of the kids. "What is that song?" he asked. Lew had come to understand that most educated Indians spoke fairly good English.

"Unofficial anthem." The teacher smiled. "You don't know it?"

"No, but I just wondered . . ."

"Yes, it is very beautiful. Do you speak Hindi?" the teacher said.

"No."

"The lyrics say, 'Of all places the best, Our India, Our India.' "

"Oh . . ." Lew said.

"You are thinking that this is not the India you see with your own eyes. Is this not the case?"

"Well," Lew began, not wishing to offend. His mind was instantly filled with bizarre images from his first week

144 Mark Leon

in India. There was one, not the most dramatic, which rose to the surface and claimed his full attention for a moment.

A few days earlier Lew was wandering through a neighborhood, not far from the sacred river. He came across a horse. He hadn't seen many horses. Cows were everywhere, wandering the streets and *gullis* at will. Water buffalo, pigs, and dogs were common, but not horses.

This one was particularly noteworthy owing to its condition. The animal was lying on its side by the narrow street. Its breath was labored, and flies were swarming on its open sores. Lew stared for a moment and ducked into a nearby tea stall for a cup.

When he emerged the horse had miraculously moved. Somehow it had gotten to its feet, walked a few torturous steps, and collapsed in the middle of the road. This was clearly the animal's last stand, breath was thinner, less regular. The eyes were open and cloudy, the jaw slack. The flies were bolder, daring to go right for the mouth and nostrils.

As Lew again stared at the unfortunate beast he thought about how the Hindus hold all life to be sacred. Among the sacred living things, he had come to understand, were parasites, intestinal worms, insects, viruses, and bacteria. And horses dying in the middle of the road. A few people stopped to casually look, but for the most part the animal was ignored, which was not easy since bicycles, rickshaws, and automobiles had to swerve wide to avoid the sorry thing.

Lew went on his way. A few hours later, as he was winding his way back to his hotel, he found himself at the same spot. The horse was gone. He asked a grinning little boy what had happened. The kid understood enough of Lew's gesture-enhanced English to respond. His expression immediately got serious, and in hushed voice he said, "*Mar gaiyii.*"

A bystander noticed Lew's blank face. " '*Mar gaiyii*' means died," the man translated for Lew. "Actually a more accurate rendering would be 'went dead.' "

"Oh," Lew said. "Thanks."

"No problem." The man smiled and continued on his

THE GAIA WAR 145

way. The boy was again grinning at Lew and holding his hand out, palm up and open.

This was a now familiar gesture to Lew. At first he had acquiesced and dropped a few paise into the waiting palms. But he soon realized that there was a bottomless pit of such eager little hands and stopped. *"Bhag jao!"* he said, one of the few Hindi phrases he had learned. A wandering *sadhu* had taught him to use it when Lew had managed to get himself surrounded by a group of street urchins all clamoring for a handout. It means "Get lost!" The irony was that as soon as the kids had dispersed the *sadhu* himself had hit Lew up for a rupee.

"I understand," the teacher said, bringing Lew out of his recollection. The kids were still singing, and the clouds were gathering for the afternoon monsoon shower. "You have no doubt seen much that is strange and disturbing?"

"Yes," Lew admitted.

"India exists in the heart," the teacher said. "If you stay long enough and open your heart, then who knows? Maybe you will see India."

"Yeah," Lew said, trying to sound positive, the image of the dying horse still before him. *Someone should have put the poor animal out of its misery before it "went dead,"* he thought.

"Life is a carnival," the teacher said.

"Yeah, I guess it is," Lew said.

"It goes on forever," the teacher continued. Then his voice became wistful. "Too bad we cannot stay around to see it all. Our time is short."

The teacher's words reminded Lew of his mission. "Do you know where I can find a guy named Swami-ji?" Lew said.

The teacher laughed. "Which one? Benares is full of Swami-jis."

Lew had noticed that India seemed short on names. Names like Singh, Mishra, Gopal, and Patel were generously shared. "Uh, just a minute," Lew said. He pulled out the card that Rainwater had given him and handed it to the teacher. "This is the guy."

The teacher smiled. "Ah yes. Mister Mishra. I should

146 Mark Leon

have guessed. You are not far. He is priest of Ganesh Temple.'' The teacher directed Lew to the proper *ghat* on the river.

Lew had been postponing the encounter with Swami-ji. He told himself that he needed the time to adjust. But now he was close and could see no reason to delay any longer. ''Thanks,'' he said, and felt his heart beat faster as he turned toward the river and the temple of the god of good fortune, Ganesh or Ganpati as he is called by those who are on more intimate terms with the elephant-headed fat boy.

Because of the monsoon the steps of the Ganesh Temple *ghat* were completely underwater, and the bottom floor of the building was flooded. The only way in was by boat. There were several boatmen standing by, eager to provide transport to the second story entrance, which stood a few feet above the waterline. Lew chose a particularly skinny one.

''Is this the Ganesh Temple?'' Lew asked.

''Ganpati. Yes, sahib. You are wanting in?'' The boatman grinned, showing bright red, betel-stained teeth.

''Yeah. How much?''

''Ten rupee.''

''Ten rupee!'' Lew knew this was an outrageous sum for so short a ride. After some haggling he got the man down to five, which was still a ripoff.

The boatman's name was Lal-ji. ''You will be wanting return?'' he asked as Lew stepped unsteadily from the wooden craft.

''Maybe,'' Lew said.

''No problem. Lal-ji is staying at your service.'' He stuffed the five-rupee note into the folds of his dhoti and rowed back to shore, where his companions were chewing betel and drinking tea. The humid pressure of the afternoon lent the scene a surreal quality, as if the billowing clouds were inside as well as outside one's skull. *What is inside anyway?* Lew wondered. For a moment he had the vivid sensation that it really was all an illusion, *maya*, as the Hindus call it, an endless show, all smoke and mirrors.

THE GAIA WAR   147

"But what's behind the illusion? There *must* be something."

He shook his head and blinked. Some of the boatmen were staring at him, waving and smiling. Lew waved back and turned to ascend the short flight of stone steps leading to the second floor of the temple. He entered what appeared to be an office and was mildly surprised to see the computer. "Hello. Anybody here?" he called.

A thin, spry old man emerged from the adjoining room. "I am here," he said.

"Are you, uh . . . Swami-ji?" Lew said.

"Yes. I am Swami-ji," the man said. "My real name is Mishra, Ram Setu Mishra actually. But no one calls me that anymore. I am, truly, *Swami-ji.*" He laughed.

"I'm Lew . . . Lew Slack," Lew said.

"Of course." Swami-ji beamed. "Your friend Alan has told me so much about you. Delighted, very pleased." Swami-ji put his hands together in the prayerlike position of traditional Indian greeting.

Lew did likewise. *"Namaste,"* he mumbled, having recently learned the Hindi word for hello and good-bye. It actually means something like, "I salute the divinity within you," or so he had been told by the clerk at his hotel.

Swami-ji clapped his hands and laughed. *"Namaste, Namaste, Namaste!"* he said, and extended his hand. "But let us now do the proper Western thing." They shook.

"I'm worried about Alan," Lew said when they were seated on the floor cushions and drinking their tea.

"He is in much danger," Swami-ji said. "I am glad you have come. The situation, I fear, is fast spinning out of control."

"What do you mean? Danger? Is Alan still in White Sands?" Lew asked.

"Yes, of course. Where else? But it is no longer *White Sands,*" Swami-ji said.

"What is it?" Lew said.

Swami-ji sighed, and his whole body appeared to relax completely although he maintained his upright posture. He closed his eyes for a moment, and, when they opened, Lew

148 **Mark Leon**

was startled by the their luminosity. "It is the New Earthly Paradise," Swami-ji said.

"Eden?" Lew said.

"One would be tempted to call it that," Swami-ji said. "But that would not be correct. Eden will no longer suffice. No, this is not the old *garden* from which we are forever outcast, but a new one, a *better* one."

"I don't understand," Lew said softly.

"Nor do I, really," Swami-ji said. "But you know how it is. The Creator is a generous spirit. When something goes bad, as it has done for us here on this earth, something better is prepared for us. I only hope that this time we will be able to receive the gift."

"If it *is* a gift." It was a familiar voice. Lew looked in the direction of the next room to see his ex-boss stooped in the short, Indian doorway.

"Hello, Lew," Skinner said.

Lew jumped to his feet, afraid. The thought flashed through his mind that he had been lured into a trap for some obscure, nefarious purpose.

"Relax, Lew," Swami-ji said. "Mr. Skinner is my newest pupil. Put away your past if you can."

"What are *you* doing here?" Lew said.

"I'm on vacation," Skinner said, entering the room. He was wearing loose, cotton, *pajama* trousers and a long, Indian *coorta* shirt, clothes far more suited to the weather than Lew's heavy, black denim jeans. Skinner sat down next to Swami-ji. "It is a *forced* vacation. Apparently there was a security breach." He gave Lew a mean look.

"Gentlemen, please," Swami-ji said. "You are in India now."

"So we are," Skinner said.

"Yeah," Lew said.

"We have much to talk about," Swami-ji said. "There is a great deal at stake. Perhaps the fate of the entire world lies in the balance. Now how about some more tea?"

Skinner nodded. Lew said, "Sure." Swami-ji filled their cups with a motion that was both grave and comical.

"If Alan is in danger, and the fate of the world is in our

THE GAIA WAR   149

hands, why are we sitting here drinking tea?'' Lew asked, spooning some sugar into his cup.

Skinner laughed at this. ''Ah, Lew,'' he said, ''in spite of your treachery, which has cost me dearly, I must admit that it is good to see you.''

''All things must happen in their own time,'' Swami-ji answered. ''What does the preacher say?''

''Preacher?'' Lew said.

''Ecclesiastes. Your Western Bible.'' Swami-ji smiled. ''To every thing turn, turn. There is a season . . . and a time to every purpose under heaven.''

''That's the Byrds!'' Lew said.

''So it is.'' Swami-ji smiled. ''But I think the Hebrews said it before the sixties rock band made it such a popular song.''

''Oh yeah,'' Lew said. ''I knew that.''

''Anyway, now is the time for tea. Sometimes the world must wait,'' Swami-ji said.

''Amen,'' Lew said. Swami-ji's words made him realize how tired he was. *It wasn't just the residual jet lag*, he thought, *it was India that wore you out everyday.*

''Have you studied philosophy, Lew?'' Swami-ji said.

''Not much. I read some Plato in college,'' Lew said.

''Plato, like most great philosophers,'' Swami-ji said, ''was concerned with the problem of reality. What is real? Questions of this sort fall under the category of metaphysics.''

''What is real?'' Lew said, recalling his experience outside the temple. For an instant the image of the boatmen smiling and waving seemed more real than anything else.

Skinner laughed.

''Yes, it is funny,'' Swami-ji said. ''So funny that some of the greatest philosophers have, in the midst of their metaphysical studies, actually died laughing.''

''Like who?'' Lew said.

''No names you would recognize,'' Swami-ji said. ''They all died young. But my point is this. Many great philosophers, Plato, Aristotle, Augustine, Scotus, and Descartes, to name only a few, have answered the question, 'What is real?' But as soon as an answer is given reality

150 Mark Leon

offers up a new, more difficult puzzle. The real *plays* with us.

"This has a curious effect. Nowadays, after thousands of years playing this game, we tend to be cynical about it. Instead of the *real* we talk about the *really* real. For example, what would you say if I told you that the teacup you hold in your hand is the ultimate truth, the *really real*?"

Lew looked at his tea cup. He saw it in a new light. It was suddenly possessed of an infinite complexity and depth. The more he looked, the more he saw. He understood, momentarily, the ancient saying, "As above so below." All the mysteries of atoms, stars, galaxies, and life itself were there to behold in the thing he held in his hand. He looked up, astonished, and said, "Wow! How did you do that?"

"It's nothing," Swami-ji said. "An old trick. Look again."

Lew looked back at the cup. Nothing had changed. But it was now just a teacup. "I don't understand," he said.

"Don't be disappointed," Swami-ji said. "That's what you need to understand. You are thinking how beautiful the cup was a moment ago. That you could see the secrets of the universe there. But you should be grateful that now all you see is a cup. What you see now is your own personal freedom. When you stared in endless fascination you were not free. You were a slave to your own conception of beauty and truth. But now you are a man again, possessed of free will, the ability to *create* meaning, no longer a passive witness to it."

"Oh," Lew said. He saw the truth to what Swami-ji said, but he was disappointed anyway. It was impossible to let go completely of such beauty.

"Don't worry, Lew," Swami-ji said. "It's a natural reaction. We all feel the same way. It is the ancient hurt. The yearning for the lost paradise. It is what defines the human condition. I think Mr. Skinner would agree with me on that point." Swami-ji looked at Skinner.

"Of course," Skinner said. "No argument there. It is in the vision of paradise regained that we disagree."

THE GAIA WAR 151

"You call the cyberion process a paradise?" Lew said.

"Of sorts. For those that can handle it," Skinner said. "Alan's alternative is worse."

"How is that?" Lew said. "At least it's a living thing, not the stinking death you tried to create."

"This is precisely the sort of argumentative scene we want to avoid, gentlemen," Swami-ji said. "The point is moot anyway. For the time being, the *Genesis Bomb*, as it is dubbed, has won. Speaking of Genesis, what do you make of the Old Testament story? Did the Garden of Eden really exist?"

"I think it's symbolic . . ." Lew said.

Skinner interrupted by laughing. "You really are too much, Lew!" he said, regaining his breath.

"Paradise is a funny thing," Swami-ji said. "You know the Indian subcontinent, as it is called, was once a paradise. It was once the most beautiful garden on the face of the earth. A tapestry of brilliant life, bounded on the north by the world's highest mountains and on all other sides by ocean." He sang part of the song that Lew had heard a few hours before, "Of all places the best, India our India . . ."

"What happened?" Lew asked. "To India, I mean."

"We happened to it," Swami-ji said. "We cut down the forests and overran the jungle. We built cities and factories. But that is a familiar story. What I am now telling you is not so familiar, but it is the truth. The Garden of Eden did exist. The story told in your Western Bible is more than a symbolic fairy tale. It is history and the history began here. India was the Garden of Eden, the home of Adam and Eve, Father and Mother to our race. It was here on the banks of the sacred Ganges that the choice was made, accept the offered paradise or strive to make a world . . ."

"OK," Skinner said. "I've heard all this before. But what sort of choice is that? We are *doers* and *makers*. What kind of a paradise is it that is already made for us? We had to reject it! We had to strike out on our own!"

"And so we did," Swami-ji said, calmly.

"Wait a minute," Lew said. "What do you mean about India being the Garden of Eden?"

152   **Mark Leon**

"Exactly what I said," Swami-ji replied. "This is where it was."

"But that's absurd," Lew said. "Ridiculous. First of all, the place never really existed. And even if it did, wouldn't it have been somewhere in the Middle East?"

"That is the popular conception," Swami-ji said. He got very quiet and closed his eyes for a few moments. He opened them at exactly the moment the setting sun edged low enough to shoot its rays through the window at his back. The effect was dramatic. The burst of light seemed to come from Swami-ji's eyes and his head was surrounded by a soft, golden halo.

Lew's jaw dropped open.

"You are easily impressed, Mr. Slack." Swami-ji chuckled. "What you have just witnessed is another cheap trick. Beware of the gurus, *sadhus*, and swamis you meet here. They are full of such tricks, and they will be happy to demonstrate them for a price."

"So you weren't really serious then?" Lew said.

"Serious?" Swami-ji laughed.

"About Eden being real and here in India?"

"I was quite serious about that," Swami-ji said. "I can even offer proof. Not that it really matters. Whether or not you believe it, the truth is still the truth."

"What sort of proof?" Skinner said.

"There were two very special trees in the garden, were there not?" Swami-ji said.

"The tree of life and the tree of knowledge," Lew said.

"Yes. I can show them to you ... or what remains of them rather." He stood abruptly and said, "Follow me."

They descended to the doorway that faced the swollen river and the city shoreline. Swami-ji called to the boatmen. Lal-ji was quickest on the draw and fetched them. He ferried all three of them to shore for only fifty paise, or half a rupee, one tenth what Lew had paid. Lal-ji returned Lew's accusing stare with a wet red grin and a shrug.

Swami-ji led them through a maze of the narrow alleyways known as *gullis*. "I'm taking you to the oldest part of the city," he said. "People have inhabited these neighbor-

THE GAIA WAR 153

hoods for thousands of years, and little has changed since the first temple was built.''

And there were temples. It seemed that every tiny intersection had one, a temple for each Hindu god or saint. Swami-ji stopped in front of one. The doorway was a low arch painted in bright purple and pink. It reminded Lew of a medical textbook diagram of a bodily orifice.

Swami-ji stepped inside and his two companions followed. It was dark. The *gullis* themselves were full of afternoon shadows, and the temple had no windows. A single candle lit the temple chamber. When Lew's eyes became adjusted, and he saw what was in front of him, he gasped. Skinner stood up ramrod straight, as if suddenly confronted with an enemy.

A man lay on a cot. The cot was a simple wood frame about three feet wide and six feet long. It supported a net of rough-looking rope. This net held the man's body. He was stretched out on his back and staring straight at the ceiling. His eyes were wide open. There was a look of suspended astonishment on his face as if he had been looking at something truly amazing for a very long time. His body was extremely emaciated. At first Lew could not believe that the man was alive, but after a few moments he noticed that the bony rib cage was slowly rising and falling.

Swami-ji stood in silence for a while. Then he spoke. ''*Namaste*, ji.''

The temple guardian closed his eyes and sat up very slowly. Then he opened his eyes and got to his feet. He put his hands together and bowed his head ever so slightly, giving a nod in the direction of his three guests. ''Welcome,'' he said. ''What can I do for you? Do you wish to make *puja*?''

''No, we have not come to pray,'' Swami-ji said.

The man was momentarily disappointed. ''Swami-ji,'' he said, ''you have not come for a very long time. And now you do not wish to make *puja*?''

''Afraid not,'' Swami-ji said. ''This is an educational visit. Not a spiritual one.''

''And what is not ultimately spiritual?'' the skinny guru said.

"You got me there," Swami-ji said. "Allow me to introduce my friends. This is Mr. Lew Slack and Mr. Larry Skinner from America. Our host, gentlemen"—he turned in the direction of Lew and Skinner—"is Shri Sharma, the priest of Sachit Temple."

Lew extended his hand and tried to smile. He was surprised at the strength in Sharma's bony grip. Skinner said, "Hello."

"Can you take us below?" Swami-ji said.

"You want to see it?" Sharma said. Deep lines suddenly creased his brow.

"Why not?" Swami-ji said.

"Do they know what you are about to show them?" Sharma said.

"Yes. But I don't think they believe it," Swami-ji said.

"Why such endless fascination with that which cannot be undone?" Sharma spoke to the room, to no one and everyone. "I will never understand. Come!"

He led them to a room adjacent to the temple. He moved a heavy trunk aside and raised a trapdoor in the floor, exposing a narrow stone staircase. He passed out candles. When they were all lit he began the descent.

They went down for a long time. When they stopped the air was difficult to breathe. Lew guessed they had gone down the equivalent of twenty stories or more.

"There. See!" Sharma pointed to an enormous tree stump in the center of the underground chamber.

"This is what remains of the tree of knowledge," Swami-ji said. "It was cut down almost two thousand years ago."

"Why?" Lew said.

"That's another story," Swami-ji said.

"So this is it," Skinner said matter-of-factly. He yawned and looked around the chamber.

"But that's all just a story!" Lew said. "It's metaphor! You are trying to tell me that this is where Eve was tempted with the forbidden fruit?"

"And Adam." Swami-ji smiled.

Lew examined the stump more closely. The wood was curiously not quite dead. It was at least six feet in diameter,

THE GAIA WAR

most of the exposed rings were fossilized. But the innermost rings gave off a faint glow. Before Swami-ji could warn him Lew reached out and touched the center, where the glow was brightest.

He screamed at the white-hot sensation. A bolt of electric energy shot up his spine and exploded in the crown of his skull. It knocked him back several feet. His back slammed into the soft earth with a thud, and he was engulfed in a small dust cloud. The vision that had just filled his head remained for a moment in the fine cloud of particles swirling about his face. He saw all the galaxies there and more. He saw the way to complete understanding of the universe. It was so simple. Why had he never seen it before? And then it was gone, leaving him empty and alone in the dirt.

"You see?" Sharma said.

Swami-ji helped Lew up. Lew shook his head and held out his hand. No damage was apparent, but his fingers still tingled. "What was that?" he said, looking first to Swami-ji and then to Sharma.

"That was nothing," Sharma said. "You had better forget all about it."

Skinner laughed.

Swami-ji said, "Take it easy, Lew. I should have warned you—Look but don't touch. Are you OK?"

"Yeah," Lew said. "I think so. So this is where it all began? All of history, I mean."

"Yes," Swami-ji said. "Do you still think it is just a metaphor?"

"I don't know, but it's hard to breathe down here," Lew said.

"Time to go," Swami-ji said.

"I might as well show you the rest of it," Swami-ji said when they were back at Ganesh Temple. The moon was nearly full, lighting all the *ghats* with the reflection from the sacred waters of the Ganges.

"The rest of it?" Lew said.

"The tree of life, or what remains of it," Swami-ji said. Then he yelled for a boat. "Lal-ji! *Juldi, juldi! Hum nadi pur jana cha-haatee tee!*"

156   **Mark Leon**

Lal-ji grinned at the prospect of more rupees. His smile faded when Swami-ji told him where they wanted to go. The other shore of the Ganges is completely deserted. Some believe the superstitious tales of a curse on the river's far side. Lal-ji was one of these.

Necessity won. Lal-ji had many mouths to feed on the few rupees he daily squeezed out of the river. They were about halfway across when something banged against the side of the boat. Lew turned his gaze from Lal-ji straining at the wooden oars. He glimpsed something white in the water. At first he thought it was the moon's reflection. Then he saw the dead infant's eyes. The tiny, upturned face stared at him for a moment and was gone. Lew turned away in disgust. A wave of nausea washed over him.

"Don't judge them too harshly," Swami-ji said, softly. "The parents are probably so poor that they cannot afford a cremation shroud. Under the circumstances the most holy thing they could do was to cast the body into the sacred river. The child likely died of dysentery."

"Or it was murdered," Skinner said. "One less mouth to feed."

"Possibly," Swami-ji said.

The boat slipped up onto the beach, shuddering slightly. It was quiet and still. Swami-ji told Lal-ji to wait. The boatman's eyes were wide-open and he looked nervously back across the river toward the city, which gleamed like a string of rough gems, but he agreed to wait.

The moon was so bright that no flashlight was necessary. Swami-ji led them through the scrubby vegetation. Lew was puzzled by the sparseness of growth. He asked Swami-ji about it.

"All the trees were cut down long ago to provide wood for the cremation piles on the burning *ghat*," the guru explained.

They were following a trail of sorts. It was difficult to see, but Swami-ji moved with confidence. He stopped in front of another large tree stump. It looked like the other one, but without the eerie glow in the center.

"If this thing is as old as you say," Skinner said, "why

THE GAIA WAR 157

isn't it buried underneath all the layers of strata that would have accumulated?''

''Not all of the ancient secrets are buried,'' Swami-ji said. ''You can touch this one, Lew. It won't bite.''

Lew knelt and ran his fingers across the smooth surface. It felt fossilized, like marble. The rings made tiny ridges. He stretched his hand flat over the center of the severed, petrified trunk. It was cool, soothing. A wave of feeling pulsed into his palm, up his arm, and slowly washed over him.

It was completely unlike the sudden, hot flash of insight he had experienced in the subterranean chamber. This was power of a different kind. It hinted at unimaginable ecstasies that could endure throughout all time, forever building to new climaxes of delight. Lew sighed. He was prepared to stay forever.

Someone spoke in a loud, harsh voice. Lew looked up to see a naked *sadhu* standing on the other side of the stump. His body was covered in grey ash. He was even skinnier than Sharma, and his eyes were blazing with a terrifying passion.

Lew jerked his hand away and stood up. The action filled him with an ancient pain. For a moment he was certain that he would die. Then he realized that the hurt was one he always carried.

''Yes,'' Swami-ji said, apparently reading Lew's mind, ''you were free of it for a moment, so now it strikes back with a vengeance. Let it be. You'll be OK. But I'm afraid we have to leave.'' He stared at the naked figure, and Lew sensed fear in Swami-ji.

When they were back on the river Lew asked, ''Who was he?''

''Not who,'' Swami-ji said.

''What do you mean?'' Lew asked.

''He means he wasn't human,'' Skinner said.

''Not human?'' Lew said.

''Not anymore,'' Swami-ji said. ''You want to go back, don't you, Lew?''

''Well . . .'' Lew began. He didn't want to admit it, but

158   **Mark Leon**

he could think of nothing else—just a few more minutes with the tree, or whatever it was.

"Don't even think about," Swami-ji said. "But if you can't get it out of our mind, then try to remember Gaur."

"Gaur?"

"That is who we saw. Or what is left of him."

Swami-ji took them to V-Jay's, one of the few bars in town. It was in a basement on a busy dirt road near the central shopping district. Swami-ji ordered big bottles of He-Man brand beer.

"So what happened?" Lew said. He took a swig. The stuff was pretty strange, but it was beer and almost cold.

"Happened?" Swami-ji said.

"He means to the trees," Skinner said. He seemed to be enjoying himself.

"Oh," Swami-ji said. "I don't know about the one on the other side of the river, but the tree of knowledge was axed about two thousand years ago. You might not believe what I am about to tell you . . ."

Skinner laughed again. The sound was starting to annoy Lew. "Tell me anyway," Lew said, giving Skinner a mean look.

"Your Jesus of Nazareth came to India. There is nothing known of his whereabouts between the ages of thirteen and thirty. *The lost years*, they are called."

"Oh yeah," Lew said. He remembered seeing a book about it somewhere.

"He came here," Swami-ji continued, "to study Hinduism, Buddhism, and all the other esoteric mysteries of the East.

"Anyway, he cut down the tree of knowledge. He used the wood to build a boat. That boat took him back to Africa. From there he went to Galilee. The rest you know about."

"Aren't you forgetting something?" Skinner asked.

"Oh, yes," Swami-ji said. "Some of the wood from that boat was used to make the cross on which he was crucified."

"Of course . . . Nailed to the tree of knowledge." Lew uttered the words as if to himself. Skinner looked away in disgust.

THE GAIA WAR 159

Later, after Swami-ji had bidden them good night, Lew and Skinner were returning to their respective hotels. "I hope we're not enemies, Lew," Skinner said.

"I don't know what we are anymore . . ." Lew said, "After what happened . . ."

"That was another time. Another place," Skinner said. "We're in India now."

"Yeah," Lew said, "I guess."

"*You* especially need to remember that." Skinner stopped walking and turned to face Lew.

"What do you mean?"

"I mean what Swami-ji was telling you tonight, the tree of knowledge, tree of life, Jesus in India. You don't believe any of that stuff, do you?"

"Well, I . . ."

"Yeah," Skinner said, "I can see it in your eyes. He has you hooked. But he warned you."

"Warned me?"

"He told you to watch out for all the swamis and gurus over here. They will pump your head full of all kinds of nonsense."

"But Swami-ji . . ." Lew protested.

"Is different. Is that what you think?"

"Yeah," Lew said.

"He is different. I'll grant you that. But he is still a swami. Don't forget it, Lew." They had resumed walking and were at the intersection where their paths diverged. "Good night, Lew," Skinner said.

"See you," Lew said.

That night Lew dreamed of killing Gaur and seizing what remained of the tree of life for himself.

CHAPTER 11

"Keep your heart a'thumpin' and your brain a'buzzin'." *Where did that come from?* Lew wondered. He woke with the phrase iterating through his mind. It was early; his body was still confused about night and day. Even so he would have slept later were it not for the strange noise. He sat up to check it out.

Lew had bought some oranges the previous afternoon and set them on the corner table in his room. Orange peels were scattered all over the floor. A big rhesus monkey was sitting on the table devouring the last orange.

"Huh!" Lew said. He stood and walked toward the monkey, making shooing sounds. The startled monkey made for the open window and the tree branches outside. But before he made his exit he turned and jumped back on the table, assuming a fighting posture. Lew stopped in his tracks. The monkey was clearly enjoying himself. The animal bared his teeth, revealing sharp fangs. With a look of pure primal aggression he advanced a step, with arms raised high.

Lew freaked. He bolted for the door and ran out into the hall, startling an Indian woman who had just emerged from her room. "Sorry!" Lew gasped. "There is a . . ."

"Monkey in your room," the woman said. "You should keep your windows closed at night. Especially if you have food in your room. They are very bold. You should also put some clothes on."

160

THE GAIA WAR 161

Lew stammered something incoherent and stuck his head back into his room. The monkey was gone. The woman stole a look at Lew's pale, bare ass before making her way downstairs to breakfast. *Not bad*, she thought.

She was finishing her coffee when Lew walked into the dining room. She lowered her paper just enough to smirk at him before he sat down. When he got up the nerve to look back her head was again buried in the *Times of India*.

Breakfast came with the room. One could choose from coffee or tea, eggs or porridge, toast or *chapatis*. Lew had switched to tea since the coffee was instant and tasteless.

"I know a place where they have real coffee." Lew looked up to see Skinner standing next to him.

"What are you doing here?" Lew said.

"You asked me that yesterday," Skinner said. "But right now I'm here to take you to a decent breakfast."

"Why?"

"Because we should talk."

Lew had expected Skinner to lead him to a fancy hotel restaurant so he was surprised when they bent to enter the low doorway of a tiny tea shop with a dirt floor. "This guy has real coffee beans from South India," Skinner said. "And he knows how to brew them."

The proprietor beamed a smile of welcome recognition at Skinner. "Two scrambled eggs, toast, and coffee," Skinner said. The man set to work with astonishing speed and efficiency. Squatting over a small charcoal pit, he cooked both meals in less than five minutes.

"You're right," Lew said, sipping his coffee, "this stuff is good."

"Now," Skinner said, "have you thought about what I told you last night?"

"About Swami-ji?"

"Yes."

"Not really," Lew said. "But one thing did occur to me. I don't know about Swami-ji and all that weird stuff last night, but the *Genesis Bomb* out in White Sands is surely no illusion."

"Nor is that Gaia creature," Skinner said.

"*Miranda* now."

Mark Leon

"Whose idea was that?"

"Hers," Lew said.

"It figures," Skinner said. "Brave new world and all that sort of thing . . . *Pandora* would be a better name for her." Skinner paused, reflecting. Then, suddenly changing gears, he said, "What the fuck is that stuff out in the desert, Lew? And how did Alan Fain manage to grow a . . ."

"Woman," Lew said.

"Yeah. How *did* he do it? I won't say I'm not impressed."

"I don't know how he did it. But he used the empathetic aether."

"The what?"

"The empathetic aether. It's a substance that we got in . . . well that's a long story[5] . . . just say we got it in another dimension."

"This on the level?" Skinner asked. "No bullshit."

"No bullshit," Lew said.

"How come you never told me about any of this before?" Skinner sounded hurt.

"None of your business," Lew said.

"You know, Lew," Skinner said, "you never cease to amaze me. Sometimes I think you may not be quite the flake you seem."

"Thanks a lot," Lew said, glaring at Skinner.

"Hey, I'm sorry. No offense. Breakfast is on me. So Alan used your *empathetic aether* to do what the ancients could only dream about. He was some guy, wasn't he?"

"Was?" Lew said. "What do you mean?"

"What makes you think your friend is still alive?" Skinner said.

"Why wouldn't he be?" Lew said, looking closely at Skinner.

"That jungle is dangerous," Skinner said. "Who knows what kind of nasty stuff is growing there."

"I'd say you are the expert on nasty stuff," Lew said.

"You misunderstand the cyberion process," Skinner

---

[5] *Mind-Surfer.*

THE GAIA WAR 163

said. "I hope to show you the truth about it before all this is over. It is that rampant, voracious jungle you should fear."

"But Swami-ji called it the New Eden," Lew said. "What's to fear?"

"There you go again," Skinner said. "But let's not argue. Eden or not, that jungle is not long for this world."

"Why?" Lew said.

"You think the Feds are going to sit around and do nothing while that jungle devours the USA?"

"But it's stopped. At least that's what the papers say."

"Yeah," Skinner said, "it has stopped for now. But White Sands is completely overrun by it, and no one knows what to expect. Alan Fain messed with the power—he has struck at the very heart of Western capitalism."

"So what are they going to do?" Lew said.

"They?" Skinner was toying with him.

"The government, the corporate power structure, you know who I mean," Lew said.

"I know very well who you mean," Skinner said. "I'm one of *them*, remember?"

"Yeah," Lew said.

"They'll deliberate for a while. Maybe even wait, but not for long. Then they'll act."

"Act?"

"You can't figure it out for yourself, Lew?" Skinner said.

"They will try to destroy the *Genesis Bomb*," Lew said.

"They most definitely will. I give it a week. No longer. If the jungle does not start to recede on its own, White Sands National Monument be damned, they will nuke the whole place."

"Alan . . ." Lew said.

"*If* he is still alive, which I very much doubt, is in deep shit," Skinner said. Then he leaned against the wall at his back and took a long sip of his coffee. "India is a trip isn't it, Lew? Don't you love it here?"

A beggar with advanced leprosy stopped outside the tea stall. He was dressed in rags. He held his hand, palm up, in front of Lew. There were no fingers left, just dirty

164   **Mark Leon**

stumps. Lew dropped a few paise into the palm. The man touched his forehead and walked on.

"Some things about India really bother me," Lew said.

Skinner, who had barely noticed the transaction with the leper, smiled.

On the other side of the world, in Washington, DC, an emergency cabinet meeting was starting. It was night; the waxing moon hung low in the sky. "I think Secretary Carp should brief us first," the president said.

But before the defense secretary could speak the secretary of the interior interrupted. "Don't you think I should get first crack at this? White Sands *is* my territory."

"Take it easy, Don," the president said. "Technically you are right. White Sands is a National Monument, etcetera. But we have something like a national *emergency* going here . . ."

"So!" Don Fields interrupted. He was the president's closest friend in the cabinet and the other officers resented his informality, which often bordered on rudeness.

"So shut up, Don," the president said. "Let Jack talk. Then we will hear from you."

Jack Carp, the secretary of defense, gave a concise briefing on the military monitoring of the situation. "So," he concluded, "the *Genesis Bomb* is no longer growing. But the jungle is not receding, either. The scientists can't tell us much. It is, apparently, some new life-form."

"What do you mean by *new*?" the president said.

"It has DNA, but it's unlike any DNA seen before. The different species of plants all share the same basic code. They aren't really different species in the usual sense of the term. They can apparently crossbreed and produce new strains at any time. This is, in fact, what happened. The initial strain, we think it was only one life-form at first, crossbred with itself, mixing and matching DNA sequences to produce the amazing variety of life we see there now. It also looks like this process of *evolution* was not random. It was directed."

"Directed?" the president said. "By *whom*?"

"Your guess is as good as mine. At first we thought

THE GAIA WAR 165

NatCo labs were responsible. But we have since ascertained that they had nothing to do with it. The stuff they were working on was far more primitive—there is no way it could have mutated into the *Genesis Bomb*.''

''What about this Larry Skinner, the NatCo rogue executive?''

''That was a major breach of their corporate security,'' Carp said. ''NatCo wants Skinner as much as we do. So far we have been unable to find him. It's hard to believe, but it really does appear that the simultaneous appearance of the cyberion process and the *Genesis Bomb* was a coincidence.''

''I don't believe it,'' the president said. ''Coincidences like that just don't happen. I don't care what it takes. Find Skinner.''

''We're trying.''

''Try harder.''

''Yes sir. But in the meantime there have been disturbing reports. Normally I would not give them any credence . . .''

''We have all heard about the UFO sightings,'' the president said with a sneer.

''I know,'' Carp said, hanging his head a little. ''I know. Grocery store tabloid stuff. But we couldn't afford to ignore any leads, no matter how absurd. And now intelligence tells me that some of the sightings seem genuine.''

''Genuine! What does that mean? People see crazy stuff all the time,'' the president said.

''I know,'' Carp said, ''but some of the sources seem credible. That would not impress me much except for the fact that there is a remarkable coherence to the reports. Several apparently reliable people report seeing the same thing or things.''

''Flying saucers!'' the president said. ''I don't believe we are seriously talking about flying saucers.''

''We aren't,'' Carp said.

''Then what! For God's sake, *what*?''

''People, sir. Flying people.''

Alan had mapped out a small portion of his new world. The job was particularly difficult because the landscape

166 Mark Leon

kept changing. Each day there were new species and new variations on old ones.

There were several large fountain plants, but the biggest was the one in which he had first bathed. When he finally found it again he immediately retrieved his clothes, and just as quickly realized he neither needed nor wanted them.

The Book of the New Creation continued to ripen, but his progress in reading it was slow. There were two reasons for this. The first was that he found the material to be dense and cryptic. But the real reason he failed to read and study it with any discipline was that he had found a new distraction—the video plant.

It had started out as an ordinary-looking fern. But soon it produced a pair of big leaves arranged like two screens joined at an angle of about 120 degrees. The leaves had first caught his attention because of their unusual color. They were a translucent silver with just a faint tint of green. The first time he stared at them he thought he saw a faint flickering in the surface of the leaves. A day later he was sure of it, and he could detect forms moving there.

Still it surprised him when, a few days later, he realized he was watching videos. They were unlike any videos he had ever seen before. Many had no clearly recognizable form. Some of these, Alan came to realize, were scenes from the world of molecular biology. The plant was showing images of its own microscopic workings. *If I can only remember this*, Alan thought. The plant was revealing answers to questions about DNA molecular dynamics that earth's scientists had not even begun to ask.

But there were also scenes of cosmic proportion. Alan witnessed supernovas from the inside out, and strange warpings of space-time that stretched his understanding of general relativity to the breaking point.

One such scene nearly drove him to tear his hair and scream. He was convinced it was an extrapolation backward in time to the initial singularity, the point from which the Big Bang originated. The screen was about to show him the ultimate secret, what went before, before there was time or space. But the screen suddenly went blank, and all

THE GAIA WAR 167

he could see on the shiny surface of the leaves was his own reflection.

Alan recalled the theory behind the empathetic aether, the stuff he had used to grow Gaia. It was simple, an old idea that modern scientists had discarded as irrelevant: the cosmic aether. The universe, according to this idea, was a plenum, a fullness. But it was filled with no ordinary stuff, not matter, not energy, not even space. It was filled with aether. Aether is fine enough to penetrate the space between atoms, between the electron and the nucleus. It even fills the space between quarks, the smallest particles yet theorized. But the aether also fills the space between the stars and galaxies.

Einstein established a cosmic speed limit with his special theory of relativity. Nothing could go faster than light. But that limit only applied to space-time. It did not necessarily impose limits on the stuff that lies underneath, above, inside, and outside space-time, namely the aether. The waves that physicists study, light, electricity, and magnetism, all travel through space-time and so are subject to Einstein's speed limit. But a wave in the aether might travel at any speed. In fact it might travel at no speed. The very concept of speed depends on the twin concepts of space and time. Waves in the cosmic aether might be infinitely slow or infinitely fast. Lew, Alan recalled, had direct experience with an aethereal wave of the infinitely fast variety, the Asklepian wave.[6]

The more Alan thought about it, the more it all made sense. The protean virus that had spawned the jungle was synthetic DNA. He had, with Gaia's help, utilized the empathetic aether in the synthesis. The result, more fantastic than he had dared hope, was all around. At least some of the new species, like the video plant, were especially attuned to the cosmic aether. The scenes Alan witnessed on those living screens were live, they were projections of information that was always there in the aether, information continually broadcast over the Asklepian wave.

---

[6] *Mind-Surfer.*

The implications went far beyond the video plant. Alan regarded that as little more than a curiosity. What really interested him were the implications for life in general. Ordinary human DNA, any DNA for that matter, was not essentially different from the synthetic DNA of the jungle. This meant, in theory at least, that humans must have the same capabilities as the the new life forms all around. These were clearly latent traits that existed only in potential. But if that potential could be *actualized*! It meant that all the secrets of the universe, from the subatomic to the extragalactic, could become transparent to the human mind.

It also meant that scientists had, as usual, gotten things backward. Current scientific theory put life in the category of a fluke, a last-minute phenomenon in the evolution of the universe, totally inessential and irrelevant except for the fact that we view things from the perspective of living creatures in one tiny corner of the universe where life just accidentally ''happened.''

What Alan was discovering was what he had suspected all along. There is nothing ''accidental'' about life. Nor is it irrelevant. Life is at the center of cosmic evolution. DNA is designed to receive the most subtle of vibrations, the Asklepian wave, as it is broadcast on the cosmic aether. This means that life has a glorious destiny and purpose. Living things have the potential to bear witness to the most incredible cosmic happenings. Beyond that Alan could only guess. Was there an ultimate purpose to life? An ultimate intelligence? Answers to those questions required more data. Alan prided himself on being a good scientist, and good scientists try not to put theory before fact.

Since his discovery of the video plant Alan's dreams had taken on a particularly vivid quality. He saw dramatic scenes, but, unlike the visions on the leafy screens, these scenes were all on a human scale. He sometimes awoke with the feeling, not that he had dreamed, but that he had been watching a movie. The characters were all unfamiliar. They were naked people with green, glowing skins, and they all could fly.

During one of these dreams the action became so intense that he woke up. He lay flat on his back staring up at the

THE GAIA WAR 169

glowing canopy of life. Gradually he became aware of the eyes that looked back. There, about twenty feet directly overhead was a beautiful, naked woman, the same creature he had chased through the jungle. Her skin gave off a green luminescence. The shimmering glow made it appear as if her body were vibrating.

Alan lay very still for several minutes, watching her. She was clearly watching him. Her expression was unfathomable. Alien yet all too familiar. Alan sensed that she knew things he could only guess at. And he guessed that he knew things she did not want to know.

He sat up slowly. Her eyes immediately got very big, apparently she had thought him still asleep. "It's OK," Alan said. "Climb down. I won't hurt you."

Alan had assumed that she was lying on an outstretched limb, but when he stood up and looked more closely he could see nothing that supported her. Then she leapt—from nothing to nothing. Alan felt as if the bottom had dropped from his stomach, and he prepared to witness a terrible fall. But she did not fall. She flew, right up into the higher reaches of the jungle and out of sight.

He rubbed his arms, jumped up and down, and shook his head. But he knew it wasn't a dream. Whoever she was, she could fly.

"This is madness," Interior Secretary Fields said, "really crazy. You *can't* be serious."

"I don't see that we have any other choice," the president said. "If this stuff starts growing again, the entire country could disappear in a matter of weeks, days even. I'm told when it's active it grows with a speed that accelerates in a geometric progression."

"I'm not sure that would be such a bad thing," Fields muttered.

"What?" Defense Secretary Carp said.

"I said, *I'm not sure that would be such a bad thing!*" Fields said. "Has this stuff killed anybody? No! As far as I can tell it has not! All it has done is turned a desert into a tropical paradise and devoured several hundred miles of highway concrete. We have been choking the life out of

170   Mark Leon

this continent for the last five hundred years. Maybe life is finally fighting back, and maybe we ought to let it win!''

"And maybe you are nuts," Carp said.

"I'm sure Don isn't serious . . ." the president said.

"Like hell . . ." Fields began.

The president cut him off with a mean look. "We can't allow ourselves to get too emotional about this. This is a political decision pure and simple. Whatever we may feel in our bones, we have to protect the vital interests of the United States of America. Those interests are primarily economic. And the economy depends on our interstate highway system."

"So you're going to nuke the whole area," Fields said in disgust.

"Only as a last resort," the president said. "Don, listen . . ."

The interior secretary was rising. "I've heard enough," he said, backing away from the table.

"I hope you remember that this meeting is highly confidential," Carp said.

"Confidential," Fields said. He had stopped at the door. He turned around. "Yeah. I remember. If I were you guys, I wouldn't want anyone to find out about your scummy little plan, either."

"You are one of *us guys*," the president said. "Remember."

"What a privilege," Fields said, and walked out.

"Don't worry," the president said. "I'll talk to him."

"I think you had better do that," Carp said. "In the meantime, I'll get things ready at our end."

"You can take action in a week?" the president said.

"We can take action tomorrow, right now if necessary," Carp said.

"No, let's wait. Our research team may come up with a less violent solution."

"OK," Carp said, "but I still think it would be better to move while the stuff is dormant."

"Not yet," the president said. "Not just yet."

* * *

THE GAIA WAR 171

"You know the story of Pandora, Lew?" Skinner said. It was midmorning and they were out on the river. A boatman, even skinnier than Lal-ji, was straining at the oars against the monsoon-swollen current on the sacred river.

"Sure," Lew said. "She opened her box and let loose a flood of evil on the world. Except Hope. Hope was spared, or something like that." Lew was trying to think of a way to get rid of Skinner, but the man had skillfully commandeered his morning and was now threatening to run roughshod over his day.

"Very good," Skinner said, "but you left out the most important parts."

"Oh?"

"Yeah. What does Pandora mean?" Skinner said.

"I don't know." Lew was thinking about how uncomfortable his jeans were in the heavy, damp heat. He resolved to get some Indian clothes as soon as possible.

"Pandora, in Greek, means 'Gifts from all' or 'All gifts.' Pandora was a synthetic woman, Lew. She was created by the gods. And the Greek gods, bear in mind, are not like the Hebrew God. The God of the Old Testament created men, women, and everything else. But Zeus and the rest of the Olympian gods did not create the world. They did not create man either . . ."

"So who did?" Lew said.

"Who knows?" Skinner said. "That's not the point. The point is that the Greek gods were really more human than divine. So when the myth says Zeus created Pandora it is highly significant. It means that Pandora is not like the rest of us. She is artificial. All the other gods pitched in, adding something to Zeus's handiwork. From Aphrodite, or Venus if you prefer, she got radiant beauty and irresistible sexual charm. From Athena a crafty cleverness. She was the original femme fatale. Remind you of anyone?"

"You mean Miranda," Lew said.

"Yeah, that bitch is artificial as hell . . ." Skinner said.

"Shut up, Larry! Where do you get off calling her a bitch . . ."

Mark Leon

"Sorry, Lew," Skinner said. "I didn't realize you two were so close."

"We aren't," Lew said. "I just don't like your talking about her that way."

"Suit yourself." Skinner smiled. "Alan's creation, that *lady*, is clearly artificial."

"So what?" Lew said. "She's no less human for that."

"What's human?" Skinner said. "Anyway, Pandora's name has a double meaning. She got gifts from all the gods and she came bearing all sorts of 'gifts' for humanity. Hence Pandora, 'Gifts from all' and 'All gifts.' But Zeus manufactured her to be a cunning bitch. He was pissed at Prometheus, who gave humans the gift of fire, making us rivals to the gods. Pandora was his way of getting even. A crafty woman with devious sexuality and some nasty little surprises in her box. From Pandora we got disease, poverty, work, all the stuff you see in such abundance, especially here in India."

"So what's the point?" Lew asked.

"The point is that Pandora would be a better name for Alan's handiwork."

"I don't see the similarity," Lew said.

"Don't you?" Skinner said.

"Isn't it about time for lunch?" Lew said.

"I suppose it is," Skinner said. He told the boatman to take them back to shore. "You know, Lew," Skinner went on, "you are lucky you ran into me over here."

"I doubt if luck had much to do with it," Lew said.

"You need someone like me to fill you in on what's really going on," Skinner said, ignoring Lew's sarcasm.

"What *are* you doing here, Larry? Why are you hanging out with Swami-ji?" Lew said.

"I don't have all the answers, Lew," Skinner said. "We all need teachers. Swami-ji is teaching me some very important lessons in mental control. Very useful stuff, really." The boatman rowed them onto shore.

"Five rupees!" Skinner said. He fixed the poor, skinny Indian with a fierce look. "Outrageous." He talked the man down to two rupees, about forty cents.

THE GAIA WAR 173

"You have to know how to deal with these people, Lew," Skinner said. "Otherwise they will steal you blind. Now where do you want to eat? I know a great little tandoori kitchen not far from here. Sound good?"

"Sure," Lew said.

CHAPTER 12

"I'm so tired, Meagan," Miranda said. She was lying on a bed in a Motel 9.

"You need to rest," Meagan said. "Just try to sleep." Meagan could not keep the fear and anxiety from her voice. Miranda's appearance terrified her. After flying two hundred miles across the Edwards plateau of West Texas, Miranda had landed in Fitoria, a truck stop community in the middle of nowhere. Miranda's appearance and the fact that the two women had no visible means of transportation caused the motel clerk to give them a slow once-over.

"She's carsick," Meagan explained when they checked in. Miranda was pale and unsteady on her feet.

Her shakes had stopped, but she was still drained of color. The faint greenish tint to her skin didn't help her appearance. "Maybe you should eat something," Meagan said.

"I don't feel hungry. Can you open the curtains? I'd like some sun."

"Of course," Meagan said. The window was small; when she pulled the curtains aside only a few small rays of sunlight came through. They fell pathetically onto the cheap, worn carpeting. "Is that better?"

Miranda smiled weakly.

* * *

THE GAIA WAR   175

Meagan woke the next morning to the sound of retching. She jumped up and went into the bathroom to find Miranda on her knees in front of the toilet bowl. There was little she could do other than help Miranda back to bed when the nausea subsided.

"I'll get a doctor," Meagan said.

"No!" Miranda said sharply. "Please, you mustn't do that. Believe me. I know."

"But . . ." Meagan was on the verge of tears. "You're sick. You need help. I don't know what to do."

"I'm not sick," Miranda said. She said it with a certainty that stunned Meagan.

"Not sick?"

"No, not really," Miranda said.

"Then you are going to be alright?" Meagan said hopefully.

"I don't know," Miranda said, grimly. When she saw the effect this had on Meagan she said, "Go get some breakfast for yourself. There is no sense in your making yourself ill over this. Try not to worry."

"But . . ."

"Meagan, please. Go. I will be alright for now." Miranda spoke with such authority that before Meagan had time to reflect or resist she found herself walking across the motel parking lot toward the coffee shop.

The place was full of truckers getting ready for another long haul on the interstate. Meagan sat down in a booth. When she picked up her menu a state trooper at the counter turned to look at her. He turned away when she put the menu down.

After ordering, Meagan thought about the scene in the motel room. Something about Miranda's condition was familiar. She couldn't quite put her finger on it, but she was convinced that she knew what was wrong, if she could just remember.

It was the sight of breakfast that brought it all back. She had felt exactly the same way once. Many years ago when she was a teenager, a junior in high school. She was sure of it. There was an empathy women had about that sort of thing. Meagan had given the child up for adoption, against

176   **Mark Leon**

her wishes. Her parents had insisted, wanting her to stay in school and go to college. It was partly to get even that Meagan had dropped out of school anyway. *Stupid thing to do*, she thought, sitting there staring at her eggs and pancakes.

It took her a while to recover her appetite. Meanwhile the state trooper was watching her, as if trying to come to a decision. He slowly got up, left some money on the counter, and left, stopping at the door to take a last look at Meagan, who was now eating.

Morning sickness. The thought sent a shiver up and down Meagan's spine. *It is beginning*, she told herself. *At long last it is beginning.*

When she returned to the room Miranda was gone. Meagan had to hug herself tightly in order to keep from becoming hysterical. She forced herself to think. *She can't have gone far, unless* . . . the thought made her heartsick . . . *she has flown away.*

She went back outside and scanned the parking lot. Heart thumping, she went around to the rear of the motel. "Thank you, Jesus," she whispered when she saw Miranda sitting with her back against the wall of the motel.

She was naked, legs stretched out in front and slightly spread apart. Her eyes were open and she was staring straight into the sun.

"What are you doing?" Meagan said. "Come back inside. You'll hurt yourself."

Miranda turned to look at Meagan. Her eyes were shining, full of sunlight. "Oh no," she said. "Oh no."

"But your eyes! You'll go blind." Meagan had taken Miranda's hands and was trying to pull her up.

"My eyes are not like yours," Miranda said. "Not anymore."

"You're pregnant . . . aren't you?" Miranda said, wonder and delight barely concealed.

"Yes," Miranda said.

Meagan clapped her hands for joy. "Praise . . ."

"But not in the way you think!" Miranda interrupted her.

THE GAIA WAR 177

Meagan bowed her head. "Forgive me, I am just a foolish woman. I . . ."

"You aren't foolish, Meagan," Miranda said. "There is nothing to forgive. But you are mistaken about me. You have to understand that. I am not who you think I am."

Meagan began to cry. Miranda stood and held her close. "Oh, Meagan," she said, "you try too hard. The universe is not less wonderful than you suppose, but more so. Your faith is good, it is just misplaced. It's all going to happen. Everything you want, but you must be patient, you mustn't try to force things. Do you understand?"

"Yes," Meagan said, not understanding at all.

"Don't worry about it," Miranda said, as if reading her mind. "I don't understand either. But you have to admit one thing."

"What?"

"Sure is strange," Miranda smiled, and Meagan laughed through her tears. "Better?"

"Yeah," Meagan said.

"There they are!" It was the motel clerk. He was standing at the rear corner of the building. A state trooper was with him.

It wasn't until they pulled up to the county courthouse that Meagan had the presence of mind to ask, "What are we being arrested for?"

The highway cop thought about it for a few seconds. "Indecent exposure," he finally said.

"Not me," Meagan said.

"You were an accomplice," he said.

"That's bullshit," Meagan said.

He had no answer to that. "Come on." They had parked and he held the door open.

"I want a lawyer," Meagan said as she got out.

The trooper said nothing. He appeared uneasy, unsure of himself, as he herded the two women into the old, limestone building.

"Nice courthouse," Miranda said. She had recovered somewhat. The cop had allowed her to dress, and she was wearing black jeans and a yellow T-shirt.

178 Mark Leon

"Yeah," he said, "a real gem. Needs maintenance though—state money just keeps getting tighter and tighter. Some counties have just given up. They tear down these old beauties and put up some kind of cheap, prefab bullshit . . ."

"Yeah," Miranda said. "That would be a real shame. Are you going to lock us up?"

"Afraid so, ma'am."

"Are there any cells with windows?" Miranda asked. "That face the sun? You may have noticed that I have a skin condition. If I don't get direct sunlight, it gets really bad."

"Well . . ." The cop was disturbed by Miranda's appearance. Her skin had turned a darker green since her morning stint in the sun. The FBI agent had given explicit instructions. Maximum security.

"Please . . ." Miranda turned on her best feminine charm, helpless dependence mixed with sexy smile.

"Well there is a cell on the south wing that gets sun most of the day. I guess I could . . ."

"Thank you so much." Miranda shifted her weight slightly, giving a sexier angle to her hips and causing her breasts to poke through the thin cotton a little more prominently.

"Sure, no problem." The cop smiled.

Creel was pissed off. His superiors just did not get it. As soon as the state trooper had called, he had put in a request to charter a plane to fly to Fitoria. He regarded it as a sheer stroke of luck that his all-points bulletin had produced results so quickly. But he had to act. No telling how long they could hold his fugitives. The woman might have additional powers. He had no doubt about the identity of the two women being held in Fitoria. They were the ones.

But he had to act, and his chief, who remained skeptical about flying fugitives, saw no reason to hurry. So Creel was barreling west on I-10, hoping to get to Fitoria by early afternoon. He flipped on the radio. "Damn!" he said, unable to find anything but country and western. He was do-

THE GAIA WAR   179

ing 110 to a Garth Brooks tune when a local cop pulled him over.

The cop was not impressed by Creel's FBI badge. "The law is still the law." He began writing a ticket, apparently in no hurry.

"Can you speed it up?" Creel said. "I'm on an important case."

"I can see that," the cop said. "You know something. I don't like you Federal boys. You've got the public fooled into thinking you are heroes when *we*"—he pointed a finger at his chest—"are the ones that do all the real work. You were going mighty fast. In fact you were going so fast that I could haul your ass in right now."

"I'm sorry . . ." Creel began.

"In fact that is just what I'm gonna do. I hope I can trust you to follow me back into town?" the cop said.

"Yeah, sure," Creel said, realizing that he would be lucky to make Fitoria by sunset. He hated local cops.

"Meagan?" Miranda said. She was sitting, with her shirt off, facing the window of their cell. A small amount of sunlight was shining on her breasts.

"Yes?" Meagan said. The adjacent cells and corridor were empty, but Meagan was worried that one of the guards would show up and take Miranda's state of undress as justification for some kind of sexual assault.

"We have to get out of here," Miranda said. "I'm not getting enough sunlight through this little window. And I think the glass filters out some of the essential light frequencies."

Meagan wondered what she meant by "essential frequencies." "I wish you would eat something," Meagan said, indicating Miranda's lunch, lying untouched on the battered metal tray.

"Alright," Miranda said, "if it makes you feel better. But food is not what I need." She cut into the cold hamburger patty. "This stuff is terrible," she said.

"I know," Meagan said, "but it's all we have for now."

Miranda tore off a piece of the stale white bread and stuffed it into her mouth. Eating the bread, bad as it was,

180   **Mark Leon**

gave her an idea. "Meagan," she said, "you now know that I'm not the Mother of God, don't you?"

"If you say so," Meagan said.

"I say so. I think it is terrible the way religious leaders exploit the legitimate faith of their followers. The stuff you see on television . . . you know what I mean?"

"Yeah," Meagan said.

"So remember that when I tell you my plan," Miranda said.

"Plan?"

"To get us out of here. This is expediency, nothing more. OK?"

"OK," Meagan said.

"Good," Miranda said. "Now listen. The next time the guard comes to check on us, tell him you want a Bible."

"Alright."

Miranda pulled her shirt back on over her head and climbed onto the top bunk. She knelt on the hard metal surface and began working at the heavy iron casing that held the window bars and reinforced glass. "Warn me if you see or hear anyone approach," she said.

Meagan nervously got up and looked out the small window in the cell door. "All clear," she said.

Within the hour Miranda had worked the casing loose.

"Someone's coming!" Meagan said.

Miranda carefully pushed the brown painted bars back in place. She hurriedly brushed the crumbled bits of plaster and chipped paint into the corner of the bunk and stretched out.

"You ladies need anything?" the guard asked.

"I'd like a Bible," Meagan said.

"And some coffee." Miranda sat up, her back to the debris on the bunk.

"I'll see what I can do," the guard said. "Coffee is no problem, but I don't know about a Bible."

"Please," Miranda said.

"I'll see what I can do," the guard said.

"And please tell the arresting officer that we need to see him as soon as possible," Miranda said.

The guard started to give a gruff reply, but Miranda's

THE GAIA WAR   181

eyes were so soft and sexy that the words stuck in his throat. "I'll relay the message," he said meekly.

"Coffee?" Meagan said, when the guard had gone.

"For appearance," Miranda said. "I've got the casing pried loose."

"Then we can leave?" Meagan said.

"We can get out, but where will we go?" Miranda said.

"Can't you . . ." Meagan began.

"Fly us away?" Miranda said. "I'm not strong enough yet. We're going to have to figure something else out. That's why I wanted you to get the Bible."

"Oh . . ." Meagan said.

"Meagan!" Miranda said. "We aren't going to work any miracles. The Bible is a prop, nothing more. Just play along, OK?"

"Sure."

The trooper showed within the hour. He carried a Bible in his left hand. The book was too thick to slide through the opening in the window, so he opened the door and came in.

"Thanks," Meagan said, taking the offered Bible.

"What's your name, Officer?" Miranda said.

"Brian," the trooper said. "You ladies religious?"

"Oh yes," Miranda said. "Do you believe in miracles, Brian?"

"I didn't used to," he said. "But I have seen things . . . I have seen some things."

"Meagan believes that the end of time is approaching," Miranda said.

"That right?" Brian said.

"Yes," Meagan said. "I think it won't be long. That's why I wanted the Bible. I need to pray. I need the Word."

"How soon do you think it will be?" Brian said.

"Pray with us, Brian," Miranda said. "I believe the time is right for a sign. You know we shouldn't be here . . . Locked up like this. I can see that you know that. We haven't really done anything." She smiled at him.

"I don't know anything about it," Brian said, stiffly.

"But you do believe in the Lord?" Meagan said.

"Yes. I do," he said.

182 Mark Leon

"Then pray with us," Miranda said.

Brian and Meagan stood while Miranda remained seated on her bunk with her back to the window. Miranda ended the prayer saying, "So Lord, we ask that you right all wrongs, free those who are unjustly bound by the wicked, open all dark places, let the sunshine in!" She reached behind her, grabbed the metal bars, and pulled. The unit came out with a loud bang as it fell onto the metal bunk.

Brian opened his eyes and yelled, "What the hell . . . !"

"It is a sign," Miranda said. "We are here on the Lord's business. The Lord wants us to go free. Will you help?"

Brian ordered Miranda down and got up to inspect the damage. There was now a two-foot-square hole in the wall. "What have you two been doing?" he said.

"We won't leave without your permission," Miranda said.

"You won't leave period," he said. "I'm moving you to another cell."

"Brian, wait," Meagan said. "If you do that, you risk the righteous anger of the Lord. Don't you see? It was a sign."

"A sign?" he said.

"Of course," Miranda said. "Don't you see? How could we have pulled those bars down? Two helpless women like us?" She conjured up a vulnerable expression, eyes like deep pools. She saw him waver and did not miss her chance. "Now listen to me, Brian, here is how we can do it. You won't lose any credibility, and we can do the Lord's will." Meagan was shocked by the glib flow of scheming lies and half-truths that proceeded to issue forth from Miranda.

For the first time since he began serving in the president's administration, Interior Secretary Don Fields felt humiliated and out of the loop. He had enjoyed unprecedented access, unusual influence for an interior secretary. This was partly because he was a close friend of the president. But it was also because the president was the closest thing to an environmentalist the country had ever had in the Oval Office.

But, Fields, thought, *all that is changing. The president*

THE GAIA WAR 183

is no longer listening to me. The crisis, this Genesis Bomb *or whatever it is, has the man scared.* When presidents get scared they typically turn to the military.

Fields did not take long to make up his mind. From the moment he left the cabinet meeting he knew he was going to act. He stopped by his office and took care of some paperwork, not because there was anything urgent, but to keep himself occupied while he got used to the plan that had already crystallized.

It wasn't much of a plan. Fields did not know much more about the situation in White Sands than did the general public. He had seen some of the classified material, but it contained little more than you could read in the papers. The explosive growth had stopped. There were sightings of strange goings-on, Unidentified Flying Objects or *Subjects* according to some sources.

He called in the young aide, the only person besides himself still working. "Lisa, I'm going to be out of the office for a few days, maybe longer."

"Yes sir," she said.

"Please tell the staff not to expect me."

"OK. When did you say you would be back? In case anything comes up, I mean . . ."

"I didn't say. I'm not sure. Lisa?" Fields looked at the young woman, noting the ambition and the drive in her eyes.

"Yes?"

"You really should get out of politics." He drove home to his Georgetown apartment and began searching through closets and garage for his camping gear. He had good stuff, but it had been a long time since he had used it. *Too long*, he thought.

On his way out of town he allowed himself to think about it. He did not doubt that the president was serious. Nuclear nightmare in the desert, or the jungle, or whatever it was out there. But whatever it was, he had to see it and he didn't have much time.

It was dark by the time Creel pulled up to the Fitoria courthouse. He was breathing hard as he showed his cre-

184 Mark Leon

dentials, "Just a moment, sir," the clerk said. "I'll get the arresting officer."

The expression on state trooper Brian Miller's face gave Creel a bad feeling. "Can I see the prisoners?" Creel asked tightly.

"I'm afraid that won't be possible," Miller said. "We've had a little problem."

"What sort of problem?"

"They have escaped."

Miller led Creel to the cell. There was not much to see. The window casing lay on the top bunk. Creel pretended to inspect it, and the square opening in the wall. Then he saw the Bible lying there. "What's this?" he said.

"They wanted a Bible," Miller said.

Something in Miller's voice made Creel suspicious. "A Bible? Why?"

"Who knows," Miller said, clearly uneasy. "Maybe they're religious."

Creel opened the book. Miller's name was inscribed on the first page. "This is yours." He made it sound like an accusation.

"Yeah. I've had it since I was a kid. Vacation Bible School—you know how it is out here."

"I wouldn't know," Creel said drily. "How did they get away after they got out?" Creel said, hoping that his conviction the prisoners had *flown* away did not show.

"I don't know," Miller said. "There aren't any vehicles missing. We have all available officers on it. So far nothing."

Creel didn't like it. He was mulling things over at the truck stop restaurant. He figured that the woman's powers were limited. Otherwise, why had they stopped in Fitoria? If she had flown off again, he guessed she hadn't gotten far. But if that were the case, why hadn't she been picked up? And the business with Miller's Bible. The trooper was uneasy about it. He was hiding something, but what? The waitress set a plate down in front of Creel. His thoughts were momentarily diverted by the big chicken-fried steak, mashed potatoes, and cream gravy. For a moment Creel was troubled by thoughts of low-fat food and smart diets.

THE GAIA WAR

185

But only for a moment. *Oh well*, he thought, *when in Rome* . . . He dug in.

Miranda insisted on driving the pickup. The route Miller planned took them far off the interstate. "I really think you should eat something," Meagan said for the third time since their escape.

"And I explained that I don't need that much food anymore," Miranda said. "Besides, those sandwiches are gross, all that mayonnaise—and the ham is so well preserved it'll be around for the fourth millennium."

"They're not *that* bad," Meagan said. "I ate one. I guess that makes me a food fool or something."

"I'm sorry, Meagan," Miranda said. "Give me a sandwich."

"It *was* nice of Brian to make them," Meagan said, handing the sandwich to Miranda.

"And to give us his truck," Miranda said. "I hope we are heading in the right direction."

"Where are we going?" Meagan asked.

"I don't know," Miranda said, but her voice conveyed more than simple ignorance. She made it sound as though she was certain they were going *somewhere*.

Meagan got very quiet.

CHAPTER 13

"Perhaps the smallest particles of all are the nouons." Alan was again reading from *The Book of the New Creation*. He knew something of nouons, having been very nearly killed by a blade of crystallized nouons.[7]

> These are the particles of thought. They exist in the aether and are not material particles, matter being a phenomenon of space-time. Just as the aether is a more subtle kind of vessel than is ordinary space-time, the nouons are a more subtle kind of particle than ordinary matter. It is this *rarefied* nature of the nouonic pulse in the cosmic aether that makes consciousness such a mysterious thing.

Alan closed the book. It was almost ready to be picked. The top of the stem, where the spine of the book joined the plant, was turning brown. In a few days, Alan thought, the book would simply fall to the ground by its own weight, like a ripe apple. But he dared not pick it himself. There were portions of the text, most notably the last few pages which were still unreadable. Would the book continue to ripen, "off the vine," as a green banana turns yellow on the kitchen counter, or not? He had scanned portions of the last chapter, where he found hints of a strange and won-

---

[7] *Mind-Surfer*.

THE GAIA WAR 187

derful destiny that awaited mankind, but it was incomplete and difficult to decipher.

The jungle was taking on a new quality. Ever since he had discovered the video plant, Alan had the feeling that there was some strange "urban planning" taking place. It was no longer difficult for him to navigate. Pathways through the dense growth were taking on more identifiable characteristics. Some resembled boulevards and many more looked like streets. No place was barren of the new life, which grew ever more varied and complex, but pathways and clearings were forming that both facilitated movement and enhanced beauty. It was beginning to look like a strange and wonderful organic city.

Alan had "sensed" music before in the jungle, but it had always been an impression, not really sound. So it startled him when he actually heard music for the first time. He was approaching the little clearing where the video plant grew. He quickened his pace and was stopped dead in his tracks by the sight which confronted him a few moments later.

The green woman was watching an erotic video. It was graphic enough to qualify as X-rated, but it was far more tasteful than the ugly porn he had seen. And the music was enchanting. It conjured images from the Arabian Nights and all the exotic tales Alan had loved as a child. The sound was distinctly Moorish, at times modulating into scales from the Far East, but always returning to the more familiar blend of Arabic and Spanish themes. The video plant had grown audio channels. Alan assumed that the music was also broadcast on the mysterious frequencies of the cosmic aether. It wasn't anything one would likely hear on AM or FM.

The woman was watching with rapt attention. Occasionally she would examine her own body, as if checking out the equipment she saw on the big leafy screens. There was nothing lewd in her actions or her fascination with the sexual images. Nevertheless, Alan felt like a voyeur. His guilt increased in direct proportion to his heightened sense of her absolute innocence.

He continued to watch, however. The woman had her back to him and he was partially concealed by a giant fern.

188 **Mark Leon**

He stood still, trying not to make a sound. The video was erotically very stimulating, but as Alan watched he began to realize that was not the point of it. It was educational.

The information conveyed was not just the standard stuff one could find in any sex manual. The theme of the material was baffling. It was that sex, in all its aspects, including, but not limited to, the actual act, had far more significance than most people ever suspected. It *was* for procreation and the survival of the species: making babies. It *was* for pleasure. It *was* to make life more interesting and complex than it would otherwise be. But, according to the video, these things were of relatively minor importance compared to something called the *Axial Awakening*.

It was this that Alan did not understand very well. Apparently the time would come when fucking would result in a new kind of pregnancy. Women would become pregnant not with child, but with themselves, new improved versions of themselves, apparently. Exactly where men fit into this was not altogether clear. Alan thought maybe that was something to be addressed in a future program.

He became mesmerized by a particularly compelling scene. The intensity of the images made him gasp. The woman heard him and turned. Alan stepped back, inadvertently revealing more, not less, of himself. His state of arousal was suddenly quite visible.

She had seemed ready to bolt, but held herself in check at this new revelation. Curiosity drew her eyes to the area where Alan's legs branched from his torso. She approached cautiously. Her eyes, Alan noted, were more green than blue. Her hair was a dusty wheat color.

"You," she said slowly and clearly, "do . . . that?" She pointed at the sexual images behind her.

"Sometimes," he said.

"Just like a handle," she said reaching with slender, green fingers. She took his erection in her hand and squeezed gently.

Alan sighed deeply. She quickly let go. "Oh!" she said, releasing him.

"No," he said. "I mean, don't stop."

She smiled at him. He was shocked by the expression.

THE GAIA WAR 189

It was a worldly smile, the smile of a corporate CEO or a powerful politician. It was not the kind of smile he would expect to see on the face of a naked, forest nymph, and so she forced him to admit that he really had no idea who or what she was.

"You have much desire," she said.

"Yeah," Alan said, "I guess I do."

"Desire is the root cause of all suffering. Or so it is *said*," she said.

"I've heard that," Alan said.

"But people say all kinds of things, *don't* they?" She managed to sound as innocent as a schoolgirl and as provocative as a high-priced whore.

"Who are you?" Alan asked.

She looked genuinely puzzled. She remained silent for a few moments, deep in thought. "Oh, I *see*!" she said, clapping her hands in delight. "Yes, you actually could ask someone that, couldn't you?"

"Yeah, you could," Alan said. When it became obvious that she had forgotten his question, he said, "I just *did*."

She frowned. "Don't be rude," she said.

"But I . . ."

"How unspeakably rude!" she said with a sudden display of white-hot anger. The intensity of it actually drove Alan back a few steps.

"I'm sorry," he said, more out of fear than genuine regret.

"No you aren't," she said. She was smiling, anger all gone. "But don't worry about it."

"May I ask you something else?" Alan said hesitantly.

"Of course."

"You can fly, can't you?"

"Sometimes," she said.

"Only sometimes?"

"Yes," she said, her hand was absently stroking the giant fern that Alan had used for cover. The green of her skin was lighter, more delicate, than that of the plant. "It has something to do with sunlight and complex energy systems."

"Complex energy systems?"

"What do you call it?" she said. "The seeds of life, the basic *molecular* structural units?"

"DNA?" Alan said.

"Yes. DNA. Our DNA has long segments that don't have anything to do with protein synthesis."

"The *silent* strands," Alan said. "Our scientists believe those portions of human DNA are just deadweight, nonfunctional stuff left over from earlier evolutionary periods."

She laughed. It was a long, near-hysterical seizure. It took her a moment to catch her breath when it was over. "Silly! Those are the most important bits. They are the future!"

"The future?"

She looked to the sky, as if that were answer enough.

"You mean that those pieces of DNA are what enable you to fly?" he said.

"Don't forget the sunlight?" she said. "Where would we be without sunlight?"

"Dead, I guess," he said.

"Or worse," she said. "We will meet again." She turned to go.

"Wait! I . . ."

She turned and said, "I *know* what you want." Her breasts rose in proud defiance.

"Well, maybe we could just talk. I mean, I don't understand what is happening."

"Who does?" she said, again taking her leave.

"But I don't know your name!" Alan said.

"What's in a name?" she said, disappearing into a thick tangle of vines that seemed to actually move slightly, opening a small path for her.

Until their encounter, Alan had not quite trusted his senses about the green woman. He had entertained the hypothesis that she was an illusion, possibly the result of some psychoactive chemical he was unknowingly ingesting when he ate the various fruits the jungle offered. But their meeting was undeniably real, or at least as real as anything ever is. What is reality anyway? Alan refused to get entangled in metaphysical speculation of that sort—he had been down

THE GAIA WAR

that road before. "That way lies madness," he said. Was it his imagination or did the slight breeze blow a barely audible agreement to his ears? He felt that the life all around was rustling in emphatic confirmation of his pronouncement.

In any case he now believed in her. And he wanted her. She was the most beautiful thing he had ever seen. He had been in love once before and blown it badly. "Ah, Pamela," he sighed as the memory of that red hair filled his mind. "I hope you're happy now."

This new passion was different. Was it love? Certainly it was lust. Then Alan realized where the difference lay. Pamela had once needed him. Their love was a passion born of mutual desire. How could this creature ever need him? She might not even be human.

This triggered another thought. He had almost forgotten about the world "outside." This innocent mistress of the jungle would need him if that other world, *his* world, began to encroach on the *New Creation*. For the first time he hoped that there was still something of the outside world left. It would give him a role as protector of this wonderful creature. Otherwise, he feared he would always be irrelevant to her, and that was a dismal prospect.

The video plant was still showing erotic scenes of almost-unbearable intensity. Alan approached, his state of arousal near fever pitch. The scenes began to change. The plant seemed to sense Alan's discomfort. The audio shifted to some familiar rock and roll chord progressions. There was a narrative.

We all want to return to the place from which we started. Not the womb, but the place where first we understood the marvelous nature of the universe and our place in it. This was before we all became hopelessly lost. Now we can barely remember that place, but a trace of recollection lingers. Sometimes a smell or any chance sensation will trigger an old feeling which will in turn give us another brief glimpse.

But it is unfortunately futile. Or perhaps this is our good fortune. After all, who wants to *go back*? Don't we all want

192   Mark Leon

to go forward? There is a serious side to things. Things can appear very *grave*. Gravity. You know in your bones that the mystery of gravity is the key to your future. Gravity is the one force which has yet to be integrated into the cosmic scheme. The electron mediates electricity. Is there a fundamental particle of gravity, the graviton? Can gravity become levity? One can hope.

The music sound track was briefly interrupted by laughter. It was the kind of laugh Alan had always wanted to laugh.

The narrative continued.

Eros is a powerful force. But you are wrong to think it derives its power from the need to procreate. At least in the way you understand the term. Eros makes babies. This is elementary. But there is also the regeneration of self; one can become newborn; this is also the work of eros. This is the way forward.

Alan was totally captivated by the narration and the music. The chord progression had built to an unexpected climax. With it the images on the screen had changed from beautiful abstract forms to a vision of deep space that was exhilarating. It lasted for only a moment, but Alan saw cities floating in the deep, starlit void, cities that were gardens like the one in which he found himself. But they were more spectacular in their beauty, their complexity more finely articulated in a rich profusion of lush form and color. And before the screen went blank he thought he saw people, people with green skins floating through the scenery.

"Things got jammed up down here," Alan whispered to himself. The video had transformed his sexual excitement into a deep intellectual ecstasy. "We belong out *there*. What happened?" Alan convinced himself that humans were not meant to be earthbound, at least not for hundreds of thousands of years. Something had gone terribly wrong. It must be the fields! The aether held all the fields, the electromagnetic force, the strong and weak nuclear forces, and even the force of gravity. The aether permeated all structure from the smallest to the largest. Somehow the

THE GAIA WAR 193

fields, or at least some of them had got jammed here on earth. The key to unjamming things was gravity. Even the very word, "gravity," hinted at this. Things were grave because the force of gravity was stuck, stuck in the mode that sticks us to the planet. And somehow eros, or sex, was the key to getting it unstuck. Then gravity could be transformed into levity, and cosmic evolution could again proceed on schedule!

Alan sat down, stunned by the thoughts and visions that were flashing through his mind. His little experiment, born of his desire to reestablish an ecological balance on earth, had turned into something far more significant. His heart was racing, hammering at his ribs. The implications were too much, too staggering. He did not want such a huge responsibility, had never intended to be so much at the center of things. He felt as if the weight of the universe had suddenly come to rest on his shoulders. The term *Axial Awakening* took on a new, unwelcome significance. It was one thing to witness the event as humanity shot forth on a new axis of evolution. It was quite another to *be the axis*. It was the difference between playing the role of midwife as opposed to mother in the rebirth of mankind. Mother must bear the full brunt of the pangs of birth.

Alan realized with a dreadful reluctance that he was full of a desperate terror. He stood up, knees shaking, heart still out of control. He wanted to run, but he was too frozen with fear. He wandered through the living streets and avenues, trying not to think.

When he came in sight of the fountain plant, he ran headlong into its flowing waters. He swam and dived and thrashed about for several minutes, finally coming to rest under a waterfall. He let the cool spray buffet his head and shoulders.

With the water another thought came flowing into his mind. It was a cooling thought, so he let it possess him. It was that he really had very little to do with what was happening. He had played a key role, but was more a pawn in the game than master chess player. This much he knew was true, and it brought tremendous relief. Another thought sneaked in on the heels of this one. It came so quickly, and was so like the first, that Alan accepted it as well. Had he been in a more reflective mood, not so desperate for any mental solace, he would not have so readily embraced it. That thought was, *So now it is completely out of my hands*.

Refreshed and free of the weight of the world, Alan went looking for the book plant. *The Book of the New Creation* promised to reveal more about the *Axial Awakening*. Clearly the last few chapters of the book dealt with it. Alan had suspected, as had many others, from the ancients to the few present-day thinkers who still bothered with such things, that there was a hidden purpose to human evolution. It was not random, nor was it to make more cars, TVs, and VCRs. The Greek word for it was *telos*, or end. End not in the sense of finished, but in the sense of an answer to the question, "What is a thing for?" Humans were *for* something. Alan had rarely doubted this.

The question, as always, was "For what?" *The Book of the New Creation* promised answers in the last chapters. Those were the pages that were still not ripe, but Alan hoped to glean something more from the text.

At first he thought he had taken a wrong turn, gotten lost and stumbled upon a different clearing, but with a sinking feeling he realized he was in the right place. He recognized it too well. Everything was just as it had been, except for one detail. All that remained of the book plant was the stem. Someone had picked it.

There was really nothing much new in the book that she had not already figured out for herself. The green-skinned lady of the jungle lay under the branches of a giant tree with fernlike leaves reading *The Book of the New Creation*. She was a fast reader. It was a good thing because, deprived of moisture from the mother plant, the pages were quickly becoming brown and brittle.

She was nearly to the last chapter and hoping to find the answer to the one question that still puzzled her. The book did not make clear exactly where this *New Creation* was to be located. Was this paradise to remain on earth, or somehow translate itself into the vast reaches of outer space?

THE GAIA WAR 195

"Excuse me," Alan said hesitantly. A day had passed since their encounter by the video plant, and he had been searching for her ever since. He had finally found her not far from the fountain plant, where she lay reading.

She looked at him over the top of the book, saying nothing.

"Uh . . . Where did you learn to read?" Alan said.

"Learn?" she said.

"Yeah, learning is a process by which we . . ."

"I know what it means," she said, as if this were enough to answer his question.

"I'd like to read it when you're finished," he said, pointing to the book.

"You may find that difficult," she said.

"Why?"

"Come here." She sat up and motioned him over, indicating that he should sit beside her. "See." She opened the book, so he could see that most of the pages were crumbling away like autumn leaves into brittle fragments.

"But!" he said. "I was hoping to learn . . ."

"Learn what?" she asked.

"I don't know," he said glumly, and hung his head. He suddenly felt very depressed.

"I'm sorry," she said. "Yesterday I didn't know about your occlusion."

"My what?" he said, bewildered.

"Your occlusion. Your kind, those of you who are native to this planet, suffer from an unfortunate suppression of important information stored in critical areas of the DNA molecule."

"How did you learn this?" he said.

"It is in the book," she said. "Or it *was*. It was one of the few things I did not already know. If I had, I would have been more sympathetic, less abrupt. You poor people. You perpetually live with deep wounds that will not heal."

A wave of sadness swept over Alan. He began to weep openly, with an abandon that he had not thought possible. Her words had hit home in a place he had forgotten about. It was an ancient place, at once personal and universal.

She pulled him to her and he rested his head on her chest.

Mark Leon

"Let it come through," she said. "And remember one thing."

"What?" he choked through his heaving sobs.

"You are not alone." She stroked his head.

When he was quiet she stood up. "You have to let go of the past," she said.

"How?" he said, looking up at her beautiful body through moist eyes.

"You are holding tight to something that was once beautiful." She reached with her right hand and closed her fist. "Like so." Then she turned to her left and reached out her left hand. "You don't want to let go, because you are afraid, uncertain whether or not there is anything else for you to hold on to. But what you hold is no longer beautiful. Now it has gone bad. You must reach out even farther." She extended her left hand higher. "And while you gently take hold of the future, you must also release the past." As her left hand tightened around some unimaginable prize, her right hand opened.

Alan watched with rapt attention. Her motions were transparently simple, yet full of grace—it was like watching an exquisite dance; she was truly poetry in motion. She stood for a moment, looking up to her left hand, now wrapped around the unseen treasure. Her right hand was open in a gesture of blissful release. "You see?" She dropped her arms and turned to face him once again, a radiant smile on her face.

"Yes," Alan said, voice barely above a whisper, "I think I do."

She sat back down beside him and again took up the book. After several minutes, Alan spoke. "Can you tell me one thing about yourself?"

"What?" She lowered the book onto her lap. Alan could not help but admire the smooth flatness of her belly. Desire threatened to consume him, and he forced himself to look away.

"How did you get here? I know something about the origins of this place, the genetic material that generated it. But I don't know how . . ."

THE GAIA WAR   197

"How the jungle could grow a beautiful woman," she said.

"Yeah."

"You should ask her," she said.

Alan scanned the clearing, thinking that she meant some new, more fantastic creature.

"She is not here. Not now, not yet, but I think she will come," she said.

"Who?"

"You know better than I," she said.

"You mean *Gaia*?" Alan said. Suddenly the likely truth began to dawn. Gaia must have done some last-minute tinkering with the protean virus.

"Is that what you call her?" she said. "Yes."

"How do you know about her?" Alan said.

"We have some common memories. She used part of her own DNA to make me."

"But why?" Alan asked.

"Every new creation needs a mother. Doesn't it?"

"What should I call you?" Alan said.

She thought about it for a few moments and said, "Raya."

"If every creation needs a mother," Alan said, "then doesn't it also need a . . ."

"Not so fast." Raya laughed. "A father maybe. Probably. Most certainly, in fact."

"Then . . ." Alan leaned a little toward her.

She pushed him back, gently but firmly. "Cool it, Daddy-o," she said. "Maybe I *was* born yesterday, or almost, but we only just met, remember?"

"Where did you pick up expressions like that?" Alan said.

"A little here and a little there," she said. "Some of what I know I have always known. Your Gaia was able to transmit a great deal in genetic code."

"But learned behavior can't be passed on through the genes!" Alan said.

"So the theory goes," she said. "Do you believe every scientific theory that comes along?"

"Of course not, but . . ."

Mark Leon

"There you have it," she said. "But there is also information in the aether that one can pick up. Unfortunately your species has lost that ability as a result of your occlusion."

"You had no childhood," Alan said.

"No what?" Raya said.

"No childhood, no long period of development in which to grow and learn. You just sprang full-blown into life, like the goddess Athena."

She laughed softly. "Oh, I see what you mean. But you are mistaken. You do do not understand."

"What?" Alan said.

"I am a child."

"But you are so . . ."

"Womanly?" she said, with irony in her voice.

"Yes."

"You really are an unfortunate race," she said.

"What do you mean?"

"I mean that when you ask questions like that you betray a woeful ignorance of the most important things."

"Tell me about the *Axial Awakening*," Alan said, wanting to change the subject.

"There is not much to tell," she said.

"But, you have read the book," Alan protested, "and now it is falling into pieces, and it is too late . . ."

"And etcetera," she said. "It is always too late if you have to read about it in a book. But here, take it." She handed it to him.

"All that's left is the last chapter," he said, "and that's still too green to decipher."

"Maybe it will ripen," she said.

She insisted they part, saying, "That's enough talking for now." Suddenly the calm was shattered by the roar of a low-flying jet. The plane was not visible through the foliage, but the sound was unmistakable.

At least it was to Alan. Raya jumped. Fear did not suit her well, Alan thought, observing her reaction. *Does it suit anybody*? he wondered.

"We will meet again," she said, her voice trembling slightly.

THE GAIA WAR 199

"I hope so," Alan said, looking up. "I wonder if we might be running out of time . . ."

"Time?" she said. "What was that noise?"

"It is one of the few things *I* could teach *you*," he said.

"Later," she said.

Alone, Alan thought about the significance of the jet. Obviously there was still some of the old world out there. "What might they do?" He knew the answer and tried to force it from his mind. But that was impossible, and so he reached an unwelcome conclusion. "I have to get out of here," Alan said.

As he reluctantly put on his clothes he reflected further. Initially he had planned to use the protean virus as a means to force the leaders of the world to adopt policies of economic growth and development that would reverse the relentless tide of ecological destruction sweeping the planet. It was a vague plan, he had to admit—half-baked. And as a result of Skinner's attempt to kill him and his subsequent experiences in the jungle, he had all but forgotten it. But now it was time to act, and his goals were far more modest. He had to negotiate for the preservation of this little enclave of paradise.

He hiked for the rest of the day and all through the next. The going was easy. The streets were open enough to allow him to keep a fairly steady pace. He was continually amazed by the beauty of the place. No two areas were the same. The jungle always surprised one with newness. None of the paths he followed were straight. They were all interconnected in twisting routes that Alan felt certain linked the entire expanse. And while he sensed that they formed an unfathomable complexity, he also found it relatively easy to maintain an eastward march.

By evening of the second day he came to the end. And it was the end in a way that brought both intense anxiety and blissful release. There was no way out. The jungle ended abruptly at a line in the gypsum sand. On the inside was the New Paradise and outside was desert. And growing up from this line was a transparent polymer wall. It looked to be about half an inch thick. It reached a height of at least thirty feet. There was no scaling it—the surface was absolutely smooth.

Alan followed for several miles along the inside circumference. There was no end to it. As far as he could tell they were sealed in. At first Alan assumed that the wall was something constructed from the outside to contain the jungle. He imagined that the Army Corps of Engineers had hastily built it.

But on closer examination he reached a different conclusion. There was a thick tangle of orange shrubbery that grew along the inside of the perimeter. The roots of this vegetation extended several feet underground and resurfaced in the form of a transparent organic polymer that grew up to form the barrier.

Naturally occurring polymers are commonplace, DNA being the best-known example. But this stuff was something else. It was hard. Alan could not scratch it with any of the rocks he found. In spite of its thickness it was transparent as glass. Alan spent a few nights in a clearing by the perimeter to check on something. By the second morning his suspicions were confirmed. The wall was obviously higher.

The jungle was growing its own barrier, isolating itself. Alan had a good idea what the barrier was supposed to keep out. He was actually relieved that he could not follow through on his plan. He had never really had any idea how to proceed. Walls keep things in as well as out, and Alan was now a prisoner in paradise.

CHAPTER 14

"We may have to act sooner," Defense Secretary Carp said.

"Why?" the president said.

"The entity is growing a protective shield."

"A shield?"

"We have our analysts at Alamogordo working on it," Carp said. "Apparently it is some kind of organic polymer. The stuff is harder than steel and almost totally transparent."

"How is it possible?" the president said. "It can't enclose the entire area... the *Genesis Bomb*, or whatever it is. We can still deliver a device from the air, can't we?"

"Now we can," Carp said, "but this shield is growing up and in. It's forming a dome.''"

But," the president said, "if it's encapsulating itself, like you say, then maybe we should hold off. I mean the stuff on the highways is dying, and if the jungle completely encloses itself, it's no longer a threat..."

"We know nothing about it!" Carp said. "This may be a defense mechanism, a way for the entity to protect itself while it gathers strength. This could be only a brief respite before the entire planet is engulfed! We need to strike while we can!"

"You refer to it as an *entity* now," the president said.

"Our botanists think it is really only one species," Carp

said. "Or a superspecies. Actually they say it's a radically new life-form which challenges the normal procedure of dividing life into phylum, class, genus, species, or whatever."

"Then it would be a shame to destroy it," the president said. "Fields is somewhat extreme in his views at times, I admit. But he has a point."

"Where is Fields, anyway?" Carp said.

"I don't know. Why?"

"I don't trust him. He is privy to information that could jeopardize Operation Take Charge."

The president hated the practice of giving every little military action a silly name like "Just Cause" or "Take Charge." And the names the top brass came up with! They reminded him of his days in the Boy Scouts. But he had learned early in his term that it was best to give in on matters like these. Men like Carp needed their code words and top secret games. It kept them out of trouble—usually. "Fields wouldn't do anything stupid," he said.

"You two are old friends," Carp said. "Maybe you should talk to him."

"I told you he's OK," the president said. "A little eccentric at times, but he has never done anything unreliable or disloyal." The president knew this was a lie. It was amazing, he reflected, that a man like Fields had made it to the highest levels of government. It was testament to Fields's intelligence.

"Alright," Carp said, "but back to the issue at hand. I really think we should act before it's too late."

"But we want to avoid a scandal if possible," the president said. "Bring me all the data you have on this new development—this shield. I'll decide what to do after I review it."

"Alright," Carp said. Privately, he was making some decisions of his own.

"We can't just print something like that," the reporter said.

"I *know* you can't," the interior secretary said. He was at a pay phone in Kansas City. "I'm telling you to get some

THE GAIA WAR   203

corroboration. It shouldn't be too hard. I'm giving you a high-level leak."

"How high?"

"Very high. What does it matter anyway?" Fields was getting annoyed. The press was always following through on low-level leaks that made his life more difficult. "This is one hell of a story I'm giving you. Just do your job!"

"Who *is* this?" the reporter said.

"You call yourself a *New York Times* reporter?" Fields shot back.

"I *am* a *New York Times* reporter," the reporter said. Fields could hear the man puff up with pride.

"Well, then, just blow that famous *Times attitude* out your shorts and listen to me one more time," Fields said. "The military is going to nuke the *Genesis Bomb* within the week. The president approves the plan. Ask the right questions at the White House and at the Pentagon, but don't bother with any assistant secretaries or presidential aides. They don't know anything. Ask the president. Ask the defense secretary. This is cabinet level only."

"Are *you* cabinet level?" the reporter asked.

"Maybe." Fields hung up. "These reporters are getting soft," he told himself.

Fields's plan was to drive to Albuquerque, where he kept a private plane. Beyond that he wasn't sure. But he had to get a look at this thing out in the desert. Then, he hoped, he would know what to do.

Meagan was worried again. Miranda had driven to the Chisos Mountains in Big Bend National Park. She had then hiked up to a remote plateau, removed her clothes, and stretched out on her back in the sun. She had been there all day, taking only a little water.

"Are you sick?" Meagan asked.

"Not really sick," Miranda said. She was again staring straight at the sun.

"Shouldn't you eat?" Meagan offered a granola bar from their small pack.

"Not now," Miranda said. "I'll eat something later." Then, emotion suddenly showing, "But *you* need to eat.

Mark Leon

You've got to take care of yourself, Meagan.''

''But I want to take care of you,'' Meagan said.

''I know,'' Miranda smiled, ''but that may not always be possible.''

''What do you mean?'' Meagan said, a new fear creeping into her voice.

''I mean, Meagan,'' Miranda said slowly, ''that I may not always be here.''

''Where will you be?'' Meagan said.

''Oh, Meagan.'' Miranda stood up, walked barefoot across the few feet of rugged terrain that separated them, and took Meagan in her arms.

Meagan gave herself completely to Miranda and sobbed for a full minute. ''Maybe I will eat something now,'' Miranda said releasing Meagan. Miranda sat on a flat rock. Her skin had turned a deeper green and the surface glow was more vibrant.

Meagan sat down next to her and handed Miranda the granola bar. Miranda broke it in two and handed Meagan half. She did it with a ritualistic ease that made Meagan think of communion, but along with the sacred connotations there was something alien and funny about the whole thing. Meagan laughed.

''Good,'' Miranda said, meaning both the granola bar and the sound of Meagan's laughter.

''Good,'' Meagan echoed. ''Really good.'' She felt a peace that came from within and from without. ''The desert mountains here are so beautiful,'' she said. ''Is the *Genesis Bomb* really going to take over the world? I mean, then there would be no more desert . . . like this.''

''That would be a shame, wouldn't it?'' Miranda said. The evening sun brought out the subtle desert colors. ''The desert is so fragile. You don't see the full beauty of it in the glaring light of day. It needs the vespers.''

''Yeah.'' Meagan sighed. She was transported by the totality of it all—their words, the sunset, even the taste of the granola bar seemed sublime. She knew the meaning of ecstasy.

''It's getting dark,'' Miranda said, breaking the long si-

THE GAIA WAR
205

lence in which they had experienced a deep communion of spirit.

"I guess we should go back to camp," Meagan said. "Lucky for us the moon is nearly full. Otherwise, I don't think the light would hold long enough for us to see the trail."

"No," Miranda said. She was putting her clothes back on. Meagan watched as Miranda's beautiful breasts disappeared beneath flannel, and her hips wiggled back into denim. It was a shame, she thought. Such beauty was meant to be seen.

"So Lew went to India?" Miranda said.

"Yeah," Meagan said, not liking this new direction of the conversation.

"To Benares?"

"Yeah," Meagan said. "That Indian, I mean that *Apache* Indian, said something about a guy called Swami-ji."

"It figures," Miranda said with a slight edge of cynicism. Then, her voice suddenly serious, she took Meagan by the shoulders and said, "Listen to me, Meagan. I have to find Lew."

"How?" Meagan said, taken aback by Miranda's sudden intensity.

"I have to go to India."

"When?"

"Now."

"Now! but . . . I don't understand." Meagan didn't want to cry anymore. She felt that she had grown older, wiser in the last few minutes, and she did not want to betray this new maturity by breaking down again.

"Yes," Miranda said, as if reading Meagan's mind. "We are both older now. You were right about my being pregnant. But what I am pregnant with is really only myself. I required sexual experience, the seed from a man, to trigger the process. Lew's sperm entered my womb and united with an egg from one of my ovaries. But my eggs are not for making babies."

"What are they for?"

"Making new life. A new life for me. It has been growing at an ever-accelerating rate since Lew and I made love.

206   **Mark Leon**

I am now strong enough to fly the Pacific and go to India. I need to see this Swami-ji. I'm also worried about Lew. He may be in over his head."

"But Lew!" Meagan checked herself. She had started to protest that Lew was not worth caring about.

"I owe Lew something, don't you think?" Miranda said, patting her lower abdomen. "We *are* animals, Meagan. But we are also more than that. I can't think of Lew as just raw material. Don't you see?"

"Yeah," Meagan said. "But when will you leave?"

"Right now. After my day in the sun I am at my strongest. My skin is now capable of an advanced photosynthesis, hence the green color. This is just one of the changes triggered by the fertilization of my egg."

"What will I do!" Meagan said.

"Go back to camp," Miranda said. "I don't think you should go home until . . ." She paused, voice trailing off into uncertainty.

"Until what?"

"Until all this is resolved," Miranda said.

"You aren't telling me the truth," Meagan said. "What's going to happen?"

"I can't tell you now," Miranda said. "I can't tell you because I don't know for certain myself. We all must have faith and hope for the best. Now here, take this." She pulled a wad of bills from her pocket.

"Where did you get all this money?" Meagan said.

"About seven hundred dollars," Miranda said. "It's not much, I know."

"Where did you get it?"

"Brian gave it to me," Miranda said, laughing a little. "You should be safe in his truck. Just stay mobile until— well, until whatever happens happens."

"I have a credit card," Meagan said. "You should keep the money."

"I won't need it," Miranda said.

"Will I see you again?"

"I think you will, Meagan. Keep your faith, just try not to push it so hard, OK?"

"Yeah," Meagan said. This time it was her turn, and she

THE GAIA WAR 207

took Miranda in her arms and gave her a warm hug.

"Thanks, Meagan. Good-bye." She was gone. Meagan looked up and caught Miranda's silhouette briefly against the rising yellow moon before it vanished in the night.

Meagan got back to their campsite full of new feelings. She wanted to be sad, but there was little room for the sadness which she had previously known all too well. Instead she felt a tension that was laced with calm excitement.

She was standing in front of the campfire reflecting on this strange exhilaration when she heard footsteps. She wheeled around.

"Where is she?" Creel said. He had his gun out. His face was alive with the light of the flickering flames.

"Who?" Meagan said.

"You know who I mean." Creel pointed the weapon at Meagan's head.

Meagan laughed. She honestly did not care at that moment whether or not he pulled the trigger. She did not want to die, but death seemed irrelevant, even funny, as she watched the way his gun barrel reflected the firelight.

"Where is she?" Creel said again. He tried to put menace into his voice, but what came out was fear.

"I don't know," Meagan said. "But I've got some hot dogs in the truck. You want to roast some wieners?"

It was cold in the stratosphere. Miranda was tempted to go higher, but she was afraid of overextending herself. The less oxygen available, the more she would have to tap into her budding energy systems. The cold didn't bother her. *Good practice*, she thought. *It's even colder where I'm eventually going.*

She rolled over onto her back so she could look up at the stars. Their pull was more powerful than ever. "Why not?" she said out loud, tempting herself. "Eventually, so why not now? Ah no, but I have promises to keep."

She knew this was not strictly true. She had made no real promises to anybody on poor planet earth, had not chosen to be born there, had not even chosen to be born at all. But she was grateful for the gift of life. That was something she told herself. And if she did not owe anything to Alan or Lew, she at least felt some responsibility. Not for the mess that they had made—that was their own doing—but responsibility in the sense that since she thought she might be able to help, she should at least try.

"Ah that word again," she said to the stars. "*Should.* What a lot of trouble from one word. When will we be able to banish it forever from our vocabulary?" She looked deeper into space and got only cold silence for an answer, which is what she expected. She laughed and did a loop, followed by an Immelmann turn. Then she rolled back, facing the black waters of the Pacific, and with reluctant determination sped even faster on her journey west to the East.

Carp was keenly aware of the implications of his plan. People assumed that the nation's nuclear arsenal was controlled by the president. And so it was. *But who really controls anything?* He had asked himself this question many times. Now that he was about to act the answer was so plain, so simple he wondered why it had always seemed so elusive. *Those who have the information.* That was the key, always had been. Information. Carp had it. The task of arming a stealth fighter with a thermonuclear device and delivering that device to a target would prove daunting for most people. But if you had the right information, it was not only possible to do, it was relatively easy. Of course, he reminded himself as he was making the necessary phone calls and travel plans, he still had to proceed cautiously and skillfully, but he had no doubt of his ultimate success. He was cautious and skillful by nature, not like that Fields, he told himself. Fields was a dreamer, an idealist. *That's why he is secretary of the interior, and I have defense*, he thought, and leaned way back in his chair and put his feet up on his desk.

What he was doing could very well spell the end of constitutional democracy in the United States. It could change the global balance of power. *Fuck it*, he thought, *it's about time somebody did something for a change.*

In the firm resolve of his will he was troubled by one loose end. He did not fully credit the UFS reports of Unidentified Flying Subjects, but they were too detailed and

THE GAIA WAR 209

too consistent to completely dismiss. He pulled the folder, clearly marked as highest-level security, from a desk drawer and opened it. The facts were few. Immediately following the appearance of the *Genesis Bomb* there had been several sightings in the Alamogordo/White Sands region of New Mexico. Locals reported seeing humanoids hovering over the area and flying rapidly away. These had quickly tapered off. There was a quote from a philosophy professor at the University of New Mexico in Albuquerque.

> I've suspected for a long time that there are more highly evolved beings out there. These are not bug-eyed monsters but humanoids. Read Plato and Plotinus on the philosophy of form if you want to know why. Don't get me wrong— I love the old pulp science fiction stories. It is just that the truth is stranger and more interesting than fiction. No surprise there.
>
> Anyway these folks aren't really watching us like the UFO freaks would have us believe. But they are *tuned in*, and whatever is happening out there in the desert is the sort of thing that interests them. And of course they can fly— they have solved the one remaining great mystery of physics. Gravity. They have the ability to transform *gravity* into *levity*. They don't need flying saucers. These are truly UFS as opposed to UFO . . .

Carp put the folder down. He was a thorough man. As much as he wanted to dismiss the philosophy professor's remarks as the ravings of a New Age flake, he could not. He was an old hand at intelligence gathering and analysis. There was a pattern here that pointed to something. Exactly what was another matter, but in the jargon of epistemology (Carp had been an undergraduate philosophy major) there was a *referent*. All the bizarre reports pointed to something. Something *real*, whatever that meant.

The one thing of which he was certain was that he didn't like it. In any military action there are always unknown factors—intelligence is never perfect. But one can usually anticipate the form, if not the particulars, of likely contingencies. In this case that was not possible, and it put an

210 **Mark Leon**

extra edge on Carp's anxiety. He had no doubt what he would do if confronted by one of these UFS creatures. He hoped their antigravity powers did not extend to objects hurled at them at high speed, things like exploding bullets and armor-piercing shells.

"I could rape you," Creel said. His gun was lying at his side and his mouth was half-full of roasted wiener. The charred dogs on white bread tasted delicious in the chill, dry mountain night. "I could do horrible things to you."

"Fucking pig," Meagan said.

"Yeah. The stars out here have the coldest sort of intensity don't they? Do you honestly believe that you two can escape the power?" he said.

"What power is that?" Meagan said with a sneer.

"The only power there is," Creel said. "Look at the world. There is order and there is chaos. There is money and there is poverty. It's clear where the real power is. You stupid New Age types are always looking for something else because you are too scared or incompetent to deal with the Apollonian forces of rightful rule."

"What are you talking about?" Meagan said indignantly. "I'm not a *New Age type*, I'm a Christian."

"Same shit," he said.

"No, it's not! You . . ."

"Shut up. I don't care what you call it. It amounts to the same thing. You believe in something crazy because you can't deal with reality. It's the quintessential characteristic of losers everywhere in every age."

"I feel sorry for you . . ." Meagan said.

Creel laughed. It was not a wicked sound; in fact his laugh was genuinely full of delight, and thus seemed especially diabolical given the context. "I *knew* you were going to say that! God how predictable you people are."

"Alright," Meagan said softly, "you're right. In fact I lied. I don't feel sorry for you. It's just that I think I should. My moral precepts tell me so, but it occurs to me now that there is some truth in what you say. My moral precepts may be at least slightly full of shit. And, therefore, maybe I have no moral obligation to feel sorry for you, which is

THE GAIA WAR 211

a relief because I just can't do it anyway. I hate you and sincerely wish that you will rot in hell forever.''

The force and depth of Meagan's words got to Creel. He hadn't expected such honesty from her. It impressed him, and, he hated to admit it to himself, disturbed him a little. ''Fuck you. Let's get back to the question at hand. Where is she? You don't think I mean business? I've done some nasty things to men and women in the line of duty. Of course, I prefer women. And you are a cute little bitch. I'd love to tie you up and rip your panties off. Big moon tonight, too. Very romantic. I'll bet you've never had it from . . .''

Meagan burst into tears. The man was clearly serious. Her last moments with Miranda had given her a deep strength. But now Miranda was gone and Creel was testing her newfound faith before she could even begin to appreciate it. *It isn't fair!* she told herself. ''So that's the way it is, huh?'' she said, voice shaking.

''Yeah.''

''I guess that's always the way it is.'' She said this more to herself than to him. It served to calm her down a little. She slowly stood up and started unbuttoning her shirt.

Creel leaned back against a rock. He idly took another bite from his wiener and chewed it with an obscene lasciviousness. His other hand reached for his gun. He did not pick it up but stroked the barrel and fingered the handle and trigger.

Meagan took her pants off. Then she slid out of her panties and tossed them aside. The cold mountain air actually gave her comfort.

Creel was impressed. She was petite, compact, and her pale skin glowed in the moonlight. She was one of those rare women who look better with their clothes off than on.

''Do what you have to do,'' Meagan said.

Creel licked his lips. ''I actually enjoy this sort of thing,'' he said, taking another bite of his wiener.

''I'll bet you do,'' she said.

''I should warn you—once I get started it's hard for me to stop.'' He grabbed his gun, tossed the hot dog aside, and stood up. He walked to Meagan and began caressing her body with the barrel of his gun. He pressed the cold steel against one, then the other, breast. He circled her navel with it and then poked at it. Slowly he slid it down.

"Turn around," he said. Meagan slowly complied. He put the gun barrel between her thighs. "You had better tell me where your friend is."

Meagan suddenly closed her thighs in a viselike grip around the gun. She had kept herself in pretty good shape by running and regular aerobics classes. Her legs were particularly strong.

"Dammit!" Creel said. "That was stupid." He tugged but could not pull his gun and hand free. "You're hurting me," he said.

"Tough shit," Meagan said, desperately fighting panic. She had not planned the action and now had no idea what to do.

"I'm really going to hurt you now, bitch," he said, still unable to get free of those powerful thighs.

Meagan thrust her hips back a little and then, with all her might, jerked her pelvis forward. "Ow!" Creel yelled as his fingers were stripped from his gun.

Meagan reached between her legs and retrieved the gun. She jumped across the flames to the other side of the campfire and pointed the gun at Creel.

"You won't be able to fire it," he said, slowly approaching her. "The safety is still on."

Meagan had once taken a class in handgun use and safety. She hadn't purchased a gun as she had intended, but she did remember a few things. She glanced at the gun and saw what appeared to be the safety and moved her thumb to it.

In that instant Creel dived for her, straight across the fire. Meagan backed up and nearly fell over the boulder behind her. She pulled the trigger. The shot missed, and Creel had her around the waist. She was bent backward over the boulder.

But she had the gun barrel pressed firmly against the flesh of his neck. A second shot was not likely to miss. "My aim is true," she said. "Get away from me."

When they were again separated by the flames Meagan

sat back on the boulder. The hard rock surface was warm from the fire, and it felt good on her bare ass. She struck a most unladylike pose, legs spread and the gun held firmly in both hands in front of her chest. Beads of sweat on her breasts glistened in the yellow glow of the flames. "I'd love to blow your dick off," she said.

CHAPTER 15

Miranda had overestimated her powers. By the time she reached the Bay of Bengal she began to panic. She couldn't go on. Hundreds of miles from land and utterly exhausted, she began to lose altitude. *I need sun*, she thought. *How foolish of me to fly at night, away from the rising sun!*

The dark waters lapped ominously close. Monsoon winds set little whitecaps foaming. They were reaching for her, eager to pull her down into ocean, where it all began and to which it all returns. *No.* Miranda shot upward back into the night. But it was a short-lived reprieve. Her climb resulted in a stall that caused a sickening wave of nausea which radiated from her bowels out to her limbs, where it manifested as a dull, aching paralysis. She fell, utterly helpless. Her toughened skin shielded her a little from the sharp smack of flesh on water. But it stung. The worst of it was her inability to summon legs or arms to the rescue. She felt the waters close over her as her momentum carried her down. *This is not the way it's supposed to be . . . This can't be right—this sinking into a cold, dark nothing.* It was her last coherent thought before slipping into oblivion.

Lew was having evening tea with Swami-ji in the guru's rooms. "I'm still interested in the tree of life," Lew said. "Was that really it over there on the other shore of the Ganges?"

THE GAIA WAR
215

"What's left of it," Swami-ji said. "But this is really an unproductive line of inquiry, Lew."

"Why?" Lew said.

"I've already told you why. What is done is done. Can't be undone. There is, after all, in spite of what dreamers and writers of science fiction would have us believe, a reality to time. Time is what it is. It has its own rhythms and beauties, but you will never come to appreciate these if you are always chasing after past glories and faded memories," Swami-ji said.

"I understand all that," Lew said. Swami-ji gave Lew a pointed look that said he did not believe for a moment that Lew *really* understood. Lew went on. "I just want to know if there is any way to make use of that awesome energy I experienced the other night."

"No, there isn't. Don't even think about it, Lew."

The sharpness of Swami-ji's voice surprised Lew. The old man was angry and unwilling to discuss the subject. This was out of character to say the least. Swami-ji was normally cool, poised, and eager to dissect any subject with philosophical or theological connotations to the point of absurdity.

Lew dropped it, but only to placate his host. If Swami-ji would not help, he could conduct his own investigation.

Swami-ji began talking about the history of Tantra, that ancient yogic art of harnessing sexual energy. "It can be used for erotic purposes. But this is really a waste of a great science. The real value of Tantra goes far beyond sexual pleasure. One can use the sexual energy to create a new life, a new self. It is the key to the next step in the cosmic evolution of mankind. Some have called it the *Axial Awakening*. In the microcosm the axis is the spinal column with the genitals at the base and the brain at the crown. As the energy of Tantra, the *Kundalini* Serpent power, awakens it ascends this axis. Tantra is the key to controlling this process so that the individual is not overwhelmed.

"But this is only the microcosmic view. The more esoteric beliefs about the *Axial Awakening* hint at a cosmic body for man where the part not only mirrors the whole,

216 Mark Leon

but actually *merges with it*. Now that would be really something!''

Lew murmured agreement and sipped his tea, but he was not really paying attention. As he looked out over the monsoon-swollen waters of the Ganges, he was planning a private trip to the other shore.

Two small boys were playing on the delta where the Howlie River empties into the Bay of Bengal when the smaller of them said in Bengali thick with the dialect of Calcutta, "Look! What's that?"

The other boy was not nearly so surprised. It was not uncommon to see dead bodies on the beach. They were either carried there by the river along with the rest of the urban filth and river silt or were washed up from the sea. "So what?" he said.

But his companion had already run to where the body lay, facedown. Jai, the bigger boy, reluctantly ran after. "Wow! wow!" Jai said a few moments later, when he stood before the body. "A *vidayshi*!" By which Jai meant that this was no typical castaway corpse. This was a foreigner. They could see that easily enough by the clothes, jeans, and flannel shirt, items no low-caste person or untouchable could afford.

Krishna, the younger boy, said, "You see! I told you." He approached the body cautiously. After poking at it with his foot he squatted and rolled it over. They both gasped.

Blue skin or blue-green skin in India is a sign of divinity. One frequently sees gods and goddesses in their various incarnations so depicted. Miranda's skin was not exactly blue or even blue-green, but the green, which was now impossible to ignore, sparked the boys' imaginations. "Pavrati!" Jai said, pronouncing the name of one of Shiva's wives.

"*Devti*!" Krishna said, which means simply "goddess."

"But she has died," Jai said sadly.

"Not possible, not possible. She only sleeps!" Krishna said.

"Then it is a very deep sleep," Jai said.

"Look!" Krishna said. "She is breathing."

THE GAIA WAR

It was hard to see but Krishna was right. Miranda's body did exhibit signs of breath. Jai began running as fast as he could toward the mud-and-cardboard shack on the delta that was their home, yelling all the way, "Baba-ji! Baba-ji!"

The first thing Miranda saw when she opened her eyes hours later were the bright black eyes of little Krishna. The first thing she thought was, *So tiny, so thin*. Miranda guessed the boy was no more than five. In fact he was nine.

Krishna began talking to her softly in Bengali. Miranda could not understand much of it, but her knowledge of Sanskrit made it possible for her to recognize some words and syntax. *What's he saying now*? she wondered. He had reached out to touch her, placing his finger on her forehead, just above the bridge of her nose, and he kept repeating, *"Devti, Devti . . ."*

Miranda suddenly realized what he was saying. The poor, half-starved creature thought that a goddess had come to visit. He was touching her where, according to Hindu belief, her third eye would have been. Krishna was probably hoping to gain some wisdom or inspiration. "No," she said. Apparently he understood and his expression made her instantly regret saying it. A look of hopeless despair replaced the brightness with a terrible swiftness.

She sat up and looked around. The effort cost her, and she had to remain very still for a few moments to fight the waves of nausea and dizziness that overcame her.

"Baba-ji! Baba-ji!" Krishna said.

Lew had a difficult time finding a boatman who would take him to the other shore of the Ganges at night. The monsoon current was getting dangerous, the moon had waned, and none of the ancient wooden vessels were equipped with lights. Lal-ji finally agreed to do it for two hundred rupees. Lew realized that this was extortion, but he was possessed of a passion that overrode any sense of propriety in business dealings.

Lal-ji chattered amiably in Hindi throughout the trip, the two hundred rupees, paid in advance, had seemingly dispelled his misgivings. He had to work hard to fight the current. It took them half an hour, but finally the hull slipped up onto the barren beach. Lew got out and told Lal-ji to wait for him. He had brought a small flashlight. It gave just enough light so that he could walk without tripping over rocks and shrubs.

Lew wandered for hours, but was unable to find the petrified tree stump. Finally, exhausted, he decided to go back to the boat and return to the city. He would have to wait for the next full moon. But neither could he find the boat. Lal-ji was waiting faithfully, but he was also asleep. The boat was nestled in a little cove and all but invisible in the darkness. Lew walked up and down the shoreline for several more hours.

Unable to go on, he lay down on the beach to sleep the few remaining hours of night until dawn. About to drop off to sleep he was brought to his senses by the sound of footsteps. "Lal-ji!" Lew said, standing up. There was no response, but Lew could sense that the person was quite near. He switched on the light and held it in front.

The sight of the naked, emaciated *sadhu* was horrific. Gaur looked like one of the undead. The ashes that covered his body and his zombielike stare added to this effect.

Gaur stared at Lew for several seconds, allowing Lew's terror to build to a suitable intensity. Then the man spoke. "*Ayee Sahub.*" Lew's Hindi was now good enough to understand. In any case, there was no mistaking the meaning. It was a summons to follow, made more ominous by the formal, polite tense in which it was uttered.

Lew tried for a moment to resist. Gaur merely smiled at this. The smile said it all: *I know why you have come. I know what you want. So I also know you cannot leave.* Gaur turned and Lew followed.

Swami-ji began to worry the next day when Lew did not show up for lunch. Lew had quickly developed a taste for the guru's cooking. "Better than Alan's," he said the first time he tasted Swami-ji's Punjabi dal.

That afternoon Swami-ji began asking around. His suspicions were aroused by the reluctance of the local boatmen to say whether or not they had seen Lew. Lal-ji, usually animated and jovial, was particularly sour on the subject.

THE GAIA WAR 219

"I know nothing Sahub!" Lal-ji protested under continued probing. Swami-ji didn't like to do it, but there was no other option, "Listen Lal-ji," the guru said, "I will make a special *puja* to Lord Shiva if you do not tell me what you know. This *puja* will make you sterile. I have used it before."

Lal-ji responded almost immediately. "Please, Baba, do not do this. My wife has yet to give me a son . . ."

"Then tell me what you know about Lew Sahub," Swami-ji said sternly.

"I took the young sahub to the other side of the river last night."

"Where is he now?"

"I don't know. I swear to you, sir, I don't know. I waited until after morning and he was still not coming. I searched and searched . . ."

"Sure you did," Swami-ji said. "How much did you charge Lew Sahub for this safe passage and loyal waiting?"

"Only ten rupee! Cheap, I swear . . ."

Swami-ji interrupted in a stern voice, "You will take me for even cheaper. You will take me for free."

"Free? But Swami-ji Sahub, I am needing to make my living on the river like any boatman . . ."

"Do you want me to make the *puja*?"

"No," Lal-ji said sadly.

"Then we go. And you will wait for me until the monsoon waters have receded and the Ganges is dry as a bone if necessary. Do you understand?"

"Yes, Sahub."

Lew was lying shirtless on a dirt floor in Gaur's filthy hovel when Swami-ji found him. "Lew, are you alright?"

Lew stared into Swami-ji's eyes, struggling for recognition, clarity of any kind. But clarity was not forthcoming. Lew's mind was poisoned by memories. They were memories only hours old but they pushed everything else away so that he could barely function as a human being.

"You spent the night soaking up the ecstatic energies that radiate from that ancient tree stump, didn't you?" Swami-ji knelt and put his hand on Lew's forehead.

220 **Mark Leon**

Lew nodded.

"It's now or never, Lew," Swami-ji said solemnly. "You must renounce it. It is a false hope that claims you. If you don't summon what remains of your will to come with me and cross back over to reality, you may be lost forever."

Lew instantly saw the truth in what Swami-ji said. But he could not hold the thought and continued to stare in silence.

"I know the real world on the other shore of the Ganges is not particularly attractive, Lew," Swami-ji said. "In fact it is rather appalling, but hope still survives there. There is no hope here, Lew. There is only a wasting of your will, which is gradually replaced by the memory of an impossible dream. Come on, Lew. Let's get out of here. Now!"

A shadow fell across the low entrance. Swami-ji turned to see Gaur, wearing Lew's *coorta*, stooped there. "You must let him go!" Swami-ji said.

"I am not keeping him here," Gaur said.

Desperate, Swami-ji grabbed Lew by the shoulders and dragged him to his feet. He led Lew out into the sunlight. "I'm taking him with me," Swami-ji said.

"Yes." Gaur smiled. "Take him."

"You filthy dog!" Swami-ji said to Gaur.

"What? You know I am innocent in this. And you also know the ancient bargain. It will be useless for you to carry him away. Unless he goes of his own free will, he won't ever regain his freedom."

"And he will. Won't you, Lew?" Swami-ji said, unable to keep the pleading from his voice.

Lew stared vacantly at Swami-ji.

"Of course he will." Gaur smiled again. Swami-ji could have killed him at that moment. He would have done it, but he realized how futile the gesture would be, and it would leave him with the bad *karma* of murder.

"I have to go now, Lew," Swami-ji said. "I know you understand. It's not so difficult if you just clear your mind. Follow me. I can't make you do it. You have got to choose. Choose life." Swami-ji turned and walked away.

Lew felt words forming on his lips. He opened his mouth

THE GAIA WAR   221

to speak, to say that yes, he *would* follow, but the words died on his lips, the memories of awesome bliss killed them and he could only think of returning to touch the source one more time.

"Go get some water," Gaur commanded. He handed Lew a rusty bucket and pointed to the polluted well. Lew felt his body obey. Gaur was rightful guardian of the power that kept them both there. And as slave to that power Lew was also slave to Gaur.

Lal-ji gave Swami-ji an inquisitive look when the guru returned alone. But Swami-ji was very quiet. "Go!" was the only word he spoke.

Lal-ji was eager to comply with the command. He knew, from his years of working the river, all the stories about the desolate other shore. He didn't know what to believe and what to dismiss as crazy talk, but if there were an ancient curse, he wanted no part of it.

Over the course of a few days Miranda came to understand that she was in a Calcutta slum. The family that had taken her in belonged to a group of untouchables. The only work available to them was "street sweeping." This meant collecting and disposing of the worst filth in the surrounding neighborhoods. It was Hinduism that had imposed such degradation upon them, but even so, all the family members were devout practitioners of that faith.

This was especially true of the father, Pandra-Lal, whom the boys affectionately called "Baba-ji." Pandra-Lal insisted that Miranda get the biggest portion of rice and lentils at each meal. This made her extremely uncomfortable since there wasn't enough to feed the family of four as it was. The little boy, Krishna, was clearly suffering from malnutrition. His hair, which should have been black, was a curious dirty blond, the result of vitamin deficiency.

Her skin color made her an object of near reverence. Miranda inadvertently reinforced the belief that she was a goddess by her speech. She knew Sanskrit quite well. Most of the languages of northern India, including Bengali, are derived from Sanskrit. Even untouchable families like Pandra-Lal's know some Sanskrit from the sacred texts. Sanskrit is still the ritual language of Hinduism.

So when Miranda began using her Sanskrit as a means to learn Bengali it made quite an impression. It was that, more than her skin color, that convinced the father there was something auspicious, if not clearly divine, about this mysterious woman.

Her sunbathing added to this aura of mystery. Indians, both Hindu and Moslem, are very modest, especially when it comes to female skin. Miranda had discarded the uncomfortable jeans and flannel in favor of a threadbare Punjabi suit of *pajama* pants and tunic top. The outfit was a gift from Pandra-Lal's wife, Jyoti. Miranda accepted only out of necessity. Her American clothes were insufferable in the sweltering monsoon heat. The suit, threadbare as it was, represented the best from Jyoti's wardrobe.

Miranda would steal time on the beach in the early morning, before most people were up and about. There she would unbutton the tunic top and expose as much bare skin as possible. Inevitably she was noticed, and it created a minor scandal in the little sweeper colony. Still she was not able to expose nearly as much of the surface area of skin as she would have liked. Consequently, her recovery was slow.

Since her encounter with Lew and the beginning of her physical transformation, Miranda's appetite had all but vanished. But in the little slum hut of Pandra-Lal and family it was returning with a vengeance. Their meals consisted of *chapati* bread in the morning with tea, more chapatis with a small portion of lentil stew for lunch, and a dinner of rice, lentils, *chapatis*, and, if they were lucky, a few scrawny carrots or some other emaciated vegetable. Although it made her ashamed, she could not refuse the big portions they always gave her. The cavern in her stomach was growing into an abyss that beckoned with gnawing insistence.

It was primarily this that forced her to strike out for Benares while she was still quite weak. She knew the reason for the new hunger. Her body was beginning the final phase of her metamorphosis, and this required a temporary, but large, intake of additional protein.

THE GAIA WAR 223

She was talking to Krishna after dinner. The little boy was daily growing more fond of her, too fond, she thought. She had been with them a short time, but her Bengali was already good enough to converse quite freely with the boy. "I must go away tomorrow," she said. Only the very young can show their changing emotions so swiftly and completely, she thought as she watched his face go suddenly dark. There was so much she did not want to see there. Her presence had been a source of light and hope for him, and even Krishna, young as he was, was beginning to understand that there was not much of either in the cards for a street sweeper in Calcutta.

"Where are you going, *Devti*?" he said, moist eyes shining in the flickering candlelight.

"Varanasi," she said, using the older name for Benares.

"Kashi!" the boy said with excitement using the mythical folk name. "The City of Light! Oh, *Devti*!" The boy's visions of the sacred city, a place he could only dream of seeing, temporarily replaced his sadness. "Take me with you!"

It broke her heart to say, "I'm sorry, Krishna, but it isn't possible."

They sat in silence for a few moments; the little boy's head was bowed. Then he got up to go. As he turned Miranda noticed something on the boy's bare back. "Wait, Krishna," she said and picked up the candle. She held it close to his dark skin and confirmed her worst fears. Miranda had been born with prodigious mental powers and a superhuman predilection for learning. Her powers of observation were also quite keen. So it was that she was able, with a sinking feeling, to absolutely identify the telltale lesion on the boy's back. There was no mistaking. Krishna was in the primary stages of leprosy.

It was impossible to spend any time in India and not see it. In her few days among the untouchables Miranda had seen cases in all stages of development. Before Krishna was a grown man he would be lucky to have any fingers left, and his nose would likely be flat and sinking farther into the wasted features of his face. Unless he got treatment, and it was certain that if he remained where he was he would not.

So she spoke before she had time to reflect or change her mind. "Yes, Krishna, you will come with me. Together we will make *puja* on the bank of the sacred river in the City of Light."

It was not hard to persuade Jyoti and Pandra-Lal. It wasn't that they did not love their child. It was harsh reality. The parents knew what sort of life awaited little Krishna. They also knew that he was not growing properly because they could not provide enough food. And, while Miranda remained a mystery to them, they had come to trust her.

Miranda did not tell them about the leprosy. They wouldn't understand and would probably assume it was some sort of *karmic* retribution and blame themselves. As far as she could tell none of the other family members were infected.

"You must take this, *Devti*." Jyoti was holding up her best sari. It was pure white.

"No, no . . ." Miranda said.

"You must wear it. Then you can get safe passage. You are a holy woman so you must dress like one," Jyoti insisted, and won in the end when she finally made Miranda understand that Krishna would be safer in her custody if she adopted the guise of a female *sadhu*.

The Calcutta train station was a swarming mass of humanity. It was a chaos and confluence of life on a scale that defied belief. And yet it was real. Miranda and the family made their way through it, one tiny, moving nexus in a huge network.

How they found the train or knew it was the right one was a complete mystery to Miranda. "Yes! No problem. This is Kashi express," Pandra-Lal insisted with such force that Miranda had to nod assent. She carried a bundle of *chapatis* wrapped in cotton, their only luggage. Little Krishna, too wide-eyed to speak, was dressed in his best *coorta* and *pajamas*.

They found the third-class ladies coach. They had no ticket and Miranda was loath to do what she had to do but

THE GAIA WAR 225

Jyoti insisted so she began chanting as they approached the car, "*Ram ka nam, Sat heh!* (God's name is truth!)"

At first the poor women in their brightly colored saris who were crowding into the car looked at Miranda with contempt. It was clear that they assumed she was just another freeloader, a poor woman trying to get a free ride by faking holy status. But when they got a better look at her some of the women began chattering among themselves.

Enough were convinced that the green-faced woman in the white sari was the real thing. Even so they wouldn't make room in the car for her. Instead they helped her climb up to the roof. Jyoti and Pandra-Lal tearfully lifted little Krishna up to her. As the train pulled away, all five of them knew it might be the last Krishna ever saw of his parents or his older brother.

The morning was dark, threatening a monsoon downpour. The train slowly picked up speed as it rumbled and creaked its way through the teeming, seemingly endless coalescence of humanity that was Calcutta. A few raindrops began to fall when they reached open country.

The landscape was flat and green. They were speeding across the Gangetic plains of northern India. Miranda was fascinated by what she saw, women in brightly colored saris carrying large volumes of water in big brass jugs balanced precariously on their heads, men herding water buffalo. These were scenes that had gone essentially unchanged for thousands of years.

The sky got darker and the sprinkle of water turned into a downpour. The women atop the train huddled closer together. "Eat." Krishna had unwrapped the bundle and held a *chapati* up. Miranda took it gratefully.

One of the women noticed how quickly Miranda devoured her snack. She offered a *dosa*. Miranda wanted to refuse, but her belly won out. It was all she could do to keep herself from snatching the thin pancake from the woman's hand.

Another woman began singing a *raga*. The voice blended perfectly with the falling rain and the rhythm of the train. Suddenly Miranda was the center of attention atop the coach. Women began passing *chapatis*, rice, *dosas*, and exotic curries in her direction. Miranda, deeply embarrassed, had no trouble devouring everything that was offered. Her prodigious appetite served to confirm her status as a holy woman or a *devti*. There was a sacred yet natural and spontaneous atmosphere atop the car. The haunting *raga* rose and fell, the ancient landscape rolled by, and the food flowed in from all directions to where Miranda and Krishna sat.

It was over in less than an hour. The morning downpour stopped and the sky cleared. The Indian sun turned the countryside into a steam bath. The woman's singing faded into silence, and Miranda's appetite was finally satiated, her belly noticeably distended underneath her sari.

Now she craved sun. The changes taking place in her body demanded solar energy in order to process the superhuman amount of food she had just consumed. A few of the women had bare breasts poking out from underneath their saris. Miranda had noticed that this radical departure from normal Indian modesty was curiously tolerated in the lower castes. Slowly she loosened the wrap that held the top of her sari in place and removed the blouse underneath. A green breast sucked hungrily at the sunlight.

The force of feeling from this was too much. Unable to restrain herself she unwound the sari, pulled it away from her skin and wadded it up to use as a pillow. She stretched out, luxuriously naked, in the sun.

A group of women quickly surrounded little Krishna and turned him away from the scene. Aside from this action which greatly frustrated Krishna (he was as curious as any nine-year-old boy about the mysteries of the female body), the women were quite tolerant of this eccentricity. They marveled at Miranda's green skin, which glowed more deeply from the solar radiance.

She sunbathed into the afternoon, until the clouds began to gather again. Euphoric and greatly rejuvenated, she rewrapped her sari and sat up in the gathering gloom. Some of the women began talking with her. She spent the rest of the afternoon in animated conversation under a light monsoon rain.

By evening they were all hungry. There was not much

THE GAIA WAR 227

food left. The women wanted to give it all to Miranda but she insisted that they divide the portions equally and felt quite guilty about that. Then they settled in for the long night's fast into Benares, called Varanasi, known as Kashi, the City of Light.

CHAPTER 16

Fields was flying low. He had taken off in the evening from his private airstrip on his ranch outside of Taos. He hoped the little Cessna would not attract attention, but was taking every possible precaution.

He was in a reflective mood as he sped south. To his right were the beginnings of a spectacular sunset of the type one only sees in the great Southwestern desert. His rise from student activist at Berkeley to a cabinet position seemed as improbable to him as ever. Fortunately for his political career, he had never been publicly linked to drug use or subversive activity. To anyone who knew him in the sixties this was a minor miracle.

Fields considered himself a patriotic, loyal American. But his vision of America was quite different from the conventional one. He saw the American dream not in terms of upward mobility, but as an ideal of harmony, an ethnically diverse country with an advanced technology that lived in peaceful balance with the natural world.

Of course this America did not exist—yet. Fields believed that it could. All that was lacking was the right sort of leadership. The president, his friend since college, was the closest thing to that sort of leader to attain the country's highest office in Fields's lifetime. But the president was far from the ideal. Political expediency saw to that.

Fields knew that what he was about to do would prob-

THE GAIA WAR

ably cost him his office and any future in national politics. This greatly disturbed him. But he felt a higher calling. He had to see for himself if the *Genesis Bomb* was the thing for which he had long hoped, a radical new way to the future. He saw a future for mankind that embraced the stars but was firmly grounded in the biosphere of mother earth. There was no reason, in Fields's opinion, why technology had to be incompatible with environmentalism. All that was needed was the vision to forge a new technology.

The old technology interrupted his musings. His radio crackled and buzzed. "You are entering a no-fly zone. Please alter your course ten miles south southeast. If you require assistance, please advise."

"A no-fly zone," Fields said to himself. "Imagine that. Right here in the good old US of A." He pushed the throttle, increasing his speed. The little craft responded with a shudder and a whine. He knew he was no match for the military craft in the area—his only hope was that they had no authorization to fire.

The warnings became more ominous. An F-16 buzzed him close enough to catch him in its wake and nearly throw him into a tailspin. He recovered and resumed his course.

"What!" Carp, informed of the intruder, was speaking to an air force major.

"What are our orders, sir?" the major said. "Do we have authorization to use force?"

"Have you been able to identify the craft?" Carp said. "Registration? Local flight plans filed? Who is flying the damn thing?" Carp thought he knew the answer. He hoped he was wrong. If the craft could be positively identified as not belonging to the secretary of the interior, they could destroy it and cover the whole thing up, make it look like an unfortunate accident or even a crash in which the military had no direct involvement. But that would be difficult if the pilot turned out to be a fellow cabinet officer.

"No, sir. All we know is that the craft is a single engine Cessna."

Carp was furious. If he took action, it would surely jeopardize his delicate plans. He needed a few more days in which to prepare. He could not afford a new blitz of media

230 Mark Leon

attention on the role of the military in the containment of the *Genesis Bomb*. "Can you disable the craft?" Carp asked. "Just damage it enough to force an emergency landing?"

"Possibly sir," the major said. "But we could easily destroy it in the attempt."

"Just a crippling shot to the rudder or something?" Carp said.

"Those little civilian planes are fragile," the major said. "And our ordnance is not really designed to maim. Its purpose is to kill. We are, after all, the military."

"And I am the secretary of defense!" Carp said, instantly regretting the momentary loss of temper. He knew how precarious a thing real authority is. An angry, overt declaration of authority usually conveys weakness or fear. Weakness and fear are the enemies of power, and Carp prized power above all else.

"Yes, sir," the major said in a carefully controlled, neutral voice.

"Force that plane down," Carp said, "but don't destroy it. Do not use lethal force."

"It could be risky, sir," the major said. "I can't guarantee . . ."

"I heard you the first time," Carp said. "However, I have confidence in your talents. They will not go unrewarded, either. I'll owe you one. I won't forget. Is that clear?"

"Yes, sir."

Fields could see the spectacular jungle. He was stunned. "I had no idea," he said, "so beautiful . . ." He made preparations. He set the automatic pilot for a gradual descent that would crash-land the plane in an uninhabited area of desert on the missile range. Then he strapped on the parachute. Fields had never jumped out of an airplane, but his rapid research into the subject (reading of a recent article in *Skydiver* magazine and conversation with the pro who had rented him the equipment) assured him that there was nothing to it. Nothing except the primal terror of falling that was beginning to surge through him like an electric charge.

THE GAIA WAR 231

As he got closer he saw that fear would not be the only obstacle to success. The dome had grown so that the outward convexity was clearly evident. There was still a large open radius above the area, but Fields realized he would have to do more than merely jump—he would have to jump with some accuracy and control. Otherwise, he would go bouncing off the side of the organic polymer barrier, his political career would be over, and he would have accomplished nothing.

And there was another factor with which to contend. The fighter was getting more aggressive, both in word and deed. "You have thirty seconds to reverse course and land before we open fire. Please acknowledge!" The jet flanked him so closely that Fields could see the pilot, who could clearly see him. The fighter pilot was gesturing with his hand. The signal was impossible to misunderstand, around and down it said.

Fields took a deep breath and turned his attention again toward the goal. *Just a few more seconds*, he thought.

He simultaneously felt and heard the explosion as the missile ripped through his tail. A moment later he lost all control. Had he been able to look he would have seen that his entire tail section was blown away. He was falling into a spin from which he would not be able to recover.

"Damn!" the pilot said.

"What's wrong?" the major said.

"We blew his tail completely off, sir," the pilot said. "He's going to crash."

"We! What the fuck is this *we*!" the major screamed. "This is on your head, Captain!"

"Yes, sir." The pilot fought against the despair that threatened to engulf him as he helplessly watched the Cessna's spiraling descent. He could not shake the conviction that he was also watching his future in the air force.

Fields had no choice. He flung the door open and jumped. He pulled the cord after he was sure he was clear of the plane. Suddenly all was very peaceful and quiet. The chute was carrying him in a delicious glide toward his target. Fields was ecstatic. All his racing, surging fear was miraculously transformed into a quiet excitement, a keen

232   **Mark Leon**

thrill. He relaxed into it and watched the beautiful foliage grow in size beneath his gaze.

The fighter pilot watched the top of Field's rainbow-colored parachute. *My career is fucked anyway*, he thought, *why not have a little fun*? He swooped down and took aim at Fields.

Fields, oblivious to the new danger from above, realized that if he did not adjust course, he was going to miss his target. The glide of the chute was taking him toward the edge of the opening. He struggled with the guidelines and only succeeded in making matters worse. He was now less than thirty yards above the jungle. He could smell it, the exotic, intoxicating aromas of new life, so close yet so far. There was only one chance left for him. If he were ever going to get in, he had to act immediately.

The pilot, venting the frustrated ambitions of a lifetime and relishing the target practice, fired. It was a direct hit. The pilot smiled and executed a steep climb. Nothing like a real kill to get the juices going.

He never knew that even though his aim had been deadly accurate, all he had destroyed were some dangling nylon cords and straps. Fields, desperate to see the new earthly paradise, had bailed out yet again and was falling, for the moment unhurt, toward the riot of life below.

When Carp heard the news his first impulse was to have both the major and the pilot detained in maximum security, but when he cooled down he realized that the situation might not be the disaster he had supposed. He dispatched an army intelligence unit to the plane wreckage. From this he got confirmation that the Cessna had indeed belonged to the secretary of the interior. Certainly, under normal circumstances, a full-scale investigation would be inevitable, and Carp's role as assassin of a fellow cabinet officer would eventually come to light. But, Carp reflected, circumstances were far from ordinary. With a little luck he could still keep things under wraps for a few more days. After that this little incident could easily get lost in the tidal wave of larger events that was sure to come. And in the meantime, Don Fields, a potential irritant to Carp's plans, was out of commission. By midnight, still at work in his office, Carp ac-

THE GAIA WAR 233

tually allowed a tight smile to steal momentarily across his face.

On the other side of the world it was high noon. "It's pretty quiet out there," Skinner said. "There isn't much news from White Sands these days. Or is it just the fickle media, tired already of the story and searching for some other banal novelty."

"I'm not surprised," Swami-ji said. "The *Genesis Bomb* operates on its own schedule. I knew it would not be what we supposed."

"What is it then?" Skinner tried, with limited success, to keep the sarcasm down.

"It is probably the next step in cosmic evolution," Swami-ji said. The monsoon clouds had blown away early and the sun shimmered on the sacred waters outside the temple.

"If it is this *next step*, why aren't we all on the bandwagon?" Skinner said. "I mean, here we are in India, where things *never change* for God's sake!"

"What makes you think you understand India?" Swami-ji said. "Your arrogance, Larry, is starting to irritate me."

"I'm honored," Skinner said. "To irritate your sublimeness is no small feat."

"Aren't you at all concerned about Lew?" Swami-ji said.

"I confess that I feel some distress at Lew's predicament," Skinner said. "All the more because his actions were so predictable. Lew is a dreamer. He's not stupid, you know."

"I know that perhaps more than you," Swami-ji said.

Skinner, ignoring this mild rebuke, continued. "He is not stupid, he just lacks . . . well, *discrimination*, for want of a better term."

"So do we all. And all of us are dreamers." It was Miranda. She stood in the doorway, sun lighting up her hair. That, plus her white sari, gave her the appearance of an *arhant* or saint. She held Krishna's hand and two of her Bengali women acquaintances stood behind her as if in attendance.

234   Mark Leon

"Well, well . . ." Skinner was very nervous. "So we meet again, Gai . . ."

"Miranda," Miranda said, coolly meeting Skinner's eyes.

"Oh yes," Skinner said. "Lew told me. *Brave New World* and all that sort of thing, right? One can hardly keep up with all your fanciful changes." Skinner looked at her more closely, studying her green skin. "And, I should add, your *metamorphoses*. You should be a big hit here in India. Blue skin is really the ticket, but a nice deep green like yours is good enough I should think—almost a *teal* really. It becomes you."

"You tried to kill me," Miranda said.

"Poor judgment on my part," Skinner said. "Perhaps you are right, and we all suffer from lack of discrimination. Surely you can't hold something like that against me. Natural human weakness, I mean."

"There are ordinary human failings," Miranda said, "and then there are things like murder. These Bengali women would kill you if they knew what you tried to do. Fortunately for you their English is not very good."

Skinner's nervousness turned to fear. Miranda watched with pleasure, noting the clammy hands and pale face.

Swami-ji intervened, saying smoothly, "How about some tea?"

"I admit that I was wrong," Skinner said. They all were comfortably seated on the floor and sipping hot, spiced Indian tea. "My time here in India has broadened my view. Swami-ji has been particularly enlightening. You see we all had our preconceived notions about what the *Genesis Bomb* is, or should be: Alan with his misguided environmentalism, Swami-ji and his Hindu cosmology . . ."

"And you?" Miranda said pointedly.

"Ah me," Skinner said. "Yes, poor me. A mere corporate serf. But my ideas weren't lacking for vision. No, I dreamed of a new world order. I saw you and the *Genesis Bomb* as things that stood in my way. Very self-centered. Childish really. I see my mistake now. But Gai—I mean Miranda, you really must admit that you yourself were blinded by dreams and visions."

THE GAIA WAR 235

"I haven't got time for such things," Miranda said. "Reality is enough for me."

"It wasn't enough for Lew," Swami-ji said. He explained Lew's predicament to Miranda.

"I was afraid something like that might happen," Miranda said. "That's why I came. I want to help Lew before—" She stopped herself abruptly.

Skinner, sensing that there was something she did not want to reveal, pressed her. "Before what?"

"Nothing," she said.

"I think we could all benefit from a free and frank exchange of information," Skinner said, trying to keep the anger out of his voice.

Miranda ignored him. She turned to Swami-ji and said, "Can you help my little friend here?" She gestured to the wide-eyed little Krishna, who was very much enjoying his tea.

"He says you are *Devti*," Swami-ji said to Miranda after conversing briefly with Krishna in fluent Bengali.

"That's not my doing," Miranda said. "But there isn't much I can do about it. Anyway, it doesn't matter. What does matter is this." She asked Krishna to take his shirt off and he eagerly obliged. Then she had Swami-ji examine the tiny lesions on the boy's back.

"There's no mistake about the diagnosis," Swami-ji said to Miranda. "Fortunately the disease is not far advanced. It is very treatable. The chances for a cure are excellent. But it will take time. He will have to stay in Benares for a year or more. The drugs are expensive, but money is no problem. The problem is the boy himself. What will I do with him? What will he do with himself, so far away from home and family?"

Miranda was clearly disappointed.

"I'll see what I can do," Swami-ji said. "But right now I can promise you nothing. Does he know?"

"No."

"Do his parents know?" Swami-ji said.

"No."

"Good. We may have to send him back to Calcutta, and

236 Mark Leon

if we do, it's best that no one know. Of course, in time they will learn.''

"How *can* you . . .'' Miranda began angrily.

"Don't be so quick to judge!'' Swami-ji interrupted. *"I'll see what I can do.* But before you become righteously indignant remind yourself of where you are. There are millions more like this poor boy, worse really. We cannot take care of them all. And if not all, why *this particular one*?''

"Because I know him,'' Miranda said. "There may be millions. That's the tragic truth of your country. But Krishna is still who he is, and I have decided to help him. That's enough.''

"Well spoken,'' Swami-ji said. "I'll make some inquiries on his behalf tomorrow.''

"Such a lot of fuss over another little leper boy,'' Skinner said, clearly enjoying the angry flash this sparked in Miranda's eyes. "But shouldn't we be talking about more important matters?''

"Larry is right, Miranda. Leave Krishna to me. For the time being he can stay here. I'll put him to work in the temple. But tell me, why did you come after Lew?''

"It's a private matter between Lew and me,'' Miranda said. "It doesn't matter anyway. What matters is setting him free.''

Skinner laughed. "What's so funny?'' Miranda said.

"Sorry,'' Skinner said. "You may be able to get Lew away from that fakir, but setting him free . . . well, that's another matter.''

"As it is for all of us,'' Swami-ji said. "It's going to be difficult. Gaur, the fakir who has Lew in thrall, has acquired much power, *siddhi* as we call it. Lew's will is now grafted to the force emanating from the petrified tree stump and to Gaur. But there is one thing we may try. With your help it might work.''

Miranda listened intently as Swami-ji told her his plan.

Later that evening Swami-ji and Miranda were dining at the Varanasi hotel. Skinner had gone off on mysterious business of his own. "I like to come here every once in a while. As pretentious as it is, the food is pretty good and

THE GAIA WAR 237

one is temporarily shielded from harsher realities.''

"Yes." Miranda found the air-conditioned comfort, wood-paneled walls, and beautiful silk tapestries an absurd contrast to the India outside.

"I can't quite believe you are real," Swami-ji said.

"What, or should I say *who*, is really real?" Miranda said.

"Don't get me started," Swami-ji said. "I'm an Indian guru remember, a natural-born philosopher. But you know what I mean. This all started so long ago, when Alan was my student. I immediately recognized him as an extraordinary talent. His grasp of science, especially biology, was so precocious. That, together with his ability to absorb the more esoteric teachings of the East . . . well, he was truly one in a million. But I never dreamed . . ." Swami-ji paused to sip his beer, getting some foam on his upper lip.

"Never dreamed what?" Miranda said, a mischievous gleam in her eyes.

"That he could create something as lovely as you," Swami-ji said. He stared silently at her for a moment. The spell was broken by the arrival of their food, chicken tandoori for him, Kashmiri lamb for her.

Miranda was ravenously hungry for meat. It was all she could do to restrain herself and eat with some pretense of civility. Her body told her to devour the entire meal with hands and mouth working as fast as possible. She managed a good show of table manners.

But Swami-ji saw through it all. "Like another?" he said when she was finished and he was still slowly working at his chicken.

"Afraid so." She smiled. "My body has been going through some rapid changes ever since . . ."

"Ever since what?" he asked.

"Well that is one of the reasons I'm concerned about Lew. We have kind of a special relationship. He is the father to my child."

"Your child?" Swami-ji was genuinely surprised, a rare event for the old guru.

"Who is me," she said. "I am mother to myself. I may look like an ordinary woman but . . ."

238 Mark Leon

"You don't look that ordinary. Haven't you noticed the stares your green skin attracts? No wonder the little boy and those Bengali women mistake you for a Hindu goddess." Swami-ji flagged a waiter and ordered a second course for Miranda.

"Yes, yes, I know." She sounded impatient. "These physical changes are the result of my *encounter* with Lew. I think this could be the future for the human race if you don't destroy this planet first. Evolution is naturally tending toward a time when your women will become pregnant with themselves and evolve into something like what I am becoming."

"And what is that?" Swami-ji said. He was very excited and trying hard not to show it.

"I'm not sure yet," she said. "But I am now able to get energy directly from the sun. The green in my skin is an advanced type of chlorophyll, more efficient than the ordinary kind found in plants. The reason I need to eat is that the changes in my body are not complete. Right now I need large quantities of protein. I think my entire vascular system is being restructured."

"To what end?" he asked, anticipating the answer.

"Well I am not sure really—" she began.

"Come on," Swami-ji interrupted. "We both know that you *know* where your future lies."

"Yes, I know," she said. Her food arrived, and she managed to eat more slowly.

"But as I was saying, I still can't believe that Alan . . ."

"You think that's what I am? A creation of Alan Fain's and nothing more!" Miranda interrupted.

"No, of course not, I only meant . . ."

"That's what your friend Larry Skinner thinks," she said, "that I'm like Pandora, an artificial woman, a creature who brings evil into the world. But he is full of shit and you know it." She was eating more rapidly now, her sudden anger stimulating her appetite.

"Take it easy," Swami-ji said. "First of all, Larry is not exactly my friend. I am hoping to educate him, maybe even change him a little. I also never meant to imply that you were a mere creation of Alan's, certainly not a bringer of

THE GAIA WAR   239

evil. But you must admit that your story is quite interesting. Most would not believe it.''

"You had some hand in all of this, didn't you?'' she said.

"Yes, I did,'' he said. "I hoped that Alan's little experiment, which includes you, would help to usher in the New Age and bring an end to this long era of darkness for mankind.''

"And now?'' she said.

"And now I don't know anymore. I see that I was a fool to think that I knew what I was doing. But isn't that always the case with us mortals?''

"I wouldn't know,'' Miranda said, without any trace of vanity or sarcasm.

"What's going to happen out there in the desert?'' Swami-ji said. He ordered another plate for Miranda.

"I don't know the answer to that either,'' she said.

"It's not going to take over the world, transform the planet into an earthly paradise?'' he said.

"I don't think so. It could, if that were what you wanted . . . but I don't think you're ready for paradise just yet. Which brings up a rather more immediate concern. Don't you feel somewhat responsible for what has happened to Lew? After all, you are the one who filled his head with all that nonsense about Benares being the site of the original Garden of Eden.'' Another plate of spicy lamb stew arrived. The waiter watched with unabashed wonder as Miranda tore into it with gusto.

"What makes you think it's nonsense?'' Swami-ji said.

"Oh come on, Mr. *guru man*,'' she said irritably.

"OK, you win,'' he said. "I guess I just got carried away. I didn't know Lew would be so gullible.''

"He isn't gullible,'' she said. "There's a naïveté about Lew that's easy to miss. It's what gives him his charm— and his vulnerability.''

"Alan would have never fallen for it,'' Swami-ji said. "But, as I said, he's unique.''

"I just hope your plan works,'' Miranda said, finally feeling almost satiated.

"It's our only hope,'' Swami-ji said. "The only way to

free a soul trapped in a false paradise is to tempt it away with another one.''

''What makes you think our bait is not the genuine article, the real thing?'' Miranda said.

Swami-ji was, for the first time in a long time, speechless. He just looked and felt a flowing, falling sensation as if he was being poured out of a pitcher into the depths of her eyes.

CHAPTER 17

It was 103 degrees when Meagan rolled into El Paso. The first thing she did was exit the expressway and pull into a Quickie Z convenience store, where she bought a Super Summer—Thirst Buster. This consisted of a full thirty-two ounces of a carbonated, artificial cherry-lime drink. She made short work of it.

"Do you have a phone book?" Meagan asked the clerk. She quickly consulted the volume that the young man slid across the counter and found what she wanted. "Thanks," she said.

She drove Miller's truck to the downtown area and parked in front of an old abandoned warehouse. She walked several blocks and realized that she was not going to find a cab to flag down. Finally she called one from a popular lunch spot.

"Where you going?" the driver said in slow, Texas tones. Meagan gave him the address. "Nice neighborhood," the driver said.

"Really?" Meagan said. This surprised her. She did not expect the church of the Loyal Army of God to be particularly upscale.

It wasn't. The driver had been right. They were in an affluent part of town, but the church was in a small strip mall. There was absolutely nothing impressive or aesthetic about it. Meagan paid the driver and included a big enough

242 Mark Leon

tip to make him grin. "Have a nice day!" He said it like he really meant it before he drove away.

Meagan walked in. "Good afternoon," an attractive Hispanic woman said, "and praise God."

"Praise God," Meagan responded, disappointed in the lackluster way she said it.

"How can we help you?" the woman said.

"I need to see the pastor," Meagan said.

"Are you a member of the church?"

"No . . . not this one anyway. I do belong to the Army of God . . . someplace else." Suddenly it *all* seemed like someplace else to Meagan, and she felt very far from anywhere.

The woman eyed her curiously. "My name is Lisa," she said.

"I'm Meagan."

"You look tired, Meagan."

"I'm very tired," Meagan said.

"Come with me then." Lisa led Meagan to a small office down a narrow corridor. There appeared to be no windows in the building, so it surprised Meagan to see an apparently healthy plant on the desk inside the office. "Please have a seat." Meagan sat down in a plastic chair in front of the desk. But as soon as Lisa made her exit Meagan got up and examined the plant. It was real.

Meagan was surprised at the appearance of the man who entered a few minutes later. He was tall, dark-haired, and good-looking. His age was of that range that Meagan would decribe as "older." But the most surprising thing about him was his suit. He was lean and wore a blue suit that was neither ill fitting nor overly ostentatious, which is what Meagan had come to expect of the male clergy in her denomination. Actually Meagan's church body insisted that they were "nondenominational," but the distinction was lost on her. Whatever they were, they had a certain look, and this man didn't fit it.

"Meagan?" the man said, extending his hand.

"Yes, I'm Meagan," she said, taking his hand.

"I'm Pastor Flynt, but you can call me Bob. I hate for-

THE GAIA WAR 243

malities. Please sit back down. Can I get you anything? Something to drink?''

"Something cold would be nice," Meagan said.

"Real brain-fryer out there, huh?" Flynt said.

"It sure is," Meagan said. Flynt left and came back with two large glasses. They were filled with iced drinks of an opaque, light brown color, obviously *not* ice tea, the standard refreshment in those parts.

"I hope you like espresso," Flynt said. "These are iced, double machiatos.''

"What?" Meagan said.

"Machiato. Coffee espressos with a dash of steamed milk froth. On ice of course.''

This was yet another surprise. Meagan took a sip. The coffee was delicious, a far cry from the ordinary, foul church brew.

Flynt sat down behind his desk and took a sip. "Ah, now that's the ticket." He sighed. Then he put his feet up on the desk. "Lisa tells me you are of our fold, so to speak." Flynt said this with more than a trace of irony.

"That's right.''

"What brings you to El Paso?"

"That's kind of a long story," Meagan said.

"Really?" One of Flynt's eybrows went up as if to say that he hoped it wasn't too long.

"You know about the *Genesis Bomb*?" Meagan said.

"Who doesn't?" Flynt said. "Funny business.''

"Do you believe in God, Pastor Flynt?" Meagan said passionately.

This caught the man completely off guard. He stammered and stuttered before he could answer, and when he did he was aware of his own singular lack of passion. "Of course," he said.

"I'm not sure I believe you," Meagan said, not quite believing her own words. She took a deep breath and then a long, slow drink from her iced coffee. The oxygen and caffeine gave her confidence. "But I have to trust someone. I have to tell someone or . . . or I don't know what. Listen to me Bob Flynt and I will tell you a story about miracles, angels, and possibly the Mother of God. I really don't know

244   Mark Leon

what to believe anymore, but I can tell you one thing. These are strange times we are living in. Strange times indeed.''

She knew she had him hooked when she began to exlain her part in seeding White Sands with the protean virus. His eyes got wider and, whether he believed her or not, he was utterly fascinated.

"So you see, Pastor,'' she said, having finally explained how she left an FBI agent handcuffed to his car in the Chisos Mountains, ''I need help.''

"Are you familiar with Genesis?'' Flynt said, after a short pause. "The Biblical account, I mean.''

"More or less,'' Meagan said, realizing it had been a long time since she had read any of that book.

Flynt's coffee glass was empty. "Care for another?'' He stood up.

Delicious though it was, Meagan was substantially charged from the stuff so she said, "Just a glass of cold water, please.''

Meagan hoped she had not made a mistake by confiding in a stranger. It seemed to her that Flynt was taking too long in fetching the drinks, and her imagination was fired with images of the pastor returning with police officers or FBI agents. She stood up on the verge of panic, ready to bolt for the exit and run for dear life in the blistering summer heat.

But Flynt returned with another iced double and a glass of water. "Please,'' he said, "sit back down. Relax. You're safe here. I can see you're exhausted. We have a place where you can sleep. But first I want to talk a little more, if that's OK.''

"Alright.'' Meagan collapsed back into her chair.

"I was talking about Genesis,'' Flynt said, sipping his drink. Meagan wondered if he drank those things all day long, and if so, how he managed to look so relaxed.

"Yes, Genesis,'' Meagan said.

"There is a little-discussed and obscure passage there, 'There were giants in the earth in those days; and also after that, when the sons of God came unto the daughters of men, and they bare *children* to them, the same, *became* mighty

THE GAIA WAR 245

men which *were* of old, men of reknown.' Genesis: chapter six, verse four.

"Anyway what is the deal about those *giants*." Flynt leaned back in his chair and took a big gulp. "Man that's good stuff!" He held the glass up to the fluorescent light buzzing overhead. Then he leaned forward, set the glass down on his desk, fixed Meagan with an intense stare, and resumed, "Those *giants*, though, that's what I want to know about."

"Why?" Meagan was bewildered.

"You think I'm nuts, or something," he said. "Right?"

"Well . . ." she began.

"You think I'm nuts after the story you just told me. Now that's really a laugh!"

Meagan lowered her head and blushed.

"But it's OK," Flynt said. "We're all in this together, and we're certainly all a little crazy. Maybe a lot crazy. The trick is to be crazy in the right way."

"Which way is that?" Meagan said.

"Why the way of the Lord, of course." Flynt smiled.

"Of course," Meagan said. She was starting to think that she had come to the right place after all.

"But who, or what, were those giants?" Flynt said.

"I don't know," Meagan said.

"Of course you don't. No one does. Not really. But there are theories, and I have mine!" He was now positively beaming, almost manic-looking, and Meagan thought that maybe he wasn't so calm and collected.

"You see," he continued, "this reference to giants occurs after the fall, after Adam and Eve ate of the forbidden fruit and were cast out of Paradise. The passage I quoted says that the sons of God and the daughters of men had children. Now I think these sons of God are the giants. They were not giants in stature or size. They were giants in that they were freaks of nature. Note the passage says they were 'sons' not 'Sons' of God. They were synthetic men, genetic experiments. God was fooling around with other humanoid creations in the garden. Adam and Eve were possibly the latest in a series of these experiments. They were the only *truly human* inhabitants.

"People have often asked, 'If Adam and Eve were the only people, how could they populate the earth without committing incest?' Well here is the answer. We, the descendants of Adam and Eve, are a hybrid race. Eve had daughters before she had Cain and Abel. These daughters and the giants gave rise to the hybrids, who are the progeny of humans breeding with humanoids.

"The giants were called giants in Genesis because many of them had special powers. Their DNA gave them extreme longevity, possibly unusual psychic abilities, and God knows what else. As I said, God was playing around. If things hadn't gone haywire with the Fall of Adam and Eve, these experiments might have been better managed, but you see what has happened."

"What?" Meagan said.

"All this." Flynt gestured to indicate the wide world. "A planet of lunatics who are bent on destroying the world. Our own church, the Loyal Army of God, in a *strip mall* for Christ sakes! The irony of it!"

Meagan was not sure see saw the irony but remained silent.

"You are probably wondering what my interpretation of an obscure passage in Genesis has to do with your story?" Flynt said, suddenly appearing calm and collected again.

"Well, yes actually I . . ." Meagan began.

"Don't get it," Flynt finished for her. "Well let me try to explain. If I'm right, there were, in ancient times, people who were not quite human. They were experiments, possibly test models for the real thing. Now this Miranda person whom you describe, she sounds like she may be one of those."

"One of the giants?" Meagan said, amazed.

"If you like," Flynt said. "Remember the giants were giant in ability and power, not size.

"But I told you," Meagan said, "Alan Fain grew Miranda in his basement. She is a new creation, not some relic from an ancient age."

"I didn't mean to imply that she was," Flynt said. "In fact this is what really intrigues me about your story. This

THE GAIA WAR   247

Alan person must have gained access to some very arcane knowledge and techniques.''

"I suppose that's possible," Meagan said. "I mean, he and his friend Lew talked about some really weird stuff that happened a few years ago. Alan claims to have gotten the catalyst or whatever it was that he needed to create Miranda from another dimension or something."[8]

"Yeah," Flynt said. "It all starts to make sense."

"Uh, one thing you didn't explain," Meagan said. "What's that?"

"If the daughters of Eve and the giants bred hybrids, part human, part humanoid, what happened to them?"

"To whom?" Flynt said.

"To the hybrids," Meagan said.

"I thought I made that clear," Flynt said. "We are the hybrids, Meagan. Ordinary people like you and me." He smiled.

"Really," Meagan said. "What does that mean?"

"It means that we never got to see what a pure race of truly human humans would have been like," Flynt said.

"But that's horrible," Meagan said.

"Horrible? I don't know about that. It has its down side I suppose. But God can make good out of evil, Meagan. Never forget that. Things didn't turn out exactly as planned, but that doesn't necesarily mean we are all doomed.''

"Pastor Fly—I mean, Bob," Meagan said, "are we living in the final days, the end times?"

"End times *schmend* times!" Flynt said. He polished off his iced coffee with a greedy gulp. "We are always near the end—and the beginning."

"The beginning? Beginning of what?" Meagan said.

"Who knows! Praise God and pass the ammunition!" Flynt was suddenly quite manic again. Meagan shifted uneasily in her seat. "Do you have a car?" Flynt asked.

"No I . . ."

"Oh that's right," he said, "that FBI agent might be able to trace it so you abandoned it. Never fear! I've got a

---

[8] *Mind-Surfer*.

248 **Mark Leon**

trusty chariot. A Suburban—for my money the best car ever made.''

Meagan just stared at him.

''You *will* come with me?'' Flynt's right eybrow arched high.

''Where?''

''North! To White Sands. To the *New Eden*, *Paradise reborn*! My God, sister, the opportunity of a lifetime. Let's take it, seize the moment!''

''It could be dangerous . . .'' Meagan began, but Flynt wasn't listening. He had already picked up the phone to call his wife and tell her he wouldn't be home for dinner.

Fields was certain he was falling to his death, and he was not thinking anything profound about his life. He was thinking about gravity, remembering his high school physics class, *This is no abstract equation, this is real force that's got me in its grip.* He closed his eyes as he crashed into the jungle foliage.

But instead of the ripping, tearing, and jabbing he expected, he felt a *concerted effort of vegetable intelligence striving to reverse the force of gravity with as much civility as possible.* At least that's how he described it afterward.

He came to rest about thirty feet off the ground in a bower of vines, flowers, and leaves. He lay there on his back for several minutes, willing his heart to slow down. When the adrenaline surge of fear had worked its way out of his system, he looked up. He was already so deep in the middle layers of jungle growth that most of the sky was hidden. But he could see a small patch of blue. There was neither sight nor sound of aircraft. After his ordeal the quiet was stunning. He opened himself to it. He was asleep within minutes.

He woke convinced that he was still dreaming. *How many times must I wake?* he asked himself. The reason for his confusion was the music. He was listening to his favorite jazz guitarist, Wes Montgomery. The music seemed to be all around him. He opened his eyes. The music did not stop. He put his hand up to his right ear and felt a small leaf there. It was vibrating. There was another at his left

THE GAIA WAR   249

ear. He carefully peeled the leaves back and sat up. The music stopped. The jungle had grown a set of earphones and piped in the most delicious jazz, just for him.

It frightened him, and he wanted to get down, out of the dense aerial growth. He began seaching for a way and felt his heart begin to throb again at the sight in front of him. It was nothing less than a staircase. The vines and leaves had rearranged and intertwined themselves so as to present him with a perfectly proportioned, velvety soft, spiral staircase all the way to the ground.

He tested it carefully before descending and still did not really trust the thing. But within seconds he set foot on the soft earth, partly covered by blue grass and delicate flowers.

"Welcome," a feminine voice said. She was standing right in front of him.

He hadn't seen her because she blended, chameleon-like, into the jungle background. When she stepped forward it looked to Fields as if she were stepping out of a living canvas to set herself off in more definite relief.

"I'm Raya," she said, offering her hand.

He took it and they shook. She carried her beautiful, naked, green body with an innocence and modesty that he found shocking. It set his mind racing, rethinking all he thought he knew and appreciated of the female form.

Finally he had the presence of mind to speak. "I'm Don Fields, secretary of the interior." The absurdity of this statement made him blush. He was convinced that she would laugh in his face.

But she did not laugh. "Since my early days," she said, "I have learned better the ways of men. So won't you join me for fruit and drink and whatever else I may have to offer that is pleasing to you."

Fields indulged himself in a moment of erotic fantasy, but when he looked into her eyes he saw that certain "pleasing" things were not included in this most generous invitation. She turned and began walking. He followed, unable to take his eyes off her body, which was more beautiful in motion. She moved with a supple grace that spoke its own language, and what it said hinted at mysteries and

250   **Mark Leon**

wonders that had always been before his eyes but somehow
never seen.

He had to force all this from his mind when they came
to her bower. It was a space enclosed on all sides by the
jungle growth. There was a small entrance and they both
had to duck.

It was cool inside and full of the sweetest, wildest smells
Fields had ever experienced. There was a table which appeared to be formed of a grassy mound in the middle of
the enclosure. On it were spread a great variety of fruits
that Fields had never seen. He could not even name the
colors, so original and strange were the hues.

She poured an opaque liquor into a hollow rind and
handed it to him. The taste was sharp but not sweet and,
at the same time, mellow, with a slight bitter tang. It was
marvelously refreshing. He started to drain the cup but was
held back by a sense of impropriety. This stuff was to be
savored, not gulped. As he was soon to learn, she had many
other drinks with flavors radically different yet equally
pleasing, and she helped him liberally to all she had.

"I was not a proper hostess with the other one," she said
after he had eaten and drunk his fill. He was so much in
awe of the fantastic tastes that had touched his palate that
he almost did not hear her. The food and drink, he decided,
was more than physically nourishing. It had also satisfied
a place in him long forgotten, something he would call
spiritual if he had to name it.

"What other one?" he asked when her words finally
sank in.

"The other man, one of your kind," she said.

"Who is that?" Fields asked anxiously.

"Alan," she said.

"What was he doing here?" Fields was surprised at the
sound of possessive jealousy in his voice. He had been
there only a short time, and already he was staking his
claim.

"I don't think he knew," she said.

"Where is he now?" Fields said.

"Gone."

"Gone. Where?"

THE GAIA WAR   251

"I haven't seen him for a while," she said, obviously bored.

Fields decided to change the subject. "You said he was one of *my kind*."

"Yes, he was."

"What kind is that?" Fields said. "I mean, how am I different from your kind."

"Ah, now that's an interesting topic," she said, brightening. "There was a book that grew here . . ."

"*Grew* here?" Fields said. He was starting to wonder about some of the drinks she had served. They were not alcoholic, but he felt a little strange, as if he were becoming aware of things in his immediate surroundings which he had never before noticed. But when he looked closely he saw only things exactly as they were. *That is it*, he thought, *things are becoming themselves to a degree unprecedented.* Unprecedented in his experience anyway.

"Yes," she said. "It was *The Book of the New Creation*."

"Did you drug me?" he asked, searching her face and seeing an enormous range of latent emotions and attitudes.

But what emerged out of all this possiblity when she answered him was so simple and transparent he had to believe it was the truth. "No, I didn't drug you. The nectars and liquors probably contain essential nutrients long absent from your diet. This would, perhaps, make you feel . . . *different*."

"Yes, I do feel different," he said. But he also realized that he felt perfectly lucid and in control of his faculties, so if he were drugged, it was not in the usual sense of the term. "This *Book of the New Creation* explains the difference between your species and mine?"

"I'm not sure the term 'species' is quite apt here," she said. "We are both humanoid. I am of an older type."

"Older?"

"Yes. At one time we existed in fairly large numbers, roaming your forests and jungles. Because of our unique abilities, we have been described variously as *fairy folk* or *giants*."

"I suppose my kind destroyed your kind," Fields said.

252 **Mark Leon**

"I can see why you might think so," she said. "You have a violent history. But that's not what happened."

"What happened?"

"Your race is a hybrid. The original humans bred with us, the *giants*, if you like. You are the result."

"But my race have none of your powers. You can fly?"

"Yes." She hovered a few feet above the grassy floor to demonstrate.

"Why can't we fly?" Fields said.

"I don't know precisely. For some reason those genes were repressed in the crossbreeding. Anyway, such things are latent in you."

"You mean we have the potential to fly?" Fields said.

"I think so. But I have no idea how you can activate those traits. Did you say you were a secretary?"

"No, I mean, yes, secretary of the *interior*," Fields said, emphasizing the importance of the title.

"Are you here on official business, *Mr. Secretary*?" It was Alan standing in the entrance to Raya's bower.

Fields turned around to look at him. Alan was again quite naked. They stared at each other for a while. "I thought you disappeared," Fields said softly. "Yes, now I remember. It was at least twenty-five years ago. You went off to India or something—one of those crazy quests for enlightenment that everybody was doing back then."

"As I recall you went on some pretty crazy trips of your own," Alan said drily.

"It *was* a long time ago, Alan," Fields said.

"Yeah, well it may interest you to know that my crazy trip to the East resulted in all this." Alan gestured to indicate their surroundings.

"*You* are responsible for this," Fields said.

"More or less. It's a long story. I won't bore you with the details. It involves an Indian guru, a computer programmer I know, and some advanced scientific theories that no *serious* scientist is ready to accept," Alan said sarcastically.

"Come in, please," Raya said. "Eat, drink."

Alan looked at her as if noticing her for the first time. "What is this man doing here?" he said sternly.

THE GAIA WAR 253

"Eating and drinking," she said. "I see that you are old friends."

"We went to college together," Alan said, "but I don't suppose that would mean anything to you." He immediately regretted his bitter, condescending tone.

She said nothing and served him a delicious nectar.

"It's actually good to see you, Alan," Fields said. "I haven't thought about you for a long time, but I always thought that if any of us were to amount to anything, it would be you."

"You've done alright," Alan said.

"Politics! Nothing really," Fields said, surprised at himself.

"You remember Larry Skinner?" Alan said.

"Yeah. Larry is in it pretty deep right now. He's got just about every Federal agency on his tail. He was an initial suspect in this whole mess."

"You call this a mess?" Alan said, sipping his nectar.

"What do you call it?" Fields said.

"I might call it paradise," Alan said, beginning to feel the effects of his drink. "Anyway, Larry had nothing to do with it. I saved the planet. If I hadn't develped the protean virus . . ."

"The what?"

"The protean virus. That's the trigger for what you see all around you. It was the only thing that could stand up to the cyberion process that Skinner had unleashed out here. Skinner's nasty microbes were designed to turn the entire biosphere into a sewer. He may have been brilliant, but he turned into a fucking pervert! Man, what is this stuff!" Alan held up his rind, still half-full.

"Nice, huh?" Fields said. "Sure beats the stuff we used to take—and *smoke*. Remember?"

"Of course, I do," Alan said. He looked Raya. "I've been eating the fruit here for a long time. But I've never come across anything like this."

"You have to know how to distill the right essences," she said. "These nectars and liquors contain amino acid complexes and special neurotransmitters that help you to see, think, and feel."

254 **Mark Leon**

"Is it addictive?" Alan asked.

"Not really. And even if it were, there is nothing harmful about what you're tasting. These are nutrients which your body and nervous system need. That's all."

"So Larry was involved?" Fields said.

"Yeah, but not like everybody thinks. Listen, Don, I've already told you too much. You know enough to get me in serious trouble."

"Don't worry, Alan. I don't think my credibility will be worth much if we ever get out of here."

"You saw the dome?" Alan said.

"Yeah. I was a damn fool to come here. But I had to see it. And it's more wonderful than I imagined, than I *could* have imagined."

"So you *aren't* here on official business?" Alan asked.

"No."

"But you must know something. What's the word in Washington?" Alan said.

"Not good." Fields looked at Alan.

Alan saw his worst fears in the secretary's eyes. He understood immediately. "When?" he said.

"Probably only a matter of days," Fields said. "You've seen the planes?"

"Yeah. Those *fuckers*! Well, it figures."

"What figures?" Raya said.

"We hybrids are about to destroy paradise," Fields said.

"How?" Raya asked.

"My people are going to send us a thermonuclear device, special delivery. You know about nuclear fission and fusion?" Alan said to Raya.

"Of course." She didn't seem disturbed.

"Do you really?" Alan said. "Do you understand the energy that will be released here? The heat, the radiation, the . . ."

"There are other more powerful forms of energy," she said simply. "Why don't you have something more to eat?" She handed him a fruit. It was white, with a delicate orange marbling.

The rind was tough, so Alan broke it open. The inside was red and juicy.

THE GAIA WAR 255

"What do you mean?" Fields asked her.

"Nuclear energy is really very crude," she said. "The Asklepian wave harbors more sophisticated forces. I don't think we should panic."

Alan looked on her naïveté with a sense of profound pathos. *How can she be so blind to the coming tragic denouement*? But when he tasted the fruit he could almost believe that she was right.

CHAPTER 18

"I really don't think the *bhang* is necessary," Miranda said. They were in the middle of the river. It was midnight and Swami-ji was rowing. He insisted, out of some obscure notion of chivalry. This neither flattered nor annoyed Miranda. Instead she found the sight of the old guru struggling with the oars amusing.

None of the boatmen had been willing to take them. They had heard rumors that something devilish had occurred on the accursed other shore of the sacred river. "We could get Lal-ji to take us if we give him enough money, but it will be cheaper just to buy a boat," Swami-ji had explained.

Miranda opened the little package of *bhang*. The waxing moon shed just enough light for her to see the sticky contents. "How will we get him to smoke it?" she asked.

"You don't smoke *bhang*," Swami-ji said. "It's not like hashish. You eat it."

"What makes you think he'll want to eat it?" she continued.

"That is where I am counting on you," he said, losing his grip on one of the oars. He nearly fell sideways into the water before he recovered.

"I could have flown us over," Miranda said, trying not to laugh.

"Too strange," Swami-ji said. "Don't start flying around here. We'll find ourselves besieged by supplicants

THE GAIA WAR 257

wanting to make *puja* or get *siddhis* from you. You have attracted too much attention already."

"But it's midnight," Miranda said. "Nobody would see me."

"This is India," Swami-ji said.

"That's what everyone says here," Miranda said. "I'm getting tired of hearing it. What does it mean?"

"Yes," Swami-ji smiled, "everyone does say it, don't they? It means whatever it needs to mean. In this case it means that no matter how dark or late it is, someone will see you. It's very difficult to hide anything here."

Miranda jumped with surprise as the boat slipped up onto the sand. "I guess I'm kind of nervous," she said.

"Tell me more about this Gaur," she said, climbing out.

"He was a wandering *sadhu* from Bengal," Swami-ji said, pulling the boat up and away from the waterline. "Actually he wasn't a bad guy as *sadhus* go. He was more or less the real thing. A lot of them are just beggars and thieves, you know. They rely on tradition in order to survive, but are not really seeking anything."

"What was Gaur seeking?" she asked.

Swami-ji just looked at her as if she had asked a very foolish question. "Enlightenment," he said finally.

"Oh." Miranda could actually feel Swami-ji bristle at the sarcasm which she could not quite keep out of her voice.

"Why do we need to get Lew stoned?" she inquired as they were walking down the barely visible path. "I thought that was the problem. He's already totally addicted to whatever it is he gets from that fossilized tree stump."

"I don't know if it will work," Swami-ji said. "But it might help momentarily to clear his senses."

"Getting stoned on *bhang* will *clear your senses*?" Miranda asked incredulously.

"Normally, no," he said. "But Lew's senses are so occluded that the THC in the *bhang* might open him up briefly. And that's all we need, a moment or two of distraction from his fixation."

"How am I supposed to get him to eat the stuff?" she asked.

258 Mark Leon

"Use your feminine wiles or something," Swami-ji said.

Or something, Miranda thought.

They found Lew lying in the dirt next to the tree stump. He was terribly emaciated and apparently asleep.

"Where's Gaur?" Miranda said.

"Probably asleep in his hut," Swami-ji said. "I'll wait for you at the boat."

"What! You can't just leave me here! What if . . ."

"Gaur is not really dangerous as long as you don't lose your will to the ecstatic pulse of the tree stump. Just concentrate on Lew. Remember, you have to get him to agree to go with you. Unless he uses what is left of his will, it won't do any good—he'll either find his way back or just waste away to nothing," he said.

"Looks like he is pretty close to doing that already," she said. "What's the deal with this tree stump, anyway? I don't for a minute believe that this was the Garden of Eden and that what Lew is so fond of is what remains of the tree of life. So what's the *ecstatic pulse* that you're talking about?"

"Later," Swami-ji said. "There isn't time now." He turned and vanished in the darkness.

Great, Miranda thought, looking down at the nude, emaciated, and dirty form of Lew Slack. "Oh, my," she said. "What paradise have you found?"

She spoke softly, but Lew stirred, rolled onto his back, and opened his eyes. Miranda decided it was now or never. She began unwrapping her sari. This got Lew's attention. When that was done she pulled the blouse off and slid out of her panties.

"Umm," Lew mumbled.

"That's good," she said. "You still remember *something*." When Lew's arms reached up for her she instinctively recoiled. *This won't do*, she thought. *I've got to concentrate*.

It wasn't easy, letting herself be caressed by those dirty hands. As Lew's passion increased he began to pull her closer. Miranda was surprised at the strength which remained in his spindly arms.

"Ouch!" As Lew's hands began to wander more freely

THE GAIA WAR 259

his long, grimy fingernails became a more serious threat. Miranda reached into the folds of her sari and grabbed a piece of the *bhang*. She held it to his lips.

He refused to eat it, but he was interested in the pungent smell. "Stop that, you're hurting me!" She pulled his hand away and kissed him. Lew's mouth tasted like dirty socks that had been soaked in sour milk and left out in the sun. Miranda came up for air. "Oh baby," she said, "you aren't making this easy."

In the end she did what she had to do. There was only one way to get him to eat the *bhang*, and that entailed putting it in a rather sensitive place. This also meant that Miranda absorbed some of the drug. Getting a little high actually made it easier for her to endure the rest of it.

All this foreplay consumed the better part of an hour. When Miranda discerned the new, drug-induced gleam in his eye, she moved to expedite matters.

She had been worried that Lew's compromised capacity as a free-thinking human would hinder his sexual abilities. But if anything, it was the opposite. Compared to his emaciated trunk and thighs, Lew's stiff member appeared ludicrously large and healthy. *If you weren't so disgusting right now, Lew*, she thought, *I might actually enjoy this*.

She pulled his head back and looked him in the eye. "Lew, you have to concentrate! If I'm ever to get your attention, it ought to be now. Do I have it?"

He just looked back with an empty expression.

"I could take that as an insult, you know," she said. Was it her imagination or did she see the trace of a smile? She was pretty sure of it. "OK, good, you can still appreciate humor, I see. Although I must tell you this whole thing is not specifically all that funny."

"Where did you get the hash?" he said, after looking at her for what seemed like a long time.

"Lew!" she exclaimed. "You're back! Excellent. Swami-ji told me that we would have a few minutes at the most. This is important. You have to make a clear, conscious decision to leave this place, forsake forever whatever pleasure you get from the energy of the tree stump. Otherwise, it's no good, and you are lost! Do you understand?"

260 Mark Leon

"Yeah," he said, dully. His eyes were starting to glaze over again.

She shook his head and slapped him across the face. "Don't fade on me, Lew! I'm going to get up and walk to a boat. You have to follow me. I can't make you go. You have to do it yourself."

She pushed him away and gathered her clothes into a bundle, which she tucked underneath one arm. "Come on now, Lew. Just follow me." She turned and began retracing her steps to the river. She inwardly breathed a sigh of relief when she heard Lew's footsteps behind.

"*Ruk Kero!*" a commanding voice called out. Lew stopped and slowly turned around.

It was Gaur, standing on the other side of the tree stump. He presented a particularly ghoulish figure. He had his arms raised high and wore a grin of demonic ecstasy.

Miranda turned around to see Lew's skinny back, vertebrae all too distinctly clear. "Lew, come on! Only death awaits you here!"

He turned to look at her. It was the most pathetic thing Miranda had yet seen in this world, still new to her. He clearly understood what she had just said, and was fighting to stay with her. Yet there was terrible fear in his eyes. It was the fear that he could not do what he had to do. It was the fear of one who helplessly sees his own doom.

The standoff continued for several seconds. Then with agonizing slowness Lew turned—back to Gaur—and slowly started walking away. Miranda, a black empty feeling stealing through her stomach, turned and headed for the boat.

Swami-ji's expression of sadness and remorse caused her to revise her judgments about the guru. "No?" he said softly.

She just shook her head. "Let's get out of here." She tossed her clothes into the boat and climbed in naked. Swami-ji pushed the craft into the dark water and jumped in. His oars cut the water with a soft splash.

"Wait!" Miranda said sharply. "Stop rowing."

"Why?" he asked, oar blades suspended an inch above the blackness.

THE GAIA WAR 261

"I thought I heard something." She jumped out of the boat and waded back to the beach. There, with his face in the water, lay Lew. "Come here!" she called to Swami-ji.

"What is it?" Swami-ji said, already out of the boat himself.

"Chalk one up for free will," she said, when Swami-ji was close enough to see. Lew was in her arms, choking and sputtering on the water he had just inhaled.

He spit out a large quantity of sacred river water mixed with phlegm, raised his head from Miranda's shoulders, looked at the guru, and said, "Paradise rephrased, Swami."

They helped him into the boat and headed for the other shore.

Rainwater was waiting for them when they entered Swami-ji's office. "Tea?" he said, holding up a still-steaming pot.

"Absolutely," Swami-ji said.

"Don't you want to get some rest, Lew?" Miranda said. She was again dressed in her white sari.

"No," Lew said, sitting down across from Rainwater. "I think I'd like some tea." His hand was shaking as he took the cup. He took a sip and looked at Rainwater. "Why did you send me here?" he said.

"That's a good question," Rainwater said, looking at Swami-ji. "You tricked me, Swami."

"Did I?" Swami-ji said evenly, pouring himself some tea. "How is that?"

"I thought we were going to reclaim America by eating up all the roads with that stuff of Alan's. But now I hear that the jungle has completely receded from the highways and is encapsulating itself with an organic polymer dome," Rainwater said.

Swami-ji, enjoying his tea with perfect quiescence, said nothing.

"I have contacts," Rainwater said. No one spoke. "I have contacts at the highest levels of the United States government. The word is that they are going to nuke the whole thing."

262   Mark Leon

Miranda spilled tea on her sari. A light brown stain spread slowly across the white cotton. Her eyes burned brightly, but she didn't speak.

"The irony," Rainwater said with a twisted grin, "is that they are going to destroy a potential moneymaker. They should make a national park out of the place—contract with McDonald's for concessions, provide RV hookups, etc. Fun for the whole family."

"Alan is in there," Lew said. "We have to do something. How much time do we have?"

"Days at most," Rainwater said.

"We'll never make it," Lew said. "You didn't answer my question. Why did you send me here?"

"I thought we were involved in a project that would free the land. I thought that Swami-ji here could bring you up to speed on it. But now I see I was mistaken. I don't know what's happening anymore. All I know is that we are in way over our heads."

"I detect hostile vibes," Swami-ji said. "Do you all really believe that I'm responsible? I am, like the rest of you, merely along for the ride. And as for tricking anyone— well, I admit, Paul, that I allowed you to think what you obviously wanted to think, and perhaps I even exploited your zeal to reclaim the North American continent for your own people. But if you think carefully, you will recall that I never explicitly encouraged such thoughts . . ."

"You never denied them either!" Rainwater said.

"No, I never denied them. As a guru I make a point of denying as little as possible. To your Western minds this may appear devious, an example of Oriental subterfuge, but I call it prudence."

"Prudence right now dictates that we take some action," Miranda said.

"I quite agree," Swami-ji said. "Now is the time for action."

"Don't you think it's a little late for that?" Rainwater said. "How are we going to stand up against the United States Air Force?"

"I doubt if the entire air force will attack," Swami-ji

THE GAIA WAR   263

said. "One or two planes will probably be sufficient—and not more than one fusion bomb."

"I'm sorry if I sound defeatist," Rainwater said, "but I'm no ghost dancer. I can't deflect bullets with my magic shirt, and I sure as hell can't stand up to a hydrogen bomb."

"Thermonuclear fusion is just another energy transformation," Swami-ji said. "There are many ways to transform energy. It's true that nuclear energy does involve rearranging matter at the level of the atomic nucleus. This was regarded by the scientists of the twentieth century as a fantastic triumph, a pivotal breakthrough. And I suppose it was of sorts. But it's really rather a messy thing, this splitting of atoms and fusing them together. The energy produced is relatively large but difficult to control."

"A hydrogen bomb is one hell of a bomb," Rainwater said.

"Yes," Swami-ji said, "but a bomb is still a bomb. *Crude* in a word. The point is there are more subtle ways to manipulate and control energy." He looked at Miranda.

She was the only one who seemed to understand what he was talking about. "You know it will be dangerous," she said.

"Life is dangerous," Swami-ji said.

Lew stood up slowly. "I don't feel so good," he said, and started for the bathroom. He got only a step before he collapsed in a dead faint. Miranda was quick enough to catch him before his head hit the floor.

"We had better see if we can get some food into that boy," Swami-ji said. "There isn't enough time to fatten him up, but he's going to need a little more stamina." Swami-ji looked into Miranda's eyes. A wordless communication of obvious significance passed between them.

Miranda carried Lew into Swami-ji's bedroom, where she laid him on the guru's mattress. Then she went to the kitchen to see what food could be had.

Skinner, who had been standing in the shadows just outside the entrance to Swami-ji's apartment, hurried away. He hired a rickshaw to take him to Clark's, one of the fanciest hotels in town. Skinner was about to test the hilarious, often infuriating idiosyncrasies of the Indian telephone system to their limits. It would be hard, under any circumstances, for a private citizen to get a call through to the secretary of defense.

CHAPTER 19

"He's very angry with you," Miranda said. It was late at night. Rainwater had returned to his hotel and Lew was sleeping.

"I suppose he has a right," Swami-ji said. "But he labors under a false assumption."

"What's that?" Miranda said. She was drinking a cold yogurt drink. Liberally laced with *bhang*, the liquid was dark green. Her experience with Lew had given her a taste for the drug.

"You should go easy on that stuff," Swami-ji said.

"I know, but the effect is so deliciously ... ah, *somatic*, I guess."

"That's what they all say," Swami-ji said. "But to answer your question, Mr. Rainwater has assumed all along that I had a clear idea of what we were doing. That's false."

"The stakes are rather high for ignorant meddling with such powerful forces, don't you think?" Miranda said.

"Normally I would agree," Swami-ji said. "But the world is in crisis. I thought it was worth the risk. Now Paul is angry because it turns out that the *Genesis Bomb* is not what he thought. It may surprise you to know that I, too, am disappointed. It turns out that it's not what I hoped either."

"What did you think was going to happen?" Miranda said.

266 **Mark Leon**

"I hoped that this would be the beginning of the new dawn, the end of a long, dark age for humanity. Now I see that hope was in vain."

"You make a grave mistake if you assume that because your specific hope has not borne fruit, there is no hope to be had from all this. There is, in fact, tremendous hope that you and all humanity should derive from these recent events. Especially from what is *about to happen*. Therein lies more than hope. Therein lies a *way*, a path to the heavens and beyond!" Miranda threw her arms up and out, fell back onto the soft pillows, and laughed.

Swami-ji laughed too. "I know I should believe you. In fact I do, but I think you have had enough. And allow me my own private disappointment. As an Indian I was hoping for fulfillment of sacred Hindu prophecy. A selfish perspective, I admit, but we all live through our imagination, which is inevitably colored by our cultural and religious heritage."

"Such wisdom, Swami! Beautiful. You really are. And you're right. I *have* had enough *bhang*."

"In that case," Swami-ji said, picking up the half-empty glass, "we mustn't waste it." He drained the glass in a few gulps. "Ah! Absolute master drink!" He lay down on the pillows opposite her and they passed the rest of the night in visions of paradise, both falling asleep just before dawn.

At the same time, across town in the more fashionable cantonment district, a clerk was trying to wake Skinner. "Sir, your call is just coming through."

Skinner roused himself from where he lay on the couch. He did not have much hope that his call was really "just coming through." There had been several such false alarms during the night. Most had ended in absurd shouting matches—one party or both screaming, "Hello! Hello!" in the receiver.

"Mr. Skinner?" A voice, remarkably clear, said.

"Yes," Skinner said.

"Mr. *Larry* Skinner of *NatCo*?"

"Yeah."

THE GAIA WAR 267

"Where *are* you, Mr. Skinner?" The voice was suddenly sharp.

"Who *is* this?" Skinner said, hope rising.

"This is Jack Carp, secretary of defense. I am calling because I have just been made aware of a whole slew of urgent messages, attributed to you."

"Mr. Secretary," Skinner said, "I have some information that will interest you."

"Your whereabouts interests me," Carp said.

"Can't you figure that out?" Skinner said. "You have my phone number."

"Never mind," Carp said irritably. "What is it you want to tell me?"

God bless the Indian phone system, Skinner thought. Even with the phone number the Defense Department could not trace the call. "I'll make this brief," Skinner said. "Certain parties, who are possibly in a position to do something about it, are aware of your, shall we say rather *explosive*, plans."

"What plans?" Carp said warily.

"We both know what I am talking about, sir," Skinner said. "And I would not underestimate the powers and abilities of these people. I made that mistake myself, and look where it got me."

"Where? Where are you?" Carp nearly shouted. Then, voice under control, "I mean, maybe we can help you, Mr. Skinner."

"Maybe you can," Skinner said. "I'll be in touch. In any case, I would expedite things. I don't think you have much time." He hung up.

Better than expected, Skinner thought as he headed for the dining room. He was ready for a big breakfast.

Bob Flynt was wolfing down a hamburger at a truck stop in Organ, New Mexico. Meagan was just staring at hers. "Not hungry?" he said.

"I don't know," she said. "I must be losing my taste for meat."

"Good policy," Flynt said. "I'm slowly working my way toward a low-fat diet myself. Very slowly." He took

268   Mark Leon

another bite. "But you know in Genesis, where God gives Adam authority over all the animals?"

"Sure," Meagan said, sipping her iced tea.

"Yeah," Flynt continued, "notice that God does not tell Adam that he can *eat them*."

"So why are you eating that cow?" Meagan said.

"Everything changed after the Fall," he said. "Hell, the animals started eating *each other*. So I guess Adam just followed their lead, but it doesn't seem quite right, does it?" He shoved the last piece into his mouth.

"You know," he said in a low, conspiratorial tone of voice, "I suspected all along that the *Genesis Bomb* was something like this."

"Like what?" Meagan said.

"Like what you said," he said, "back in my office, you know, the millennium or something."

"What are you talking about?" Meagan said.

Before he could answer the waitress brought their check.

"I know some back roads," Flynt said when they were again seated in his Suburban. "We can cut up into the San Andres range. Some of those roads are pretty rough. They say you got to have four-wheel drive. But I swear this baby can handle it!"

A few miles farther he left the highway and they were barreling down a dirt road, leaving a small dust storm in their wake. With very little to hang on to, Meagan was getting badly bounced around. "Slow down!" she yelled.

The AC was cranked to the max. That and the noise from the road shielded Flynt from Meagan's cries. Finally she reached over and grabbed him by the shoulder. "Slow down." She mouthed the words very slowly.

"Sorry," he said. "I get on a roll sometimes."

They hit a military blockade. "This area is off-limits sir," a boy in a soldier suit said.

"We are on a religious retreat," Flynt said. "I'm Pastor of the El Paso Chapter of the Loyal Army of God, and this is my secretary. We're gonna pray out here in the wilderness until we get some answers. And we will, too!"

"Sorry," the boy said. "I'm not supposed to let anyone through. The *Genesis Bomb*, you know?"

THE GAIA WAR   269

"Of course I know," Flynt said. "That's why we're here. These are the *end times*, son. Do you know your Bible?"

"Well . . . a little, I mean . . ."

"Revelation, son. Book of Revelation. You better start studying. There may not be much time left." Flynt opened his glove compartment and grabbed his Bible. He got out of the car, winking at Meagan as he put his arm around the boy.

They walked to an open tent and went inside.

An hour passed and Meagan was still alone. The insufferable heat had forced her to abandon the car within a few minutes. She was sitting on the shady side of the vehicle, leaning against a tire and scratching the desert with a stick.

She finally got up and walked over to the tent. She had heard familiar noises coming from inside. They were things she had heard at her church—it now seemed like ages ago—prayers to the Holy Spirit, speaking in tongues, etc. She didn't care. She was hot, tired, hungry, and bored. Just as she was about to walk in, Flynt and the young soldier came out. Meagan recognized the look on the boy's face. She had seen it on other faces and felt it on her own. He was transformed. He was in the Spirit, no longer of the flesh; he was *reborn*.

Wait till tomorrow, kid, Meagan thought.

"Meagan," Flynt said, "I want you to pray with Glen and me. Glen has just received a wonderful gift, isn't that right, Glen?"

Glen just beamed and took Meagan's hand. Meagan sighed and tried not to look disgusted as she joined hands with Flynt and they closed a prayer circle.

When it was over the poor boy didn't seem to notice that they had driven the Suburban right past his post. Flynt kept his speed down, and Meagan maintained a stony silence.

"I don't think it's a good idea to take Krishna," Swami-ji said. "It's going to be hard enough with Lew, but you *need* him. The boy serves no purpose except as an object for your misplaced compassion."

"You're one cold guru, Swami-ji," Miranda said, "and

270 **Mark Leon**

if you say *This is India* one more time, I'll kill you."

"OK," Swami-ji said. "We've wasted too much time already, sleeping off our *bhang* high. That was really irresponsible."

"You're also far too serious sometimes," Miranda said, "but you're right. It's late afternoon, which makes it the middle of the night in White Sands, New Mexico. I would like to get there before morning."

"I don't see how you can do it," Swami-ji said.

"Do what?" Lew was up. He was dressed in clean white *coorta* and *pajama*. The clothes hung loosely on his emaciated frame.

"Our lady is going to take you home," Swami-ji said.

"Home?" Lew said. "Where's that?"

"My sentiments exactly," Miranda said, "but we have work to do. Leave us alone for a little while, will you, Swami-ji. Lew and I need to talk."

Miranda explained the situation to Lew as she felt she had to. She told him that they risked death by thermonuclear explosion.

"So why do it?" Lew said. "I don't want to desert Alan, but this sounds like madness, to head straight for ground zero."

"I don't think we'll die. It wouldn't be prudent to explain exactly why. But I do need your help, Lew. Trust me?"

"I want to trust you. I owe you that much. You didn't ask to be born into this world—"

"None of us did," she interrupted.

"No," he continued, "none of us did—you least of all. But you're asking me to believe too much too fast."

"You have believed far stranger things, Lew," she said.

He hung his head, ashamed of his recent escapade on the other shore of the sacred river.

"Don't, Lew," she said. "No shame in what you did. You were chasing a dream, a fool's paradise. It is the human condition. Now I'm asking you to help me chase mine."

"OK," Lew said. "When do we leave?"

THE GAIA WAR 271

"Right now. It is going to be cold. That won't bother me, but you and Krishna . . ."

"Krishna? Who's that?" Lew asked.

"Meet your Bengali traveling companion," Swami-ji said. He had returned with the little boy in tow. "I only have one sleeping bag." Swami-ji sounded concerned.

Lew volunteered to let Krishna have it. He took some of Swami-ji's wool blankets. They went up to the roof. Most Indian buildings have open roofs. The walls of the rooms below extend up above the top floor. This gives an extra set of rooms on top that are open to the sky.

Good-byes were short. "Where's Skinner?" Lew said.

"I haven't seen him for a while," Swami-ji said. "I suppose he'll turn up."

"Yeah," Lew said, "I suppose he will."

Little Krishna's eyes got wide as Miranda unwrapped her sari, and took off her blouse. "*Zurur, heh,*" she explained to him. He nodded, but still gaped at her.

She said a few more words and Krishna crawled into the sleeping bag. Lew wrapped himself in the blankets. He immediately began sweltering in the monsoon-laden heat.

"*Namaste*, Swami-ji," Miranda said. She held Krishna close to her chest and told Lew to stand behind her and wrap his arms around them both.

"*Namaste,*" Swami-ji said. He placed his palms together in the traditional manner. "And good luck."

The unlikely threesome shot skyward. Swami-ji watched as they sped across the river toward the setting sun.

This time Miranda had wisely chosen to follow the sun. Most of her skin surface was covered by her two passengers, but any sun was preferable to none.

It wasn't long before Lew regretted giving up the sleeping bag so easily. It was hard to breathe and his ears hurt badly, but the numbing cold was the worst. He finally had to tell Miranda that his fingers were too cold to hang on. She bound Lew's arms with her own hands while squeezing Krishna to her chest.

The wind was so painful that Lew thought he would lose consciousness. He merged with the agonizing feelings of cold—embraced them. It was the only way to keep from

272 Mark Leon

going mad. Their course took them over Pakistan, Afghanistan, Saudi Arabia, the Middle East. And then the Mediterranean. "The cradle of your culture!" Miranda screamed when they were over Greece.

Lew looked down. He wished she would just drop him so he could sink blissfully into the wine-dark sea. It looked warm. Anyplace would have.

"That's all you can tell me!" Carp said. "The call came from someplace in India?"

"Probably, sir." The military intelligence officer badly wanted the conversation to be over.

He got his wish. Carp slammed the phone down. *It doesn't matter*, he told himself. *Larry Skinner and NatCo were never the key to the mystery.* But it was another loose end. *One had to handle loose ends carefully: if you ignored them, they could get tangled in the works, and if you pulled on them too hard, they could cause the whole thing to come unraveled.* He didn't like doing what he did next, but felt it was the only prudent course of action. He picked up the phone and punched a number.

"Tomorrow morning, sir?"

"Yeah," Carp said.

"I was hoping for another day, sir, we . . ."

"So was I, but circumstances have a way of dashing our fondest hopes and dreams."

The other party had no response to this.

Military! Carp thought. *No imagination.* "It's a go," he said. "I don't care what you have to do. Just do it. You can *do it*, can't you? Because if not, I'm sure . . ."

"Oh no, sir! I mean yes, sir. We'll be ready."

Rainwater and Swami-ji were walking along the river *ghats*. The sunset was another one of those yellow, pyrotechnic displays that you only see in India. "So that's it as far as I can tell," Rainwater said. "Up in smoke. Everything."

"Not necessarily," Swami-ji said. "The story isn't quite over. Don't assume catastrophe until the final scene is played."

THE GAIA WAR 273

"And when will that be?" Rainwater said.

"Ah!" Swami-ji smiled. "Good point. Maybe never. Is there really an end?"

"There's death," Rainwater said. "That seems pretty final."

"You Americans," Swami-ji said.

"I'm not an American! I'm an Apache . . ."

"Mescalero," Swami-ji finished it for him. "But you *Native* Americans have more in common with the *invaders* than you realize, or, in your case, than you care to admit."

"How's that?" Rainwater said drily.

"Your fierce individualism. This, for example, is what's behind your characterization of death as *final*. It's a dramatic event in the life of the individual. No one would deny that, except possibly some Buddhists I know, but nothing more. There is nothing final about it."

"So what?" Rainwater said.

"So lighten up, Paul."

They walked along in silence for several minutes. "I'm going north," Rainwater said finally.

"North?"

"Yeah, to Central Asia," Rainwater said.

"Oh no, don't tell me . . ." Swami-ji began.

"Yes!" Rainwater said. "I mean no offense, Swami, but this whole Hindu Vedanta thing is *bogus*. You guys are all a bunch of tricksters as far as I can tell. Some more honorable than others, I admit—you, for example. And the *Buddhist* trip? Same thing—maybe with a little more reserve and finesse.

"But they say Central Asia is where it all began—with the ancient *shamans*. My people probably originated there."

"What do you expect to find?" Swami-ji said. "The whole area is in political upheaval right now because of the breakup of the Soviet empire. Do you really hope to find a *shaman* who can put you in touch with the ancient roots of your culture?"

"Maybe. I have to try."

"I'm not surprised," Swami-ji said. "I'll miss you.

274　Mark Leon

Where can I ever hope to find such a dedicated partner in the quest for the *Great Symbol*.''

''Your *Great Symbol* is about to go up in flames,'' Rainwater said.

''Our *Great Symbol*,'' Swami-ji corrected. ''And don't be so sure. It ain't over till it's over.''

CHAPTER 20

Miranda chased the sunset. At one point, midway over the Atlantic Ocean, she began to drop back into the dusky darkness that marks the interface of night and day. "This is more like it." Lew's teeth were chattering uncontrollably and he could barely speak. As they lost speed and altitude the air became warmer and the windchill lost its deadly bite.

"Yeah," Miranda said. "I hope you can swim."

"Anything to ease up on the cold," Lew said.

"I don't think you'll find the water very warm," she said grimly.

"What's wrong?" Lew said, the import of her words finally registering.

"I'm losing the sun, Lew," she said. "My powers have been increasing ever since . . . well ever since we made love that first time. I thought I was strong enough to take all three of us back. But I need the sun, and I'm losing it."

Lew looked down at the dark water, getting closer by the second. "I'm a good swimmer," he said, and immediately wondered why.

"It is our only chance, Lew," she said.

"Oh no," Lew said. "I didn't really mean . . ."

"Otherwise we'll all die. There are no warm beaches to wash up onto out here. I have to get to White Sands or else Alan will be vaporized." They were falling now.

276 Mark Leon

"What do you want me to do?" Lew said.

"Just let go," she said. "I can't promise you anything. I may not make it even without your weight. But I know we are doomed if you hang on. Sometimes you just have to let go."

"Alright." Lew was amazed at his reaction to all this. It was not what he thought it should be. He didn't feel brave, noble, or joyful. He didn't feel much at all. He tried to conjure up some sort of terror—even a mild fear of death would have been nice, but the best he could do was a sense of tense expectation. "Let's do it."

Miranda opened her arms, and Lew released what little grip he had left. " *'Tis a far better thing I do now . . .'* " he screamed as he fell. That actually made him smile. *Literature has its place*, he thought.

Miranda was not smiling as she watched him hit the water with a dull splash. She clenched her jaw and raced to catch the sun, gaining altitude by centimeters and speed by seconds.

"Not quite a flaming sword, but every bit as effective," Pastor Flynt said. He pounded again on the polymer surface. They had cut across the San Andres mountains and were parked on the western side of the dome.

"What sword?" Meagan said.

"You know the story," Flynt said. "After Adam and Eve were taken from Eden by the Archangel Michael, God put a flaming sword at the eastern gate of Paradise."

"Why?" Meagan said.

"To keep them from getting back in, of course."

"No, I mean why the *eastern* gate?" she said.

"I don't know!" Flynt snapped. "The eastern entrance was the easiest way in, I guess."

"Sorry," Meagan said. "I was just asking."

"Damn!" Flynt said. "Just look at it. I couldn't have dreamed it any better." He was gazing fondly, lustfully at the jungle within.

"It *is* beautiful," Meagan said, "but so is the desert." Flynt's behavior was beginning to worry her. The man was

THE GAIA WAR 277

obsessed with the scene inside the dome. The barrier just fanned his fires.

"The desert!" he said. "My God, woman, how long have we lived in deserts of one sort or another? I thirst, I tell you! I *thirst*! It is true what they say about you women! You're all blind to paradise! The very paradise which you ruined for our great forefather. You never appreciated Eden the way Adam did, and he only went along with your folly out of love. Oh misplaced love! Oh faithless creature! Woman is thy name!"

"Hold it right there, mister!" Meagan said. "I've had it with you pious male pigs lording your bogus spiritual authority over me! What the fuck do you know, anyway? A bunch of stories your daddies told you is all! I've been abused sexually, economically, and spiritually by you assholes for as long as I can remember, and I don't care what kind of know-nothing bunch of ninnies call you *pastor* at your half-assed church, I'm not going to listen to you—"

"But Meagan," Flynt interrupted her, his demeanor suddenly calm and peaceful.

"What?" she said, bewildered by his sudden change.

"For a half-assed church," he said, "we do make a pretty mean cup of espresso, don't you think?"

She stared at him for a long time. Finally she said, "Yeah, you do. So, Pastor Bob, of the Loyal Army of God. What do we do now?"

"I'd say this might be a good time to pray," he said.

"I think I'll just watch the sunset if you don't mind," she said.

"Suit yourself."

"I've got to hand it to you, Swami-ji," Skinner said. "You have class. Like Zeus. In all the old Greek myths Zeus calls the shots, but he rarely gets involved directly. He just plays on the desires of lesser gods and mortals. He does it so skillfully that his power is never in doubt even though it's seldom used."

"Except that I'm not really interested in power," Swami-ji said.

278 **Mark Leon**

"No, that's true. It's the only thing about you I don't understand," Skinner said.

"I doubt that," Swami-ji said. "But let's talk about you. What will you do now?"

"I'm afraid I may have to remain here for a while," Skinner said. "It's just you and me, Swami. Any ideas?"

"India is a vast place," Swami-ji said. "We're on the brink of great changes in this country. There are many in the West who say India is the next emerging market, that there is a lot of money to be made."

"Money." Skinner said it like a strange sound in an alien language. "Money to be made. Yes. Maybe we should form a partnership. I can still raise some capital. I am not totally without resources."

"No," Swami-ji said. "Thank you, but no partnerships. That's really not my thing. It was merely a suggestion. India might be able to use a man of your talents if you are inclined to stay."

"I may not have much choice," Skinner said.

"Pharmaceuticals," Swami-ji said.

"What?"

"Pharmaceuticals. Drugs. Your old friend Alan Fain brought me a root that grows only in Tibet. It produces strange visions. I still have some. I suspect that if one could isolate the active chemical ingredient, there might be a lucrative patent in it. Pharmaceuticals are rumored to be one of the hot new Indian markets."

"May I see this stuff?"

Swami-ji went into his bedroom and returned with a small bundle. Skinner unwrapped it. There, on the coarse wool cloth, lay a thin black root about two inches long. "Have you tried it?" Skinner asked.

"Oh yes. Quite remarkable. The Tibetans say that it induces the after-death state, the *Bardo* as they call it. I don't know about that, but I was transfixed by the most-intriguing visions for a period of about two hours. The side effects are minimal."

"What sort of market is there for something like this?" Skinner said. "There are plenty of hallucinogenic drugs around."

THE GAIA WAR 279

"This is different," Swami-ji said.

"How so?"

"I have long held a theory about the nature of life," Swami-ji said. "It's commonly held that plant life is inferior to animal. But that's nonsense, the natural prejudice of the rational animal. If the entire global ecosystem is a single superorganism, a *Gaia* if you will . . ."

"Not this Gaia crap again!" Skinner said.

"Bear with me," Swami-ji said. "I'm not just spouting some half-baked New Age nonsense. Consider, for the sake of argument, that all life on the planet is interconnected in ways that we still do not understand. One might be tempted to say *subtle* ways. But that would be wrong. To say our interconnection is subtle is just to restate the concept of global ecology. This was a new concept fifty years ago, but now it's old hat.

"No, I'm saying that the connections are not subtle at all. We seem blind to them not because they are subtle, but because they are big, powerful, *overt*.

"There is a planetary central nervous system that is more centralized than your brain. In a nutshell, my theory is that the plant kingdom is the nexus of this nervous system. That's why the destruction of global rain forests is more of a catastrophe than even the most radical environmentalists realize."

"So what does your *theory* have to do with this drug?" Skinner held the little root up.

"I think that stuff puts you in direct contact with the planetary nervous system," Swami-ji said. "More than that really. It puts you inside it. Your brain, your central nervous system, becomes a *conscious, active participant* in the global life network."

"How much does it take?" Skinner asked.

"Very little," Swami-ji said. "Only a gram or two."

Creel leaned on his horn outside the El Paso FBI field office. Finally an agent came out. "What's the deal, Jim?" he said, amused by the scene. "How did you get yourself handcuffed to the steering wheel?"

"It's a long story. Just get me out of here," Creel said.

280 Mark Leon

"Want something to drink? It's 110 today," the other agent said.

"Dammit, Scott, I have to take a leak. Get me out of here!"

"I don't suppose you have the keys?"

Creel glared at his colleague.

Later they were inside drinking coffee. "God this stuff is terrible, Scott," Creel said.

"Coffee's coffee," Special Agent Scott Byrd said.

"No, it's not," Creel said.

"So she handcuffed you and took your keys?" Byrd said.

"Yeah. Don't tell anybody around here, OK?"

"What about your report?" Byrd said.

'Fuck the report. I'll just leave that part out."

"Nothing to be ashamed of," Byrd said. "Sounds like this chick was pretty tough." He smiled.

"And fuck you too, Scott," Creel said.

"So if she took your keys, how did you get here?" Byrd said.

"I hot-wired it, man. Don't you know anything?"

"Guess not," Byrd said.

"I've got to find them," Creel said.

"Do you have any leads?" Byrd said.

"I *know* where they are."

"Where?"

"White Sands, you fool. The *Genesis Bomb*, or whatever that mess is out there," Creel said.

"That's a problem," Byrd said.

"No problem. Just detail some agents and let's get our butts up there. We can make it in a few hours."

"You should take a look at this." Byrd handed Creel a fax.

"Off-limits!" Creel said. "Why? What the fuck is going on?"

"I don't know, but this comes from high up," Byrd said.

"How high?"

"High enough for you to forget about it," Byrd said. "I got a call from NSC today. There is some spooky shit about

THE GAIA WAR 281

to break out there, and they don't want anybody to know about it.''

"Listen, Scott," Creel said, "I've seen some spooky shit myself. I'm the only one who has firsthand knowledge of the UFS.''

"Not the flying people bullshit. Not you, Jim?" Byrd said.

"I'm telling you it's true. All bets are off, Scott. I have to get out there!''

"And lose your job?" Byrd said.

"It is clear you do not *fully grasp* what I am saying! There may not be a Bureau, there may not be a Department of Justice; hell, there may not even be a United States of America if we don't act!''

"Jim, I'm going to have to recommend that you take some time off . . .''

"Oh hell, Scott!''

"Let me finish. It is burning up out there. You ever heard of sunstroke? It affects your judgment, Jim . . .''

"My judgment is fine!" Creel got up and stormed out.

"Don't do anything stupid, Jim," Byrd yelled as Creel screeched out of the parking lot back onto the blistering road.

Only mad dogs and Englishmen, Byrd thought, shaking his head as he retreated to his air-conditioned office and bad coffee.

CHAPTER 21

Miranda hit daylight and strained for the sky, looking straight into the sun. The skin of her naked back, now exposed to the solar rays, also began soaking up energy. She murmured some comforting words to little Krishna, still inside the sleeping bag and clasped tightly to her chest, and then she wheeled around and raced back into the darkness.

She summoned latent, yet dimly perceived, navigational powers to try and locate the spot where Lew had fallen. *Please be here*, she thought as she hovered above the black waves and called his name. She circled until she felt her strength ebbing again and started to depart when she saw something glimmering below in the faint starlight.

It was Lew's wristwatch. He was waving, trying to shout, but unable to make much noise with lungs that were rapidly collecting seawater.

"I thought I was a good swimmer," he sputtered as she grabbed his arm, "but I was about to go down."

"You're a great swimmer, Lew." Miranda pulled him from the water.

They made it back into the light and she flew far enough to give them a few minutes before the darkness overtook them once again. "You have to help me, Lew," she said. "I can't make it with both of you unless I can keep my back exposed to the light. The sun is my energy. Can you hold on to my legs?"

THE GAIA WAR   283

He shook his head. "Look at my hands."

She did and saw his blue fingers.

"I'll be lucky to keep them," he said.

"Don't worry about that," she said. "You're not going to lose your fingers. Right now we have to keep moving. Let's try this."

It was awkward, but they finally managed to get Lew and Krishna half in the sleeping bag. Miranda was able to hold them both underneath with her arms, thus keeping her back exposed to the sun.

Lew lapsed in and out of a weary sleep. He thought he saw Cuba at one point and later a familiar coastline. "Texas," he said to himself, "home."

Miranda was fatigued beyond what she thought was possible, and they began to lose time; the darkness was once again on their tail. But she made it to the eastern edge of the dome in time to see the sunset. She set her passengers down on the white gypsum sand.

Lew crawled from the sleeping bag and stood, shaking. Krishna was fast asleep. Lew held his fingers up to catch the golden rays of the sun as it dipped into the western horizon. Some color had started to return. He clenched both hands, making fists that caused all his knuckles to pop.

"Ready to fight with Helios?" Miranda said, smiling.

"What?" Lew said, dazed and not quite aware of his pose, which could easily be mistaken for a challenge to the Sun God. "Oh yeah," he said. "I mean no, just trying to get some blood back in my fingers."

"I'm afraid there's no time to rest," Miranda said.

"Why not?" Lew said.

"I didn't count on this barrier. We have to find a way in. I'll have to scout it by air."

"Do you have the strength?" he said.

"No, but that's beside the point. We have to get in." She took a running leap and hurled herself up. Somehow she managed to keep going.

She was soon back. Her return was not graceful, more a falling out of the sky than a landing. "OK," she gasped. "There's an opening in the top. It's only about a hundred yards in diameter, but I think I can get us in. One more time, gentlemen." She picked up the still-sleeping Krishna and turned to stare into the last rays of the sun. Then the orb was gone, as Helios drove his chariot from mortal view. "Hold on, Lew," she said.

Lew grabbed her around the waist. "Run with me," she said. They ran together for several yards and then, on cue from Miranda, they both leapt. Lew felt their parabolic arc play out to its apex under the pull of gravity. Miranda's counterforce took them about midway up the dome. With a sickening feeling that Lew recognized from nightmares, he knew they were going to fall. But she dug in with new resolve and slowly they began to rise.

They just cleared the upper lip of the dome. "Sorry, Lew, but I'm all in. We are each on our own now. Watch out for Krishna." She released the boy, and Lew let her go. Then they fell into the lap of Paradise.

Meagan caught the edge of the sun's disc in her eye just before it went down. *It will make you go blind*, she thought, and laughed. She had just looked at Flynt, perched on a rock and still deep in prayer when the evening desert silence was shattered by the sound of a Ford Bronco. "Oh shit," Meagan said. She recognized Creel's car.

"Friend of yours?" Flynt said, rousing himself.

The car skidded to halt, kicking up a cloud of dust, and Creel leapt out. He immediately crouched, leveling his gun at Meagan and yelled, "Freeze!"

"Guess not," Flynt said.

Two thoughts came in rapid succession when Miranda opened her eyes. The first was that she was finally home and the second was that the woman looking at her could be her daughter.

"Hello," Raya said, handing her a hollow gourd filled with clear nectar.

Miranda drained it and instantly felt a delicious, warm surge of energy begin to flow through her body. "Are the others . . ."

"They're fine. You need to rest," Raya said. She got up

THE GAIA WAR   285

and disappeared into the jungle, returning with another gourd full of the same liquid.

Miranda made short work of it. The juice was rapidly recharging her energy systems. She still needed the sunlight for a full recovery of her powers, but she felt that soon she would be able to fly short distances.

"I'm Miranda."

"I'm Raya," Raya said.

"Of course," Miranda said. "Raya."

"Welcome home, Mother." Raya kissed her on the cheek.

"I really would prefer a night mission," Carp said. He was talking with Major Franklin in Alamogordo.

"Too risky, sir. Normally I would agree to it, but under the circumstances . . ."

"What if the circumstances were that I ordered you to proceed immediately?" Carp said. "I could have you court-martialed."

"With all due respect, sir," Franklin said, "I don't think so."

Carp turned quite red, but remained silent for a full minute. When he did speak it was in a very quiet, deliberate manner. "Alright, Major. You win this round. But we go at dawn. Everything is ready?"

"Yes sir. Dawn."

"We are going to add a little something to the early light," Carp said smiling.

The major, not smiling, saluted and left the office.

Carp wrestled with a dilemma. He had promised the major a big promotion for taking command of the operation. But the man had just come very close to insubordination. *Should I, for the sake of morale, make good on my promise and promote the man or should I have him shot*? He pondered this for a while without resolving it and finally poured himself a drink. He drank to the coming New Order. He wanted to drink to his own place in that order but could not for lack of an appropriate title. *Emperor, Dictator, Supreme Commander, Autarch*—none of them seemed quite right.

286   **Mark Leon**

* * *

"I have to go back out," Miranda said.

"Why?" Raya offered her another gourd and Miranda gladly accepted.

"I caught a glimpse of something on the western side," Miranda said, finishing her drink. "I have to check it out."

"But nothing can penetrate . . ." Raya began.

"It's not that," Miranda said.

"Then what?" Raya said. "You're still not at full strength. You should rest."

"Just a hunch," Miranda said, "and I'm sure I can make it." She stood up. "Where are the others?"

"I've got them resting in my bower," Raya said.

"Take care of them. We have work to do and not much time," Miranda said.

"Work?" Raya said.

Miranda laughed. "I know. It's a difficult concept. But I finally got it. I'll explain when I get back. I won't be gone long." She jumped up and rose through the layers of jungle growth. Night had set in, but the soft vegetable light had begun to glow with cool intensity. Miranda, again feeling a strong sense of home, hated to go back out.

"Look at the light," Flynt said, gazing with wonder at the multicolored display that was lighting up the inside of the dome.

"It's beautiful," Meagan said.

"It's the fucking devil's light," Creel said, still holding them at gunpoint.

"What do you intend to do with us?" Flynt said.

"I'm going to find out what's going on and save this country is what I'm going to do!" Creel said. He was shaking. "Where is your witch friend?" he demanded, pointing his gun directly at Meagan.

"She's right here." A voice came from above and behind Creel.

Creel wheeled around and fired into the air. The shot went wild. Miranda landed and moved toward him. The second shot was more accurate. The barrel of Creel's gun

THE GAIA WAR 287

was inches from Miranda's chest when he squeezed the trigger.

She gasped and stepped back, clutching her chest. But before Creel could get off another she straightened up and kicked him so hard between the legs that he crumpled into the fetal position and screamed in agony.

Meagan ran over to her. "Oh my God! You're hurt," she said.

Miranda collapsed into Meagan's arms.

"We have to get you to a hospital," Meagan said.

"No," Miranda said, stepping away. "My skin's a lot tougher than yours. I'll be OK."

But Meagan was looking at the green blood on her blouse and shaking her head. "He shot you!" she said, and looked at Creel, still whimpering at their feet. "I'll kill you, you bastard!" She started to kick him.

"Meagan," Miranda said, "there isn't time. Forget him. I have to get us inside the dome. Hold on to me. And you . . ." She looked at Flynt, who stood there with his mouth open. "Do you want to come in with us? It will be safer, I think."

"Are you serious?" Flynt said. "Can you get me inside there?"

"Yes. Do you want to go?"

"Why take him?" Meagan whispered to Miranda.

"We can use him," Miranda said.

"Paradise regained," Flynt said to the sky.

"It may not be quite what you think," Miranda said.

Flynt didn't hear. "I'm ready," he said. "I've been ready for a long time."

"Hang on, then," Miranda said. She put her arms around Meagan and Flynt wrapped his arms around her waist from behind.

Miranda groaned on the ascent, and Meagan said, "You need help. That chest wound looks bad."

"No," Miranda said, breathing hard, "nothing vital hit . . . I'll be . . ." She never finished, slipping into unconsciousness as they tumbled over the rim and back into the welcoming life below.

CHAPTER 22

Meagan climbed down from the middle layer of the jungle after ascertaining that she was not hurt. She headed for the voices she heard below.

"Help me carry her." It was Raya talking to Flynt. Meagan dropped the rest of the way to the ground, landing next to Raya.

"Please help us," Raya said. "She's hurt."

Another one? Meagan thought, looking at Raya. She was surprised to discover that she was not disappointed.

Miranda lay unconscious in Raya's bower. Raya attended her. Krishna still slept peacefully.

Lew was somewhat recovered and restless. He emerged from inside the green haven to stand in the jungle's weird, yet strangely soothing, half-light.

"Hello, Lew." It was Meagan.

"Meagan," Lew said, "I . . ."

"You don't look so good," Meagan said.

"India was hard on me," he said.

"God, you're skinny!" she said, coming closer.

"What happened out there?" Lew asked.

"They shot her," Meagan said.

"Who?"

"Who do you think?" It was Flynt, emerging from the shadows.

THE GAIA WAR 289

"This is Pastor Bob Flynt," Meagan said.

"Please, call me Bob," Flynt said. "No need for formalities here."

"Lew Slack," Lew said, holding out his hand.

"My God, son!" Flynt said when he took Lew's hand. "Your hands are ice-cold."

"I had a little trouble with the stratosphere," Lew said.

"What?"

"Never mind," Lew said. "But what did you mean— just now, about whoever it was that shot Miranda?"

"I mean," Flynt said, "this is all-out war. You know what this place is, don't you?"

"No," Lew said.

"This is the New Eden. This is that which was promised to Adam when the Lord said, ' . . . your heel shall bruise his head . . . ' "

"I don't follow you," Lew said.

"Don't worry about it," Meagan said.

"The serpent's about to get his head kicked in," Flynt said, ignoring Meagan's sarcastic tone, "and he's fighting back. We ain't seen nothin' yet."

"I know," Lew said.

"Why did she bring you inside?" Lew asked Meagan.

"Fuckin' FBI pig was about to kill us," Meagan said. "Why did she bring you here?"

"We're about to get nuked," Lew said.

"Yes!" Flynt said. "Fire!"

"You're not making any sense, Lew," Meagan said.

"I mean," Lew said, "they're going to try and wipe this whole place out once and for all with a nuclear bomb, but Miranda has some sort of plan. She and Swami-ji, Alan's guru, worked it out. For some reason she needs me. I still don't know why."

"Right before she brought us in she said we could use Pastor Flynt, too," Meagan said, "but I can't imagine what for."

"I can." It was Alan. Fields was walking behind him. They came into the clearing from a path leading back into the jungle.

"Alan!" Lew moved quickly to his friend's side.

Mark Leon

"Man, you look terrible," Alan said. "What happened?"

"I went to India," Lew said.

"Ah"—a knowing look came into Alan's eyes—"that explains it. This is Don Fields, secretary of the interior. Do you remember Don, Lew?"

"Only from the evening news," Lew said.

"He was a classmate of mine back in college—along with that son of a bitch Skinner," Alan said.

"Larry's still in India," Lew said.

"Where?" Alan's eyes flashed with hostility.

"In Benares, with Swami-ji," Lew said.

"That asshole!" Alan said. "I've got to . . ."

"I think we have more important things to worry about right now," Meagan said. "I'm sure your personal vendettas are very interesting, but—"

"Alright!" Alan cut her off. "For once you're right, Meagan. If I'm right about Miranda's plan, which may be the only chance we have to escape vaporization, then there are certain things I should try to explain to you all. This may offend some of you, especially you, Pastor . . ."

"I said call me Bob," Flynt said sharply. "And I doubt if there is anything you can say that will shock me, son. I presume you are going to tell us all about Tantra?"

"Well, yeah, actually . . ." Alan faltered, reappraising the pastor.

"I think I get the gist of it," Flynt said, "and I'm not bothered. There is no sin here. We are restored."

"What?" Meagan said, bewildered.

"Everybody sit down," Alan said, "this may take a while." He proceeded to explain the theory of Tantric energy and the channeling of all energy along the central axis of creation.

A few hours later, deep into the night, Meagan sat with Raya beside Miranda. "Is she going to live?" Meagan said.

"I don't know," Raya said. "The bullet is very close to her heart. I can't extract it. I've applied some fungal essences, but . . ."

"She said her skin was tough," Meagan said.

THE GAIA WAR 291

"It is," Raya said. "One of your race would be dead."

"What do you mean *my race*?" Meagan said. "Aren't we all human?"

"Yes, and no," Raya said. "Certainly we are human in form. But she and I"—Raya indicated the still-unconscious Miranda—"we're not really of your world."

"What world, then?" Meagan said.

"This world." Raya smiled, indicating the glowing jungle. "This is what might have been for you."

"Might have been? I don't understand," Meagan said.

"It is in all of your greatest myths," Raya said. "A legend of a golden age, before the downfall of your species, before you became . . ."

"Monsters?" Meagan said.

"What you are," Raya said diplomatically.

Miranda stirred. "What you still can become," she said weakly.

"Mother!" Raya said.

Meagan's eyes flashed when she saw that Miranda did not correct Raya.

"Don't be angry," Miranda said. "I guess I am her mother . . . sort of. When Alan and I worked on the protean virus that exploded into . . . the *Genesis Bomb*, I included a little something extra, something of myself. Raya is the result.

"But"—Miranda looked at Raya—"I'm not anyone's mother really. Please, Raya, call me Miranda."

"Miranda, then," Raya said.

"You look worried Meagan. Are you alright?" Miranda said.

"Yes, but . . ."

"What?"

"Is it true?" Meagan said.

"Is what true?"

Meagan repeated the gist of Alan's talk.

"Yes, Meagan. I'm afraid so. It's our only chance. I hope it won't compromise your . . ."

"No," Meagan said, "it won't. But I had to hear it from you."

292 Mark Leon

"I have much work to do." Miranda sat up. She gasped and clutched her chest.

"No!" Raya said, "you must rest."

"I'll be alright," Miranda said, taking a deep breath. "It may not matter anyway, but I have to try. Can you take me to the communications center?"

"Yes," Raya said.

"Then let's go." Miranda, in pain, stood up. "I'll see you soon, Meagan. You should rest." Miranda put her hand on Meagan's shoulder.

"Where are you going?" Meagan said.

"I have to talk to your people," Miranda said.

"My people?" Meagan said, sitting down on the grassy bed where Miranda had lain.

"*The people of earth*," Miranda said, following Raya out into the sparkling new world.

Meagan fell asleep almost immediately.

On the other side of the world, Skinner was holding a piece of the black root in his palm. "How do I take this stuff?" he said.

"Chew it up thoroughly," Swami-ji said, "and wash it down with tea. The alkaloids in the tea will help buffer the stronger ones in the root."

"But what *is* it?" Skinner said.

"I don't know. That's work which remains to be done. Maybe it's something you can take back to NatCo—get your job back, redeem yourself in the eyes of the corporate fat cats," Swami-ji said.

"You're a devious one," Skinner said. "I don't mind telling you I'm nervous. You sure this stuff is OK?"

"I found the side effects to be minimal," Swami-ji said. "It was an awesome experience, however. You don't want to have any distractions."

"No side effects?" Skinner said.

"I didn't say *no* side effects, and of course they may vary with individual response."

"Great," Skinner said. "You really inspire confidence. Do you have a name for it?"

"I call it *Zindagee*."

THE GAIA WAR 293

"Zindagee . . ." Skinner repeated softly.

"It means . . ."

"I *know* what it means," Skinner said.

"Don't take it if you feel anxious," Swami-ji said. "I merely brought it to your attention as an interesting possibility for further research."

"OK," Skinner said. He popped the black *Zindagee* root into his mouth and began to chew. "Ugh! This is the foulest-tasting . . ."

"Have some tea," Swami-ji said, handing Skinner a cup.

Skinner gratefully gulped it down and continued chewing. When he was finished he said, "What now?"

"Now you make yourself comfortable," Swami-ji said, "and wait."

Raya took Miranda to the video plant. "What are you going to do?" Raya said.

"I'm going to try and get through, warn the whole world of what is about to happen. There has to be somebody left out there with some sanity. Maybe they will stop it."

"And if they don't?"

"Then we have to do what we can," Miranda said.

"Will it really work?"

"I don't know. It has never been done before, but in theory, at least . . . Anyway, let's get to work. We only have a few hours before dawn, and my guess is that's all the time we have left."

The two women busily engaged themselves in what could only be called an advanced form of horticulture. Anyone watching would never again doubt the reality of what gardeners call "green thumb." They pruned, grafted, and created. The plants responded in ways that indicated a vegetable sentience. Miranda was able to coax rapid growth by touch alone, and Raya induced flowering with the sound of her voice.

Skinner began to notice the tree that grew across from the temple. There were several monkeys playing and jabbering there, but his attention was drawn to the tree itself.

294   **Mark Leon**

"It's *alive*," he said, and immediately thought he heard a mocking voice from somewhere deep within answer, *Of course it's alive, you fool!*

Soon the tree was all he saw, and all he felt. There was depth in that tree, and Skinner wanted to explore that depth, get lost in it. It was surprisingly easy to do. He felt a mild dislocation as his spirit merged with the tree. He flowed down long corridors of sap to roots deep in the ground, where he thrilled to the damp smell of earth. He shot down green tubular tunnels to leaves that vibrated in delicious ecstasy to the touch of the sun.

And there was more. Skinner sensed a nexus of plant life that was, indeed, global. He tapped into it and traveled to rain forests in Brazil, where his joy was cut short by the sound and fury of a chain saw. He swayed to the aquatic rhythms of underwater sea meadows and surveyed the earth from Alpine aspens.

"Amazing," he said, and the global network of vegetable life answered in the affirmative, with laughter and a joy full of spontaneous life. Skinner sensed a center to the network, and he kept trying to work his way toward it. But the distractions along the way were endlessly seductive, and so he kept getting lost in ways that were more delightful than frustrating.

The sound sent an electric jolt down Carp's spine that caused him to straighten out suddenly with such force that his whole body jumped an inch off the mattress. It was the telephone. He snatched it and was unable to speak until the tension in his jaw slackened.

"Carp!" he said, looking at the clock. "It's 4:00 fucking A.M. for Christ sakes . . ."

"We have a problem, sir." It was the major.

"What kind of problem?"

"You better turn on your television."

"My television! Why?"

"Or your radio, any damn thing, and listen."

Carp punched the clock radio on. He kept it tuned to a country and western station. They went twenty-four hours—it was a popular station for the truckers on their

THE GAIA WAR 295

long hauls, so Carp was surprised to hear static. And then the white noise began to resolve itself into a voice. But it wasn't a glad-happy midnight DJ that he heard. It was a woman, and she was saying the same thing over and over again.

"People of Earth! People of Earth! This is an emergency. This is not a test. I am coming to you live over the Organic Broadcasting System via the Asklepian wave. I am speaking from deep inside the *Genesis Bomb* in White Sands, New Mexico. My voice is carried on a nouonic pulse, a more subtle form of cosmic resonance than any radio or television frequency. I am trying to reach you all. I will continue to broadcast this message until my instruments show that I have significant reception in all time zones. My words are automatically translated on the Asklepian wave into your mother tongue. I want to speak to all of you.

"People of Earth, People of Earth . . ."

"How long has this been going on?" Carp said.

"I don't know," the major said. "We were testing our secured radio frequencies and all we could get was this."

"You mean that this is on all radio bands?"

"And television," the major said.

"We have to move!" Carp said. "Can you go now!"

"No we . . ."

"I'm sick of your 'no's,' Major! This is an order. Proceed immediately with Project Clean Slate."

"We don't have the device on board yet. It will take at least another hour . . ."

Their phone conversation was interrupted by the same repetitious message, ". . . significant reception in all time zones. My words are automatically translated on the Asklepian wave into your mother tongue. I want to speak to all of you.

"People of Earth, People of Earth . . ."

"My God!" Carp dropped the phone as if it were suddenly red hot. "The telephone too! That's not *possible*," he hissed. He grabbed a pair of pants lying on the armchair. He was quickly dressed and out the door.

296 Mark Leon

By the time he got to the airstrip Miranda had progressed beyond the introduction. It was on every radio and television station. All telephones, including cellular, were buzzing with it. Those who logged on to personal computers were surprised to see the text of her speech scrolling down the screen.

The major was waiting for him. "We go now!" Carp said, jumping out of his car and slamming the door.

"I told you, the bomb isn't even on the plane yet. It wouldn't do any good for us to go now."

"I don't care how you do it!" Carp said. "Just get the thing on board and the plane in the air, pronto! Now! Move!"

The major just stood there, watching Carp's fury build. When the defense secretary was nearly apoplectic, the major said, "We're doing that, sir. Please understand that a nuclear device is not a big firecracker or piece of dynamite. The loading and preliminary arming procedures are quite precise and technical."

"How long?" Carp practically gasped the question.

"Thirty minutes more," the major said.

"Make it ten. Any coffee around here?"

The major pointed to a small building adjacent to the hangar which housed the stealth craft. Carp strode toward it, and the major followed.

Inside the major switched on the radio. Carp glared at him but didn't say anything as he poured himself a cup. He let the major pour his own.

Carp took his first sip and Miranda's voice said, "Good morning," as if on cue.

"It is morning for me, and very early morning indeed for my listeners on the western half of the North American continent. I owe you all an explanation. I have commandeered all of your communications systems. This is a radical action. I would not do such a thing if it were not justified. Many of you wonder that such a thing is possible

"In my announcement I told you that I speak through the Organic Broadcasting System. This is how I am able to reach you all, on your televisions, radios, telephones, and

THE GAIA WAR 297

computers. The basis of life is information. Your scientists already understand that much. What they do not yet understand is that this information is held in a network that is both larger and smaller than any of the energy fields known to your physicists. This network forms a Unified Field, and it both permeates and supports all structures, from the smallest subatomic particle to the largest galaxy. It is alive. Your ancient philosophers called it the *cosmic aether*.

"The *Genesis Bomb* is life as it is intended to be. It grows here in the desert without the interference patterns that impede the other living things of your world. Therefore, it is always intimately connected to the Unified Field. The microphone into which I speak is a living plant stalk. I am, right now, watching my image on a monitor which consists of a specialized leaf from a video plant.

"I tell you these things knowing most of you will not believe. But these things are not miracles. They are the norm throughout much of the universe. Your world has been isolated and impoverished for so long that what is a simple fact of life will appear to you as a miracle.

"But these are things which, either you will grow to understand or you will reject, and thereby destroy yourselves. This is certain because I am talking about life, and life is the one thing you must have. Your life suffers a temporary setback. It will not always be so. Either you will become part of the healing process here on your planet or continue down your path of self-destruction.

"I did not choose to come here. Like each one of you, I did not choose to be born. That is the way of life. I am like you but I am not one of you. My place is not here. Those who helped midwife my entrance into your world wanted to call me Gaia.

"Gaia, the mother earth spirit. There may be a Gaia; in fact I know there is. She is you and your planet. She is powerful, she is intelligent. She can clean up much of the ecological mess you have made. She can help you to re-create your planet in the living image of what it is supposed to represent when, and if, you choose life over death. But she cannot survive neglect and abuse forever. She will die,

298 Mark Leon

you will die, and your planet will die if you do not begin a new age of partnership with her.

"In any case, I am not Gaia. I am not a goddess. I am not Eve. I am not the Virgin Mother of God. I am the mother of no one except myself. I will tell you who I am. I am . . ."

The transmission was suddenly shattered by a burst of static. Skinner had finally found the center, the nexus of the organic network. His traversal of it had landed his awareness in the life systems of the *Genesis Bomb*, and he quickly penetrated to the heart of the Organic Broadcasting System.

"She is no mother!" he screamed. His anxious voice was harsh and abrasive compared to Miranda's cool, reasoned tones. "I will tell you all what her real name is. It certainly is not Gaia. It is *Pandora*! Yes, Pandora, the artificial bitch! Pandora, who, in the guise of a beautiful and cultured lady, brings pain, sickness, suffering, and all manner of evil into the world! Don't listen to her.

"There is right now"—Skinner's voice was starting to pick up static as Miranda fought back for control—"an air force stealth craft on the way to liberate us from this alien! The United States government is about to deliver a thermonuclear device into the heart of the *Genesis Bo* . . ."

Miranda briefly regained control. "He's right about that!" she said. "Please, if there is anyone out there who can stop it—*do something*. I appeal to the president, to the Congress, to anyone who can stop this mad scheme. We mean no harm. Do not destroy us and travel farther down the path of death . . ."

"She lies!" It was Skinner's voice again. He was in his element and enjoying the battle.

Miranda turned to Raya, who watched helplessly as their signal was once again jammed. "I can't fight him," Miranda said. "He's too strong. How did he penetrate the net so thoroughly?"

"He used the *Zindagee* root," Raya said. "It allows your consciousness to merge with the planetary life web to which we are temporarily linked."

THE GAIA WAR 299

"*Zindagee*, the Urdu word for *life*," Miranda said, sounding far away. Then, with force, "Do we have the root?"

"Yes," Raya said.

"Get it for me," Miranda said. "I must follow and fight him from inside."

"No!" Raya said. "You are still weak. And we need you here. I'll go."

"No, *I'll* do it." It was Alan. He had left the others and had been listening for a few minutes. "You don't need me here. There are four men and three women. I'm superfluous. Give me the drug, and I'll go after the *sonofabitch*."

Carp might have ruptured an artery when Skinner started talking about the stealth craft and the bomb, but at the same time a young man in uniform interrupted them, "Excuse me, Major, sir. We're ready to go."

Carp followed the technician out to the hangar with the major close behind. He breathed a little easier when the pilot climbed in and closed the hatch. He almost sighed with relief when, after a short run down the strip, the plane lifted off and banked gracefully up into the sky.

CHAPTER**23**

As Alan chewed the bitter, black Zindagee root the others assembled around Miranda. They all gaped at the studio, clearly a transmission center but completely organic; all the technology was alive.

"Alan has explained the situation?" Miranda said.

"We know what to do," Meagan said.

"There's no time to waste," Miranda said. "We may have only minutes." She removed her clothes and the rest of them disrobed. Then she took Lew by the hand.

"Try to emulate our actions as much as possible," she said. "This is Tantric sex. The goal is not pleasure in the ordinary sense. And, most importantly, we must all control the climax. It must be timed and synchronized. You will know when that time comes."

She showed Lew what to do. He sat on the soft, velvety grass and assumed the lotus position of meditation. Miranda did what was necessary and then slid down on top. She wrapped her legs around Lew's back, assuming a mirror image of Lew's posture.

Meagan and Pastor Flynt followed their example. Raya took the secretary of the interior, who had been watching it all with a glazed expression, by the hand. She gave him a shy smile. "Anything I can do to help?" she said.

He turned red. Within a few minutes they were all properly engaged.

THE GAIA WAR 301

"Take it easy, Lew," Miranda whispered in his ear. She could feel his excitement surging to the point of no return. "Stay with me, think of something—anything for distraction."

All the images that came flooding into Lew's mind were not helping to distract him. He thought of a toothbrush, but bristles grew into long, silky hair, and the plastic handle molded itself into seductive curves.

"Lew!" Miranda said. "Please, this is crucial! Our lives hang in the balance . . ."

She was interrupted by the sound of the jet. So was Lew. It brought him back from the edge. It was a quiet, innocent sound, but as it grew in volume it began to acquire sinister overtones. This was a messenger come to deliver the *word*, and the word was *death*.

The root was so awful-tasting that Alan could barely choke it down. He chewed quickly and thoroughly and so began to feel the effects within seconds. He lay on his back and stared up at the jungle. He wondered why he had ever seen vegetable life as random or disorganized. He now saw that it was all expressive of endless pattern. Pattern upon pattern that never repeated yet always had reference to some grander, hidden pattern. He was drawn into the plant life by the pull of this fundamental, yet unperceived pattern that is the inspiration and mold for all life.

He didn't find it. Instead he found a deeper structure of profound beauty. He trembled in ecstasy just to behold it.

His bliss was rudely interrupted. "Don't believe what she was telling you." It was Skinner, still broadcasting his message and now free from any interference. Alan directed his will toward the voice he knew so well.

He was surprised to confront a body. He had assumed this was all in his mind, and he knew his physical body was still lying in the grass. But he saw Skinner standing in a blaze of energy. Around the figure there was a white aura, which crackled and popped. Alan looked down at his hands to see that he had a similar form. Skinner's attention was all on his speech. His back was to Alan. "The *Genesis Bomb*," Skinner said, presumably to a world audience, "is

302 Mark Leon

the first wave of an alien invasion. We must destroy it before . . .''

Alan quickly moved in and punched Skinner's strange body in the right kidney. Skinner screamed and wheeled around. His face lit up with a demonic intensity when he recognized Alan. ''So!'' he said. ''It has come to this! What do you propose to do? Kill a spirit?''

''Yes,'' Alan said, coldly. ''I only wish I could kill all of you.''

''All of *us*?'' Skinner said.

''The enemies of life,'' Alan said.

''You're dreaming, Alan Fain,'' Skinner said. ''There is no *us*. There's just a *you* with a head full of half-baked delusions. Did you ever think for one minute that bitch could really change things.''

''It doesn't matter,'' Alan said, advancing.

''This is all a big hallucination you know,'' Skinner said.

''Maybe,'' Alan said, throwing his fist into Skinner's face. Hallucination or not, the punch connected solidly. Skinner jumped back, clutching his jaw.

They went at it, Alan throwing body punches and striking his enemy's face whenever possible. Skinner, who had studied various martial arts, relied on powerful kicks. These were extremely effective. One nearly smashed Alan's knee and he was forced to retreat.

Skinner hurled himself on Alan and began biting and scratching. Alan threw him off and ran several yards. He turned to see Skinner, bloodied and grinning, just a few feet away.

''We're pretty evenly matched,'' Skinner said.

''Yeah,'' Alan said, panting and tense with pain.

''You still want to kill me?''

''Yeah.''

''Then come on!'' Skinner's eyes lit up with a terrifying fury and he lunged at Alan.

The pilot was speaking to ground control. ''The hole in the roof of the dome is less than ten meters in diameter.''

''Your window is smaller than that,'' the major said. The

THE GAIA WAR　　　　303

hydrogen bomb was sealed inside an extremely accurate "smart bomb" delivery system.

"I know, sir, but there is not much room for error."

"No, there is not, Lieutenant. Do your job."

"Yes, sir." The pilot was young. He was not supposed to know that he was dropping an H-bomb. But he knew. His hands were clammy and his forehead glistened with cold sweat. It was easy, a piece of cake. At his altitude, with his equipment, there was no way he could miss. *But*, he couldn't help thinking, *what if I do miss?*

He didn't. As soon as he released the bomb he knew it was a direct hit. He didn't want to see. He was going to do some serious recreational flying over the desert, as far away from White Sands as possible. He banked sharply and opened the throttle wide. The violent g force shoved his body down into his seat and stretched the skin across his face. It felt good. Anything would have.

Miranda tracked the bomb. Her senses were more acute than ever, as accurate as radar and, at that moment, totally integrated with her sexual response. The bomb went through the center of the opening. She said, "Now!" They all knew what she meant.

The fission trigger went first. As the blinding flash of light expanded out in a spherical wave, the heat set off the fusion reaction. An even bigger wave of light followed.

Miranda sucked the radiant energy in through her optic nerves. Lew and Miranda's simultaneous orgasm transformed both their spinal cords into energy columns. The first wave went from Miranda's eyes into her brain and down her back. There the energy poured through her genitals into Lew's, where it shot up his spine.

Lew went ramrod straight as he felt a bolt of white light explode at the crown of his skull. The heat waves came next. The red, radiant energy traversed the same path. First Miranda, then Lew. As the energy left Lew's body Raya absorbed it and passed it on to Fields who in turn passed it to Meagan. It emerged from the top of Flynt's skull.

Lew felt himself fuse and separate from Miranda millions of times. It was as if their sexual union were re-creating, on a biological level, the two nuclear processes of fission

304 Mark Leon

and fusion that were releasing such vast amounts of energy. This yoga, this Tantric sexual discipline, was the key to modulating the release of atomic energy from the scale of atomic nuclei to the scale of organic life. This modulation was really a series of recapitulations of the two basic paradigms of fission and fusion, differentiation and unification.

Lew felt throughout the process that he was witness to the revelation of a great mystery, the mystery that has puzzled philosophers since the very beginning of philosophy, the One vs. the Many. Sameness and difference. It is expressed in billions of ways from the smallest to the largest. It is articulated at the organic level through sex. And by a disciplined practice of sex it could all be brought into the organic level in a nondestructive way.

There was one white-hot blast of deadly radiation that Miranda directed outward. It shot out the top of her skull, out the opening in the dome, and down the side, where it struck Special Agent Creel in the face. His retinas were immediately burned out. Screaming, he fell to his knees, hands rushing up to cover his face.

It seemed to go on for hours, days. Time itself was dissolved in the endless display of unity and difference. The shock waves which followed the waves of radiant energy were coarser, but they went through the same channels, eventually dissipating through Flynt into the jungle life.

When it was all over everything was more alive. The jungle radiated a new, vigorous energy that was intensely powerful, awesome even. But unlike the raw thermonuclear energy, this new power was not life-threatening. Lew, after he and Miranda separated, stood up and surveyed the scene. Nothing had really changed, and yet he was keenly aware of the new power. It thrilled him, but he would not have thought to call it "safe." It was certainly not dangerous in the way the bomb had been, but there was nothing benign about it.

They were all standing now. There was no need for words. What they had just experienced was both profoundly personal and communal. Each one knew that the others knew. It was Miranda who finally broke the silence. "I

THE GAIA WAR 305

need to finish my broadcast.'' She went to the tall, green stalk that served as her microphone and began speaking.

"People of earth, throughout your long history you have sought much and found little. You have unraveled secrets of the atom and beyond. You map the stars and possibly the structure of the cosmos itself. And still it is not enough, not nearly enough.

"If you would attend to the things that are always before you, shining of their own individual radiance, you would discover signs to amaze and astound. And more—you will be led to greater power than the silly destructive force of an atomic bomb, creative powers beyond your wildest imagining.

"One of your greatest poets[9] said,

> *'That which before us lies in daily life,*
> *Is the prime wisdom: what is more is fume,*
> *Or emptiness, or fond impertinence,*
> *And renders us in things that most concern*
> *Unpractised, unprepared, and still to seek.'*

"This wisdom is lost to most among you. If you think of it at all, you think it means that you should be small-minded. Not so! There is the secret of great things concealed in these words. The secret is in what always lies before you. By looking far away, and always into the places most hidden, you have missed the greater part, which is always the *prime wisdom*.

"Before we were interrupted, I was going to tell you who I am. I am quite simply the future. I am what you can all be if you will stop attending to your violent fears and fantasies and start attending to life.

"Those of you who know anything about genetics know that there are long strands in your DNA—the code of life that programs who you are—which are 'silent.' Your scientists say they are silent because they are not actively in-

---

[9] John Milton, *Paradise Lost*, Book VIII.

306 Mark Leon

volved in the synthesis of protein. But this is information which is waiting to be activated. It is the key to the next step in the great game of cosmic evolution, a step which some call the *Axial Awakening*.

"If, and when, these silent strands become active, you will begin this process of awakening and go forward to claim that which you lost so long ago—your birthright, your destiny.

"But this will not happen unless you bring your human life into harmony with the life of the planet. That's the trigger which will begin the process. The universe is not some inert, dead thing. It's alive. It's intelligent. We have just demonstrated here that life and intelligence can tame the energy released from a nuclear bomb. One of your government tried to destroy us. A hydrogen bomb was detonated here this afternoon. We would have been vaporized were it not for the life force which is still coming alive here in me and in the *Genesis Bomb*. I call on the authorities who are still in charge to take responsibility for this reckless action and bring the perpetrators to justice."

Defense Secretary Carp was running to his car. "You can't just leave me holding the bag on this thing!" The major was yelling after him. "I'll tell them all! I was just following orders." Carp ignored the major, speeding away and thinking furiously about plausible deniabilty.

"Where's Carp!" the president demanded.

"I can't find him," the chief of staff said. "He seems to have disappeared."

"And Fields?"

"There are rumors that his private plane was destroyed over White Sands."

"Oh My God . . ." The president held his head in his hands.

Miranda continued. "So I'm a possible future for you all. I am not *Gaia*, your mother earth, but unless you learn to live in a relationship of mutual nurturing with your real

THE GAIA WAR 307

mother, you will never see this glorious future. I'm not Pandora. I bring no harm. I bring nothing. Soon I will be gone.

"Another of your greatest writers has said, 'To insist that all things are exactly as I have said would not be the action of a sane person, but it is reasonable and good to believe that something like this is true.'[10] I don't know exactly what your future will be. I know it can be wonderful, an endless living adventure, or, if you persist on your present course, it will be a disaster. I also know that whatever your future is, I will not be a part of it.

"So now I'll tell you who I am. I am Miranda. I am the creature of a brave new world. And there are other such creatures like me in it. You never were alone. Some of you have heard the rumors of UFS, Unidentified Flying Subjects. They are true. When the *Genesis Bomb* first exploded its wonderful New Creation in White Sands, others like me, the children of tomorrow, came to see if possibly you had finally learned the secret of life over death. They quickly saw that you had not, that this was a freak accident, and that you would probably try to destroy it. So they retreated and have not returned.

"It is to this community that I go. I leave you in peace."

Swami-ji turned off his radio. "Impressive," he said. "*Brave new world* indeed!" He laughed. He had a problem—what to do with Skinner's body. Something had obviously gone wrong. The drug should have worn off, but the man's body lay in a deep coma, barely alive.

He finally decided to take the body to a temple deep in the heart of the old Hindu section. He left the body with an old fakir, a man he trusted. "You will notify me immediately if there are any changes?"

"Yes, Swami-ji"—the emaciated Hindu priest smiled broadly—"he is in absolute master, safekeeping with me."

---

[10] Plato, *The Phaedo*.

Mark Leon

* * *

Alan could not kill Skinner, but he had beaten the man to a bloody pulp, lying in the nexus of the inner reaches of life. Alan felt himself being pulled away from it, back to his earthly body. He picked up what was left of Skinner and was surprised to find how light it was. *It's not really him anyway*, Alan thought. He squeezed and pushed the mess until it was compressed into a wet baseball-sized mass. He compressed it further until he had a little seed. He pushed the seed deep into the earth, or whatever it was that supported them.

Alan opened his eyes. He was back in the jungle, and Lew was standing over him. "What happened?" he said.

"So it worked," Alan said.

"Yeah." Lew looked embarrassed. "It worked."

"Sex," Alan said. "I always figured it was good for something."

"Why do you think they call it the gravitational *field*?" Miranda said. She had ferried Lew, Alan, Meagan, Flynt, and Krishna back outside the dome.

"But won't you get lonely?" Lew asked. "Out *there* I mean?"

"Oh no," Miranda said. "There really are others out there. I've begun to make contact already. They call to me. Besides, I have Raya and the secretary of the interior."

"But what will you *do*?" Meagan said, trying to keep the petty envy and possessiveness, which she could not help feeling, out of her voice.

"Oh brave new world," Miranda said, "that has such people in it! What are fields *for* anyway? I go to play, to play in the fields of the universe."

She flew back inside. The dome closed behind her, sealing off the New Paradise forever. The ground around them shuddered. They watched as the new biosphere lifted off the earth, leaving a shallow depression behind. It was a living city, encased in a living polymer dome, and it was ascending to the sky, leaving the earth forever.

"Are you sure you want to do this?" Raya said.

"Absolutely," Fields said.

THE GAIA WAR 309

"You could emerge as the hero in all this," Miranda said. '*Secretary of the interior survives nuclear attack inside* Genesis Bomb.' I can just see the headlines. You might have a brilliant political future. It's not too late. I can still get you out of here."

"No thanks," Fields said. "After seeing this, I could never look at a national park again with anything but regret. This feels more like home." He looked at Raya. "Besides—" He was cut off by her passionate embrace and long, lingering kiss.

CHAPTER 24

Meagan and Flynt took Krishna to El Paso to begin the proper treatment for his leprosy. The doctor could find no trace of the disease.

"I'm not surprised," Flynt said later. They were having coffee back at his church. "My prostate isn't acting up anymore. Whatever happened in there has cured us all."

"Cured us of what?" Meagan said.

Flynt didn't answer. "You know I'm going to keep little Krishna."

"Yeah," Meagan said.

"I've always wanted a son."

"That's nice."

"My wife's leaving me."

"I'm sorry to hear that," Meagan said.

"It isn't easy being a preacher's wife. I'm quitting the business anyway."

"What will you do?"

"This town needs a good espresso bar," Flynt said. "I've always wanted my own business."

"Great," Meagan said.

"Did it mean anything to you?" Flynt said.

"What?" Meagan said.

"You know, what we did out there," Flynt said.

"Sure it meant something to me," Meagan said. "It saved our butts."

THE GAIA WAR 311

"That's not what I meant," Flynt said.

Meagan just sipped her coffee. The tinkling of the ice filled the little windowless room.

"I've been thinking," Flynt said. "A child needs a mother."

"I've been thinking, too," Meagan said. "I have some money saved up. I've never been anywhere, no place interesting, I mean."

"El Paso isn't so bad."

Meagan just looked at him for a moment. "No, it isn't. But I want to go to Greece, Italy, India, Malaysia, Australia . . ."

"So the answer is no?" Flynt said.

"I didn't say that."

"You'll think about it?"

"I may not be back," Meagan said. "Ever."

"But you will still think about it."

"Yeah," she said. "I'll think about it."

They found Creel, blind, with radiation sickness and badly dehydrated, stumbling around near US Highway 70. "At least he has his pension," the El Paso bureau chief said to the doctor outside Creel's room.

"Yeah," the doctor said. "He may not need it."

"That bad?"

"I predict," the doctor said, "that if he survives the week, he has about a year before his body is riddled with more kinds of cancer than I know the names of."

"Hell of a prognosis," the FBI man said.

"Could be what's in store for us all," the doctor said.

The FBI man stared at the doctor. "You didn't buy any of that crap, that People of Earth speech, did you?"

The doctor just shrugged and looked away. It was clear to him. The battle lines were drawn.

"Don't tell me Swami-ji showed you the tree of knowledge?" Alan said. They were watching the sunset in White Sands.

"Yeah," Lew said.

"And the tree of life?"

312 Mark Leon

"Yeah, that too."

"You didn't *believe* all that stuff about India being the site of the original Garden of Eden and Jesus going there?"

"Well . . . I . . . it makes a damn good story," Lew said.

"Oh man! Didn't Swami-ji warn you that India is full of charlatans and fake gurus?" Alan said.

"So it was all a line he was feeding me? I mean I *touched* them both. The tree of knowledge . . ."

"Shocked you, right?" Alan said.

"Right."

"You were suckered, Lew," Alan said. "Well, don't worry about it. It has happened to wiser men than you. They know all the tricks over there."

"But I thought Swami-ji was different," Lew said.

"He is," Alan said. "And he's one of the smartest guys you'll ever meet. He could be a great philosopher or scientist if he cared about that sort of thing. But he's a swami. You can never forget that. Once a swami, always a swami."

They wandered out into the area where paradise had grown. It was remarkable. Except for a slight depression in the desert floor, there was almost no sign that anything had been there. Alan stopped where he thought the marvelous fountain plant had been.

"Ah, Lew"—Alan sighed—"what is it? We seem to have a knack for losing paradise."

"At least we have had it to lose," Lew said.

"Yeah," Alan said. "I guess that's one way to look at it."

"Was it just another crazy dream, Lew? We almost had it—the *New Earthly Paradise*." Alan was looking into the brilliant orange-and-pink clouds on the western horizon. "But the time for regrets is over. No need to cry for Paradise Lost all over again. We have been down that road."

"What then?" Lew said.

"I have something here, Lew." Alan pulled a sheaf of papers from the inside pocket of his parka.

"What are those?" Lew said.

"These are the last fifty or so pages from the *Book of*

THE GAIA WAR 313

the New Creation. I xeroxed 'em before they disintegrated.'' Alan grinned.

''Anything interesting?''

''Yeah. The last chapter was more technical than the rest of the book. It's a manual.''

''A manual? What kind of manual?''

''It's not very detailed, but for someone with the right kind of knowledge, someone like *me*, it shouldn't be too hard to figure out.''

''Figure *what* out?'' Lew was becoming annoyed with Alan's grin.

''How to grow a spaceship,'' Alan said.

''*Grow* a spaceship?'' Lew said.

''How else would you do it?'' Alan said. ''The nuts and bolts, tin can, liquid hydrogen/oxygen, faulty O-ring, fireball space shuttle technology is ancient history. We are on the cutting edge of the future. *You* saw it. An entire celestial city, a self-contained organic biosphere ascending to the heavens. *That's* the future. Didn't you notice?''

''Notice what?''

''That place wasn't just a jungle anymore. It had grown into a whole city. Avenues, fountains, a broadcasting center . . .''

''Movie theaters?''

''Eventually,'' Alan said, ''entire organic shopping malls.''

''A celestial city.''

''Yeah, that's the point,'' Alan said. ''She told me the secret of antigravity, Lew. I mean not the technical part. I hope to find that in here.'' He held up the sheaf of papers.

''What secret?'' Lew said.

''*Levity*,'' Alan said.

''Levity? I'm afraid that doesn't sound very impressive, Alan—the secret of antigravity is *levity*.''

''You know how scientists have discovered the fundamental particles that mediate all the other forces, the electrical and the two nuclear forces?''

''More or less,'' Lew said.

''The big mystery is gravity. No one has been able to find the *graviton*. The graviton is key to antigravity or levity. *Miranda told me the secret of the graviton.*"

"Yeah?" Lew said. Alan was obviously playing the scene for all it was worth.

"*We* are the gravitons, Lew. It's us. We have the potential to mediate the gravitational force, the potential for *levity.*"

"Alright," Lew said. Alan's words were beginning to intrigue him as they always did, but he felt he had an obligation to resist. "Suppose we *are* the gravitons. Suppose this is the key to *levity*. Why would you want to grow a spaceship?" Lew said.

"You need to ask?" Alan said, looking at the few stars, barely visible in the evening afterglow.

Lew said nothing. His question had been merely rhetorical, and he was thinking furiously, imagination fired to the melting point.

"You have any pressing plans for the coming millennium, Lew?" Alan said, turning to face his friend.

"Nothing that can't wait," Lew said.

RETURN TO AMBER...
THE ONE *REAL* WORLD, OF WHICH ALL OTHERS, INCLUDING EARTH, ARE BUT SHADOWS

The Classic Amber Series

NINE PRINCES IN AMBER	01430-0/$3.99 US/$4.99 Can
THE GUNS OF AVALON	00083-0/$3.99 US/$4.99 Can
SIGN OF THE UNICORN	00031-9/$3.99 US/$4.99 Can
THE HAND OF OBERON	01664-8/$3.99 US/$4.99 Can
THE COURTS OF CHAOS	47175-2/$4.99 US/$6.99 Can
BLOOD OF AMBER	89636-2/$4.99 US/$6.99 Can
TRUMPS OF DOOM	89635-4/$4.99 US/$6.99 Can
SIGN OF CHAOS	89637-0/$4.99 US/$5.99 Can
KNIGHT OF SHADOWS	75501-7/$4.99 US/$5.99 Can
PRINCE OF CHAOS	75502-5/$4.99 US/$5.99 Can

Buy these books at your local bookstore or use this coupon for ordering:

Mail to: Avon Books, Dept BP, Box 767, Rte 2, Dresden, TN 38225   D
Please send me the book(s) I have checked above.
❑ My check or money order—no cash or CODs please—for $_____ is enclosed (please add $1.50 to cover postage and handling for each book ordered—Canadian residents add 7% GST).
❑ Charge my VISA/MC Acct#_____ Exp Date_____
Minimum credit card order is two books or $7.50 (please add postage and handling charge of $1.50 per book—Canadian residents add 7% GST). For faster service, call 1-800-762-0779. Residents of Tennessee, please call 1-800-633-1607. Prices and numbers are subject to change without notice. Please allow six to eight weeks for delivery.

Name_____
Address_____
City_____ State/Zip_____
Telephone No._____

AMB 0595

AVONOVA PRESENTS
AWARD-WINNING NOVELS
FROM MASTERS OF SCIENCE FICTION

MIRROR TO THE SKY
by Mark S. Geston   71703-4/ $4.99 US/ $5.99 Can

THE DESTINY MAKERS
by George Turner   71887-1/ $4.99 US/ $5.99 Can

A DEEPER SEA
by Alexander Jablokov   71709-3/ $4.99 US/ $5.99 Can

BEGGARS IN SPAIN
by Nancy Kress   71877-4/ $4.99 US/ $5.99 Can

FLYING TO VALHALLA
by Charles Pellegrino   71881-2/ $4.99 US/ $5.99 Can

ETERNAL LIGHT
by Paul J. McAuley   76623-X/ $4.99 US/ $5.99 Can

DAUGHTER OF ELYSIUM
by Joan Slonczewski   77027-X/ $5.99 US/ $6.99 Can

NIMBUS
by Alexander Jablokov   71710-7/ $4.99 US/ $5.99 Can

Buy these books at your local bookstore or use this coupon for ordering:

Mail to: Avon Books, Dept BP, Box 767, Rte 2, Dresden, TN 38225   D
Please send me the book(s) I have checked above.
❑ My check or money order—no cash or CODs please—for $_____ is enclosed (please add $1.50 to cover postage and handling for each book ordered—Canadian residents add 7% GST).
❑ Charge my VISA/MC Acct#_____Exp Date_____
Minimum credit card order is two books or $7.50 (please add postage and handling charge of $1.50 per book—Canadian residents add 7% GST). For faster service, call 1-800-762-0779. Residents of Tennessee, please call 1-800-633-1607. Prices and numbers are subject to change without notice. Please allow six to eight weeks for delivery.

Name_____
Address_____
City_____State/Zip_____
Telephone No._____   ASF 0695